ROB ROBERTSON'S

ICY
SHADOWS

The Jericho Trilogy
Book I

A novel featuring
Agent Nolan "Jet" Jericho

Warren Publishing, Inc.

Published by Warren Publishing, Inc.
Charlotte, NC
www.warrenpublishing.net

ISBN: 978-0-9960506-9-2

Library of Congress Control Number: 2014936950

Published by Warren Publishing, Inc.
www.warrenpublishing.net

DEDICATION

*To my wife Dana for her continuing love and faith
in me, her support and encouragement of
this project being paramount. Without her,
Icy Shadows would only have been a
wisp of my imagination.*

*To my daughters for sharing their Dad:
(from oldest to youngest):*

*To Kirsten, for her strength, perseverance, and belief
in family; for her support of my writing, having
proofread an initial draft of Icy Shadows.*

*To Katelyn, for her mature approach to life, her
academic excellence, and the well-balanced,
engaging, fun-giving person that she is.*

*To Dominique, for her continuing striving for
perfection, for always doing what's right, and
her unspoken challenge to me to follow suit.*

*To Michaela, for her wacky, fun-loving, and
infectious personality, having a zest for
life that few people manage to obtain.*

*To my granddaughter, Laila, for making me laugh
and keeping me young; who, at five years old,
couldn't care less what a novel is.*

CHAPTER 1

Icy Springs—July 20, 1972

They say that sometimes you can feel death hover in the air. . .

Without a doubt, Miss Viola Krenshaw was heralded as quite the authority around Icy Springs within her chosen pursuits. First and foremost, the elegant spinster of seventy-four years was the longhaired musician of the village—a music guru able to throw down a mean piano lesson for only fifty cents a half-hour. And if *The Mary Tyler Moore Show* was not holding her hostage for a half-hour, the aging hands of this frail culinary wizard were often busy conjuring up a Devil's food cake that Satan himself would declare as being manna from heaven. Equally contributing to her notoriety was the fact that little Miss Krenshaw was Her Highness of Highway 64 when seated at the throne of her charcoal-gray 1949 Plymouth four-door sedan.

Not that "my old chariot," as tagged by Miss Krenshaw, was on the road all that much. A year in which the quarter-century-old car put in 1,200 miles would actually be considered well-traveled, for the odometer barely indicated 29,000 miles driven since '49—and most of these miles had been executed at a prudent thirty to forty miles per hour.

Miss Krenshaw's weekly excursions required a round trip of twenty-four miles each Saturday to the county seat of Sharpton, a dozen miles west of Icy Springs. Time was never a leisurely commodity for the spinster when in town, as her jaunt typically began with a guerilla raid on the A & P grocery store to seize necessary supplies for the week. Then there was the mad dash into The Pill Peddler pharmacy just long enough to procure precious salves and ointments, all the while being aggravated by "Mr. Lyerly, that flirtatious pill pusher behind the counter." When the gray chariot's trunk was sufficiently stocked with groceries and medicine, its driver sped back toward Icy Springs with the speedometer pushing forty. Every three months, though, Miss Krenshaw was forced to make a pit stop on her way home and spend her hard-earned piano money on some fuel for her sedan. She ultimately conceded that biting the bullet and patronizing the filling station was a necessity required of the symbiotic relationship between her and the Plymouth—after all, if she took care of her prized chariot, it would take care of her.

Once every three or four weeks on a Thursday, Her Highness' chariot cautiously headed west across the county line on a ten-mile medical pilgrimage to her trusted physician in Monksville. Without fail, Miss Krenshaw's anatomy maintained an orderly rotation of ailments which staged periodic but predictable uprisings requiring a doctor's attention, so every third or fourth Thursday, it would be "off to Monksville."

July 20, 1972 happened to be one of those "ailment Thursdays"—sciatica, to be precise—and the old Plymouth sedan was cranked at exactly 6:45 a.m. Oh, yes, Miss Krenshaw's appointments in Monksville were *always* scheduled at 8:30 a.m., leaving Her Highness of the Highway an hour and forty-five minutes to cover only ten miles in her chariot. Contrary to her guerilla grocery raids and mad medicine dashes in Sharpton, the overly-punctual Miss Krenshaw was content to sit in her Plymouth with its doors locked while skimming through her recipe books—content, that is, until the receptionist unlocked the door to the doctor's office.

The spinster's favorite part of the Monksville journey was when she passed by her "second home," the revered Icy Springs Lutheran Church. In spite of her ingrained familiarity with the looming edifice, it never failed to capture Her Highness' attention during the sedan's slowly mounting acceleration from her driveway. The church was only a quarter-mile from her house, allowing Miss Krenshaw to walk to her beloved house of worship every Sunday to provide piano music for the eleven o'clock service. With its position atop the highest man-made building in the village, the church's steeple was the pinnacle of the community, architecturally *and* spiritually. The steeple, bearing its majestic cross proudly at the top, symbolized the stalwart faith of the village citizenry, a tightly woven fabric uniting the people of Icy Springs with a God they worshiped without falter. For most citizens, the humble spire served as a type of giant lightning rod insulating the village from all that was evil. Other than the notorious cotton gin murders which had occurred a half-decade earlier in January 1967, Icy Springs appeared to be the epitome of a safe haven secured by the ever-present sentinel of the church and its steeple.

And, oh, how the citizens were mesmerized by the shadows lent by the steeple! Throughout any given sunny day, the steeple would cast an assortment of illusions upon the ground, holding the villagers captivated. The continual interplay between light and dark teasingly distorted the boundaries between earth and sky, with the fickle movement of the shadows connoting a battle between God and Satan being waged upon holy property. Most villagers found it downright creepy to set foot within the shadows cast by the steeple, for doing so suggested that one might be interfering with that otherworldly struggle between good and evil.

There was *one* exception, however, which seemed to permit human intrusion upon the steeple's shadows, a phenomenon occurring not long before sunset in the middle of summer. It was at this time that the steeple would cast an extremely long shadow that stretched all the way to Highway 64, where the tip of the steeple's cross would find itself firmly planted smack in the middle of the road in its silhouetted form. The people of Icy Springs relished standing on the shadow of the cross in that God-kissed spot, their exact motive remaining unclear. Maybe they felt that a shadow projected with such precision signified a kind of direct portal to God. . . Who knows? Drivers would often bring their cars to a halt in the middle of the highway right in front of the church, merely to allow the cross to bless their vehicles. Yes, indeed, the steeple of Icy Springs Lutheran appeared to offer large metaphysical doses of the Lord's hedge of protection, and the villagers certainly treasured these smoke signals directly from God!

As Miss Krenshaw passed by the church at 6:48 a.m. on that fateful morning of July 20, she felt the customary magnetic pull of the steeple obliging her eyes to study the sacred parcel of land. Although rapid-shot glances disengaging one's eyes from the road are usually not recommended for most drivers, the spinster's habit was not entirely negligent of safety due to the *very* slow speed of her Plymouth as it passed the church. At eighteen miles per hour and climbing, Her Highness of the Highway had more than adequate time to take in a succession of images at this part of her journey.

Glancing at the church's invitational doors, she scanned upwards to the majestic stained glass windows which, believe it or not, were once designated as an expendable item on a budgetary list when the church was in its construction phase. After admiring the stained glass windows, Miss Krenshaw proceeded optically toward the steeple. *Just one peek at the lovely steeple, then I can get on down the road to my medical appointment.* Continuing in her ritualistic from-the-bottom-up fashion, Miss Krenshaw allowed her eyes to ascend toward the cross on the steeple as a means of re-charging her personal hedge of protection. Suddenly, her frail hands gripped the steering wheel with a tremendous firmness that could only have been induced by sheer terror. She glanced away quickly, shaking her head violently as if she were trying to clear her eyes of something and her brain of *everything*, then she looked back once again. Her heart pounded like a pile driver, with her not-so-powerful grip on the wheel going completely limp. With no one holding the reins, the faithful old Plymouth sedan rolled off the right side of the road into the ditch.

Luckily, the panic-stricken spinster had only accelerated to twenty miles per hour in the quarter-mile from her driveway. Thanks to having gone limp and easing off the accelerator, the diminishing speed offered Miss Krenshaw a courteous impact upon the Plymouth's abrupt union with the ditch.

The terrified spinster flung open her door and trotted as fast as a seventy-four-year-old piano teacher possibly could. Racing toward the porch of the little white house on the property adjacent to the church, she chanted breathlessly, "Oh, my dear heavenly Father! Oh, my dear heavenly Father!" Miss Krenshaw kept repeating her abbreviated prayer while bolting to the porch. Once there, the overtaxed woman literally fell against the front door in a leaning position, her exhaustion accompanied by the strangled breaths of intense asthma.

Miss Krenshaw pounded on the screen door with as much energy as her frail body could summon. "Miss Eden! Miss Eden! Come quickly!" shouted the panicky spinster. "Are you in there? Miss Eden, please answer me!"

After a few seconds, the front door was flung open and Miss Eden stood there, peering through the screen. Frankly, the surprised resident looked quite hideous, as she still had curlers in her hair and her face bore some kind of anti-aging, greenish-blue mask composed of God-knows-what. Was it an avocado crème of some sort? Or, was it pomegranate? One thing was for sure: it was a blessing to the villagers that sighting Miss Eden in her facial mask and curlers occurred with *much* less frequency than sightings of Bigfoot.

"Land sakes, Miss Krenshaw! What in the name of the Holy Ghost has you acting like a madwoman? What can possibly be this—"

"You've got to call somebody, Miss Eden—the police, the hospital, somebody! But first, please step off the porch and come see what I, oh . . . I mean, oh . . . it's just terrible! PLEASE come and look, and tell me if you see what I'm seeing! And then you tell me if I am going crazy!"

By now, Miss Eden had dropped her incensed routine and settled into a sincere state of fright commensurate with that of her long-time neighbor and friend. "Okay, Viola! For corn's sake, I'll look—but, I tell you, you certainly have me scared to kingdom come!"

As the frightened ladies nervously stepped off the porch, another figure approached them. Both women immediately recognized the man now addressing them with a shaky voice. "Ladies, this can't be real! Am I seein' what I think my eyes are seein'?"

Burley Rankin was the local tire guy, who owned a tire repair and replacement business on the outskirts of Icy Springs down near what the locals called the "bridge that always floods." It was not unusual at all for him to be heading to Sharpton during the wee hours of the morning to conduct some early-bird business.

"Burley, come on! Miss Eden is walking with me over to the church so I can show her what I saw, which I guess is what you've seen, too! Come with us right now, please!" Upon her plea, the three frightened figures started walking somberly toward the church while keeping their eyes trained on the ground. It was as if the trio subconsciously felt that avoiding eye contact with the steeple would simply banish the sword of terror piercing them so.

"Viola, I was goin' to get some parts in town when I saw yer car in the ditch. I thought maybe ye blacked out or somethin'. When I got out, I saw ye wasn't in the car—and that's when I looked up toward the church and seen somethin' that I sure hoped wasn't real."

"I'm afraid it is, Burley! I'm afraid it is!" The motley three came to a stop roughly fifty feet from the church as the spinster continued. "Miss Eden, Burley—look up there at the steeple. Both of you look up there and tell me if that is who I'm afraid it is!" The terrified trio could no longer hide their eyes and avert the sword of terror impaling them, for the time had come: it was time to look upward and triangulate what each was seeing.

The soul-shattering fright gripping these disbelieving on-lookers was immediately validated by the unmistakable image before them. "Oh, Lawd be with us! Lawd be with us!" murmured Burley as he fell to his knees in a prayerful position and started sobbing. Miss Krenshaw's body transformed to jelly as she fainted, collapsing into the arms of Miss Eden. Miss Eden managed to steady the spinster's body while crying and trembling quite forcefully herself. "The world must be coming to an end," whimpered Miss Eden.

It is often a single, isolated moment in the complex fabric of time that forms the most haunting of memories, and the stark sight hovering above them would be forever etched in the minds of Miss Krenshaw, Miss Eden, and Burley Rankin. The shared vision they were beholding would connect these three citizens of Icy Springs for the rest of their lives; their souls would forever ache from the fright-imprinted snapshot now burned within their memories. For it was on this morning of July 20, 1972, that three pitiful souls in Icy Springs found the lifeless body of Pastor Paul Christmas strapped to the steeple of the village church.

The robe of the minister flapped gently as a small breeze began to materialize. The house of worship was now stripped of the symbolic sanctuary its parishioners had so relished. Having once served as a beacon of a place isolating all comers from the evils of the world, the steeple's hedge of protection now seemed slashed to the roots. For the citizens of this idyllic community, the shadows of the steeple would now symbolize portals to the very bowels of Hades—for now it appeared that the shadows had surely allowed Satan himself to enter the heart of Icy Springs.

CHAPTER 2

Enter Jericho!

Reaching for yet another Almond Joy, the man with a well-deserved day off had settled in to see his favorite TV show, *Star Trek*. And, better yet, not only was he getting to watch the great space opera, the cosmos had granted him the serendipity of his day off coinciding with a re-run of his all-time favorite episode, the one where Captain Kirk fights the lizard man!

Although the relaxed man's quirky nature usually found him pulling for the alien underdogs rather than the all-too-perfect Kirk, the outcome was always the same. At the end of each episode, Kirk would be back at the helm of the Enterprise being his bossy ol' self with his glossy ol' hair. *Man! They just do not make entertainment like this anymore!*

Yes, State Bureau of Investigation Agent Jericho had indeed earned this day of vacation in the summer of '72. He and Agent James had just closed a tedious case which had dragged on for three years and, at one point, had been deemed by the rest of the SBI as unsolvable. So, considering the fact that his lover "Cat" did *not* have the day off, Jericho was content simply to spend some time with a little *Star Trek*, some Nehi grape soda, and a questionable amount of Almond Joys.

Despite these decidedly simple pleasures on his days off, Nolan "Jet" Jericho had become somewhat of an enigma in his complex thirty-four years of living. Formerly a member of the NYPD and living in the heart of the Big Apple, Jericho had resigned totally from the urban scene amidst the fallout from an explosive situation which left him bearing a nasty aftertaste of big city politics. Accepting an offer he couldn't refuse from a mysterious voice on the phone, he was suddenly whisked away to the mid–1960s Southern landscape of Raleigh, North Carolina. Once in the South, Jericho suddenly found himself the proverbial square peg in a land full of round holes.

For sure, Nolan Jericho could have easily relegated himself to the status of a misfit during his initial years of living in a state of the U.S. undergoing so much racial transition. Granted, North Carolina had not experienced quite the degree of explosive fusion exhibited in the forced brotherhood of Alabama or Mississippi, but the "Tar Heel State" had still suffered many of the growing pains in the sixties' decade caused by the New World Order of the South. Even as public schools and other institutions were just being desegregated upon Jericho's arrival in Carolina, stereotypes and the N-word still floated freely from lips in a state where "First in Freedom" would be stamped on its license plates in the not-so-distant future.

Discrimination practices were still rampant in North Carolina, for the racial demographics of its population at the time of Jericho's arrival comprised an extremely limited palette of colors—primarily, black and white. Consequently, a good many of the state's citizens still had black-and-white vision. It was common to hear phrases like "the black guy who . . ." or "the white guy who . . ." Whether love or hatred of one's neighbor was the dominant doctrine of the household, an underlying awareness of color was always present in the Carolinian consciousness. Simply put, there was hardly any gray area in how people viewed each other. Home-grown North Carolinians of the mid-to-late 1960s had been indoctrinated early in life as to who was an equal neighbor and, of course, who was not.

So then it must have been the most provocative of additions to the force when Nolan Jericho joined North Carolina's State Bureau of Investigation in February 1966. As a non-Caucasian SBI agent, the man with a life already steeped in paradoxes became the rarest of breeds in Raleigh's high-level law enforcement. And, to make matters more perplexing for Southern traditionalists, the new arrival on the force was a creature in the form of a human melting pot—for Jericho was a man whose internal diversity was divided evenly among four quartiles of heritage. His African-American paternal grandfather had married a Puerto Rican woman, with their union producing a proud, fiery, Latino/African-American blend of a man known as Roberto Jackson Jericho. Before tragically becoming just another soldier labeled "MIA" during the Korean War, Captain Roberto Jericho had fallen head-over-heels for the lovely Xiaoling Ogawa, herself the rare product of a Japanese man and a Chinese woman. Before his eventual disappearance in Korea, Roberto sired a child by Xiaoling, a boy to be known as Nolan.

So that was how the SBI ended up with an African/Puerto-Rican/ Japanese/Chinese-American agent. Yes, Nolan was indeed the poster child for multi-culturalism. Somehow, though, all of these fractions of heritage had managed to meld together in forming a most unique and incredible man, the sum of the individual parts having indeed produced a much greater whole.

At first, the people of North Carolina were baffled by Jericho, a man like none they had ever set eyes on. He was a challenge to the unenlightened citizenry and their gray area issues, a citizenry whose black-and-white vision required any degrees of tolerance or acceptance to be defined by clear, limited boundaries. Simply put, anyone encountering Jericho was at a total loss to readily pinpoint a single heritage as a target for their hungry bigotry. *Is he black? Is he Chinese? Is he Hispanic? Is he Japanese? Just what is this guy?* People simply could not isolate a quality about the agent quickly enough to ridicule—and the incredible Jericho never gave them enough time to do so, for the breath-taking persona created by his striking appearance, his unforgettable charisma, and his remarkable abilities always slammed the door shut in the face of prejudice.

At 6'1″ tall and thirty-four years of age, Jericho had a formidably lean, tight body, somewhat akin to that of a young actor named Bruce Lee who had gained some notoriety in the U.S. for his portrayal of Kato in *The Green Hornet* TV series. Even though the agent's muscles didn't bulge excessively through his clothing, a person could throw a C- or D-battery at Jericho's chest and it probably would bounce off about two or three feet. With a beautiful, Hispanic-tinted skin that one might describe as a light, creamy brown, Nolan had his father's wiry African hair, which he kept short and impeccably trimmed. Perhaps most fetching of all were Jericho's evocative, slightly slanted green eyes, lending the agent what others considered his most exotic quality. He immediately conveyed the mystique of a person from "far, far away." He looked Oriental . . . sort of? . . . maybe? . . . who knows?

Jericho's charisma was equally mesmerizing, starting with his voice. Although not very low in tone, his voice possessed a somewhat hypnotic, monotone quality perceived by most people as cool, in-charge, and—to some listeners—slightly aloof. The drone of his voice was further enhanced by his often quirky and interesting word choices.

Women, especially, were entranced by Jericho's appearance and charisma. Upon encountering the agent, a woman instantly sensed that she had encountered a "one-off," a type of man that nature had never before constructed and probably wouldn't get around to again for some time. As a "God's gift to women," he had the ability to immediately transform a woman into a gelatinous zombie with the potential to wander out into the street in front of a steam roller or to fall into an open manhole while staring at him out of hormone-fed curiosity.

Although Jericho could have easily abused his effect on women, the restraint he practiced with the feminine gender remained one of his more admirable paradoxes. He possessed the gift of holding women spellbound, yet the agent was content to remain a one-woman man and—for the present—that honor went to Catherine Marshall, a.k.a. "Cat." Yes indeed! Almond Joys, Nehi grape, *Star Trek*, and a gal named Cat—this complex man liked things kept simple!

Jericho appeared content to live in a rather small upstairs apartment not far from the SBI office, surviving off cheap cuisine, with cheeseburgers and foot-long hotdogs being the primary staple of his diet. Therefore, when it came to living quarters or fine food, definitely no interior decorator or food connoisseur was he. As a contradiction to his many simple preferences, however, clothes and cars were the two champagne-level vices often rearing their expensive heads in Jericho's beer-level budget. Most of the agent's meager salary went toward his threads and his wheels, two of the prime factors in his fascinating appearance and alluring persona. His closet was full of silk suits—dark ones and gray ones—ordered from a tailor in New York City. Often he wore his personal version of casual wear: a pair of black pants, a black t-shirt or polo shirt, and a black sports jacket. Such an all-black ensemble generally turned heads in contemporary North Carolina, a land populated by Sunday suits and farming overalls. At the time of Jericho's arrival in the state, James Bond movies such as *Goldfinger* had been in full swing, creating a spy craze. Whether in his silk suits or his all-black garb, Nolan Jericho always commanded a look of "one of those spy fellers" to the citizens of Raleigh and beyond. With virtually no effort, the agent created the illusion of a dangerous man with a mysterious purpose.

Clothes aside, it was Jericho's two cars which were his true guilty pride. The "sisters," as he called them, were an ocean-blue 1965 Corvette Sting Ray Coupe and a candy apple-red 1967 Corvette Sting Ray convertible. He referred to the blue sister as "Polly"; the red sister he called "Anna." Jericho spent weekend after weekend washing, waxing, and polishing the sisters, with his primary objective always being to produce a reflection clear enough that one could literally hold a picture to each car's hood and see the image clearly. At times, his girlfriend Cat—whom the agent considered to be of equally-high maintenance—was jealous of the petting Jericho lavished upon the sisters. Often, when speaking of his vices, Jericho jokingly acknowledged his tailor and his mechanic as the two key people in his life—and that little running gag certainly didn't sit well with Cat.

Despite his appearance and charisma, the SBI would not have been as mesmerized by the agent as the average citizen had not Jericho possessed incredible abilities. The agent's deductive logic seemed infallible and was instrumental in solving some of their most lingering cases. He was one of the sharpest shooters in the organization. In describing his marksmanship, Jericho once said he was "able to uncrown the king on a playing card from thirty or forty feet." However, it was his incredible fighting skills and seeming invulnerability that perhaps fascinated his colleagues the most. Whereas the agent had inherited his logical thinking, serious demeanor, and iron determination from both parents, he had been trained in karate by his black-belt mother. Jericho often joked with fellow agents that—even with his father being the one who gave him a royal spanking for any wrongdoing—his mother had a most unique approach to handling undesired behavior. Xiaoling had been trained in the art of kendo, that is, fighting with cane poles, and she would often utilize household objects at hand as a source of punishment. "Quite frankly," said the agent, "I never showed my mother any disrespect when she was near a broom. In a matter of three seconds, she could grab the broom, spin it like a wheel, and knock me about six feet."

The martial arts were relatively unknown in North Carolina at the time of Jericho's arrival. As citizens were just then receiving their first exposure to karate in spy movies and shows like *The Green Hornet*, very few people in law enforcement actually engaged in the fighting skill. However, after the "human melting pot" arrived at the SBI and actually nullified a hostage situation, with his karate skills playing a key role, Jericho's fellow agents came clamoring for him to demonstrate some of that Oriental "fightin' crap." It wasn't long until his good friend, fellow agent Bennett James, became a brown belt himself. Although Bennett could never out-spar Jericho, he had easily become the second best in the entire force at karate.

In fact, it was Jericho's skills in the martial arts that led to him becoming affectionately known as "Jet" within the SBI. It was Bennett who had started the nickname, claiming that Jericho moved faster than a jet plane and pointing out that the agent's arm and leg thrusts had the *whoosh!* of a jet engine. At first, Jericho didn't know how to take the nickname, tending to shrug it off a little. Neither his father nor his mother had ever displayed a sense of humor, thus nicknames were not a standard practice in the Jericho family. However, the rational side of his nature—instilled in him by both parents—eventually prevailed. It was not long after being first called "Jet" by Bennett that the agent realized his colleagues labeled him so out of affection or respect, as a result of having proven his immense worth to them. Thus, Jericho really came to appreciate their admiration, and the moniker "Jet" became a vital part of his self-identity. In keeping with his charisma-laden nature, Jericho decided he enjoyed the explosive nature conveyed by "Jet Jericho." It seemed to imply a stronger "Follow me!" message when issuing commands such as "I'm Agent Jet Jericho! Immediately exit the building!" For some reason, commands from "Nolan Jericho" seemed to beg for a "pretty please" to follow.

So, yes, indeed! After solving what he and Agent James referred to as the "three-year case," Agent Jericho had certainly earned this day off to enjoy his Almond Joys, Nehi grape, and *Star Trek*. After his fourth Almond Joy, it looked like the episode was finally at the part where Kirk was about to climb the mountain and push the immense boulder down on top of the incredibly sluggish and unsuspecting lizard guy.

Finally! It seems like I always get interrupted in this part of the episode. There's always somebody needing something, and I never get to finish this scene. Jericho watched intently as Captain Kirk prepared to dislodge the boulder from the cliff's edge. *Go James T.! Nobody can move a two-ton boulder like you! They just do not make TV shows like this anymore!*

Jericho's phone suddenly began ringing. He immediately had that "Good grief!" feeling similar to the one many men experience upon finding out their mother-in-law is coming to visit. *Oh, great! Why at this part? I never get to see Kirk push the rock on the lizard dude!*

Although he attempted to ignore the phone, each ring jabbed at him like a needle and grew progressively sharper with each jab. After all, the agent did not typically receive many calls—but what if it was from Cat? Or, what if his mother in New York City was having an emergency? On the seventh ring, he buckled under and put an end to the unsettling ringing. *This had better be good! Kirk's wiggling the boulder; he's just about loosened it. It's about to be "Bye-bye, you Godzilla wanna-be."*

"Jericho here." The agent always identified himself immediately on the phone with his last name in a low monotone rather than initiating the tired old thrust-and-parry banter characterizing most telephone conversations. It grated his nerves immensely to participate in cumbersome, redundant dialogue such as *Hello? Is this Nolan Jericho? —Yes, this is Jericho.* In Jericho's mind, answering the phone with two words logically prevented the waste of many.

"Jet, Fowler here. I know it's your day off, but I need ya down here at my office—looks like I'm gonna have to mail ya somewhere."

"Okay, I'm on my way. I'll be there in say, uh, forty?"

"That'll work, Jet—at least sometime within the next hour."

Jericho put the phone down and stared at it a few seconds, then glanced back at the television. Captain Kirk was descending the mountain and was approaching the Gorn, now in a supine position after having been seemingly kayoed by the big rock. Within a few seconds, the diabolical man-lizard moved slightly and started hissing once again.

"Damn, missed it again . . . never fails!"

CHAPTER 3

Gettin' Mailed Outta Town

Since it was a gorgeous Friday afternoon, Jericho opted for Anna, his red '67 Sting Ray convertible. He cranked her up and, backing out of the driveway, blew a subtle kiss over to Polly, Anna's blue sister. *Aieee! Did I turn off the television? Well, no matter now.* The agent sped off after deciding it wasn't worth the climb back up the steps to his apartment.

Rapidly accelerating to the speed limit, Nolan began mentally picking apart his vacation strategies. SBI agents typically received two weeks of vacation per year, with options of either taking one day or several days at a time in small here-and-there doses *or* taking an entire week or two at a time in one or two large doses. Virtually any combination of vacation lengths were permissible within the two-weeks-per-year allotment. Jericho had always leaned toward a whole week off in the winter, heading to somewhere like Florida or the Bahamas, then using the other week by taking off a day here and a day there in the summer. However, the continual monkey wrench within Jericho's a-day-here-and-there strategy was that Fowler tended to view any agents taking off for only one day as being "on call" rather than on vacation. And so, here he was, heading toward downtown Raleigh on his day off.

With the breeze feeling *so* good as he traveled down Hillsborough Street, Jericho realized he had not yet consumed a *real* meal today—a hand full of Almond Joys, yes, but nothing offering actual sustenance. Fowler could wait another ten or fifteen minutes, for it was time to pay a visit to the cinder-block building just up ahead!

The agent sighted the quirky red, white, and blue structure that many a hungry N.C. State student raided upon their salivary glands reaching overdrive. Whipping his Sting Ray into the parking lot, Jericho smiled as he remembered joking with Cat that he could probably let go of the steering wheel coming down Hillsborough Street and Anna would turn into the establishment by herself, somewhat like a horse freed of its reins on a frequently trod path. Yes,

Char-Grill! *There truly is no better cheeseburger on the planet than at this place!*

Jericho got out of his car like a kid arriving at F.A.O. Schwarz in New York City. *Great! No crowd at all, a granted bonus for being here at an "off" time!* His salivary glands were now definitely ensnared in the same magnetic pull felt by the local college students, and there was no going back! Fats Domino's music came to mind, only in a slightly twisted manner. *I found my thrill, at Raleigh's Char-Grill!*

"Hey, Jet! How 'ya been? Haven't seen ya lately!" The often gruff man behind the counter had the luxury of being especially friendly during slower hours, for it was the harried hours around lunchtime which escalated his gruffness.

"Good to see you, Smokes, but it'll be even better to see two of your Char-burgers and *pronto!*"

"Have 'em right out, Jet! Hey, Carney, fix two of Jet's usuals. Cheese, mustard—"

"Yeah, yeah, yeah . . ." boomed the grouchy voice from the grill. "Aliens didn't kidnap me yesterday! Cheese, mustard, ketchup, chili, and onions!"

"Hey, Jet, ya ain't gotta suit on," noted Smokes. "I've never seen ya in the black tee. What's up?"

"It's supposed to be my day off, Smokes, but Director Fowler chased me out of the bushes. I guess I need to learn to lay low. Anyway, the home office isn't going to get a guy with a suit on during my day off—they'll have to deal with 'Jet-casual'."

Smokes started laughing vigorously. "'Jet-casual' . . . 'Jet-casual'! Hey, did ya hear that, Carney? 'Jet-casual'! Jet, you sure are one funny joker with words."

"I'll see you, Smokes. Thanks for the protein blast—best cheeseburgers on the planet!" As Jericho walked away, he could still hear Smokes chuckling a little and muttering "Jet-casual" to himself. Jericho couldn't help liking the lumbering oaf, basically a street-corner pusher whom the agent depended on to feed his ground beef addiction. Smokes lived life one customer at a time and a laugh at any given moment.

Jericho consumed his two cheeseburgers rather quickly. He liked eating while standing, preferring to take in the shade offered by the Char-Grill sign. He never ate in Anna or Polly, for to desecrate his prized Sting Rays or his clothes with Char-Grill's stain-threatening chili would piss him off big-time. As he ate, he thought again about Cat and smiled, thinking of how she ranted and raved about the agent's diet. He could just hear her now. *"How can you have such a HOT figure and be so lean?—and yet, you take in the same nutrition as a garbage truck! You are—ugh!—such a MAN!"* Cat would go on and on and on. The more she worked herself up, the more Jericho would take pride in having baffled her with his contradictory metabolism. It was much more entertaining to make Cat's fur bristle up than to keep her static.

As Jericho headed down the last several blocks toward the Department of Justice, he replayed Fowler's phone call in his head. The tactless director always used the phrase "gonna mail ya" when he was assigning his agents to an out-of-town mission. Therein dwelled the total illogic of Jericho's vacation dilemma, its Catch-22: If he stayed in town and Fowler caught wind of it, he would get "mailed outta town." In order to avoid getting mailed out of town from now on, it seemed that the agent would indeed have to leave town for a week! Fowler just could not seem to abide his agents relaxing on their home turf.

As he left Anna in the parking lot of the Department of Justice and headed up the steps, his heart started racing a little. It wasn't Cat's day off, and she would be manning her station unless Fowler had sent her on a "go-fer" mission of some type. Cat was the Jill-of-all-trades around the SBI office. She was the receptionist/secretary and could make *killer* coffee. Two different agents had actually proposed to Cat upon sampling her Chase & Sanborn. Even though Cat was her name, with coffee-brewing her game, Fowler often utilized Cat as a go-fer. During tougher times budget-wise, it was hard enough to justify a cadre full of field agents, and, increasingly, Director Fowler was finding it even more difficult to justify having both a receptionist/secretary *and* a go-fer. So, when agents out in the field needed some assistance in the form of equipment or other resources transported to them, Cat was the go-fer who was sent on the errand. Cat didn't mind it, either: it was indeed wonderful to escape the domain of stodgy ol' Director Fowler every now and then.

Now, there were two things Jericho knew could easily get one fired from a government office if strict protocol was not followed: finance and romance! As Fowler always said, "When it comes to finance, one should never dip his pen in company ink; and, when it comes to romance, one should never dip his, uh, pen in company ink." Well, Cat was company ink, pure and simple. It was clearly stated in the rules that agents were not to fraternize with other employees in the organization. In the eyes of the government, sexual relations created the potential for sticky, complicated situations, no matter how big the smiles on any guilty parties might be. For that reason, Director Fowler, Agent James, and the rest of the clueless SBI crew were kept in the dark regarding the after-hours relationship between Jet and Cat. Yes, Jericho publicly engaged in a little mutual cat-and-mouse flirtation with Cat at the office now and then, but so did most of the other agents—some of them married! With Jericho's reputation as a potential boy-toy in the eyes of every woman, it might have actually raised a little suspicion if he and Cat played it *too* cool.

As Jericho left the elevator and rounded the corner, he first caught a glance of Cat's shiny black vinyl boots as she was oddly leaning over from the customer's side of her desk and talking on the phone. Evidently, she had been on the run when the phone had pulled her like a magnet back to her desk.

Stephanie Catherine Marshall ate and breathed the motif regarding all things "cat." In addition to everyone addressing her by the shortened version of her middle name, the lovely Caucasian girl's eye shadow seemed to somehow accentuate the cat-like quality of her eyes. Although virtually anyone's eyes are inherently asymmetrical upon close examination, Cat's makeup seemed to highlight her alluring optical misalignment, yielding a slightly evocative look— a somewhat feline look, perhaps, or maybe a Far Eastern look . . . or *something.*

Of all the women Jericho had ever known, Cat was the only one of whom he could distinctly visualize every aspect of their first meeting. Having been introduced to her just outside Fowler's office when he was hired, the agent could vividly recall *exactly* the spot where she had stood, *exactly* what she had worn, *exactly* the way she had fixed her hair, *exactly* the manner in which she had looked him over, *exactly* all the words she had said and *exactly* how she had said them, and *exactly* how her intoxicating perfume had seemed to permeate, but not dominate, her presence.

Cat sometimes seemed to purr when she talked, due to little tonal nuances in her voice. For example, Cat had a funny little way of responding sarcastically to people with the phrase "Yeah, right." She would keep her mouth nearly closed, slurring the words together quickly from the bottom of her throat to produce a strange, swallowed-up "Yehroit" utterance. Jericho had heard no one else on Earth say it that way, and even that little nuance was an extreme turn-on for the agent.

And her wardrobe was equally nuanced. Cat had ultra-soft cashmere sweaters that seemed to almost blur one's vision into soft focus. She looked extremely fine in the longest dresses or the shortest skirts. The agents around the office often marveled at her glittery tops, referring to her collection of shirts adorned with sequins. And boots! Cat had boots of all kinds and colors for any occasion: vinyl boots, leather boots, suede boots, cowgirl boots . . . you name it! It was quite obvious that—as with Jericho—much of Cat's salary went toward clothes. There just wasn't another woman to be found in Raleigh who dressed quite like Cat. Whereas the female world seemed to have anointed Agent Jericho as the perfectly exotic male, Cat easily qualified in the eyes of most men she met as the perfectly *erotic* female.

Cat's primary hobby, in keeping with the cat theme, was her nine cats. Although her cats could suddenly disappear off the face of the Earth without Jericho going into a state of mourning, Cat worshipped her feline children. Each of the nine felines was a different breed and, interestingly, they were named after Presidents: Nixon the Siamese, Truman the Persian, Kennedy the Maine Coon, Roosevelt the Himalayan, Lincoln the Manx, Jefferson the Scottish Fold, Madison the Russian Blue, Fillmore the Egyptian Mau, and

Hoover the hairless Sphinx. On one occasion, Nolan casually mentioned that Hoover was the ugliest cat he had ever seen and looked more like a giant, anemic rat, leading Cat to give him the silent treatment for the rest of the week.

At work, Cat referred to Jericho as "Agent Jericho," both out of professional expectation and to perpetuate the "strictly co-workers" façade of their relationship. Privately, Cat did not prefer the name "Jet" at all, instead calling him "Nolan." Only two other people on Earth currently referred to the agent by his given name: Xiaoling, his mother, and Ricardo Baldini, an Italian intelligence agent with Interpol and an old friend of Jericho. Ricardo knew nothing of the "Jet" label that Nolan's Southern comrades had slapped on him. Additionally, a fourth person in the form of a mysterious, shadowy operative from an unknown organization identifying himself as "Dr. Rob" had referred to the agent in a deep, emotionless tone as "Nolan Jericho" in the few instances he had contacted the agent on the phone.

Therefore, Jericho's first name had become virtually obsolete due to his line of work, for he rarely heard it during any given day. Because of this rarity, hearing Cat purr his name during off-hours—especially while in a loving embrace—classified her as practically having exclusive copyrights on the use of the name "Nolan." She alone empowered the word with that special magic, moving the agent emotionally upon hearing it spoken. When things were getting hot and heavy between them, Cat would often call Nolan her "Indian Tiger," an extreme turn-on for the agent which brought out his more predatory side.

Jericho eased up near Cat's desk—he hoped to catch her by surprise on his day off—but, hanging up the phone and spinning around, she beat him to the punch. "Why, Agent Jericho! What has you gracing my presence on your day off? What happened to your date with, uh, Captain Kirk?"

"It seems that a Klingon named Fowler invaded my galaxy. I got a phone call saying I was needed right away. Cat, you would think that by now I would have learned to blow town to avoid our 'klingy' director's transporter beam."

"I know what you mean, Tiger!" muttered Cat, glancing around to ensure that no one heard her address Jericho that way. Although Cat was known for her flirtatious manner, with Jericho she truly felt it, and that made her all the more self-conscious of her conduct. "Yeah, Tiger, the chief manages to 'beam me aboard' also on my days off when he needs me to go-fer for him."

"Well, I guess I'll get in there and see what's going down. I'll stop back by and brief you. And, later on this evening, perhaps you can, uh, de-brief me."

"Oh, naughty, naughty, agent," said Cat in a singing manner as she rubbed her two index fingers together in a *tsk-tsk* motion. "You'd better watch that fraternization, Tiger. You might end up with a very big smile on your face if you're not careful and leave us with no jobs."

"Consider me admonished, Kitten dearest." Having been injected with a good dose of light-heartedness, the agent left Cat's desk feeling that seeing her had definitely been worth the interruption of a vacation day.

Passing by the desk of his friend Agent James, Jericho was surprised to find him there shuffling some papers. "Whoa, Bennett, I figured you would be out in the field today. What's up?"

"I might ask the same, Jet. I figured you would be in disguise as a couch potato scarfing down Swiss cake rolls."

"Actually, Bennett, they were Almond Joys today. I had to give up Swiss cake rolls for a while—you know, too fattening!"

"Okay, Mr. Calorie Counter, Almond Joys, then. At any rate, I figured you'd be takin' it easy."

"I tried that, but the Great Fowler summons. . ."

"Yeah, he sort of took me hostage, too. I would have loved to have been doing some kind of leg work today out in the beautiful sunshine, but the boss thought I needed to catch up on some paperwork. So, here I be!"

"Okay, catch you later, Bennett. Now to see what's up. . ."

Jericho found Bennett to be the perfect co-worker and friend. He always had your back in the field and was always up for anything fun or interesting during off-hours, yet he was never clingy or needy. Like Jericho, Bennett had his own pet interests and was perfectly content with people giving him his space to pursue them. Primarily, the sandy-blonde, curly-haired agent— reminding one of a surfer dude—was an aspiring artist. Bennett was especially attuned to the work of a local artist named Bob Timberlake, whose paintings were really beginning to sell. Recently, he had mentioned to Jericho in confidence a desire to sit in on some seminars offered by the rising artist. Jericho felt that Bennett really had the soul of an artist and would rather be wielding a palette of paint than a holster and gun.

Approaching Fowler's office, Jericho could see the bulldog of a man hovering around the filing cabinet digging for something. The agent breathed deeply as he knocked on the door and the bulldog spun around, a cigar jammed in his mouth with its ashes hanging by a thread. That was the aspect he liked least about attending Fowler's office: the rancid stench of his cigars. Jericho provided his dry cleaner with a high frequency of patronage in trying to keep the smell of Muriel out of the expensive suits he wore to work.

"Hey, Jet, get on in here! I really need ya today." That was about as close to an apology as Fowler ever offered for intruding upon an agent's day off.

"I suppose, perhaps, it's for something for which you thought of me as best suited after consideration of other agents, Director?" That was about as tactful as Jericho dared to be concerning the matter, in lieu of saying "Why me?—and today of all days, when you have other guys on the payroll just sitting around?"

17

"Yeah, Jet, this one has your name on it, all right. Ya remember Icy Springs and the homicides ya tackled there in '67?"

"Yes, I do. And very clearly, Director. How could I forget? Icy Springs was viewed by its citizens as a rural utopia until the cotton gin crimes turned their paradise inside-out. It's taken a half-decade, but the village has seemed to return to relative normalcy—uh, *hasn't* it?"

"Yeah, Jet, that is, until two days ago! I got a call this morning from Sheriff Niblock. He said the citizens were full of panic and wondered if I would officially send ya down there. I'm really surprised he didn't get ya on the phone."

"He might have tried. I went jogging later in the morning than usual since I had the day off." Indeed, Jericho was sure the sheriff had tried him, and he regretted missing the call and delaying assistance to his good friend at Icy Springs. After helping Sheriff Walter Niblock with the '67 murders, Walt and Jet had kept in contact with each other. Although Jericho was an incredible marksman, he had never been hunting, so Walt had invited Jet down on several occasions to go hunting in the woods around the old Yates place. Jericho always thoroughly enjoyed those expeditions with Walt.

"Well," continued Fowler, "seems that yesterday morning, several citizens found Reverend Paul Christmas dead, with his body tied to the steeple of the church."

Astonishment swept across Jericho's face. "My stars, Director! I remember Pastor Christmas very well. I mean, my God, he was the spiritual leader of the entire community! For the villagers, his murder has to be as hard on them—or harder—than the assassinations of Kennedy or Martin Luther King were for our nation. My heavens, what a bad hand!" Being an avid poker player, that was the phrase Jericho often used to size up a tough situation.

"Yeah, that pretty much sums it all up! Sheriff Niblock indicated to me that he really could use your help. I know ya worked good with those people down there back in '67."

"I'll leave right away, Director."

"No, Jet, hold off leaving today—and don't bother trying to call the Sheriff this evening. He said he will be attending to a bunch of clean-up matters and other logistics and may not get in 'til real late. He said, if ya could, to just head that way tomorrow. I told him I'd getcha down there first thing. I just wanted ya to know today what was going on so ya could be prepared for me to mail ya out."

"Thank you, Director. I'll play my cards right."

"Oh, and Jet—I'll probably send Cat down there in a couple of days to assist ya. I know that the situation there has to be an emotional powder keg, and Cat's so good at calming people down and distracting them from their worries.

I truly think that she could be of good use. By that time, you may need her go-ferin' some stuff for you anyway."

For the sake of appearance, Jericho played things cool as he downplayed his reaction to the news of Cat's assistance. "Well, Director, only if you think she might be helpful . . ."

"I do in this case, Jet—and good luck! Get down there and find some justice and peace of mind for the citizens in Icy Springs."

"Okay, sir, will do!"

After walking out of Fowler's office, Jericho thought, *Hot damn!* Although the task at hand was very grim and he truly felt for the people of Icy Springs, Jericho was elated at the prospect of Cat being assigned as his assistant on the assignment. Little did Director Fowler realize that, by sending Cat down in several days, he would be supplying this lonely agent in the field with a round-the-clock booty call. *Man, can you imagine—some good loving shipped directly to me, all courtesy of the state government at the expense of the taxpayers. And why not? I pay my share of taxes.*

Still pondering the situation, Jericho walked by Bennett's desk and put his right hand on Bennett's shoulder. "Careful not to overdo the paperwork, chum. I'm heading out in the field for awhile. Fowler's mailing me out towards Charlotte." Jet really didn't feel like taking time to share the details of his assignment with his friend, for he hadn't totally internalized the situation yet himself, so it was best to change the subject. "Bennett, what are you painting these days?"

"Believe it or not, a scene the next block over from our building—the grounds of the Capitol! You'd be surprised what good inspiration that area offers with those awesome trees providing such a great backdrop for the Capitol." Jericho nodded his head up and down slightly as he processed his friend's interesting revelation, for it was true. As many times as Jericho had ridden and walked by the Capitol, he really never had considered the plot's value from an aesthetic standpoint. "*Hmm!* Well, partner—happy painting!"

As he arrived at Cat's desk, the luscious woman's voice once again purred quietly in his ear. "Well now, what ball of yarn did our nasty ol' director toss around for the Indian Tiger to play with?"

"I'm goin' out tomorrow morning, Cat . . . uh, to Icy Springs."

Suddenly Cat's demeanor changed from alluring to concerned. "Oh, my—there? What could possibly be happening back at that beautiful little village?"

"I'll fill you in later, Cat. One good thing, though—and act clueless when he tells you—Director Fowler said he plans to send you down in a few days to assist me."

"*Oooo*, come to Papa," Cat slyly intoned.

"Well, I'll arrange a room for you beside mine at the local motel. You can at least use the room to store your wardrobe. And remember, no cats!"

"I know, I know, agent—looks like my sister's going to be doing some drive-by feeding for me again while I'm gone."

"Say, uh, Cat, just in case Fowler were to change his mind about sending you down, do you want to get together this evening? Say, for supper and some, uh, dessert? Remember, Kitten, 'dessert' is 'stressed' spelled backwards. I've been feeling some, uh, stress today from my day off being interrupted. Perhaps you can relieve me of some of it," said the agent with a wink.

Cat knew exactly what Jericho meant by dessert. "Sounds good, Tiger. However, we always go out to eat and then go to your place. Let me cook for you for a change. Be at my place at, say, 6:30? How does a great pan of homemade lasagna sound?"

"I'd be a fool to resist it!"

"You got that right, Tiger!"

CHAPTER 4

In the Lair of the Cat-Woman

Lasagna, huh? I can't wait to see what kind of spin Cat puts on that dish!
Agent Jericho was fairly well packed and ready to head out for Icy Springs the
next morning. He didn't dread tomorrow's trip, for he always enjoyed driving
one of the sisters around on a Saturday morning with little work traffic to be
found. In fact, this Saturday's journey would be an extreme pleasure if the
agent didn't have such a tragic scene waiting for him at his destination.

Nolan had decided to take his blue Sting Ray Coupe, Polly, on the trip to
Icy Springs. For sheer pleasure, he generally preferred to ride in Anna with her
top down, feeling the sun against his face and the constant breeze against his
skin. When on a tense assignment, however, Polly proved to be more practical.
It seemed that Anna offered too much temptation to put her top up and down
every time the weather changed, proving to be more distraction than the agent
needed. Anna also left him feeling like a sitting duck with the top down,
potentially inviting some lunatic to take a pot shot at him. At any rate, Jericho
decided to ride Anna over to Cat's apartment on this perfectly sunny Friday
afternoon. It was only fair, since he would be out of town with Polly during the
upcoming week—or would it end up being *weeks*?

Nolan hadn't spent much time at Cat's place since he had started seeing her
privately. He offered just about every excuse in the book to make sure they
usually ended up at his apartment. Even though Cat's cooking was great, he
constantly offered to treat her out; invariably, he would end up taking her to his
place for the evening, *or* entire night, eventually dropping her off back at her
place. The agent's reasoning with Cat was that he wanted to treat a hard-
working girl out to eat rather than have her slaving over a hot stove. He also
told her that having her over at his place all the time forced him to be vigilant
with his housekeeping. After all, he was a *man*—the place would be an absolute
wreck were it not subject to periodic inspection by his lover. Over time, Jericho

had executed nearly every reason he could generate in order to avoid going over to Cat's apartment.

The truth was that on the home turf of the capital city, Nolan simply felt a sense of control at *his* apartment. The agent knew exactly how many paces away his gun rested from his bed . . . from his couch . . . from his dinette table. He knew where every stick of furniture was located and could maneuver around them in the dark as effortlessly as during the day. Granted, no agent would ever have that degree of control when out on a field assignment, but, by God, he could at least have some say about his security when on the home front.

Besides, there were all those presidential cats at Cat's apartment—meowing and purring and puking up hair balls and litter boxing and kneading their claws into his expensive pants and so forth and so on. Jericho would tell Cat that going to her place was like visiting a pet store, except her place had no cages. Cat would always respond with, "Well, all of my sweet little pussies are out on good behavior and are free to roam about as they wish—so there!" Keeping his feline angst to himself, the agent would think, *Good behavior? Jeesh! It's like having a bunch of wrecking balls with legs and claws. Crash! Bang! Shatter! Spill! Doesn't Cat ever get fed up with this continual demolition derby in her apartment?* Regardless, Cat's invitation in the office suggested to Jericho that it was time to make a concession on her behalf and go to her place. Hopefully the evening at her place wouldn't turn into Feline Friday. *Maybe they'll all be asleep . . . or off in the corner humping or licking each other.*

Cat's apartment was actually a modest little 1,200-square foot house, which she rented from the landlord next door. The house was located at the end of a dead-end street, at least giving Jericho some assurance his prized red Anna could sit there somewhat discreetly without screaming: "Look, everybody! Guess who's at Cat's place? Jericho!" The agent pulled into Cat's driveway and sat there a second listening to Anna idling. *Now, that's the kind of purring I like to hear—no fur . . . no claws . . . and no litter boxes to empty!* Nolan shut off the engine and, bypassing the two steps to the front porch, took one hop onto the creaky planks of the porch. Known for his punctuality, Nolan glanced at his watch. As he prepared to knock on the door, the second hand passed over the twelve just as the hour and minute hands were denoting 6:30. *Yes sir, Mr. Johnny-on-the-spot! Right on time! You've either got it or you don't! And you've definitely got it!*

He tapped on the screen door three times with a moderately soft knock, then, several seconds later, tapped three times about twice as loud. Cat headed toward the door and started to unlock it. Before managing to open the door, she hollered "Hold on, Tiger!" Through the thin lace curtain on the door, Nolan could see her suddenly bend over and then pop back up. She reached for the door knob once again, but then bent over a second time and sprang back up. "Just a minute, Tiger!" As she repeated this lather-rinse-repeat routine of plopping down and popping up a third time, the agent pressed his nose against the window of the door and angled his eyes downward to see what was going on. *Well, that figures—of all the craziness!* Nolan rolled his eyes when he realized that Cat was feverishly grabbing at cats left and right in an attempt to keep them from bolting outside. It was like putting your thumb in a dike to stop the leak: leak after leak would keep springing up, but in this case it was cat after cat.

Finally, the door opened to reveal an apologetically smiling Cat. "They really are so precious and well-behaved. You know that, don't ya—at least you'd better *say* you know it!" cautioned Cat in defense of her babies. "They just like to explore, being so intelligent and all. Now, allow me to take your jacket, Babe. Just go on over to the table—dinner's on! I'll put the cats up in the laundry room." Cat took Nolan's sports jacket, as the agent had come in casual dress, anticipating a relaxing evening.

As Cat re-entered the room from subduing and containing her pride of miniature lions, Nolan's mouth slightly opened, as if somewhat in awe. "You look simply gorgeous, Cat!" The brown-haired gal of 5'7" was adorned in a lovely green dress made of a velvety cloth. Accompanying her dress were black leather boots. Cat just had a way of being appetizing, no matter what she wore. Whether a full-length dress or a bikini, Cat was a breath-taking sight whom Jericho found *achingly* beautiful.

"Oh, yeah—one more thing I nearly forgot, agent: hand it over!" commanded Cat, reaching out with her right hand.

"Yes, ma'am!" responded Jericho, loosening his shoulder holster and placing it into Cat's outstretched paws. She immediately did a 180 and headed back toward the bedroom, for the agent's gun was to spend the evening alongside his sport jacket on the chair at Cat's makeup table. It had taken a while, but Nolan had finally become compliant with Cat's ritualistic requisitioning of his firearms anytime they spent the evening together. She maintained that she wouldn't attempt to satisfy a man that could go off at any minute—ammo-wise, that is.

After seating himself at the dinner table, the agent began to stand up out of politeness upon Cat's return. "Oh, please, stay seated, dear, and just relax. I'll bring out the meal. Would you like a salad?" Even though Cat was going to have one herself, she had asked Jericho out of courtesy, knowing full well what the response would be. "Uh, no thank you—I'm in a rather carnivorous mood." This was *always* the agent's response when anybody asked if he desired salads or green vegetables. Whether eating out or eating at home, Cat's gun-toting honey was a meat-eater, plain and simple—so much so, in fact, that she always claimed Nolan held cows in higher esteem than the Hindus did.

Cat served the hungry agent a hearty portion of lasagna, then placed a salad and a much smaller portion of lasagna at her place. As he took a succulent bite,

Nolan couldn't get over how good the lasagna tasted—the perfect ratio between meat, noodle, cheese, and tomato sauce. "This is simply outstanding! How did you learn to cook so well, Cat? As I recall, I don't believe I've ever asked you that, have I?"

"Actually, no, you haven't. You see, my older sister had to grow up mighty quickly when Mother abandoned us. At the time, I guess I was two years old and she was around ten. Sis immediately grabbed some recipe books the week Mother left and began experimenting so that she could cook for Father and me. She quickly became a great cook and passed the skills on to me when I was around nine years old, enabling her to eventually leave and get on with a life on her own."

Man! I learn something new about this remarkable woman every day. She is definitely a puzzle of pieces that continue to assemble before my eyes. What a classy lady! Silently, Nolan gave thanks for this miracle of a woman twenty-four years of age, with whom he was sharing such a fantastic dining experience.

While they were eating, Cat initiated a conversation that she had been incubating in her head for some time. "You know, Nolan, sometimes you confuse me. We've talked over and over about the need for secrecy regarding our relationship, due to our jobs. Yet, instead of dining in at one apartment or the other, we quite frequently eat out in public. Surely you know that Raleigh isn't the biggest state capital in the country, and it doesn't exactly have a monstrous selection of restaurants. So, my question is: How have we managed to escape getting caught the past several months during our public appearances? You know? I mean, how are you so sure we won't run into Director Fowler or Bennett or Engelbretsen or Dalmus or Donnelly or Flagg or Stonestreet or Ayteck—or any others from that snoopy herd of agents in the department?"

"Whoa, wait a minute—Stonestreet? I don't remember a Stonestreet. Who's that?" asked Nolan, wearing a confused look.

"Sorry, uh, Stonestreet was someone I dated in high school. I got a little carried away when I starting rattling off names," explained a slightly embarrassed Cat.

"Good Lord, let's not get into listing your past boyfriends—the cheese on the lasagna will grow mold," replied the agent in a smart-alecky tone.

"Very droll, Agent Jericho. Why don't you see if you can join the cast of *The Carol Burnett Show!*? However, clever man, you never answered my question! Once again, how are you *so* sure we won't run into any of that vast array of geniuses we work with?"

Nolan gulped down a bite of lasagna rather uncomfortably as he tried to come up with an appropriate answer for Cat's question. Meanwhile, the atmosphere, which had been relatively quiet for the past five minutes, was slowly becoming contaminated by a din of noise coming from the laundry room. All sorts of sounds—thumps, meows, hisses, and scratching at the laundry room door—began to dominate the impromptu conversation. And the crescendo of the hubbub was becoming exceedingly distracting, making fluent conversation a challenging prospect.

"Well, Cat, as to our colleagues: I do my homework. For example, I've researched *[crash]* the eating habits of our closest associates—you know, casually asking them what kind of cuisine they like and names of their favorite restaurants. I have also noted the agents' work schedules that are posted weekly. In other words, I think most of our *[bang]* good fortune in avoiding our acquaintances is due to my expert planning. Honestly, though, I'll have to confess that some of our good fortune is perhaps due to just *that*—merely good luck. I suppose *[thump . . . hiss]* if someone ever does confront us at a public venue, I could just say you and I went out as friends. I mean, I could always say I appreciate *[slam]* the hard work you do for all of the agents at the office and am thanking you with a proper meal out."

"Yehroit! Nolan, that sounds so ludicrous! Do you honestly think anyone from our *[meow]* organization would fall for that lame explanation?"

"Why not?"

"Well, for one thing, your reputation as a chick magnet. Every girl that enters a room in which you *[bang]* happen to be imagines having your baby."

"Cat, that's crazy!"

"Is it, Nolan? Is it really that crazy?"

"Well, Cat, by the same token, attention from the opposite sex doesn't all fall just on my side. Every guy *[crash]* at the office fantasizes about you—and, unfortunately, I have to hear the lion's share of their dirty daydreams."

"Case closed, Nolan! You're making my point for me! Would anybody in his or her right mind who is able to count from one to ten or recite the alphabet fall for some contrived story about us just being friends if they saw us out together?"

"Well, Cat, I, uh—"

Suddenly, a *tremendous* crash came from the laundry room and the meowing, thumping, hissing, and scratching suddenly stopped, similarly to when kids commit a no-no and wish to camouflage the act with complete silence. "Sorry, Babe—be right back!" exclaimed Cat, hopping up immediately with a worried look, and flinging open the door to the laundry room.

"Oh my gosh! There is Tide detergent *all over* the floor! Nolan, I'm sorry, darlin'. Uh, since we were about finished eating anyway, would you mind finishing up your meal by yourself and making yourself comfortable? I'm going to sweep up the detergent real fast and put away the leftover food and dishes. I think that it's time to let the cats out of the laundry room."

Thank goodness for those little wrecking balls on legs and claws. For once, Jericho was indebted to the Society of Walking Fur Balls. The detergent fiasco initiated by the cats had brought an abrupt end, at least temporarily, to a conversation that the agent was finding increasingly tedious and awkward. When Cat got on a certain track of thinking, it took an earthquake to derail her—either that or a completely-dumped box of detergent, compliments of Kitty Central.

However, Nolan realized Cat was right. The two lovers *were* indeed cheating the odds that someone from the department would eventually witness one of their rendezvous and rat on them. For someone typically so obsessed with security and prudence, the agent was definitely walking a tightrope in his public appearances with Cat, and repeated gambles like that were truly against the agent's nature. Secrecy would be much more assured if, in lieu of taking Cat out to eat, he would just take her to his apartment and then drop her back off at hers. *I don't know, anymore—maybe I'm just being defiant against the regulations. Maybe I'm just daring them to catch the 'Great' Jet Jericho and tell me I'm wrong, and then try to reprimand me. Perhaps it is a wild streak in me wanting to lash out at authority and assert my right to love Cat publicly. Thanks a lot, Cat! Now, I'm more confused than ever. I just might have to re-think some of this.*

Jericho decided to retreat to the bedroom—after all, Cat would be releasing the feline army into the living room any minute. Normally at this time, he and his lady were often watching television at his apartment. However, with the cats back on the prowl, watching television in Cat's living room would mean rubbing and licking followed by more licking and more rubbing—and, darn it, only a small percentage of the rubbing and licking would be coming from Cat, for she would be busy paying attention to the little home-wreckers. Closing the door behind him, the agent mentally declared martial law on the entire perimeter of the bedroom, with all members of the feline species to be officially considered contraband and denied access. *I'm putting my foot down, yes, I am!*

After a brief period of calm during which Jericho assumed his lady was busy sweeping and dust-panning Tide, he heard the clamor of pots, pans, and dirty dishes being put away. The piercing ring of Cat's telephone suddenly drowned out the happy homemaking sounds. Since the only phone in her apartment was the one beside her bed, Cat yelled out, "Nolan, would you please get that?" The agent barely heard her hollering from the kitchen through the bedroom door.

"Hello, uh, Catherine's Cat Farm, with many cats of exotic varieties for sale! May we help you?"

Three seconds of silence . . . and then *click*. Nolan put the receiver back down, with a devilish grin on his face.

"Babe, who was that?" arose Cat's faint voice from the percussive symphony of kitchen cleaning.

"Wrong number—they hung up on me!" *Hey, wait a minute, Ms. Double Standard! You worry about our relationship being discovered, and you just had me answer the phone at your place! Big mistake! Or was it? Cat, are you maybe deep-down defying people to catch us just like I am? Or were you just not thinking? Now, I'm REALLY confused!*

Jericho went over to Cat's makeup table and surveyed her arsenal of cosmetics. Picking up a metal eyelash curler, he eyed the instrument curiously and visualized the device being applied in a torture chamber somewhere behind the Iron Curtain. Placing the weapon of death back down on the table, the agent then lifted up his shoulder holster that Cat had left hanging on the back of the chair next to the table. He carefully re-positioned the holster on the chair's back so that his gun was angled just so. *Okay, let's see now: I'm in bed, I hear a disturbance, I do a simple shoulder roll on the floor, I reach toward the holster, I retrieve my gun, I pivot around, and BLAM!* Satisfied that he now had a crisis plan in place, Nolan opened the bedroom window to savor the wonderful breeze filtering through the screen on the unusually cool July evening. He pulled off his black t-shirt, transforming the breeze into a cool gel sliding across his smooth, tan chest. *Sweet Jesus, there is nothing like a Carolina breeze!*

Jericho pulled off his pants, and then, wearing only his briefs, he walked over and reclined on the bed; he could still feel the soothing breeze. Through the door, he could still hear Cat restoring her kitchen back to normal and, for some strange reason, the most peaceful, calm feeling his soul had ever experienced washed over him. Truly indescribable, the sensation was euphoric. *Wow! Home! This feels like what a home should sound like—should feel like.* Within minutes, he found himself yielding to the gradually increasing force of his heavy eyelids.

◆ ◆ ◆ ◆ ◆

"Oh, won't you stay just a little bit longer . . ." The beautiful melody and words of the song "Stay" by Maurice and the Zodiacs was the next thing Jericho was aware of. *Cat's favorite song. The music . . . where from?*

Somewhat groggy, Nolan twitched as he felt a kiss upon his cheek. *What? Cat!* With his head still sideways, he opened his eyes slightly and spied Cat's record player with a '45' spinning on its turntable. The room was now dimly lit, as Cat had substituted the light of her nightstand lamp for the overhead lighting.

"Won't you press your sweet lips to mine . . ." The haunting music and Cat's kiss had merged to simulate the effects of a heart-reviving defibrillator shocking the agent back into consciousness. Jericho opened his eyes wider as he pivoted his head slowly toward the foot of the bed. The next view transfixing his eyes could have literally justified the application of an actual defibrillator straight to his heart, for views much less than what he was now seeing had certainly brought many a heart to a screeching halt.

There was Cat, still in her black leather boots, but she had now donned a sheer black lace négligée with her breeze-touched hair dancing lightly upon it. *My Lord, I now thank you that I am not a priest.* Indeed, at this very moment, Jericho could fathom no way at all that any man alive could even pronounce the word "celibacy" when in the presence of Cat in a négligée.

"Cat, heavens above! You certainly are providing Agent Jericho here with one amazingly babe-a-licious dessert. Are you expecting me to die on my next mission or something?"

Cat went into her soft, purring voice. "Shh, Agent Jericho, you think too much. It's time for the, uh, 'Indian Tiger' to start stalking his prey—*or*, perhaps, to get stalked." Cat started tickling Nolan's toes with her tongue. Unexpectedly, she lunged forward and started biting him playfully all over his chest. She continued her path of nibbling up the arch of his neck until maneuvering herself into his arms. As she lay down beside him and looked into his eyes, Nolan gently initiated half-nips/half-kisses against her moist lips.

"Why, agent! I detect that your, uh, submarine has put its periscope up," Cat whispered in a naughty tone.

"Uh-huh, but it's still only at half-deployment," Nolan slyly suggested as he continued to massage her lips with the gentle nipping of his teeth.

"Yehroit!" purred Cat, smiling at Nolan's grandiose self-assessment.

"Careful there, Cat, you know what your 'Yehroit' does to my warped libido. I think it's time for the submarine to go into deep dive." Nolan immediately entered into what Cat designated as the agent's 'Indian Tiger' mode, comprising a spontaneous transformation from his usual soft-spoken, passive demeanor of a gentleman to the dominating, purpose-driven personality of a Mr. Take-Charge. The agent immediately swung his body rapidly so that now Cat was completely flat on her back while he stared downward into her asymmetrical eyes. With his forearms straightened stiffly and serving as pillars holding his chest above Cat's, the agent began an intense alternation of kissing her passionately and biting at her neck. Cat's motor was definitely now purring, for this particular sequence of maneuvers drove her absolutely wild!

"Owwww! What the—? Yeoww! Cat, my toes! What the hell is biting my toes?" Nolan quickly collapsed his arms and allowed his body to fall beside Cat. His surprised lover sat up quickly and looked toward the foot of the bed.

"Uh-oh, Tiger, kitties on the loose! I'm afraid that was Roosevelt. He loves biting and pawing at toes—the precious little thing nearly tore my feet to shreds the other night."

Jericho felt both violated and annoyed that the bedroom ban on cats he had declared had now been obviously rendered void. "Well, hell," mumbled the irritated agent, "how did *she* get in here?!"

"Roosevelt's not a she. She's a he . . ."

"He . . . she . . . it . . . shit, whatever! Why didn't you close the bedroom door?"

"Well, Nolan, uh, honey, I did, actually. It's a long story." She drew breath and then, all in a rush, her explanation poured forth. "You see, the floors of this old house aren't level, so the latches on the doors won't quite line up with the slots in the doorjambs unless you lift the doors up a little by their knobs while closing them—I've notified the landlord, and he has said that he'll fix 'em, but he hasn't." Cat took another deep breath to recover from this rapid-fire explanation and then resumed in a more normal tempo of speech. "Anyway, Roosevelt has learned how to push open those sorry ol' doors when they're not securely fastened. He was just showing you that he loved you. Here, Tiger, I'm putting him out right now, see?"

After ejecting a perturbed Roosevelt and coming back to bed, Cat knew she needed to step up her feminine wiles a notch to settle down her wound-up partner. "Tiger . . . uh, let me be in the driver's seat for a little while you just lie back and relax."

Leaning over Nolan while seated beside him, Cat started giving Jericho some of her famous A-1, super-spicy, non-refundable kisses. Once again, the agent's mind was now fully focused on his lady and he began to tingle at her touch, her smell, her taste, her—

"Holy craaaap! What—? CAT!!! Owww! I thought you put Roosevelt out. He's clawing my groin. STOP IT!" Nolan reached down toward his privates and grabbed the orb of hair attacking him. As if he had a live grenade, the agent slung the fur ball toward Cat's makeup table.

"Rraaaooh!!" The cat's wail sounded like a siren as he sailed across the room.

"Careful, Nolan! He didn't mean any harm—and that was Kennedy, not Roosevelt. I guess Kennedy must have been in here all the time hiding under the bed. Kennedy is, uh, fascinated by genitals."

"Tell me about it! Cat, I've had about enough of these *anti*-sex kittens for one evening. I'm about fed up!"

Cat had already rushed to Kennedy's rescue and was stroking the distressed Maine Coon's long tufts of smooth hair. "There, there . . . that mean ol' spy guy didn't mean to sling you half-way to Timbuktu. Here you go, precious. . ." Cat opened the door once again and expelled the second little anti-aphrodisiac responsible for delaying some good love-making. "Okay, Tiger, no more kitties—I promise!"

Nolan was now on the floor on his knees, with his eyes frantically scanning back and forth beneath the bed, searching for cats. He was now in a state of accelerated paranoia about what might lie ahead.

Cat knew she had her work cut out for her. Yet again she initiated her masterful techniques of distraction. "Now, darlin', I know you have some wounds and are upset. Let's see if I can lick those wounds and make everything *all* better." Achingly aware of the spot in which he had last been wounded, Jericho found Cat's offer most enticing. Just perhaps, even with all the calamity having transpired, the outlook could still be *"All systems go; periscope up!"*

"Uh, Cat . . ." said the agent in a somewhat calmer tone, obviously trying to disguise any forthcoming measures toward self-gratification. "I'm not altogether selfish, you know. I know you feel slightly embarrassed about this whole affair tonight and that you're wanting to make it better. So, out of my intense love for you, I'll graciously accept your offer to lick my wounds. Please proceed."

"Yehroit! Oh, brother!" murmured Cat. She began kissing and nibbling upon his chest, working her way down rib by rib toward his flat, tan stomach.

BAMM!—

Agent Jericho felt a crash against his skull suddenly, and then, as though he were submerging under a wave of darkness, he started losing consciousness. He fought against it, barely managing to rise above the impending darkness and back into the now-blurred light. He shook his head violently in an effort to clear his visual focus. Instinctively, he pushed Cat off one side of the bed onto the floor and thrust his body over the edge of the other side. Rolling once on his left shoulder over to his holster, the agent snatched up his gun and swung his body quickly around. With a straightened right arm guiding his gun, he pointed in the direction of the bed. "Cat, are you okay??"

"Yes, Nolan, I'm fine—although I think I broke a nail when you shoved me off the bed!"

Jericho eyes quickly fished for who—or what—had rendered him nearly unconsciousness. Quickly assessing the scene of the vicious attack, he noticed that Cat's alarm clock was resting on the bed. "That big-ass alarm clock," as Nolan referred to it, had fallen about four feet from the shelf above her bed, where Cat kept it as a means of forcing herself out of bed each morning.

The agent lifted his gun toward the shelf. Then, upon sighting the culprit, he started feeling his blood boiling. He couldn't believe his eyes. *A cat! A sorry-assed, stupid, butt-lickin' cat!*

"Tiger, please don't shoot! It's Truman."

Jericho kept his gun trained on the cat, which was contently licking his rump. "Do I have clearance to open fire and remove a couple of his nine lives?"

"Hold on, soldier!" commanded Cat. "You kill *any* of my pussies, and this little pussy goes bye-bye." With that threat, Nolan lowered his weapon, walked back to the chair, and holstered it.

"Truman's my high-flyer, Tiger—he loves climbing. He must have been up there watching us all along. He really didn't mean to crack your skull open, the poor little kitty. Are you okay, Babe? Uh, Babe?"

"Are you talking to me or the cat, CAT!?"

"Why, Nolan, I'm talking to you, of course," responded Cat in a pitiful tone. The agent started putting on his pants.

"What's wrong, Tiger? Are you furious with me?"

"Cat . . " Nolan paused for a long time and then began speaking in his most deliberate monotone to convey his seriousness with clarity. "Cat, I love you." Again he paused to marshal his self-control. "I appreciate the great meal you fixed for me. What a meal! But, the dessert tonight has just about killed me." There was another long pause, as the agent pulled his shirt over his head before continuing. "In the course of less than ten minutes, I've been gnawed," he deliberately spaced out his words, pausing to let the magnitude of the indignities sink in, ". . . clawed . . . and nearly knocked unconscious! Makin' love to you has to be one of the most dangerous assignments I've ever undertaken."

"Nolan . . . do you still love me?"

Another short pause. "*Well*, that I do, Cat."

Cat playfully patted the bed right beside her. "Then give it just one more chance tonight, Tiger, huh? What do you say?"

As fetching as Cat looked sitting on that bed with her pouty lips and even poutier eyes, Jericho simply had to declare an end to the evening. "Cat, I have at least three or four long days, probably more than that, waiting for me at Icy Springs. Besides, even *if* I wanted to give in to your offer, which I am sorely tempted to do, I can safely say that the periscope is fully lowered and the submarine has headed back to port." Nolan paused and then aimed his best I-could-just-kill-you look straight at Truman. "For tonight, I think I've had too many torpedoes launched at me from the enemy."

The cat looked up toward the agent and meowed, then continued licking his posterior. "Anyway, Cat, I'm just gonna head on back tonight and hope to get a good night's sleep free of dreaming about psychotic cats with hyperactive thyroids. Don't worry, I'll try to call you in a couple of days from Icy Springs."

Nolan went over to the bed and kissed Cat gently on the forehead as she tightly wrapped her arms around his abdomen. "I do love you, Cat—and thanks for the great lasagna. I'll see you when Fowler mails you out."

"You promise that we're okay?—that the cats haven't ruined things for us?"

"Aww, Cat, I'll continue to take life, uh, one cat at a time."

CHAPTER 5

Arrival in the Village

Weather-wise, Saturday morning turned out to be a gracious morning for Jericho's trek to Icy Springs. The agent always savored the hypnotic hum of Polly's engine and, at least in Nolan's mind, the blue Sting Ray seemed particularly fond of cruising down Highway 64. *Man, Polly, you are purring today.*

Ooh, that itches, that itches, that itches! Stupid cat! Jericho's feet stung and itched from Roosevelt's surprise attack last night at Cat's apartment. To try to relieve the irritation, he had been driving with one shoe off and one shoe on, using the heel of his shoe to scratch the itch on the other foot, and then switching shoes and roles. The relief this dance of shoes provided was only partially effective and definitely distracting from his normally efficient driving, as he was constantly glancing downward to locate the displaced shoe for the next trade-off. *Man! Who'd have thought a stupid ol' cat scratch could ITCH so bad . . .! If Roosevelt ever pulls that again, I'll strangle the little son of a—"*

BEEEEEP—!!

The agent jerked his head upwards to see that he and Polly were now crossing the center line and heading right toward a station wagon. Nolan quickly dropped Polly back into the right lane. *Whew! Get it together, man! Roosevelt may have turned my feet to confetti, Kennedy didn't do my balls any good, and what a sore lump on top of my head, thanks to Truman, but no damn cat's going to be the death of me!!* Once Nolan managed to calm his mind somewhat from dwelling on the felines, he re-directed his thoughts toward his lover. *I wonder how Cat's doing this morning?*

Thinking of Cat made Jericho somewhat melancholy, for he felt a little unsettled inside about leaving her on such an insecure note last night. True, it was the most bizarre evening he'd ever spent with any woman, but it was exactly this type of wacky unpredictability that attracted him greatly to her. Realizing he had it *bad* for the woman, he regretted that he had perhaps relinquished a wonderful opportunity, not just to satisfy his carnal desires with Cat, but to passionately show his appreciation for her attempt at an extremely thoughtful evening. *If only those damn cats hadn't rattled me so . . .*

Okay, I'll drive myself crazy if I think of Cat all the way down 64. Maybe listening to some music will take care of that.

Nolan reached for the radio as he was about to enter the traffic circle around the courthouse in Pittsboro.

"All right, folks, now we have Percy Sledge melting some hearts with his great hit from '66—so by request, enjoy some Percy . . ."

"When a man loves a woman, can't keep his mind on nothing else. He'll trade the world for—"

Sighing, the agent abruptly turned the radio off. *Well, that wasn't what I had in mind! Thanks a lot, Percy!*

Around 11:00 a.m., Jericho entered the municipal limits of Siler City. *Boy, I am starving—shouldn't have skipped breakfast this morning. I'm in the mood for a couple of good cheeseburgers.*

A hint of a smile appeared in the agent's face as he saw the little brick building ahead on the left side of the road. *Ah, yes! Johnson's Drive-In Restaurant! There truly is no better cheeseburger on the planet than at this little place!*

Jericho wasn't able to visit this little jewel very often, but any chance to stop was always a mouth-watering delight. Mr. Johnson performed the most unique culinary hocus-pocus in preparing his cheeseburgers. Each flattened patty was cooked somewhat well-done with the extremely thin outer fringes of the patty grilled to a slightly crunchy texture. Serving as a royal crown, the burgers were smothered with a melted blanket of Velveeta cheese. No matter how foul a mood the agent might be in, biting into a Johnson's cheeseburger immediately transported him into taste bud paradise.

Mr. Johnson looked up from the grill as Nolan entered the restaurant. "Howdy, fella, good to see you again!" As opposed to his acquaintance with Smokes at Char-Burger in Raleigh, the agent did not frequent Siler City enough to be on a name-recognition basis with Mr. Johnson, but then, after most people had seen Jericho once, they were bound to recognize him forever. His vividly handsome appearance, enhanced by its fusion of harmonious multi-cultural elements, ensured that an impression of the agent was forever indelibly imprinted on one's mind. At times, this could be a disadvantage, like when Jericho needed to blend in with a crowd in order to follow a suspect without any fanfare.

"Good to see you, sir. Man, you seem to have those little treasures jumpin' the sizzle, today."

"Sure do, son, and I'm sure you're planning to have a few!" said Mr. Johnson with a smile, brandishing his spatula.

Jericho hung his suit jacket on the coat rack and sat at the counter. The waitress walked up, whipping her pen and order pad out faster than Matt Dillon. "Whad'ya have, Doll Baby?"

"I'll have two cheeseburgers with mustard, ketchup, chili, and—oh, yes—some onions."

"Sweety, I heard you say two cheeseburgers. What else did you say?" Typically never having problems writing down a customer's request, the waitress had been too busy staring at Jericho.

"...two cheeseburgers with mustard, ketchup, chili, and onions."

"Okay, sweet thing, thank you! They'll be right up!"

In less than two minutes, two burgers wrapped in wax paper appeared in front of the agent. *Ahh, if I were in San Quentin and awaiting execution, I would request a half-dozen of these babies for my last meal. Ummmm!* The delicious meat was saturated with its warm glue of Velveeta, coating his tongue and the palates of his mouth. Upon making contact with his taste buds, the heavenly blend transmitted an explosion of indescribable flavor to the agent's brain. *Incredible, simply incredible!*

With the last bite still in his mouth, Jericho stood and began putting on his suit jacket. "Sir, the burgers were as fantastic as usual. I'm sure I've never mentioned this, but I'm an SBI agent from Raleigh. I hope you realize, sir, that if your burgers are ever outlawed, I'll rush in immediately to confiscate them!"

"Son, I would go down in the gunfire with my spatula in my hand."

Both men chuckled and exchanged a polite "good day" nod with each other. Upon easing back into Polly, Jericho offered her his apologies. *Sorry, old girl! All the wonderful food I consume and all you taste is gasoline and motor oil—'tis a terrible, terrible shame!*

Around an hour-and-a-half later, Jericho passed through Monksville. The last several times he had driven this way was in anticipation of an entertaining hunting romp with Walt Niblock. Today's trip was unfortunately the flip side of the coin, as a piercing, icy tinge of anxiety filled his chest. He knew that the picturesque village of Icy Springs would be in a state of mourning, with an intense fog of gloom choking its citizens. Reverend Christmas had been their hero for nearly a quarter of a century, and his legacy would be tightly interwoven within the fabric of daily life in the village for many years to come.

Jericho's first glimpse of Icy Springs in heading west from Monksville was Big Blue's Feed Mill and Fertilizer Warehouse, a hulk of a business only surpassed height-wise in the community by the steeple of the late Pastor Paul's Lutheran church. Nestled along the banks of Atkins River, the normally bustling establishment was tranquil today, with no vehicles gathered around. *Looks like they're closed—I guess they've shut down until Monday to cope with the shock of the pastor's death.*

After crossing the Atkins River Bridge adjacent to the mill, Jericho glanced to his right as he ascended the hill. Sitting on a knoll roughly a mile in the distance on another road was Mimosa Grove Baptist Church, spotlighted by the golden mid-afternoon sun. This vision stirred a vivid recollection in the agent's mind of having once visited the inviting little African-American house of worship for the funeral of Red Chambers, caretaker of the Icy Springs Ginning Company.

Upon cresting the slope from the river bottom, he saw the Icy Springs Hotel standing proudly on the right. Actually a bed-and-breakfast inn reincarnated from its previously life as a Victorian-era residence, this hotel-of-sorts was touted by the Montmorency family as being situated on the same property as *the* Icy Springs, that is, the actual aquatic source from which the community took its name. According to local legend, a Revolutionary War soldier once stopped by the tucked-away underground springs for a revitalizing sip and remarked, "Great Balls of St. Elmo's Fire, these certainly are icy springs!" Supposedly transcending the legend is the true phenomenon that the springs are really fifteen degrees cooler than any other springs in the county.

After rounding a slight curve from the Icy Springs Hotel, Jericho spied Icy Springs School on the right. The agent somberly cruised by the deserted school. However, since it was a Saturday, Nolan quickly remembered that the vacancy of the premises was appropriate for this day of the week. Immediately past the school was the "downtown" of Icy Springs, if one dared to call it that. The tiny business district included Switzer's Hardware Store, followed by Doc's Store, both to the right of the highway and both being prominent establishments comprising the heart of Icy Springs. At these local watering holes, older men of the community would sit around mustard-stained checker boards sharing war stories, weather reports, and the same ol' tired gossip they accused their spouses of transmitting.

Being unincorporated, the village of Icy Springs did not have an official elected mayor. But unofficially, the position of mayor was recognized by villagers as being filled by the proprietors of Switzer's and Doc's in alternating years. During Jericho's first visit to Icy Springs in '67, the very German Heinrich Switzer was mayor. If the principle of yearly alternation still applied, Jericho figured ol' "Doc" Lassiter now had the privileges of the mock title during this even year of '72. As the agent passed by Doc's Store, he fondly recalled the icy-cold 6½-ounce glass bottles of Coke and the giant one-cent Jack's cookies. What a treat! However, the fanciful memory was quickly shattered by the fact that Switzer's and Doc's were both locked up tight, as quiet as a cemetery on a day of the week typically inviting much activity.

If the business district of Icy Springs could be considered the heart of the village, then its soul lay straight ahead on the left at the big curve: Icy Springs Lutheran Church. Jericho was suddenly struck by an intrusive thought. *You know, I've never before considered that all establishments in the village are on the right—Big Blue's Mill, the hotel, the school, Switzer's, and Doc's. However, the church is on the other side of the road! Is this perhaps the manner in which the villagers separate their commercial and worldly lives from their hallowed ground? Could it be, whether consciously or subconsciously, a way to enforce spiritual purity within their community and not offend God with their petty human day-to-day activities?*

Jericho had no more time to ponder the esoteric side of Icy Springs, for now he was passing by the church. It was truly eerie seeing the normally serene temple of spiritual invitation and salvation adorned with crime scene tape cordoning off a large area in front of the building. Currently, a shadow from the steeple was darkening a significant portion of the restricted zone. The agent slowed to approximately five miles per hour, glancing up at the steeple and visualizing the image of the pastor in his black robe adorning the tower. He felt a shudder, as he had met Pastor Paul on several occasions and was always so impressed by his appealing, larger-than-life character. *Who could have done such a thing? Well, I guess that's why I'm here.*

Nolan wanted to stop at the site and begin screening for clues, but he had to suppress the desire. *I need to get with Walt first. He can help me get my bearings quicker than my piecing everything together from scratch.*

A quarter-mile past the church, Jericho saw a form walking toward him alongside the road, a form he recognized from past visits to the village. Long-haired, scruffy-bearded hermit Bud Holly frequented the local highways, scouting out out-of-state license plates in the same manner that bird watchers seek to catch a glimpse of rarely seen feathers. *Still up to your meaningless meandering, are ya, ol' fella?*

Without slowing, the agent continued heading down the road on the western side of Icy Springs toward Sharpton. About two miles past the church, the Icy Springs Volunteer Fire Station stood gleaming in the sun, thanks to its aluminum framework, as did the Icy Springs water tower not far in the horizon behind the station.

Another two miles found the agent riding by the place he considered "ground zero" of his association with the eccentric world of Icy Springs—the Icy Springs Cotton Ginning Company on the right. *It looks even more chilling now that it has shut down and has ivy climbing all over it.* Many uninvited, horrible images of a half-decade ago began twisting and burning within Jericho's mind as his eyes revisited the defunct business. After being momentarily hypnotized by the gin's foreboding presence, Nolan looked away, trying to clear his mind of the blood and cotton mixed horribly together. *How can such a wonderful slice of this world, a utopia such as Icy Springs, be plagued by such evil—both then and now? Man, what a bad hand!*

Three miles past the gin, Jericho finally spotted the most distant outpost of Icy Springs: the Icy Springs Sheriff's Office. The unassuming brick structure housing area law enforcement represented what citizens of Icy Springs considered the gateway to their village, with a five-mile limbo separating the Sheriff's Office and the town of Sharpton. There really wasn't much to speak of between the Sheriff's Office and Sharpton other than the Chat & Nibble Café and Motel.

Well, here I am in "Walt's World," mused the agent as he turned right off 64 into the parking lot of the Sheriff's Office. Sheriff Niblock had coined the nine-mile strip of 64 stretching from his office to Big Blue's Mill at Atkins River as "Walt's World." Although the noble sheriff had jurisdiction over the whole county, he had a particularly strong affinity for Icy Springs. His home was located on Elmwood Road along the outskirts of Icy Springs, so the county commissioners had granted him permission to establish his base of operations at the satellite office in Icy Springs rather than the slightly larger office in Sharpton.

As Nolan opened the door, a tinkling bell above announced his arrival. "Hello! Uh, did anybody here summon an African/Puerto-Rican/Japanese/Chinese-American SBI agent?"

CHAPTER 6

The Idiot's Guide to Meeting a Dobermann

"Well now, friend, you sound *exactly* like just the guy I sent for!" barked a voice from behind one of the portable partitions dividing the modestly spaced office into individual work stations. A 6'2" frame suddenly elevated itself into a standing position, with the face and curly black hair of Sheriff Walter Niblock now appearing above the makeshift wall. "Yeah, you not only sound like the guy I sent for, you look like 'im, too!" Having vigorously maneuvered from behind the partition, the smiling sheriff walked gamely toward Jericho. He extended his right hand for a handshake, with his left arm half-hugging Jericho and his left hand administering two quick back pats. The two lawmen then cleared their throats and pulled apart cleanly and quickly, having just exchanged the awkward sort-of-hug that guys of the era felt remained within acceptable boundaries of manhood.

"Man, it's good to see ya, Jet!"

"Same here, Walt, although I kind of wished your invitation involved needing a hunting partner for some deer or game fowl running wild on the old Yates place. I hate our reunion is under these conditions. The afternoon drive through Icy Springs was like going back in time to, uh . . . ."

"1967? Yeah, the climate around here is similar to that, except only much more intense."

"I guess you mean because of *who* the victim is?

"Yeah, Jet, Paul Christmas was like Jesus to the citizens of Icy Springs. People here are taking it hard to the max. His death has not only paralyzed the village of Icy Springs, half the county is in a state of mourning. Even some businesses in Sharpton and Monksville have closed their doors today out of respect to the reverend. The people around here generally have a tremendous amount of faith in me to solve crimes, but I knew this one was *big*! You know, Reverend Paul sometimes said in his sermons that 'a prophet is not wise in his own country,' and that's the way I felt in this situation. The people here were so distraught Thursday that I felt I just had to show them that the outside world was rallying to support them—and Jet, to the people around these parts, you are definitely the best of the outside world. To this day, partner, you are still the most talked about out-of-towner—why, let me even go as far as to say 'celebrity'—due to how you put an end to the cotton gin murders."

Jericho nodded his head in a slight bow of respect and appreciation for the faith Walt was exhibiting in him. "I am again honored to help this community *and* you, my friend." Indeed, close friends were few for the agent, with Walt being one of the few males of the species that Nolan could call a buddy.

Walt was unlike any local lawman that Jericho had encountered in his cases around the state. Most hometown guys bristled up when some know-it-all in a suit from Raleigh came poking his nose in local business, but the wise Sheriff Niblock was a different breed. Only two years in office at the time, Walt had had the guts to call Raleigh for help back in '67 against the wishes of county bigwigs. From the first minute Jericho had set eyes upon the sheriff, Walt had shown Nolan nothing but respect and willingness to assist in any way. At times, the sheriff seemed almost as a sponge, soaking up any tricks of the trade and miscellaneous tidbits he could from Jericho. The humility and wisdom of the sheriff in desiring to push his own learning curve beyond its limits was a quality Nolan always found refreshing in Walt. So, from the get-go, the state agent and the local lawman were compatible, both on duty and off.

"What say we go on down to the church and let you have a look-see? Or did you stop there already?"

"No, Walt, I didn't. I didn't want to waste time trying to assimilate information that you would be able to readily point out."

"I swear, same ol' Jet—always thinking before you act. Bad habit of yours, ya know!"

"I guess so, partner, but I am indeed anxious to see the crime scene." As an impatient sort, Nolan was now ready to get on with things.

Just as they pulled the door closed, with its tinkling bell signaling their departure from the now vacant office, a patrol car pulled up and parked next to Nolan's blue Sting Ray. The driver hopped out energetically.

"Jet, you remember Deputy Maness, of course."

"Sure, Sheriff," replied Jericho. "How have you been, Deputy?"

"Fine, sir, just fine!" exclaimed the deputy, looking over Jericho's car. "Wow! Raleigh must be treatin' you right. Love the Ray!"

"Ol' Polly here treats me well. Don't be fooled, though, I'm on an SBI salary—therefore, I have to give up fine food, shelter, and other necessities to keep ol' Polly up."

The agent was familiar with most of Sheriff Niblock's men, so he was quite taken aback at the other deputy exiting the vehicle. Finding himself face-to-face with a new deputy, the usually eloquent Nolan attempted an introduction. "Hello, I'm out from, uh, Raleigh. I'm an, uh, SBI agent named—"

"Deputy Dobermann, this is the famous Jet Jericho," intervened the Sheriff, sensing that Nolan was a little awkward with his self-introduction. "Jet's a good friend of mine. He's the guy you've heard everyone talk about who solved those murders five years ago. Jet, this is the newest member of the force, Deputy Dreama Dobermann."

"I'm pleased to meet you, Deputy." Jericho was rather amazed at the rarity he was witnessing—a she-deputy in rural North Carolina. Standing about 5'6", the obviously very young woman had flowing, straight, blonde hair of the type that Jericho associated more with West Coast girls. Her uniform was the tightest the agent had ever seen on *any* government employee, looking as if it had been literally painted on. She was wearing quite a bit of makeup, displaying a particularly heavy hand with the eye shadow. Despite the excessive paint job, the deputy's eyes reminded Nolan of Cat's. In similarity to those of his lover, Dobermann had noticeably asymmetrical eyes, imparting to her a slightly exotic appearance. This exoticism was perhaps even more magnified by the fact that the she-deputy was staring in awe at Jericho.

"Why, Agent Jericho, how I have *so* longed to meet you. I've heard you are *quite* a man! You certainly look the part of a hero." Her over-emphasis of certain words left Jericho noticeably embarrassed in front of the other two male lawmen. At that point, Deputy Dobermann began gently biting her bottom lip not so unnoticeably as she stared intensely at Nolan. She reached out and started rubbing the material on the left sleeve of his suit. "Where do you get these soft, silky suits?"

Walt rolled his eyes and started fidgeting. "Jet, we'd better, uh, get on to the church."

"Definitely, Walt! It was good to see you again, Maness. Nice to meet you, uh, Deputy Dobermann."

Maness indicated goodbye to Jericho, saluting with his index finger from his forehead. Turning around, the deputy opened the door and set off that aggravating tinkling. Remaining outside, Dreama kept her eyes transfixed on Jericho as he and Sheriff Niblock seated themselves in Walt's patrol car. Watching intently as the two men backed out onto the highway, she waved goodbye with her left hand as her right hand played gently with the antenna of Nolan's Sting Ray. Her hand slid up and down the metal rod ever so slowly as the sheriff's car disappeared in the distance. Still gently biting her bottom lip, she watched until the vehicle was lost in the horizon and, with a slightly mischievous grin on her face, turned to go inside.

There was certainly no lack of conversational fodder to chew on while riding to the church. "Okay, Walt, you owe me an explanation, my friend! Before we get down to business, I've just got to ask. *What* was that all about?

Where did you get her? Bimbos-Are-Us? And buddy, before you explain, let me guess: she's one of the county commissioner's daughters and arm-twistin' little ol' Daddy asked you to hire her with a handshake and a wink?"

"Whoa, partner, hold on a minute! It's nothing like that! She's, uh, an experiment of a type. You see, things are typically slow in this county. I mean, the biggest crime in this neck of the woods is somebody taking money from a pay phone or stealing a license plate from an out-of-state guest at Byers Lake Campground. Recently, I felt the morale on the force was plummeting to an all-time low, so I hired Dobermann. Before she took the job, she had been a pre-school teacher who couldn't handle the children. One day, she just up-and-decided she would rather go into a line of work where she could shoot her clients if they were misbehaving. I needed more help and, uh, well, I figured I'd pretty-up the office a little bit with her presence—you know, brighten up the environment for my men. She's been here about three months."

"Okay, so how has this great experiment worked out for you?"

"*Well*, it's been interesting, to say the least. At first she wore very little makeup on the job so that I would take her more seriously. These days, she cakes it on like a Gabor sister. I'm *really* trying to work on that and get her to tone things down *big*-time!"

"Okay, so how have the men reacted overall to Dobermann?"

"*Well*, that's also been interesting. Competition among my deputies is at an all-time high. They don't stink like they used to, coming in all cologned-up. Deputies Hodges and Sanford have even taken off some pounds in the last three months in an attempt to look their trimmest. There seems to be a definite correlation—the more makeup she wears, the better they smell and the more weight they lose. So, some aspects of Dobermann have been good. The men really seem to enjoy her, having even given her a nickname. Get this, Jet: they call her 'Triple D'. Do you get it? Deputy Dreama Dobermann, uh, Triple D—seems to fit, doesn't it?"

"I won't argue that point, Sheriff!"

"However, there is one problem: the woman is *so* damn promiscuous. Dreama sees a man she wants and she's like a guided missile—so, you'd better watch out for yourself! She made a play for me the first week I hired her."

"Okay, and what did Sarah think about that?"

"Well, Jet, you know how much I love Sarah. She and I have a great marriage in which we're open and honest with each other. I immediately told Sarah about Dobermann flirting with me. *Do you believe* that my sweet little wife went to my office the next day with one of my hunting rifles and shot a hole dead center through the front side of Dobermann's desk?"

"That explains a lot, Walt. You know my powers of observation—I noticed that hole when we were in the office, and I assumed one of your detainees had raised a little ruckus while in custody. *Hmm*, so it was Sarah, huh?"

"Yeah, Jet—not a bad little shot, is she?" Walt inquired quite proudly. "Anyway, Dobermann doesn't flirt with me anymore with that bullet hole there reminding her of Sarah. However, Dreama's still so hot-to-trot in her walk and her talk, flirting with man after man. I'm really trying to work on that and get her to tone things down *big*-time!"

"Well, good luck on that one, Sheriff!"

"Jet, I hope you don't think I've been silly. Do you blame me? I mean, you agents in Raleigh have that fantastic-looking Cat working in your office."

"Yeah, Walt, but there's a big difference. Cat is extremely competent and efficient. She's an incredibly intelligent woman, with a fantastic brain."

"Well, Jet, I realize that Dreama isn't going to win a blue ribbon at the county fair in the brains exhibition. However, rest assured, I'm really trying to—"

"—I know, let me guess!" Jericho interrupted his friend. "You're really trying to work on that and get her to tone things *up* big-time in the brains department, eh?"

"Yeah, Jet, bingo! You got it! I don't have the heart to let her go, but trying to get her to think beyond her hormones is like trying to get the Pope to preside at a tabernacle."

Jericho mused for a few seconds about the so-called problems of small-town law enforcement. In his job, the agent placed his life on the line quite frequently, only to be chewed out by the ogre-like Fowler for bypassing certain obscure procedures. In Icy Springs, Walt was dealing with constantly having to reprimand an extremely voluptuous woman in a skin-tight uniform, telling her "Bad girl . . . bad, bad girl!" *Boy, Cat would go ballistic if this little piggy of a deputy ever went to market in her turf, that is, hitting on me. It would not be pretty.*

Suddenly adopting a somber tone, Walt softly uttered, "Well, Jet, here we are. Still gives me a sick feelin'." The patrol car rolled to an easy stop underneath a tree between the church and Miss Eden's house.

CHAPTER 7

Shadows and Cigarettes

Jericho and the Sheriff stood facing the church and stared quietly for several seconds as if offering an unsolicited moment of silence. The sun was beaming intensely behind the church, projecting a rather lengthy shadow of the steeple not yet quite reaching the highway.

Walt hesitantly broke the silence. "Jet, why kill Reverend Paul? I mean, the man didn't have a mean bone in his body and had never offended anybody to the best of my recollection. And, my gosh, Jet, why tie him to the steeple? Why not just kill him plain and simple?" These were rhetorical questions, of course, for Walt knew that Jet had no answers to soothe his confusion. However, talking things out with Jet always seemed to result in useful knowledge of either the informative or the comforting kind. Jet just had a way of re-framing one's thinking into a different perspective.

"Well, Walt . . . at this point, the only conclusion I can draw is that someone, a person with a really deranged way of thinking, either had a compelling vendetta against the reverend *or* that person had an unexplainable hatred for the church congregation. Perhaps that person was attempting to make a statement against the entire community of Icy Springs."

Walt now looked more confused than ever. "The church? The community? Jet, usually when a person kills someone else, it's because he is only concerned about ending the life of the victim."

"Usually, but not always. And, technically, we need to say he *or* she at this point. Don't forget, partner, our killer could be male or female."

"Wow, I'd hate to see a female that could drag a man's body up a roof and hang him on a steeple like that!"

"You ought to see some of the, uh, 'ladies' that we put away in the state penitentiary, Walt!"

"Gender aside, you mean to tell me it's possible that someone killed the reverend just to drive home a point of some sort to our community?"

"It's a possibility of uncertainty. Walt, I realize that you generally deal with a rural population of stable, like-minded citizens in this county. I suppose when somebody around here is out of his or her mind, so to speak, it's more than likely a personal issue—you know, a one-on-one difference of opinion. But in my travels around the state, I witness a larger sampling of behaviors—craziness of all kinds."

"So, you think someone was out to get the people of this area?"

"I didn't say that, Walt. I just said it's merely a possibility. The fact that the corpse was put on display for all the world to see leads me to think that our killer might have been obsessing about something other than simply killing the pastor. Sheriff, I caution you about drawing conclusions too soon one way or the other. When dealing with someone mean *or* insane enough to do this, the actual motive is still a wild card."

"I do know one thing, Jet: whoever is responsible for this has left an eternal wound in the spirit of the villagers, and that pain will still be around for several generations."

As the two lawmen started slowly walking toward the front of the church, Jericho deduced it was his turn to start asking questions. "Walt, you've indicated to me how hard the citizens are taking this, with the businesses being closed and all. Do you have any suspects at all?—and I mean the slightest suspicion of *anybody*."

"That's the problem, Jet. *Nada* . . . nothing . . . nobody. I swear to you, Paul Christmas had never crossed anybody on any matter. I've never heard one citizen utter an ill word about the man—that's what has made this investigation so sluggish. Usually, I have at least *some* bare threads of information to go on in various cases I handle around the county. I mean, someone somewhere always has a zipper unzipped or a button unbuttoned, figuratively speaking. You know yourself that you usually find *somebody* lacking an airtight alibi or not entirely motive-free . . . but in this case, amigo, like I said—*nada*! Jet, Paul was regarded so highly by the people of this county that if he forgot his checkbook, he could fashion a check using the back of a piece of brown paper torn from a grocery bag and the banks would accept it upon recognizing his signature!"

"Damn! That's quite amazing, actually," responded the impressed SBI agent.

"Yeah, Jet! I'll bet no one in Raleigh could get away with writing a check like that *or* cashing it."

"They'd be laughed out of the city," verified Jericho.

The lawmen had now reached the area nearly beneath the portico of the church. With his right hand, Nolan began fidgeting with the crime scene tape while staring straight up the profile of the steeple. "So Walt, from what you're saying, you have no witnesses of the actual body being placed on the steeple. I assume that this hideous act was done at night, perhaps just before sunrise. Tell me, who stumbled upon this terrible scene?"

Walt pointed with the index finger of his left hand toward Miss Krenshaw's house, her drive-way visible a quarter-mile away from the curve at the church. "Technically, the first person to notice the body was little Miss Krenshaw, a spinster in Icy Springs who teaches piano and plays for the services here at the church. She was on her way to Monksville at about ten to seven that morning when she spotted the body. It startled her so much she ran into the ditch."

Lifting the index finger of his right hand, the Sheriff then pointed to the little white house adjacent to the church and continued. "After getting her senses back, Miss Krenshaw hightailed it to the porch of Miss Eden's house. Miss Eden is a divorcée, uh, many times over, and she operates a travel agency in Sharpton. Miss Krenshaw got Miss Eden to come out in curlers and all. 'Bout that time, Burley Rankin pulled up, alerted to the scene due to Miss Krenshaw's car in the ditch. Burley operates a tire business down on Garden Valley Road. Anyway, the three of them fell to pieces once they sized up the situation and reality hit home. Miss Eden called my office immediately from her house."

"Did any of them see or hear anything at all suspicious—in addition to, of course, the crime scene itself?"

"Nothing at all. And, I promise you, these three are clean as a whistle. All three thought the world of the reverend and were shattered to pieces by their discovery."

"Well, Walt, you know that I believe you and I trust you, but . . ."

"I know, Jet, I know: you'll want to talk to each of them yourself."

"Yeah . . ."

"Jet, I don't take offense. I remember one of the things you told me not long after we first met. You said that sometimes a stranger can get a person to recall bad memories more vividly than an acquaintance could. If I remember correctly, it had something to do with the interviewee feeling more emotional in the presence of a person he or she knows."

"That's right, Sheriff. As long as the stranger can keep the person being interviewed generally at ease without being in an extremely nervous state, the interviewed person will generally react to questions in a cognitive manner—thinking more clearly without being emotional. It has something to do with the fact that a person instinctively remains a little on edge around a stranger, not letting his or her defenses down. The trouble *you* have, Walt, is that everybody around here knows you and respects you. Let me guess: when you interviewed Krenshaw, Eden, and Rankin, they were probably grieving extensively, right?"

"They were indeed."

"There you go, Walt. You see, a shepherd of the community—a person regarded as a comforting friend—is more likely to *enable* the person being interviewed to be more emotional. So, I truly doubt if each of the three had that edge and were thinking clearly when talking with you. They probably used you as a welcome release valve to vent their emotions—you might say, they were *feeling* answers to your questions rather than *thinking* answers. It makes a difference in the memories a person can conjure up."

"Sorry, Jet . . ."

"Don't apologize, my friend, that's why you called for me. Now, I'm not promising I will get anything out of the trio. If there is nothing, then there is nothing. However, maybe I'll keep them on edge just enough—that is, thinking cognitively enough—to recall something distinct or unusual. Plus, they've had a day or two since talking to you to calm down a little. Walt, is there anybody else living nearby who might have detected anything odd happening early Thursday morning?"

Looking in the direction of Icy Springs' so-called business district, Walt again raised his right index finger and pointed. "Well, not really . . . I mean, you can see Doc's Store and Switzer's Hardware in the distance. But, neither one was open yet for the day. Both Doc and Mr. Switzer said they were home, oblivious to everything going on."

"Okay, then I don't think I'll pursue interviewing those two formally. I think I can conclude that their lack of proximity to the crime scene from their houses creates a high probability that they saw and heard nothing. And, with their stores not being open until eight o'clock, it's safe to say that downtown Icy Springs was dead of any activity at ten to seven in the morning other than those unfortunate passers-by, Miss Krenshaw and Mr. Rankin."

Jericho glanced back upwards at the steeple. "Walt, how do you suppose the killer got the body up there?—and how did *you* get the body down?"

"We actually retrieved Paul's body with the help of a cherry-picker that we borrowed from Crescent Power Company in Sharpton. We took a little time getting the body down, as I wanted to make sure we imposed as little disruption on the crime scene as possible. I decided to use a cherry-picker just because I felt it might be more secure for everyone involved in the process. It's awfully precarious up there that high, especially on the front side of the steeple. It ended up that we had to wait until about two o'clock that afternoon for Crescent to jump-start their cherry-picker and bring it to us."

Changing his posture somewhat and staring at the ground, the sheriff continued as he adopted a grim-sounding tone in his voice. "Man, Jet, I'll never forget that spooky scene. As the guy standing in the bucket of the cherry-picker was hoisting ol' Paul off the roof of the steeple, the shadow of Paul's body was etched into the landscape. It was as if the pastor's body was floating by itself, with his shadow creeping along below. We had closed 64 to all traffic that morning and afternoon, detouring all comers and goers down Swann Road and Turkey Farm Road past Mimosa Grove Baptist. The only on-lookers were some of the locals walking up whose curiosity had been aroused enough to watch everything as it happened. It was spooky! Everyone there was gasping in horror as Paul's shadow seemed almost alive, sort of mocking them, maybe like it was mocking death itself. I know it sounds crazy, but you've got to understand that imaginations were feeding on the frenzy of the day. A couple of the villagers standing near the edge of the shadow commented on how cold the area was. One of them said it felt downright icy. Oh, well . . ."

"Mighty grim indeed, Sheriff, especially for this little Shangri-la of a village. Okay, so back to my other question: how do you think the killer got Paul's body up there?"

"Well, this is just speculation, albeit with some forensic backing. As you already see, the A-frame architecture of the church brings the eaves of the roof within eight feet of the ground. Getting on that roof is not that tough. It would have been easy to loop a length of rope around the chest of the pastor just under his armpits and haul him up. The county coroner, Jack, has verified some abrasions of the skin—rope burn—on Paul's body. And, we did find a lot of shingles on the roof that had tattered edges, as if something heavy had been dragged toward the steeple. And dragged it certainly was—a helluva drag up that steep roof! Anyway, before you ask, friend, there were no fingerprints, no blood, no clothing fragments, no hair . . . nothing else."

"What conclusion did the coroner, uh, Jack, draw as to the cause of death?"

"A very sharp blow to the head with an unknown blunt object, like a baseball bat or something."

"How long had he been dead before being discovered?"

"Jack thinks that Paul had been dead for six to eight hours before the abrasions from the rope occurred."

"*Hmm*! That long before, huh? Walt, when's the last time anybody remembers seeing Paul?"

"The last time anybody recalls seeing the pastor was Tuesday evening on his visitation rounds at Sharpton Memorial Hospital. According the hospital officials, Paul trumpeted his usual 'Have a blessed evening!' to the receptionist on his way out. We checked the hospital parking lot and detected no sign of foul play there."

"Then, may I assume his car is in the parsonage garage?"

"Yeah, Jet. We think he arrived back home safely Tuesday night. However, nobody remembers seeing him at all on Wednesday *or* seeing his car on the highway. Paul could often be found in his office on Wednesday evening during choir practice but, seeing as Paul was renowned for his excessive visitation, the choir thought nothing of it if he *wasn't* buzzing around the church. And the congregation thought nothing of it if they called the church and no one answered. Jet, Paul was a visitor-and-a-half, always visiting like crazy. He

47

came and went, came and went. But as I said, I haven't yet turned up anybody who saw him after Tuesday."

"Walt, mind if we climb up on the roof?"

"Sure don't! That's why I had them leave the ladder over there against the eave. I knew you'd be chomping at the bit to go up there."

As the men stood at the base of the ladder, another question suddenly hit Nolan. "Walt, something I about forgot to ask you: I know Paul wasn't married, so did he have *any* family?"

"His father's dead, but his mother lives in a nursing home somewhere down in Spartanburg, South Carolina. She's nearly blind and cannot walk without assistance, but she has a pretty sharp mind, from what I've heard."

"What's her name?"

Walt suddenly grinned like a Cheshire cat. "You're not gonna believe this one, Jet. Her name is Mary! Yep, that's right: Mary Christmas!"

"You're right, I don't believe you!"

"Well, it's true. Anyway, Paul had no sisters, but there is a brother. *And,* another interesting tidbit: his brother is only about twelve minutes older than Paul. From what I've learned, Paul and his brother were twins—the spittin' image of each other!"

"What is his brother's name? Where does *he* live?—and don't tell me his name is something like Jolly or Happy Christmas. I'll have you hauled away by the men in white."

"No, partner, hold off on the mental crew. His brother's name is Ronald—goes by Ron. He lives somewhere down around Columbia, South Carolina."

Nolan had started easing up the ladder to the edge of the low overhang, with Walt right behind him. In the midst of climbing, the agent asked, "So, how was the relationship between Paul and his brother?"

"Well, from what I understand, Paul and Ron had sort of grown apart. They hadn't really seen or called each other in quite a few years. In fact, I don't know if Ron has ever visited Icy Springs to see his brother since Paul received his appointment as minister here."

As Nolan was about to give a hand to Walt to help him onto the roof, he stopped moving and looked confused. "Wait just a minute, Sheriff! I thought you told me a few minutes ago that you could think of no one in the pastor's life meriting any degree of suspicion?"

Throwing his weight onto the roof and sitting beside the agent, Sheriff Niblock puffed out a breath before mounting his defense. "Whoa, Jet, I clearly said that I couldn't think of anyone who had a motive to kill Paul. Remember, I said that the pastor never crossed anybody and didn't have a mean bone in his body. So, I can't see that he gave Ron any reason to kill him. More to the point, I just can't see a motive on Ron's behalf."

"Sorry, partner, perhaps I was a little too quick on the draw. Please keep talking . . ."

"Well, from what Paul once told me, Paul had nothing against Ron, and I don't believe Paul gave Ron any reason to despise him. I think Ron's misfortune might have been the wedge that separated him from Paul and, I suppose, from everybody else."

As they gently crab-walked backwards up the steep incline, Nolan eyed the shingles closely. "Go ahead, Walt, I'm listening. What's this about Ron's misfortune?"

"Well," continued the sheriff as he huffed and puffed some deep breaths, "Ron was a big-time investor, operating between Columbia and Atlanta. Supposedly, he was one of the richest men in Columbia at one time. Then, in a short amount of time, it all came crashing down."

As Nolan continued to ease up the roof, Walt came to a stop midway. "Jet, you remember my one fear, don'cha? I don't like heights, never did. You keep on going, and my ass will be entertained enough right here."

"Okay, Walt . . . So, what about Ron's fortune crashing down?"

"Well, within the time span of a year and a half, all his investments went south big-time *and* he lost his beloved wife—Linda, I believe, was her name. In other words, Ron went from being a wealthy, happily married man to being penniless and lonely in the blink of an eye."

Speaking a little louder as he neared the steeple, Nolan looked back to assure Walt was okay. "How did he lose Linda?"

"Well, you know, socialites . . ." commented Walt with an equally loud voice. "From what I've heard, they were celebratin' it big one night in the middle of Lake Murray outside of Columbia in Ron's boat. It was a rather rowdy party from what I gathered, and Linda took a spill into the water. Partygoers maintained it was accidental, and no evidence ever contradicted otherwise. When her body washed up days later, she had a higher alcoholic content than Sharpton's liquor store—verification that there was no reason to suspect foul play. Ron took Linda's death very hard, and having to trade in his expensive fleet of European cars for one used Volkswagen only added insult to injury. Now remember, Jet, this is all stuff Paul told me a good while back when telling me about him and his brother having lost contact."

Now sitting still beside the steeple and leaning against the base, Nolan gathered his breath a second. "So, Walt, why do *you* think the relationship between Paul and Ron deteriorated?"

"Well, I don't think Ron consciously held anything against Paul, for Paul certainly didn't kill Linda and Paul certainly didn't lose Ron's money for him. Even so, Ron's life had spiraled downward, thus you had a Ron that was drowning in a pool of loneliness each day of his life. In his previous life as a well-to-do, I suppose Ron always felt superior to Paul to some degree. I mean, here was a rich investor with a beautiful wife who had become a master of all things worldly. In Ron's eyes, Paul was a pitiful servant of the people, always performing the lonely and thankless function of bringing godless people closer to a God that Ron didn't think existed to begin with. Think about it: in the blink of an eye, Ron became the lonely one. The poor soul's misfortune and loneliness were probably intensified in his mind by the stark contrast with his brother's fulfilling life—you know, with Paul having such support and love from the people of Icy Springs. In Ron's eyes, Paul had a rich, fulfilling marriage to an entire village. In fact, the only times I think Paul ever left Icy Springs in all the years he lived here were when he went to South Carolina to see his mama and the one time he took a vacation overseas to the Holy Land—that's the degree of commitment Paul had to his church. I just think that eventually Ron could no longer handle the love this entire community had for Paul, especially when love and happiness were now so absent in his own life. Jet, I'm sure Columbia is a nice city, but you just don't find the same love and caring among people in a state capital that you do in Icy Springs."

"Tell me about it! They didn't exactly roll out the Welcome Wagon in Raleigh when I moved there from New York." Nolan was now standing up beside the steeple and propped against it looking down at the ground.

"Jet, do you think I was stupid to not even consider Ron as a suspect?"

"No, Walt, not at all. As you implied, just because Ron was lonely, bitter, and perhaps even a little jealous of the life Paul had, all of that doesn't necessarily add up to a motive for Ron to kill his brother. I'm sure Paul still treated Ron as any great pastor would treat his own brother, with brotherly love. However, I think I might like to meet Ron because of the complexity behind his circumstances—you know, drowned wife and all. Again, please don't be offended, friend—it's just my thorough nature. If and when I do see Ron, I'll probably turn up nothing. The reality is that merely suspecting somebody of the possibility of committing a crime is one thing; the more difficult aspect of the process is obtaining concrete proof that the suspect did it, if—-and *only* if—things move beyond mild suspicion."

"Thanks, Jet, at least I feel a little bit less incompetent. I guess lately I've just not been able to think with my usual clarity and precision."

"Well, Walt, I tell ya, it's nothing that can't be solved by finding Dreama Dobermann another line of work. Even though you're happily married and said you wanted to keep your deputies on their toes, I think you were thinking more with your pecker than with your brains in the decision to hire Triple D."

"Aww, Jet . . ."

"—Hold on a second, Walt! From up here, I can see something down there on top of the portico. It looks like a cigarette package."

"Aw, that idiot Hodges! I should have known better than to send him up to the steeple. I would-a seen it myself if I didn't have this dang fear of heights. I should have known Deputy Hodges would be about as attentive as a gay guy at a girlie show. Damn!"

"Hey, don't beat yourself up, Walt. Let's check it out!"

Several minutes later, the lawmen were back on solid earth, standing underneath the portico. "Should I bring the ladder over, Jet?"

"Nah, just lock your hands together and give me a lift up. The package is right along the edge—I think I can reach it."

Complying with his friend's request, Walt interlocked the fingers of both hands and held them about two feet off the ground; Jericho stepped into the makeshift cradle and, with a "1, 2, 3, up!" and a boost from Walt, was soon gripping the top of the portico. With Walt half-supporting Nolan and the agent half-suspending himself by hanging by his left hand, he was able to rake along the top edge of the portico with his right hand. As if on cue, the cigarette package came tumbling over the edge of the portico.

"Got it! Okay, Walt, you can back away now!" The sheriff let go of Nolan's foot and backed up about three feet. Now fully hanging from the portico by both hands, Nolan dropped with ease to the ground.

"Hey, Kool cigarettes! A popular brand, eh, Jet?"

"Yeah, you know anybody who smokes 'em?"

"Well, it might have been Paul's brand."

"Hold on, Walt—you mean to tell me that the 'perfect' reverend smoked?"

"Yeah, he'd been trying to quit for years. That's the one aspect of Paul that people did complain about a little bit. He had some fussy women of the congregation who smelled it all over him from time to time and ranted about him being a bad role model for the youth of the church. I mean, we're all human, but to his credit, Paul never smoked in front of anybody as far as I know. He told me a time or two how smoking soothed him late at night when he was conjuring up a sermon."

Bending over and examining the package closely, Nolan saw that it wasn't empty. "Hmm, there are a few cigarettes in here. And, wow—look at this, Walt! Check out the tax stamp on this baby!" Not wanting to handle the item, Jericho carefully took a pen from his pocket and used it to angle the package appropriately so the sheriff could see the tax stamp.

"Holy Toledo, Jet, a *South* Carolina tax stamp! And take a gander at the date on the overprint covering the stamp: July 12, 1972. With this package coming so recently from South Carolina, that certainly makes—"

"—our friend Ron a *lot* more interesting!" interjected the agent. "Unfortunately, Walt, the fact that these cigarettes were taxed in South Carolina and the fact that Ron lives in South Carolina jive only enough to produce the weakest circumstantial evidence at best. Any defense lawyer would enlighten a jury in a split second on the absence of proof that it was Ron who purchased them. However, along the same vein of thinking, the coincidence of the two facts certainly doesn't eliminate possible guilt, either. Call it a gut feeling, Walt, but South Carolina sounds like it might make a good tourist destination for me."

"It's a real slim proposition," noted the sheriff while scratching his head, "but it's the *only* morsel of a lead we have at the moment."

"Sure enough, Walt. Don't pick up the package. I didn't touch the front and back of the package with my hands when I retrieved it—I knocked it over the ledge by bumping one of its narrow sides with the edge of my hand. What I'm trying to say—and it's a shot in a million—is that we might have some intact prints on this baby." Walt was already heading to the trunk of his patrol car to obtain a plastic bag into which to scoop the cigarette package.

"Do me two more favors concerning the cigarettes, Walt. Would you have your deputies check the parsonage for any packages or cartons of Kool cigarettes? And, would you also check with Jack to see if tobacco residue was documented in his autopsy on Paul's body?"

"Sure thing, Jet—uh, check for prints, check for residue, gotcha! As far as cartons of Kool cigarettes at the parsonage, we didn't see any when we went through it yesterday."

"Thanks, Walt! Oh, yeah, about the parsonage—"

"I know, partner. Have no fear. We fine-tooth-combed that sucker, inside and out, upside and down—desk drawers in the study, notepad at the telephone, calendar, *everything*. You name it, we searched it. I went through everything personally with the assistance of Maness. I didn't trust Hodges or Sanford with that task—nor, of course, did I trust Dreama."

"Good enough, Walt, I'm sure you did a fine job. However, just do me the courtesy of one more glance around for some Kool cigarettes—just in case. I mean no offense, buddy. But with Paul being a known smoker, cigarettes would not have been something extraordinary to have seen at the time—they would have blended in with the background. Now that the cigarettes *are* a possible lead, would you mind one more glance?"

"Sure, Jet," replied the understanding sheriff. "No problem!"

"My Lord, it just hit me—" mused Jericho. "Tomorrow is Sunday! I just now thought about it."

"Yeah, it's Sunday all right, and Paul's funeral is at two o'clock tomorrow afternoon."

"Are Ron and Mrs. Christmas coming to the funeral?"

"That I don't know. Church representatives contacted law enforcement officials around Columbia and Spartanburg, asking them to inform the next of kin. But, I don't know if either Ron or Mary has responded with an intention to come—in fact, I don't know if Mary has the health to attend or, for that matter, if Ron has the desire to attend."

"Walt, what is the congregation doing tomorrow for their church service? What are the plans for the funeral?"

"Actually, they've canceled the normal service for tomorrow morning. I had offered to have all the crime scene tape and barricades removed after your visit today so they could have the morning service and the funeral here tomorrow, but the church elders wisely counseled against it. They felt that the congregation was not emotionally ready to resume worship in the place where the body of their beloved leader was so brutally displayed after his life was so, uh, tragically ended."

". . . and the funeral?"

"Interesting outcome there, partner: the wonderful congregation over at Mimosa Grove Baptist Church graciously offered the use of their facilities for the funeral. As you know, Jet, Mimosa Grove is a black church. The elders of Icy Springs Lutheran politely declined, saying that they needed more space for the funeral, which is not altogether dishonest, I suppose. I mean, there will be a ton of people at Paul's funeral. But, I think the main reason the elders didn't consider the offer was because of the color difference. Jet, I will have to say that people in these parts generally get along respectably as neighbors regardless of color, with blacks and whites often reaching out and helping each other in times of crises, at least to a degree. So, I'm proud of Icy Springs for being a place with relatively little racial tension, a place where people tend to live in harmony. However, when it came down to brass tacks and the congregation at this church was invited to mourn for their dead in a black church, I don't guess the church elders of the Icy Springs Lutheran were quite ready to blend gods of different colors. I suppose they still feel that heaven must be segregated even though they're acting all brotherly down here."

"Okay, so where's the funeral going to be held?"

"The principal of Icy Springs School okayed the use of the gymnasium through the school system's superintendent. The church elders hopped right on that one and, petty hidden agendas aside, they probably made a good decision. I'm betting the gymnasium will be packed. Jet, do you think you will begin questioning the neighbors this evening, or will you start tomorrow?"

"Neither, Walt. I think I'll actually hold off until Monday morning. I mean, people right now are still probably emotional powder kegs. They need a funeral for some closure, and I'm certainly not about to intrude upon their day of mourning. No, I need to leave their Sunday alone—for them, God, and probably me, too. I think Monday will offer me a better shot at getting people to respond to me cognitively and sensibly rather than emotionally."

"Hey, Jet—" interjected the sheriff, snapping his fingers. "I did almost forget to mention one guy who lives near the church you might want to question."

"Who's that?"

"Bud Holly—uh, Bud E. Holly, to be precise. And no, he's no relation to Buddy Holly, the singer. You know, you've seen him walking along the highway before. He's the hermit who lives down there in the holler beyond Miss Krenshaw."

"Yeah, I saw him wandering along the highway earlier today on my way to your office. He's the guy that wanders the highway looking at license plates through his binoculars or some such nonsense, right?"

"Right! But, I doubt you'll get much of anything from him. I already talked to him. I asked him if he heard or saw anything weird happening up toward the church in the wee morning hours. He said everything seemed quiet and normal to him. But, I *know* you, and you'll want to talk to him. Watch out, though, for he's a nut—a real interesting nut, however."

"Exactly where is his house?"

"Actually, only about fifty feet off the highway down in the holler."

"I've passed through the holler many times and I've never seen a house by the road. All I've noticed is a gravel drive right beside the highway disappearing into the ravine."

"Yeah, you'd never notice the house! The ravine beside of the road is *so* deep! His house is down in there though, camouflaged by the thick overgrowth of trees and brush."

"And just what makes *him* so interesting, Walt?"

"Well, sort of like Ron Christmas, they say some years ago Holly was extremely rich—a Wall Street man that flew back and forth from New York to London. Supposedly, he even owned a small island near St. Croix of the Virgin Islands. However, I've heard he engaged in some bad ventures like some crazy restaurant franchise, first losing all his money and then losing all his marbles. He's a nice guy, though—to me, he's totally harmless. But he's still a nut—a real interesting nut, as I said. You'll see some evidence of his past wealth down there around his house. Don't ask me, you'll see what I'm talking about!"

"One more question, Walt, and then I can consider this debriefing finalized. How's the media been treating Paul's murder?"

"Well, it's been predictably sensationalized beyond measure—you know, enabling the community to feed on its own terror. I've been hounded the last two days by reporters from the Sharpton *Sentinel* and the Monksville *Tribune*. However, thank goodness Iris Towers is my first cousin—you remember me talkin' about her, don't you?

"Yeah, I do—from what I remember, she is one of the most powerful business women in North Carolina. She owns the radio station in Sharpton, the one in Monksville, and several others, right?"

"You got it! Pays to know someone! All I had to do was sic ol' cousin Iris on the newspaper guys and she immediately called off the dogs. With a crack of her whip, all the reporters got sent back to their kennels with their tails tucked between their legs."

"Perfect! We definitely don't need mass mania being perpetuated and our jobs being made ten times harder. Well, we've done all we can here, I suppose." Upon that, each man opened his respective door to the patrol car and crawled in.

"Hey, Jet, where are you staying tonight? As always, you are welcome to stay with us. Sarah wouldn't mind a bit."

Although the invitation was sincere, Walt already knew what the agent's answer would be. Jet didn't sleep well in other people's houses. An independent sort, the agent felt as if he were imposing and wished not to bother hosts with his tendency to be a night owl.

"Walt, I think I'll haunt my usual hideaway out toward Sharpton, the Chat & Nibble Café and Motel. I always sleep so well there when I visit you to go hunting. Besides, the people that run that café make what has to be the best foot-long hotdog on the planet!"

"Wait a minute, agent!" grinned the sheriff. "If I remember correctly, you said that exact thing about Miller's Truck Stop in Monksville after our hunting trip last year. Jet, I could swear you said their foot-long was the best on the planet! But then, come to think of it, I believe you also said the same thing about Hap's Grill in Salliston. If I recall, you claimed that the chili at Hap's elevated their dogs to a height no other dog could touch."

"*Did* I now, Sheriff? I think perhaps your memory has been severely contaminated by your constant exposure to Triple D. Anyhow, I do love the way Chat & Nibble tortures their hotdogs in the deep fryer, turning them tough, wrinkled, and almost brown. Then, as if that's not enough, they toast the buns to a crisp, flattened state of perfection. What a dog!"

"I swear, Jet, you never change a bit!" Walt laughed vigorously as he started the ignition and backed up the car. "By all means, let's get you back to that blue Ray so you can go confiscate the perfect hotdog!"

"Now your thinking is clear again, Sheriff!"

CHAPTER 8

Funeral for a Legend

Yes, Sunday was a day of mourning in Shangri-La.
It was a hot day, and the gymnasium felt like a sauna.
The place was packed, with many standing outside.
White people were there, and black people were there.
Niblock and his force were busy managing the crowd.
Jericho sat in the corner underneath the scoreboard.
The Lutheran preacher from Sharpton presided.
The Lutheran preacher from Monksville eulogized.
Reporters' pencils danced to the rhythm of the words.
The music was sad, offered by a slightly off-key choir.
Photographers' cameras clicked rhythmically.
Many cried to the choreography of floating tissues.
The casket was closed and carried down the aisle.
"Paul Christmas has left the building!" Gone for good . . .
Sweaty people left the building, nursing empty souls.
Cars rolled off one by one, a darkened gym left behind.
Icy Springs was one citizen less, deprived of a legend.
Their caretaker was gone! Who would mind the store?

Despite her son's death, Mary Christmas had not come!
Despite his brother's death, Ron Christmas had not come!

CHAPTER 9

A Triple D Breakfast

Jericho knew this would be a long Monday as he hoped to interview the three citizens who had happened upon the body of Reverend Christmas plus the long-haired hermit who wandered up and down the road. Sheriff Niblock had called his motel room at 7:00 a.m., with the two agreeing to meet in a half-hour at the motel's adjoining café for breakfast—the best way to attack a long day! Having showered just before Walt's phone call, Nolan had his dark-blue dress suit laid out for the tasks at hand. When questioning people for any leads, the agent generally preferred to look most professional.

And Jericho was indeed ready to get on with things, having had a good night's sleep. He always rested well at the Chat & Nibble Café and Motel. A quiet environment with soft lighting was vital to the agent for sleeping well, and he thought Chat & Nibble's Motel had the quintessential atmosphere for catching "Z"s. The one-story motel had a total of ten units, laid out in two rows, with five units in each row. The clean, carpeted rooms were of functional simplicity, each having a bedroom and a bathroom and a tiny kitchenette area, containing a refrigerator, stove, and sink. The lighting in the hotel room was of low wattage, providing a somewhat dim interior. During summer months, the small air conditioner unit in the window ran continuously, its hum providing a sonic backdrop that masked out the sound of the occasional passing automobile.

Jericho loved neon, and he appreciated how the soothing multi-colored aura of the Chat & Nibble sign peeked around the edges of the window shades, allowing just enough spectral illumination on the walls in the pitch-black room to induce a deep sleep. At both ends of each five-unit row were bug lights casting an eerie, bluish glow. Nolan always requested Room #5, farthest in its row from Highway 64. Tucked against the corner of a wooded area, this room seem the quietest. With the drone of the air conditioner and the hypnotic blend of the bluish bug light and the neon motel sign, the agent was lulled instantly into a peaceful slumber under the covers in his slightly chilled room.

As Jericho finished straightening his tie, he thought about how his sheriff associate had handled Pastor Paul's murder thus far. Yes, it was true that Walt typically used his heart a lot more than his head, and if his friend had been working for a by-the-book type like Director Fowler, he would have found himself out on the street hunting for a job. Granted, Walt could be a little too easy-going and sloppy, such as with the oversight of the cigarette package. But to hell with procedures and over-zealous investigation, for this was Walt's World! Sheriff Niblock *knew* his constituents and knew them well, and they respected his manner of peace-keeping. *As the old saying goes*, pondered Jericho, *those you serve don't care how much you know; they just want to know how much you care. Yeah, Walt's way works effectively in his world, I guess; it's only the big cases every decade or so that bewilder him.*

Jericho looked at the clock on his nightstand. The agent thought this would be the perfect time to check in with his director, for Fowler usually arrived at his office by seven o'clock most mornings. According to Fowler, he could wade through a little paperwork before the "boy scouts" reported to work at eight. Jericho knew he would have Fowler's full attention before the office got busy, and besides, it would be nice to get his daily report out of the way before a full day of interviewing. Fowler didn't expect his agents to report on Sundays, so Nolan had benefited from a free pass of sorts yesterday. However, the agent knew his director was probably blowing a gasket by now, wondering what was going on here in Icy Springs.

"Hello, Director Fowler. Jericho here!"

"Okay, Jet, what's happening down there in Icy Springs? I even saw coverage of the preacher's funeral on the news here in Raleigh."

"Well, Director, we don't have any strong suspects. As you probably know, Paul Christmas was more popular than the Pope. The crime scene was almost squeaky clean, with only a cigarette package left behind. Sheriff Niblock is currently having it checked for prints."

"Okay, agent, so what's your next move?"

"Well, I'm meeting with the sheriff in a few minutes for breakfast. Hopefully, he'll have verified some prints on the cigarette package and possibly have some other useful info. I am going to question the three witnesses today that came across the pastor's body, along with a hermit-type guy that walks along the highway a lot near the church. Tomorrow, I might go down into South Carolina to talk to the pastor's mother and his brother; neither of them came to the funeral. They say Paul and his brother had become estranged. Interestingly enough, sir, the tax stamp on the cigarette package at the crime scene was from South Carolina."

"That may be, Jet, but unless you get a good set of prints, the fact that the cigarettes were purchased in South Carolina is—"

"—circumstantial," interrupted Jericho. "I know, sir, but it *may* be all I have to go on. However, I don't know that for sure—that's why I'm interviewing the villagers today."

"Sounds like you've got a plan, agent—at least, uh, for no more than you have to go on. I guess I would be doing the same if I were in your shoes. Watch your back, Agent. Remember, it took an insane guy to do what he did to the preacher and that community, and he's running around loose. The fact that you're a public servant hunting for him paints the bull's eye directly on you, not him. As long as the killer's identity is unverified, he's the one with the advantage of anonymity—so be careful out there, Jet."

"Yes, sir." Jericho was nearly floored by Fowler's unsolicited concern for his safety, a side of the crusty curmudgeon he had rarely, if ever, seen. *Fowler, ol' boy, I guess you do have a big heart after all.*

"Where are you staying, agent?"

"The Chat & Nibble Café and Motel, Room #5."

"Uh, Jet, one more thing—I'll probably mail Cat out to ya on Wednesday. Today, I had her run some paperwork out to Agent James on an assignment in Fayetteville. I'll probably let her stay in the office tomorrow. So, for right now, count on seeing her on Wednesday. I can probably leave her out there with you for the rest of the week."

"Yes, sir, no problem there, sir!" *Yes, sir, no problem there, no problem at all! Cat will be great help, as intelligent as she is—and, of course, looking as great in a négligée as she does.*

Minutes later, Jericho was seated at his favorite spot in the Chat & Nibble Café, the corner booth with the round table by the window. A waitress stumbled up to the table in a slumping posture, rubbing her droopy eyes and yawning. She robotically set a glass of water on the table in front of the agent. Setting her eyes upon Jericho, she immediately shape-shifted into a dramatically different life-form. Suddenly standing in a chest-out/tummy-in/bottom-out pose, the waitress tilted her head slightly and focused her eyes toward Nolan as seductively as she could. Swallowing her next yawn, she launched the cheesiest, breathy Marilyn Monroe imitation possible. "Well, baby doll," whispered 'Marilyn.' "What would a strong, well-dressed, nice-looking fella like you desire to start your day off right?"

"I don't recognize you," said Jericho. "You're new here, aren't you?"

"Just started last week, honey—however, we can make up for lost time and become acquainted real, real fast."

"Well, I tell you, uh, Miss. Let's just start our relationship off one meal at a time with me doing the ordering and you fulfilling my order." *Oh, great! I just left that one wide open for her to run wide with.*

"Sure thing, baby—I take orders real good!" assured the waitress in her breathy whisper-tones as she winked at the agent slightly.

Clearing his throat, Jericho glanced at the menu a final time so as to dodge the wink. "I think I'll start off with a large glass of freshly-squeezed orange juice and, for my meal, I'll have ham with three eggs sunny side up, hash browns sprinkled with diced onions, and toast with strawberry jam; coffee will be fine, with cream and sugar. If you would, walk the juice on out here first thing straight from the juicer—I prefer it with that rich citrus aroma."

Bending over the table slightly and positioning herself with the agent face to face, the waitress whispered, "I get into a man who really knows what he likes."

Glancing at her name badge, Jericho quickly responded, "Funny thing, uh, Lora—that's exactly what my one and only back in Raleigh says about me."

"Well, she's in Raleigh, and I'm right here, handsome!"

"Yes, you're right here, but my orange juice is nowhere in sight. Now, why don't you just trot along and start a-squeezing?" With a quick look of indignation coming over her face as if she had just been outbid at an auction, Lora shape-shifted back into her original form and slumped off in a huff to fulfill the order. . .

While sipping his orange juice and glancing at an extra copy of the newspaper he had borrowed from a barstool, Jericho heard the tinkling of the bell at the entrance. He glanced in that direction and spotted Walt, wearing his usual jovial disposition. *Great! All right, Sheriff, let's find out where we are on possible fingerprints.* The door halfway closed behind Walt, but continued tinkling as it fully re-opened upon the appearance of a deputy. *Hmm, Deputy Sanford. I remember him—his elevator doesn't quite reach the top floor.* Sanford held the door open for a couple seconds until another deputy's uniform started merging into view. *Oh, my God! Dreama! Walt, why did you have to bring that helium-filled head with a body hangin' from it? I don't need any silly distractions this morning.*

Sheriff Niblock and Deputy Sanford waved to a customer sitting on a barstool and came to a halt, the patron presumably an acquaintance. As they were chatting, Deputy Dobermann charged ahead like a locomotive upon eyeing Nolan in the corner booth. *Aw, man! Am I a sitting duck!* thought Nolan as he grimaced and partially sank in his seat. *Danger! Incoming missile!*

Jericho had no difficulty at all in executing his loyalty to Cat, for no other woman in the world could tempt him into bed. However, it was always such a hassle dealing with insistent, horny women without having to be overtly rude. This type of woman reminded the agent of whales: big, goofy creatures that he truly didn't relish harpooning emotionally. He'd do it if necessary, but it sure was a nasty chore to perform. *Hopefully, she'll sit across from me, not next to me. Uh-oh . . .*

"Hi there, hero. You look all bright-eyed and bushy-tailed." Dreama literally threw herself down in a sitting position on the booth seat right beside Nolan while he took another sip of orange juice. Thanks to the springs in the cushion, the agent was trampolined upward about three inches without warning.

With orange juice now running down the sides of his face, Jericho fully closed his exotically-slanted eyes while breathing a full breath in and a full breath out and lowered his glass to the table. Picking up his napkin, he wiped the juice off his face and muttered, "Thar she blows!" *Thank goodness the juice didn't end up on my suit. How does she manage to defy physics anyway? She plopped down so hard in that painted-on uniform, something had to have split!*

"What did you say, sir?" asked Dreama, quite confused by Jericho's whale-sighting call.

"Uh, nothing, Deputy Dobermann. Just thinking about whales and such— do ya know where I can find a good harpoon?" Jericho's voice now had a much more stoic tone than Dreama remembered from their brief first encounter.

"Huh? What do you mean, sir?" asked the still-confused blonde.

"Oh, nothing."

Oblivious to the fact she had just given the agent a Vitamin C bath, the deputy seemed baffled by his stern demeanor. "You're not much of a mornin' person are you, Mr. Jericho? Maybe sitting beside an admiring fan can get the rockets in your engine all fired up!"

Oh, God! Walt, GET OVER HERE! You and Sanford can talk to that guy later about lowering the speed limit on his street or whatever it is he's hitting you up for. Help! MAYDAY!

"Hey, listen Tiger, before the other troops arrive, let me ask you—would you like to go out together one night while you're here? I can be *loads* of fun!"

Tiger!? Nobody calls me Tiger but Cat! And where did her addressing me as "sir" suddenly disappear to? And going out together!? Man, she certainly shifted into a much higher gear in a flash. Walt was right about her promiscuity!

"Deputy Dobermann—please, uh, don't address me as, uh, 'Tiger'!"

"Oh, I'm sorry, sir! May I call you Jet, sir?"

"Might as well, I allow everyone else to." Jericho was now carefully monitoring every syllable he uttered to the deputy so as to leave no room for misinterpretation.

"Well, Jet, would you go out with me? What do you say to you and me, uh, *jetting* away together one evening? I'll bet you can create quite a sonic boom with that body of yours." Dreama was practically begging in the silliest manner possible, accompanied by equally silly giggles powered by only a few brain cells.

"Let's see, Deputy," replied Jericho, attempting his most matter-of-fact voice while clearing his throat nervously. "Uh, how I can put this? It's like this . . . I, uh . . . I mean, aren't you a little on the young side?"

"Oh, Jet, you're so ridiculous! How could you possibly think I'm too young to go out with you?"

"Well, Deputy, rather than answer that question, shall I order you something to eat?—perhaps some mashed-up carrots or a sliced-up wiener with a cup of warm milk?"

"Mashed-up carrots? Warm milk? Oh, *you*! You're just being funny—after all, I'm twenty-one years old! Anyway, quit calling me Deputy. Call me Dreama!"

"Well, regardless of your age, Miss Dreama, I am not available as I am currently seeing a wonderful—"

Suddenly the cavalry appeared at the last minute.

"Morning, Jet!" trumpeted Walt. "I see Dobermann sniffed you out. How did you sleep last night?"

Jericho breathed a sigh of relief as Sheriff Niblock and Deputy Sanford took root in the circular booth across from Dreama. Their interruption was even more well-timed than the Great Detergent Spill by the presidential cats that had put an end to the rather awkward conversation with Cat in her apartment.

"Hi, Walt! I had a great night's sleep—you know, good ol' Room #5!"

"That's great!" replied Walt. "I was real restless last night. I got up and just started thumbing through one of those *National Geographic* magazines. Interesting stuff, Jet-—did you know there is a certain species of penguin that only has sex once a year?"

Suddenly, a look of bewilderment came over Deputy Sanford's face. "Oh my God!" Sanford moaned. "Then, I'm married to a penguin!"

Jericho did his best to contain any hint of a smile, while Dreama simply rolled her eyes and mumbled, "Oh, brother!"

Walt sensed it was time to interject and keeps things moving. "Jet, you remember Sanford don't you?"

"I certainly do—good to see you again, Deputy," responded Jet, holding out his hand.

"And you, too, sir! You, too!" Sanford gave Nolan one of those over-exuberant, seemingly never-ending handshakes that tempts the recipient to yell, "Enough, already!"

Just then, Lora the waitress appeared with Jericho's meal, looking even more indignant than previously. As she set his plate down, Nolan couldn't resist himself. "As you can see, fellow lawmen, I've ordered already. There's not really anything more I'm needing from Lora here, but I'm sure she's dying to give the rest of you *anything* you desire."

"Hmmph," grunted the waitress at Jericho's smart-assed routine. "Mornin', everyone, I'm Lora. Here's your water; just let me know when you're ready to order."

"Just bring me a Western omelet, ma'am," chirped Sheriff Niblock. "And you can probably bring a coffee pot for all of us. I don't ever see these two deputies here drink anything but cups of joe in the morning!"

"Yep, coffee's just fine by me," replied Sanford heartily, "and I'll have a stack of pancakes with maple syrup."

"And you, ma'am?" asked Lora unenthusiastically as she looked toward Deputy Dobermann. Just then, Jericho nearly gasped as he felt a hand suddenly lying on top of his leg.

Dammit, Dreama, what are you doing? Stop that! Nolan's thoughts were in turmoil upon the sudden onslaught of Dreama's hand. Dreama's fingernails started massaging the material of Jericho's trousers and moved upwards closer to his thigh. *Stop it, bitch! Personal property! Quit doing that!* Desperately trying to physically telegraph the message *Get off!*, Nolan shook his leg as much as he could in the hopes of not drawing the attention of Walt and Deputy Sanford to the weird escapade happening under the table.

Still rubbing Nolan's leg, Dreama said, "Bring me one egg over-easy, some grits 'n' butter, and the biggest piece of Polish sausage you have."

"Are you sure of that?" inquired the waitress. "I think some of the kielbasa links back there are rather hefty."

"I'm positive," snapped Dreama. "I thoroughly enjoy oversized hunks of meat!"

On that note, Deputy Sanford nearly dropped his glass of water and started coughing, which was followed by gurgling sounds emerging from his throat. "You okay?" asked Walt, looking at his choking deputy.

"Pardon me—" strained Sanford between coughs. "I must have . . . *cough, cough* . . . swallowed my . . . *cough* . . . water the wrong way . . . *cough.*"

As the waitress walked away, Jericho took advantage of the distraction provided by Sanford's coughing cacophony to reach down and pinch Dreama's hand sharply with his fingernails—and not a moment too soon, for Dreama had almost worked her way up to massaging *his* kielbasa.

"Ow!" half-whispered Dreama, glaring quickly at Jericho with pouty lips. Without uttering a sound, she mouthed to him *"Why'd you do that?"* The agent immediately conjured up his infamous "crazy look" and flashed it at Dreama. His frozen-faced still-shot of insanity had taken Nolan many years to master, but it came in quite handy with even his toughest clientele. The look was similar in nature to what some educators refer to as their "teacher look," a look that means "Enough is enough! I'm fed up and I mean business!" However, Jericho's crazy look had an accelerated tinge of implied psychosis, complete with stiff, twitching cheeks and glazed, serial killer-like eyes. Thankfully, the crazy look worked and Dreama put her promiscuity temporarily back into its holster, taking her hand away from the agent's leg.

"Sorry, gang," croaked Sanford, still clearing his throat.

"Think nothing about it, Deputy," assured Jericho. "It was actually pretty good timing."

Dreama suddenly stared at Nolan in disbelief. She had a nervous, "Are ya gonna rat on me?" look on her face.

"What do you mean, 'good timing'?" asked an equally puzzled Sanford.

"Well, look at it this way, Sanford," clarified Jericho. "You could have gone into a coughing fit while you had a mouthful of hot coffee—so, what is one man's hardship can actually be another man's good fortune." Walt and Sanford laughed at that observation, with Dreama supplying a giggle of relief.

"Jet, eat your breakfast while it's hot," urged Walt. "While we're waiting on ours, let's get down to business. Unfortunately, the cigarette package came up negative for prints. So, what we're left with is the fact that the tax stamp and overprint on the package identify them as being sold in South Carolina in July. I hate that's all we've got. It would'a been nice to've had a stronger lead to go on."

"Well, Walt, the fact that no prints turned up doesn't automatically designate the package of Kool cigarettes as insignificant. Perhaps down the road, the item could still play a part in the grand scheme of things regarding the crime."

"I guess it's possible, Jet . . . that's a good way to look at it, I suppose."

"What about tobacco residue on Paul's body?"

"Jack said that was a definite positive from the autopsy. Although he had tried to give it up, Paul evidently smoked 'til the end."

"And what about any packages or cartons of cigarettes at the parsonage?"

"Negative on that one, Jet."

"Well, Walt, thanks for checking. Of course, all that tells me at the moment is that Paul may have just run out of cigarettes and needed to replenish. Anyway, I'll drop the matter of the cigarette package at the crime scene for right now, and we'll just go on the assumptions we have. So, consider that bit of evidence temporarily on the back burner."

"Okey-dokey," replied Walt. "Hey, you're still interviewing the three villagers who discovered the body as well as Bud Holly down in the holler today, right?"

"Yes, Sheriff, that's my plan."

"What about tomorrow?"

"I called Fowler this morning, Walt. I told him I was probably going to venture down into South Carolina tomorrow to pay a visit each to Ron Christmas and Mrs. Christmas. You noticed, of course, that they weren't at the funeral, didn't you?"

"Yeah, both were no-shows," acknowledged the sheriff. "But that doesn't mean they're guilty, though."

"Right, Walt. However, with literally nothing to go on at this point, something about Ron's loneliness and his potential jealousy of Paul is pulling me like a magnet in his direction. Trust me, I never have any right to hope *or* pre-judge that any particular person is guilty. Therefore, I don't wish guilt upon Ron or any other specific person. After all, I really have no tangible evidence making Ron a worthy suspect other than a South Carolina tax stamp happening to be at the crime scene. But, there *is* the slightest chance that Ron's loneliness and jealousy could have snowballed and plummeted him into an extremely psychotic plane of thinking. Who knows?"

"Yeah," agreed the Sheriff. "I guess any thin hunch or suspicion at this point is worth investigating in a case where the victim seems to have had no enemies at all. I wish I could ride down with you, but I have to appear in court on a domestic dispute case. Would you like a deputy to accompany you?"

"NO!" shot back Jericho tersely. *Oops!* thought the agent immediately of his quick outburst at Walt's offer. He didn't mean to deny such a generous suggestion so sharply, but he feared Dreama might attempt to hop on the ol' Jericho train, and that would most certainly make for a *long* round trip to South Carolina and back. "Uh, I mean, no thanks—but I appreciate the offer. I anticipate tomorrow being quite a non-eventful, trivial day, so I'll be fine. There is one thing I do want to ask you though, Walt. What was the deal with the big guy in the overalls at the funeral yesterday serving as a pallbearer? I didn't recognize him. He seemed to be an oddball among the crew of suit-and-ties carrying the casket."

Deputy Sanford horned in, now that his throat was completely clear. "Oh, that was Big Blue. He's the guy that owns Big Blue's Feed Mill and Fertilizer Warehouse down at Atkins River."

"Ahhh, so that's Big Blue, huh?" responded Jericho. "As many times as I've passed by his business, I have yet to meet him—so why was he a pallbearer?"

"Oh, you don't know?" asked a surprised Walt. "I'm sorry—I thought you were aware. Reverend Christmas did a little part-time work down at Big Blue's mill."

"Really, now? Yeah, that one fact has escaped me, I'm embarrassed to say. I must have overlooked Paul's part-time employment in his obituary, and they didn't mention it at the funeral."

"Well, Jet, his part-time work there wasn't a big part of his life, with the mill work just giving Paul a little extra money toward his retirement and such. You know how it is for ministers. Congregations think that just because they are providing housing for pastors by putting them up in parsonages, they are not obligated to pay them much of a salary. And, as hard as ol' Paul worked, his church was really getting an incredible deal. They were receiving nearly everything for nearly nothing."

"Okay, Walt. So how was Paul's relationship with Big Blue and his co-workers at the mill?"

"Pristine, as usual for Paul—no problems there."

"As expected. Well, thanks for the info, Sheriff. I think I'll let you lawmen enjoy your breakfast while I go out and start my interviews."

"Hey, Jet, you're gonna need a good meal tonight to set you right for your journey down South tomorrow, right? I'll pick you up at 7:30 this evening and take you for some of the best barbecued chicken you've ever put to your lips."

"Best on the planet?" posed Jericho with an impish grin.

"Yeah, definitely the best on the planet!" smiled Walt.

"Done deal! Well, then, excuse me, Deputy," requested Jericho, indicating his intention of departure to Dreama. As she stood up to let Nolan out, the agent bowed his head slightly toward Walt and Deputy Sanford. "Gentlemen," said Jericho politely. He stood and attempted to ease past Dreama, but she wasn't giving him enough clearance to do so without rubbing against her. Slightly annoyed but still minding his manners, Nolan bowed his head toward her. "Good day, ma'am." As Jericho walked toward the register to pay, Dreama stared at him while gently biting her bottom lip as she had done during their first encounter.

"Snap out of it, Dreama," asserted Sheriff Niblock. "He's too complex for you."

"Why, Sheriff Niblock, whatever do mean by that? He's just another man, I'm sure," sighed Dreama, thinking she could redirect her boss's intuition with such an obviously phony representation of her thoughts.

"*That*, he's not, Dreama! That, he's not!"

As Deputy Sanford stared at the well-groomed, exotic man standing at the cash register and bowing his head slightly to the cashier, he saw this moment as an opportunity to ask something he had been pondering for quite a while. "Sheriff, I've actually never seen Agent Jericho in action. Is he everything they say he is?"

"That and more, son—much, much more. I don't know quite how the North Carolina SBI was lucky enough to end up with such an agent. Jet has an incredible brain, and he's a marksman unlike any I've ever seen. He puts me to shame on our hunting trips. *And*, none of us would stand a chance against him in hand-to-hand combat. He can easily incapacitate four to five men in less than ten seconds. Yeah, don't let the expensive suit and the soft talk fool you. That's a helluva man walking out that door!"

CHAPTER 10

Jericho and the Amazon Beauty Queen

As Jericho headed down 64 in the direction of Icy Springs Lutheran Church, he replayed the extremely awkward breakfast in his mind. Dreama had come within a razor's edge of violating his male privacy, which, of course, hadn't happened since Friday night with Kennedy the cat. *Maybe having Deputy Dobermann on the force seemed like a good idea, but I need to somehow get it across to Walt that Dreama's got to go! She's really melting away the legitimacy of his authority. I mean, would Steve McGarrett allow Elly May Clampett to join Five-O? C'mon, Walt . . .*

The agent had decided that Miss Eden would be the most logical person to question first among the trio who had discovered Paul's body. Walt had mentioned that business hours at her travel agency in Sharpton generally ran from 10:00 a.m. to 6:00 p.m. So, as it was now around quarter to nine, Miss Eden ought to be out of the shower and in the final stage of primping by the time he arrived—or so he hoped!

Just past the church, Jericho turned into Miss Eden's drive. He quickly stepped up onto the porch and, upon noticing the front door was open and that there was no doorbell, knocked on the screen door. *Man, what if she does actually appear at the door in the curlers and spooky facial mask, as Walt had described?* As he waited, Nolan glanced in the direction of the church and then back at the highway. *Okay, Bride of Frankenstein, c'mon! Open sesame!* Suddenly, the screen door swung open and a somewhat husky female voice inquired, "May I help you, sir?"

Okay, let's have a look at Miss Franken— Whoa! As Nolan spun around, he found himself in a most disconcerting position—that of being unintentionally face-to-breasts with one of the tallest women he had ever encountered. *Man, she must be six foot seven! Walt never told me she was an Amazon!* Miss Eden was definitely not in her incubating stage, with curlers and a facial mask, nor was she in the primping stage. She stood fully dressed, wearing lots of sparkly jewelry, with her makeup just so. Apparently in her later forties or early fifties, she had what Nolan could only think of as a beauty queen look. Indeed, Miss Eden had an unexpected elegance the agent had not anticipated.

Looking up toward her face, Nolan opened his billfold and displayed his identification. "Uh, ma'am, I'm Jet Jericho, a field agent for the State Bureau of Investigation. Please do not be alarmed, you are not in any trouble. I am simply seeking your assistance with some information about what you experienced last Thursday morning."

"Thank you for the proof, sir. I trust you, so please do come in. I truly don't know how much help I'll be, but I'll make every effort. Come, let's sit down." She turned around and walked with one of those high society gaits usually manufactured in a charm school.

As Nolan entered, he immediately noticed a shrine of sorts that Miss Eden had erected to her past. In addition to framed magazine covers adorning the walls, there was a cluster of pictures featuring the tall blonde in an assortment of classic poses one would expect to find in a fashion model's portfolio. *Who would have thought you would find an Amazon beauty queen in the middle of Icy Springs?*

Nolan paused in front of a magazine cover in which a young Miss Eden was wearing a one-piece swimsuit, a tiara, and a sash bearing the title "Miss Bahamas."

Sensing he had ceased to follow, Miss Eden turned immediately turned around. "Oh, I see you spotted a youthful Miss Bahamas. That's actually my favorite cover, but the cover days have come and gone, Mister, uh . . . I'm sorry, my memory has already failed me . . .?"

"Jericho, ma'am, and I'm very impressed with your accomplishments."

"*Au contraire*, Mr. Jericho, don't be misled. The beauty queen in the picture you're studying did not possess the official Miss Bahamas title that competes in international pageants. You definitely see no future *Miss Universe* in that photo! Actually, the starry-eyed beauty queen you see was the result of a marketing contest that *Coppertone Suntan Lotion* was sponsoring in their Caribbean division."

"Nevertheless, ma'am, very impressive!"

Turning around, the former Miss Bahamas resumed her charm school stroll toward the living room, with Nolan in tow. As he passed by an open door on the right, the agent glanced into the room and again came to a halt, this time in awe. "Whoa! Miss Eden, if you'll pardon my obvious nosiness, that has to be the most makeup I've ever seen in any place, with the exception of the cosmetics section at Woolworth's. I have a lady friend back in Raleigh and, honestly, your makeup station looks like a Las Vegas dressing room compared to hers."

Smiling elegantly, Miss Eden continued the procession toward the living room. Once through the living room door, Miss Eden slowly extended her arm and made a grand sweeping horizontal motion of invitation. "Wherever you prefer, sir."

"Thank you, ma'am. If you don't mind, I'll try the rocking chair. I think better when I'm rocking."

"By all means, Mr. Jericho." Upon that, Miss Eden sat on a very long satin couch in a ladylike position definitely confirming her charm school etiquette and giving the illusion she was riding the decorative piece of furniture side saddle. Her imposing stature remained quite pronounced, even while sitting.

"For some reason, Mr. Jericho, your name has been teasing my memory, and it just struck me! You are the man who came from Raleigh a good while back and solved those horrid cotton gin murders, aren't you?"

"Your memory serves you well, Miss Eden."

"My, my, sir! You are quite the hero in this village. I was still living in France at the time of those murders, but I have heard people talking about the crimes and your exploits since returning."

"If you're not offended, Miss Eden, I would appreciate your first name for my reports."

"Actually, Mr. Jericho, Eden *is* my first name. You see, everyone in Icy Springs calls me 'Miss Eden' in the grand ol' tradition of Southern gentility, I suppose. To tell you the truth, no one around here can keep up with my last name due to my history as a multiple divorcée. And, I've *no* doubt that you've surely heard that bit of gossip in this little pea pod of a village."

"Yes, ma'am, the wind has carried that information in my direction."

"I must say, you are a gentleman full of tact, Mr. Jericho. I shall have a cigarette now. Shall you?"

"No thank you, ma'am." Smoking definitely explained the reason for Miss Eden's husky, Lauren Bacall-like voice. As she gracefully lit up, Nolan noticed that the package was Benson & Hedges, not Kool—just an observation.

"Yes, Mr. Jericho, for your report, you may label me as Miss Eden Perdue Jansen Jones Hornby Jones Marchinko. And yes, the two Jones were the same man. Actually, I'm a divorcée three times and a widow twice."

"Are you originally from Icy Springs?"

"Born and bred here, sir. However, whereas my sisters were content learning meat loaf recipes, raising chickens, and marrying men with whom they are miserably happy to this day, I preferred to explore the world, and see it I did! I started out as an airline stewardess, a quick and easy way for a Southern village girl to become well-traveled. Anyway, I met men and I left men, and I married men and I buried men. You're looking at the former wife of an airline pilot, a banker, a major league baseball coach, and a gigolo."

"Miss Eden, you complimented my tact earlier; therefore, I'm afraid this next observation may betray your compliment. Uh, this is quite a small house you live in—that is, considering the professions of some of your ex-husbands."

"Mr. Jericho, never once did I say to you that I lacked in money. As they say, sir, don't let the cover shade your impression of the book. I'm probably the wealthiest business woman in the county, other than that meddling busybody Iris Towers, who owns the radio stations. No, Mr. Jericho, this is actually the house where I enjoyed my childhood. Before they died, my parents left it to me in the will—feeling sorry for me, I suppose, as I was between marriages at the time. They always hoped this house would be the magnet to pull be back home. It eventually did, but too late for them and, I suppose, one gigolo too late for me."

"I'm sorry, Miss Eden, sounds like life has been a bad hand for you at times."

"Oh, don't weep for me, sir. I took on the world, put up a great fight, and it kicked my ass—if you'll pardon the euphemism. In the long run, however, I was able to commercialize my worldliness, for I now run a flourishing travel agency in Sharpton. The travel business is all about bringing a place of dreams to reality in the life of a person with a pocketful of cash, and there is no better authority to transform any place in the world into a reality than someone who has actually been there!" Miss Eden looked at the agent with a curious smile and extinguished her cigarette. "Now, my turn to ask the questions, Mr. Jericho."

"Fair enough, ma'am, fire away!" Although he sounded confident, Jericho started rocking more vigorously, a symptom of his discomfort in being sized up by women. He'd had enough of that this morning at the Chat & Nibble.

"Mr. Jericho, you are a most unique-looking man, of the kind I've only encountered in distant exotic places throughout the world. In fact, to be completely honest, I must confess that I have never seen another man who had such a rich blend of physical traits from your beautiful brown skin to your deliciously Oriental eyes. It doesn't take a genetic scientist to know you're not from these parts. What's *your* story, sir? After all, you've been made privy to mine."

If that same description of his "delicious" eyes had been uttered by Lora the waitress or Dreama Dobermann, Jericho's horny-woman siren would have been wailing away and he would have run for the hills. However, Miss Eden had made him feel one-hundred percent comfortable with the question. She had such an air of class that the question reeked of sincerity fueled by raw curiosity, not raw sexuality. Nolan perceived that Miss Eden had "been there, done that" to such an extent in her life that she was left with no interest to "go there, do that" again. Pretty things—jewelry, clothes, men—were so much a part of her

70

past that he supposed she couldn't help finding him a curio of sorts, an odd spectacle to look at for a few minutes before moving on to another curio.

"Well, Miss Eden, you see, I was in law enforcement in New York City before I moved down to Raleigh for personal reasons. It's funny that you say have spent your whole life running around the world for I, on the other hand, have had the entire world running around *inside* of me my whole life. My African-American grandfather married a Puerto Rican woman and my Japanese grandfather married a Chinese woman."

"And how have you dealt with this world inside of you through the years, Mr. Jericho? I mean, how have you felt inside? Did you ever manage to piece yourself fully together?"

Jericho was stunned. No one, not even Cat, had ever cut to the psychological chase with such penetrating, sharp-bladed questions. In the household of his serious parents, no discussion *ever* centered around feelings. Talk in his family had always been about taking action, moving forward, creating the future. There had *never* been any time for reflection! So, hell yes! Having the genetic constructs of four races synthesized within his body, his psyche was bound to have had a field day with that booger of a beast through the years. And now, this Amazon woman in Icy Springs was forcing him to confront the beast.

There were several moments of uncomfortable silence—awkward, that is, for Jericho. "I, uh . . . hmm . . . I guess, Miss Eden, that I just force all those faces of the past residing inside me to live in harmony. Although my blood does seem to boil intensely at times for reasons unknown, I've always attempted to glean the best from my four heritages and attack the future head on—you know, leaving any unwanted scraps behind."

"Interesting answer, Mr. Jericho, but you *still* didn't tell me how you *felt* inside."

Jesus! Who is this woman? Sigmund Freud's wife? I'm surprised she doesn't have me lying on the couch while sitting beside me wielding a pad and pencil! Nolan had become extremely disquieted with this spontaneous, albeit well-intentioned, invasion of his inner thoughts. *Okay, Lady, it's time to bring a halt to Psychology 101!*

Without warning, the unexpected happened. Miss Eden farted! It was the paradox of paradoxes, hearing such a crudely manifested sound erupt between expensive satin upholstery and the aristocratic, poised lady adorning it. A noticeably embarrassed Miss Eden shifted her position slightly and, for the first time during Jericho's visit, glanced away from Nolan while softly speaking. "I beg your pardon, sir—terrible, terrible tummy bubble trouble I am having this morning. I hope it wasn't that noticeable."

Not that noticeable! That faux pas was no slight feminine oopsy daisy! That so-called tummy bubble trouble was something direct from Mt. Olympus!

Hercules couldn't have outdone that! A moose could have walked through the room and been less noticeable! Not that Jericho was ungrateful, for this was the third in a series of perfectly timed distractions having rescued him from recent situations most awkward, from the spilled detergent on Friday at Cat's to the waterlogged Deputy Sanford at breakfast this morning and now to the flatulence of this ex-beauty queen—a trilogy of fate's good timing. *Somebody up there's looking after me!*

While the off-balanced socialite struggled to regain her composure and decorum, Jericho seized the opportunity to regain control of the dialogue. "Miss Eden, I came by here to ask you about Thursday morning and, partially due to your wonderful hospitality, I haven't done so yet. I would still like to ask you a few questions about Thursday morning, but I don't wish to make you late for work."

"Don't fret about that, Mr. Jericho. Remember, I *own* the establishment. The doors are open when I wish them so."

"Thank you, ma'am. Do you attend the church next door on Sundays?"

"No, but I have often been invited. Pastor Paul's shadow darkened my porch frequently, as he would visit me to try and, let us say, recruit me to his flock. An extremely nice man he was, and I now wish I had seized more opportunities to become better acquainted with him. But, such are the priorities of the second wealthiest business woman in the county, the first being that ol' cantankerous Iris Towers, of course."

"From your perspective, what-all happened Thursday morning leading to the discovery of the Reverend's body?"

"It was all so surreal, if you know what I mean, like when something is really happening, but yet you can't believe it. You feel sort of out of sync with time itself because your mind is so desperately scrambling to try to make sense of the given moment and piece reality back together. It was truly the strangest moment of my wealthy, sordid life."

"How did Miss Krenshaw and Mr. Rankin come into the picture?"

"Well, it was Viola Krenshaw who alerted me with her persistent knocking. The poor old soul had run her car into the ditch when she saw the pastor's body up there. She was in a bad state of mind, or so I perceived. I didn't know what was happening at first. I thought she was about to have a heart attack or stroke or something."

"What about Mr. Rankin?"

"Well, he came up to Viola and me as we were stepping off the porch to go have a better look. Viola still hadn't told me exactly what it was that had her so frightened. Then, Mr. Rankin told us he had seen Viola's car in the ditch. He said he was driving to Sharpton to get some car parts of some kind. He said he couldn't believe his eyes at the horrible sight. I still didn't know what they were talking about, therefore they had me scared half to death. The three of us walked closer and closer and . . . oh, Mr. Jericho, if you will pardon me, I now prefer to cease my recollections at this point."

"I understand, Miss Eden, you've been more than cooperative. Just one more thing, ma'am, and I wish you to think as clearly and as thoroughly as you are able. With you living the closest of any citizen to the church, can you remember any unusual noise, light, or other strange occurrence happening early that morning? Please think clearly: did you see or hear anything out of the ordinary late Wednesday night or early Thursday morning?"

After a minute of silence, Miss Eden clasped her hands together apologetically. "I'm so sorry, Mr. Jericho. As a service to both you and the late Reverend Christmas, I wish I could provide the information you need. However, I generally sleep with blinders on my eyes to maximize the darkness and I play a record on the record player to also help me fall sleep. It's hard for me to fall asleep, but when I do, I *really* do. I am a heavy sleeper."

Standing up, Agent Jericho extended his hand. "Miss Eden, I can't thank you enough for the wonderful visit and the helpful information."

Miss Eden's gargantuan figure rose from the couch and gently shook his hand. "I really wasn't helpful, Mr. Jericho. I mean, what did you find out from me?"

Looking upward into her face, the agent smiled and said, "Miss Eden, it takes all bits of information to form a complete picture—both the things one discovers *and* the things one does not. Lack of information can be as equally informative in the long run." As soon as he had imparted those words of wisdom, Nolan's thoughts immediately rewound to Miss Eden's interrogation of him only moments ago. *Hmm, maybe one can learn much from what one doesn't know or refuses to confront.* The agent bowed his head slightly and, winking one of his deliciously-slanted eyes, spoke with all sincerity "To repay you for your hospitality, Miss Eden, I'll make you a promise! I'll try to do a little better in the future at seeing how I feel inside about, uh, stuff."

"Oh, Mr. Jericho, you would the wiser for keeping that promise. The 'stuff,' as you call it, is what forms the dragons inside us that we all have to slay. Please take that advice from a worn out old socialite who spent many years battling her own dragons."

Nolan sat back down in the plush seat of his blue Sting Ray and watched the Amazon waving goodbye to him as she nudged her door closed. In fifteen minutes, Miss Eden would be heading toward her travel agency to resume her daily dance of making exotic places come to life in the minds of restless people and depositing their dreams in her cash register. For some unexplainable reason, he felt simultaneously melancholy *and* uplifted. Every once in a while, when questioning strangers, it seemed that this field agent managed to find a pearl among all the empty husks out there.

CHAPTER 11

The Amphibious Attack!

Next on the list to question was Burley Rankin, the entrepreneur of a tire business somewhere on Garden Valley Road. Walt had provided a brief, homespun profile of Burley to the agent, and it appeared the tire expert was a bit of a character—a simultaneously genuine *and* offbeat fellow. Apparently, no citizen of Icy Springs could mention Burley's name without breaking into a smile, as Walt himself had proved with an impish grin while describing Burley.

Supposedly, the most prominent characteristic of Mr. Rankin was his fascinating *ultra*-Southern accent. Walt said you just had to hear it to believe it, for 99.9% of the people in North Carolina did not speak nearly as Southern as Burley. It always seemed that whenever a North Carolina accent was depicted in a Hollywood movie or TV show, the result was a dialect that would leave a true North Carolinian scratching his head in confusion and thinking, *What North Carolina are they talking about?* Burley's accent, on the other hand, was twice as exaggerated as the pseudo-Southern talk heard in any show.

Actually, his unique brand of conversation had made Burley quite a local celebrity. People found the extremity to which Burley butchered the English language rip-roaringly funny. There was no better company to have sitting by a campfire, regaling campers with tales of redneck escapades. In fact, swore Walt, attendance at the volleyball games of the county church league supposedly doubled when Burley was appointed as referee. For example, people just rolled on the ground when he pronounced the word "four" as "fo'." So, when the score was four to four, people had a field day with that one. A spectator was bound to ask, "Hey, Ref, what's the score?" to which Burley would reply, "Ah say-yed, ye deaf dawg, the sco' is fo' to fo'."

Thanks to Walt's colorful profile, Jericho sensed that Burley was without a doubt a one-of-a-kind oddball. But other than mentioning the accent dipped heavily in Southern, Walt had refused to inform Jericho of any additional oddities, having mischievously insisted he didn't want to spoil all the surprises in store for the agent. "You've simply got to meet this guy for yourself," Walt kept insisting. "He defies description—visiting Burley is better than going to Disneyland!"

About two miles down Garden Valley Road, Nolan guided Polly around a horseshoe curve and immediately began descending a steep slope alongside the Atkins River. Midway down the slope, the agent noticed a narrow bridge over the river in the distance. He also spied what he perceived as two people standing on opposite sides of the bridge with their backs to each other. Nearing the bottom of the slope, the bridge and its two occupants disappeared as the cattails and brush on the riverbank temporarily obscured Jericho's view of the river.

At the bottom of the hill, a sign just before an extremely sharp bend in the road warned of the one-lane bridge that Nolan had just spied from the upper portion of the slope. *Ahh! Just ahead is the famous bridge that always floods during a heavy rain.* The explanation of the bridge's flooding was actually quite interesting. According to Walt, a heavy rain didn't necessarily have to happen in the vicinity around Icy Springs to flood the bridge. A sudden heavy rain in the mountains forty miles northerly could flood the bridge as the river's overflow worked its way south. Therefore, a flash flood could actually overtake the bridge while the sun was shining in Icy Springs.

The agent carefully maneuvered Polly around the ninety-degree curve leading immediately to the fragile-looking bridge, which seemed barely above the water. As if a curtain had just been raised in a stage play, the characters of the drama were now revealed in clear focus. Standing on the bridge, two young ladies, appearing to be older teenagers, were fishing with bamboo poles, each girl's cane rod extending over a rail of the bridge. The girl on the right side of the bridge appeared to be redheaded, while the female opposite her was brunette. Each angler stood slightly bent over the rail toward the water, with the composite view framing the two figures as perfect bookends decorating the bridge. Both girls were wearing blue jean shorts barely there and halter tops even more barely there.

A chauvinistic high school English teacher had once told Nolan that essays should be held to the same standard as women's clothing. "An essay, like a lady's skirt, should be long enough to adequately cover the subject, but short enough to maintain a high degree of interest." *Hmm, ol' Mr. Cameron would certainly say these two standing before me have not adequately covered their subjects at all.* The two scantily clad females gave a whole new meaning to the word "clothing"—although Nolan thought that, in the circumstances, the term applied only loosely. And, what made matters worse, there was no way Nolan could proceed across the bridge as the two sentries arched over the rails formed a barricade with too narrow an opening for his Sting Ray to pass through. *Great! I wonder what the toll is going to be to get by these two!*

Never having received any specialized training in the event two half-naked females were obstructing passage across a river, the agent brought the creeping Polly to a complete halt at the foot of the bridge. He tapped the horn lightly twice in a staccato fashion. Neither girl seemed distracted at all by Nolan's polite request to move and kept her concentration solely aimed toward the river. *Okay, if that round of medicine had no effect, let's up the dosage.* This time, Nolan blew Polly's horn using the old "shave-and-a-haircut, two-bits" rhythm, but leaving out the "two-bits." Like zombies, the girls still stared unflinchingly at the water below.

Okay, enough's enough. Polly, it's time we give 'em the maximum dosage. The frustrated agent then extended a stiff arm, pressed his hand firmly against the steering wheel and sent a several-second unrestrained blast of warning.

Jericho's blaring decree to cease and desist the fleshy blockade proved successful: both girls suddenly glared at the blue Sting Ray as if the agent had some gall to show up at *their* bridge without an invitation. The redheaded girl placed both hands on her hips while the brunette walked over toward the driver's door. Jericho immediately rolled down the window and started to address the approaching female but was not quick enough on the draw.

"Oh, I'm sorry, mister! My sister and I didn't mean to block you from crossing over. When you blew your horn at first with those short little ol' toots, I thought you was flirtin' with us. Daddy told us to ignore any of the local coon dogs with two legs that might come a-sniffin' around. So, I mumbled to my sister just to pretend you wasn't there. Anyway, I could see you meant business when you sat on the horn that last time—again, I'm sorry."

"That's quite okay, Miss, uh . . .?"

"Rankin. My name's Ronda. My sister's name is Randi."

Jericho glanced toward Randi, who was already waving with one of those silly-little-schoolgirl waves which involved keeping the palm still while moving the fingers real fast up and down. *Very quaint,* mused Jericho. *Oh well, as the old saying goes, "When in Rome . . ."* Nolan lifted his right hand off the steering wheel and duplicated Randi's imbecilic micro-wave, making sure the gesture was accompanied by an equally goofy, insincere smile on his face.

Nolan immediately turned his attention back toward the brunette. "Well, Ronda, Daddy certainly has trained you well. Yes, indeed! Always ignore any dogs a-sniffin'. I believe you said your last name was Rankin—your daddy wouldn't happen to be Burley Rankin, would he? The Burley Rankin who owns the tire business?"

"Yes indeedy, that's my Daddy! Our place is a mile on over the hill past the bridge. If you come to the big white church on the left, you've gone too far. Our driveway's on the right and goes on down into the woods a little ways. There's a little wooden sign at our mailbox with 'Burley's Tire Place' carved on it."

"Thank you for the information, Ronda. You've been a great help to me. Have you and, uh, Randi caught anything today?"

"I'm startin' to think I have," replied Ronda, suddenly shifting her voice to a lower, naughtier tone. "You know, mister, you're kinda cute! I've never seen a man that looks quite like you. You sorta look like one of those Greek god fellas I've seen pictured in the school books."

Oh, no! Here we go again! Nolan quickly abandoned his casual voice which was usually characterized by a modicum of warmth, choosing instead to adopt a more serious, all-business tone. "Okay, Miss Rankin. I've—hey, what is she doing to my car?"

Nolan's peripheral vision had caught Randi easing up to the front of his Sting Ray. The redhead was now half-straddling the fender over the right front wheel-well of his car, with her left foot planted on the ground and her right leg stretched horizontally along the gleaming metal of the hood. With her torso and head now lying on the warm, blue surface, she seem to be massaging her body on Polly in a strange, erotic fashion by moving her anatomy slowly back and forth.

"Ronda, tell your sister to stop whatever she's doing. She'll ruin my wax job!"

"Oh, calm down, mister, she's harmless. You see, Randi has a thing, uh, what d'ya call it?—a fetish! Oh yes, that's it! Randi's got a fetish for sports cars—they drive her absolutely wild. Now me, on the other hand, I have a thing for the guys who drive 'em!" Upon that grand revelation, Ronda grabbed Nolan's steering wheel with her left hand and began moving her face toward the agent's, with her lips initiating the formation of a pucker.

Lord, what do I do now? I really don't want to punch her. Immediately switching his thoughts to the contents of his vehicle, Nolan reached down and grabbed a small vial positioned under his front seat. "I hate to inform you Ronda, but I'm taken!" He quickly raised the bottle, pointed it at her, and sprayed two short blasts.

"Ughhh!" shouted Ronda as she recoiled her head out of Nolan's car and stood upright. She immediately started rubbing her eyes and—with a lemon-sucking, sour expression on her face—began spitting out the contents of Jericho's spray. "*Puhhh, puhhh*! What was—*puhhh, puhhh*—in that bottle? Ughhh!"

"Don't worry, Ronda. It's nothing toxic, or at least not poisonous in small quantities. 'Twas a little of my car's interior air freshener, a scent called 'Newborn Baby,' as I recall."

"Yeeuck! It tasted more like 'Baby Diapers'. You are so mean! Why'd ya have to do that?"

"As I told you, Ronda: one, I'm taken, and two, I need to get on up the road and see your daddy." At that point, Nolan turned his attention toward Randi, who was oblivious to Ronda's plight and still enjoying the husk of Polly's exterior. *Now, to get rid of this redheaded little car-humper!* The agent poised his fist and mashed the Sting Ray's horn with vigor. The redhead shot to her feet so fast, she nearly lost her balance and fell over the rail of the bridge. Since the metal of the hood amplified Jericho's enthusiastic honk, Randi now stood beside the car with her eyes crossed while pumping her right ear with her right palm in an attempt to clear the sudden onset of loud ringing.

Jericho super-revved his engine, pushing the accelerator all the way to the floor, and then seized the opportunity, throwing his gear shift into drive. The car lunged forward like a thoroughbred coming out of the gate in a major derby. In seconds, Nolan was looking in his rear view mirror at the two girls standing with their hands on the hips, each possessing a Lora-the-waitress look of indignation as his Sting Ray sped toward the crest of the hill.

That was definitely weird! I am SO glad Cat wasn't here because, at this very moment, I would have to be fishing those two fine examples of nubile jailbait out of the river before they drowned. Ol' Cat would've seen to it that they cleared the rails by at least three feet as she sent them sailing into the Atkins.

Jericho soon noticed the sign Ronda had mentioned, pointing the agent to a long gravel drive. Following the trail, Nolan's car disappeared into the woods for a few moments before merging into a clearing. Situated at the end the end of the drive was a brick house with a huge garage-type building on the right. Attached to the garage was a small annex, presumably an office or perhaps an on-site store where tires and parts could be purchased.

Nolan pulled up slowly between the house and the garage, turning the ignition key and quieting Polly's softly-purring engine. Stepping out of the car, the agent was immediately struck by the powerful "sound" of silence—it was *dead* quiet! No roar of vehicles in the distance . . . no noise of air wrenches or other mechanical sounds from the garage . . . nothing!

"Hello! Anybody here?" the agent called out, hearing his echo slightly reverberate down the holler toward the river. With the absence of a response, he started walking slowly toward the garage. About fifteen feet from the immense, partially opened sliding door, the air was suddenly filled by an unsettling sound, bringing the cautious agent to a halt.

Buhhreeeep!

Nolan instinctively perceived the noise as somewhat amphibian in nature, but he questioned his judgment slightly. As he started to proceed forward, the eerie, frog-like sound erupted again.

Buhhreeeep!

The agent's inner alarm began eating at him. *Something's not quite right. It sounds like a frog of some kind, but . . .*

Buhhreeeep!

At that third iteration of the quirky noise, a startling realization struck Jericho: *That's not a frog—it's human! Somebody's imitating a frog!* Nolan quickly reached inside the breast of his coat and drew his gun. He made a quick dash and planted his back against the outside wall of the garage around the corner from the sliding door. The agent could sense his pulse increasing slightly as he attempted to size up the situation. *I've heard similar sounds before, in other cases when people are trying to replicate the voices of creatures. An extremely good imitation of a frog, all right, but it still has a slightly unnatural quality in the timbre. No, I'm not wrong—it's definitely human!*

Before tragically disappearing during the Korean War, Roberto Jericho had often told his son stories of the many tactics used in combat scenarios across the world. Warriors at home in a jungle habitat often confounded their enemies with sounds of various jungle creatures. In fact, *faux* animal sounds often proved an effective means of communication in coordinating an ambush. *Why the frog sound in a deserted garage out in the middle of nowhere? Did somebody see me arrive and is trying to remain hidden? Is someone coordinating with a partner, setting a trap for me? Come on, Jericho, get it together! Proceed with caution, but don't be too paranoid. There's a reason for this, and you'll find the answer. Just be cool!*

Buhhreeeep!

The sound is definitely coming from inside the garage. Okay, boy, take it easy. Nolan eased along the slightly open sliding door and darted quickly through its opening into the darkened interior of the garage with his gun pointed at full arm extension. At first, his eyes had to adjust to the sudden absence of daylight, denied by the nearly closed door. After scoping the area panoramically, he retracted his arms somewhat closer to his chest. *Seems clear—but careful, Jericho, careful. Let's have no surprises!*

Jericho stared intensely at the right side of the garage, limited in space due to approximately a dozen tall stacks of tires rising from the floor. Having around fifteen to twenty tires in each stack, the somewhat crowded forest of tire trees could easily camouflage an attacker waiting for his prey. As the agent proceeded slowly toward the tire stacks with his gun poised, a thought hit him. *What if Mr. Rankin saw something or has knowledge of something that happened Thursday morning? Has the killer gotten to Burley before me? Am I about to find Burley's body among the stacks of tires?*

Jericho eased ever so cautiously and quietly from one tire stack to the other, constantly surveying the landscape with his peripheral vision. He was ready to blast away at any time if need be. As he neared the tire stacks toward the back right corner of the garage, an inconspicuous doorway permitted some fluorescent light to pierce the pervasive dimness. From the direction of the light, the now-familiar sound once again bathed the atmosphere—only it was much louder!

Buhhreeeep!

So, the sound is definitely coming from in there. Okay, here you go, agent. Don't do anything stupid! Moving quickly toward the illuminated doorway, Nolan breached the opening between the garage and its annex. He was afraid of what he might find—the body of Mr. Rankin slumped over his desk, perhaps?

The agent came to an abrupt halt and stood in amazement at the sight he was beholding. Before him was a stoutly built man, a fireplug of a guy having virtually no neck, sitting at a desk against the wall with his back toward Nolan. The man seemed to be engrossed in a book of some kind. Unaware of Jericho's presence, the man's upper torso seemed to slightly quiver for a second as if he were trying to work up a great burp and then— *"Buhhreeeep!"*

Relieved but still puzzled, Jericho put his gun back into his holster. "Excuse me, sir. Do you make sounds like that on a regular basis?"

Not startled at all, the fireplug spun around on the rotating office seat. "Oh, I'm sorry, fella, didn't hear ye pull up. Sure is a slow day; sure can use some business. I've been workin' on my frawg chirps. See? I'm studyin' up !" The stout man held out the book in which he had been so immersed: *The Complete Encyclopedia of the World's Frogs and Their Chirps.*

"Uh, frog chirps, sir?" asked the confused agent.

"Yeah, frawg chirps! Did ye know that different kinds of frawgs make different sounds? And, each frawg makes a different sound, depending, of course, on what he's tryin' to accomplish!"

"Of course, sir! I, uh, guess I've let my knowledge of frog chirps fall by the wayside."

"Well, what ye heard wuz me practicing' for the big Frawg Chirpin' contest they have once a year at Shady Corner—out East not too fer from Raleigh."

"I have passed through Shady Corner a time or two, sir. I didn't realize they had an annual contest there."

"Oh, yes! Mercy, son, it's the Kentucky Derby of Frawg Chirpin'. Anyways, I've been the grand champeen five years in a row. I always have to practice my frawg chirps durin' slow bizness moments so I can hold on to my title—very competitive stuff, that frawg chirpin'."

"I'll bet, sir. You definitely wouldn't want to lose that claim to fame, would you?" intoned Jericho with a subtle dose of sarcasm.

"Oh, no! No, I wouldn't! What you heard me practicin' when you wuz a-comin' in wuz the danger call of the red-eyed tree frog. Listen here: *Buhhreeeep!"*

"Impressive, sir. Uh, I don't think I've ever heard a red-eyed tree frog portrayed so accurately—that is, of course, by anyone except a *bona fide,* red-eyed tree frog!"

"Of course you haven't, sir! Nobody can do a perfect alarm chirp of a red-eyed tree frawg except a red-eyed tree frawg, but I come the closest of any human bein'."

"I'll bet you do."

"Now, listen to how different the hunting chirp of a yellow-banded poison arrow frawg sounds as compared to the danger chirp of the red-eyed tree frawg." The stout man then put his thumbs up to his lips. He blew intensely, with his face starting to turn a light shade of purple. At first, no sound emanated from the exhaling man, then suddenly—

Freeerrrppp! Freeerrrppp!

"Incredible, sir, but I was afraid for a second I was going to have to pick you up off the floor if you had kept on."

"I know, son," said the man, with his face slowly resuming a healthy pink tone. "That's a difficult frawg chirp—in fact, it's one of the hardest. Now, let me show you the mating call of the Brazilian tree frawg!"

As the man lifted his hands toward his mouth, Jericho quickly intervened. "Oh, I'm sorry, sir, I don't mean to be rude. But, I've actually come by here for a reason other than being educated in the art of frog chirping. I'm guessing that you are Burley Rankin, sir?"

"Sure am, son! I'm afraid ye have the one-up over me. Who are ye, buddy, and how can I help ye?"

Nolan immediately displayed his identification and launched the scripted introduction he had used with Miss Eden. "Sir, I'm Jet Jericho, a field agent for the State Bureau of Investigation. Please do not be alarmed, you are not in any trouble. I am simply seeking your assistance with some information on what you experienced last Thursday morning."

"Why, good Godamighty! Ye're da man! I mean, ye are DA MAN! Ye're the secret agent dude that solved those ol' killings at the Cotton Gin back a few years ago, aren't ye? I always wanted to meet you! Ye're da man!"

"Why, I'm most certainly humbled by your glowing assessment, sir. Yes, I am the one to whom you are referring, but I am not a secret agent. As I said, I am an agent with the State Bureau of Investigation. I won't take much of your time. I just want to ask you a few questions."

"Boy, ye spy guys tickle me silly. Do ye drive one of those cars with a seat that can hurl yer carcass through the roof?"

"No, sir, I can tell you have seen some James Bond movies. I'm afraid my car seat just keeps my, uh, carcass firmly resting in it."

"Ye mean, ye can't shoot no missiles from yer car, neither?"

"No, sir. . ."

"No instant oil slick from the back of the car to make bad guys spin out of control?"

"No, sir, I think that was in *Goldfinger,* perhaps?"

"Aw, shucks—well, anyways, it's a big pleasure to have a spy guy from Raleigh here in my garage. I sure did think ye's awful duded up in that 'spensive suit just to be a normal guy wantin' a tire patched."

With a slight smile and his eyes squinted more than usual, Nolan thought he'd have some fun. *Oh, what the hell, I'll feed the guy's escapist fantasies just a wee bit.* "Trust me, sir, I am a normal guy—that is, when I'm not flying over the state with my jet pack on or dodging criminals shooting at me with laser guns."

"Da hell ye say? Man, I'd sure like to spend a day in yer shoes, Mr. Jericho!"

"Well, Mr. Rankin, it's not all it's cracked up to be, although I did have the privilege of meeting your lovely daughters back on the bridge. Ronda was kind enough to tell me exactly where to find you."

"I tell ye, Mr. Jericho—even though I would like to have a shot at being a secret agent fella, I am still a proud, proud man. I do love my two little gals. They are the purdiest, most innocent little angels a daddy could have."

"Yes, sir, they are indeed quite pretty." *I think I'd better stop at the innocent part. What Daddy doesn't know won't hurt him—at least for today, maybe.*

Jericho knew the morning was quickly diminishing, and he still had two citizens after Mr. Rankin that he wished to question. "Now, Mr. Rankin, let me ask you about Thursday morning."

"What about it, sir—and, please, son, call me Burley!"

"Yes, sir, uh, Burley. First, are you a member of Icy Springs Lutheran Church?"

"No, sir, never have been much of a churchgoer. Oh, I believe in Gawd, and He is certainly mighty good up there at looking after ol' Burley. But, I just don't like to dress up in no suit and put on airs around people. I feel I can talk to Gawd right here in dis here garage better'n I can dressed up in front of ever'body."

"Fair enough, sir, I'm not here to judge your religious practices. Did you know Reverend Christmas?"

"Aw, son, who didn't? That man wuz ever'body's friend. He visited ye when ye wuz sick. He brought ye a little money if ye had a little run of bad luck. I recollect that when my first garage burnt down, here come ol' Pastor Paul with some money he'd collected to help me rebuild."

Tears slighted swelled in Burley's eyes as he looked toward the floor. He paused for a second, then continued. "Yeah, Pastor Paul was a good soul. He tried and tried to git me to come to church, but I wuz a stubborn cuss to the end. No matter how much he visited and invited me, I never did darken the door of the church. He bugged the crap out of me, but I held my ground. His death sure has me thinkin' a lot, though. Would it have hurt me to try at least once or twice sittin' in on a few borin' sermons? Maybe he did have somethin' to say that wouldn't-a hurt ol' Burley in the least to hear."

"Well, Burley, don't beat yourself up. Sometimes we are all guilty of turning a deaf ear to someone or something that is trying to speak to our souls. But, you're right—from what I've heard, Pastor Paul indeed spent his life like a shepherd looking after his flock whether they were members of his church or not. Now, next question, Burley, what happened that Thursday morning when you were going by the church and saw Miss Krenshaw's car in the ditch?"

"Well, that's purdy much when all it started. I was headin' toward Sharpton to git some car parts. I saw Miss Krenshaw's Plymouth sittin' in the ditch between the church and Miss Eden's house. I thought maybe ol' Viola had passed out. When I git out of the car, I happened to take a look-see up toward the church and there I seen 'im tied to the steeple—Pastor Paul! Gawd help me, that was the worst sight a man could see. Then, I looked over at Miss Eden's house. Miss Krenshaw wuz just a-poundin' on the screen do' and out comes Miss Eden. I run over to the porch to join 'em, and the three of us walked back to the church together to see that gosh-awful sight. Miss Eden then went inside her house and called for help."

"Mr. Rankin—uh, I mean, Burley—do you know of anybody that had any ill will toward Reverend Christmas? Anyone who would have had a motive to kill him?"

"Oh no, sir, Mr. Jericho. If anyone in the village had harmed a hair on that man's head, it would've been like killin' the Easter bunny or Santy Claus."

"I'm beginning to believe that, Burley. Anyway, I can't thank you enough for your time. You have been most helpful to me."

"Glad to try, Mr. Jericho. Hope ye find the killer. I'd like to see 'im go to the gas chamber."

"We'll see what emerges, Burley. Please relay my thanks to your lovely daughters."

"Oh, ye can tell them ye-self when ye go back across the bridge."

Jericho knew he would drive to hell and back to avoid another encounter with Ronda and Randi. "Well, Burley, if I remember my map correctly, Garden Valley Road eventually circles back to Highway 64 going the other direction. When I exit your drive, I'll just head toward the white church and take the long route back. Anyway, tell Ronda to watch out for Greek gods bearing gifts in the form of little spray bottles."

"Sure will, Mister Jericho, whatever that means."

"Oh, I'm sure your sweet-smelling daughter will understand."

CHAPTER 12

Three-Cent Cookies, Devil's Food Cake and Mary Tyler Moore

As Jericho was passing by Big Blue's Feed Mill on the roundabout route from Burley's Tire Place, his stomach sent messages to his brain that it was time for a little nourishment. *Man, not long 'til noon—I might pay ol' Doc a visit.* Walt was still insisting on taking the agent to an establishment for dinner later that evening, where he swore they had the best barbecued chicken ever, so it seemed more sensible to opt for a light snack as opposed to a full lunch.

It was a ritual for Jericho and Walt to make a pit stop at Doc's Store on their occasional hunting trips. Conversing with ol' Doc Lassiter was truly a blessing, for the mild-mannered store owner seemed to be one of those souls bestowed with the rare gift of making sense of a world growing crazier every day. Even though Doc was designated by the villagers as one of the two rotating "mayors" of Icy Springs, there was a complete absence of pretentiousness in the proprietor's personality. Nolan often compared Doc to the character of Sam Drucker on *Petticoat Junction*, but without the quirks. Similar to a bartender at one's favorite hangout, Doc just seemed to offer a refuge of stability in Icy Springs, where one could stop by occasionally to bend an ear and borrow a cup of sanity.

Nolan felt perfectly at home as he pulled Polly slowly through the covered shelter attached to the store, then eased by two old gas tanks, and parked her precisely underneath the overhanging American gas sign. For years, the red, white, and blue sign adorned with its prominent metal torch had served as somewhat of a landmark in the village, with much the same status one might afford a lighthouse or a clock in a town square. As he seemed programmed to do upon each visit, Jericho paused for a split second to savor the inviting screen door with its Merita Bread logo imprinted upon the somewhat rusted wire mesh of the door.

"Why, Jet Jericho! Long time no see, young fella!"

My, how good it felt to hear Doc's always-warm greeting, as if a prodigal son had finally made his way back home to a waiting father. "Hello, Doc, it has seemed like quite a while. I'm just sad that this visit to Icy Springs involves business, not pleasure."

"I know what you mean by that, son—a sad, sad day in our little 'slice of heaven' here, losing such a wonderful man as Pastor Paul. He was irreplaceable, and I mean *irreplaceable*! But honestly, I was countin' on seeing you on this round. As you know, word travels like a fire in a dry forest around here. I heard that Sheriff Niblock was asking for assistance from Raleigh. That kind of stuff is usually supposed to be kept under the covers, but I figure it was that blabbermouth Deputy Hodges who spilled the beans. Anyway, whatever the circumstances, it is great to have you back in my humble store, agent."

Nolan nodded slightly with his head and began slowly surveying the store, not as much out of curiosity as from the need to verify that everything was intact, that perhaps, at least within Doc's time warp, there was one place on this planet the agent could always depend on being resistant to change. The crude cedar floorboards, partially camouflaged under several thick coats of brown varnish, still creaked at the slightest shift of the foot. The rectangular soda cooler against the wall to his right was making its familiar thumping noises, compliments of a tired compressor providing refrigeration for a chest full of delicious bottles of pop, a litany that Nolan knew by memory—Coca-Cola, Pepsi-Cola, Nehi Grape, Nehi Orange, Brownie Chocolate, RC Cola, Dr. Pepper, Mountain Dew, 7-Up and Sundrop. The three wire racks full of empty pop bottles next to the cooler served as a testimony to the cooler's importance as a Mecca of sorts for the ever-thirsty villagers.

On the brownish oak counter in front of him sat the Holy Grail of the community, a giant canister of Jack's delicious one-cent cookies. *Yes!!! They're still here!* For some strange reason, Jericho always felt like Jack's cookies would be the first precious commodity in Doc's commercial Nirvana to bite the dust in its battle against time. The view on down the counter toward Doc's ancient cash register featured a parade of candies, ointments, salves, and other assorted sundries. For some reason, the gleaming cobalt blue glass of the Vicks and Noxema products always caught the agent's eyes. The tall, long shelves on the left side of the store were filled with canned foods such as Van Camp's Pork and Beans, while the shelves on the right side of the store contained Oxydol, Borax, Clorox, Ivory Soap, and other necessities for maintaining a clean home and a clean body.

One could often find older men of the village sitting at the back of the store behind the lunch counter playing checkers and munching on thick bologna and mustard sandwiches on white bread. Doc had sometimes prepared freshly-trimmed meat sandwiches wrapped in brown paper for Walt and Jericho as fuel on their hunting trips. Yes, Doc's Store was the most special of escapes for the agent, for nowhere in Raleigh could one find an establishment that offered such a personalized, homespun experience.

Today seemed to be a first as Jericho found himself Doc's sole customer. The agent eased over to the cooler and lifted the lid of its chest. Leaning over and feeling the cool air against his face, he took out a Coca-Cola with a thin layer of ice hugging the neck of the bottle. After prying the cap off the bottle with the opener affixed to the side of the cooler, Nolan turned back toward the welcoming proprietor. "Doc, it really is good to be in your company, but I have to say that I don't think I've ever stopped by here when there weren't some fellas playing checkers or some housewives picking up a few odds and ends." Upon sharing that observation, Nolan opened the lid of the "canister of the Gods" and picked out three of Jack's giant cookies.

"Can I fix you a bologna and mustard sandwich, Jet? I can put an extra-thick slice of fresh-cut cheese on it. I know how crazy you are about cheese!"

"Cheese! Ah, another food of the Gods! But no, thank you, Doc. Walt's wanting to take me out later for supper at some place he says has killer barbecued chicken."

"Gracious, son! I know just where you're heading. Walt's taking you down near Beaver Junction, but I'll say no more. Sounds like Walt is wanting to, uh, surprise you."

Thinking about the fiasco with Deputy Dobermann at breakfast, Jericho rolled his eyes slightly. "I'd have to say Walt's had enough surprises for me lately. I hope the surprise tonight will be a little more, uh, hands-off."

"Umm," nodded Doc with a look of slight confusion. "Oh, sorry, Jet, back to you noticing the store being so lonely—yeah, it's been *real* slow today. I think most people are still grievin' over Pastor Paul and can't find it in 'em to get back in their routines quite yet. I guess it'll take a little time."

"I suppose so, Doc." Normally, Jericho would never consider discussing his work-in-progress with private citizens, but he really trusted Doc. And since nobody was in the store . . . "Speaking of Pastor Paul's murder, I know you've already told Walt you were at home and unaware of what was happening Thursday morning. I'm at least trying to get around today and talk to the three who discovered Pastor Paul's body—in fact, I just came from Burley Rankin's."

The old storeowner launched a sly grin. "Ohhh, son! Let me guess, you heard the mating call of the Brazilian tree frog!"

"No! Thank God, I deprived myself of that. However, I heard enough of his other frog chirps to say I've safely met my amphibious quota for quite a while."

"You know, Jet, all kiddin' aside, ol' Burley really is pretty good at imitatin' those croakers. He's won that contest down East five years in a row.

In fact, even Ed Sullivan's talent scouts came out one time and visited Burley. I think they found his act a little too, uh . . ."

"Cerebral?" interrupted the agent whimsically.

"Yeah, that's a good word. Let's say it was a little too sophisticated for the average viewer. Did you by chance meet his two daughters?

"Yeah, boy! They can certainly put molasses in the gears of a man who's in a hurry."

"Sure can, Jet—even though Daddy thinks he's got two sweet little darlings on his hands, those two are hornier than Marilyn Monroe at a YMCA. Ronda, in particular, will throw herself at a man quicker than Raquel Welch can take off a prom dress."

"I must agree with you, Doc. Anyway, before I went to Burley's, I paid Miss Eden a visit."

"Well then, son, I will attest that you certainly visited a swanky dame if you visited Miss Eden. She is a one-of-a-kind woman, a real touch of class! Now granted, she *is* the pootin'-est woman you'll ever hear. She passes gas like a 200-pound prostitute. When I'm outside at the gas tanks, I can hear her cut one all the way from her mailbox—something to do with a digestive disorder, I believe. Still, she is a real catch. Sad thing is, most men around here are frightened of her. I think it's 'cause each man is afraid he could become husband number, uh . . ."

"I think it would be husband number six, Doc—that is, if you count the Jones fellow as two men, being that his two marriages to Miss Eden were inconsecutive."

"Yeah, I guess he was sort of like the Grover Cleveland of marriage, huh, Jet?"

"Yeah. Anyway, as accommodating as Miss Eden and Burley were, I really didn't uncover anything enlightening for now. I'm on my way to visit Miss Krenshaw and Bud Holly."

"Good luck, son. I really hope you find some helpful information pointing you to the killer. It certainly would allow the people of Icy Springs to feel some sense of justice in their topsy-turvy world, and maybe the village could regain some semblance of normalcy down the road. I think you'll enjoy meeting Miss Krenshaw. Just don't let her talk you into a piano lesson. As for Bud Holly, on a scale of weirdness, your visit with him will probably rank on up there with meeting Burley and his girls."

"*Great!*" replied the agent with a slightly sarcastic tone. "Oh, Doc, one more thing: You really keep up on people and what's going on. What do you know about Pastor Paul's brother, Ron?"

"Well, Jet, Paul and his family were originally from South Carolina, as you probably know. His brother was living around Columbia from what I recall Paul saying. Now, whether he still does, who knows? I have never seen the man. You'd be shocked if you did see him, seeing as he and Paul were identical twins."

"Yeah, Walt mentioned that to me."

"Anyway, they say Paul's brother was rich as a skunk and had a wife who was a real looker. Paul told me one time that his brother lost his wife in a boating accident and then went flat broke not long after that. The only other thing I remember Paul saying about his brother was that the man was bitter beyond belief and wouldn't have anything to do with him. Can you imagine?— shunning a brother like Pastor Paul?"

"No, that I can't imagine. Anyway, thanks, Doc, it's always refreshing to visit you. What do I owe you for the Coca-Cola and the three Jack's cookies?"

"That'll be twenty-four cents--fifteen cents for the Coke and nine cents for the three cookies."

"Hey, what happened to the famous one-cent cookie?"

"Sorry, Jet, Jack's has raised the price. I just haven't changed the 'one cent' on the canister to 'three cents' yet."

"All right, Doc, here's your money. I hope your business picks up later on. I'll be seeing you soon, if I'm lucky."

"Same to you, Jet."

After paying Doc triple the price to which he was accustomed for the cookies, Jericho felt a little melancholic as he walked out the door. He sensed Doc's time warp finally being compromised by the not-so-welcome changes of the outside world. Cranking up Polly and looking down the road toward the church, the agent placed his chin on the steering wheel for a few seconds. *I guess there is no place left on Earth where things remain unchanged, even at Doc's.*

It was literally a hop-and-a-skip to Miss Krenshaw's house from Doc's store. As Nolan walked on the stepping stones in front of the old two-story wooden house, he was somewhat impressed by the invasive vines horizontally overtaking the porch columns. The limber planks of the porch seemed to sag precariously with each footstep toward the front door, and the agent expelled a light sigh of relief upon reaching the door mat. He paused momentarily to assess the custom for announcing one's arrival at the house, concluding that the ornate device implanted in the center of the door was an old-fashioned manual doorbell. Firmly clamping the metal key-shaped shaft protruding from the doorbell between his thumb and index finger, Nolan could feel the mechanism's gears shudder as he twisted the key clockwise and set the bell ringing.

Soaking in the nostalgic, metallic call of the bell, Jericho glanced downward at the black mat underneath his feet. Highlighted against the dark surface of the mat were numerous miniscule paint chips from the door. Fully alerted to the disrepair of the ailing home, the agent's eyes scanned the now obvious overabundance of tiny paint chips all along the porch at the base of the outside wall. *Hmm, Miss Krenshaw evidently has little help in keeping up the premises. Oh, well . . . I hope she's available.*

As if on cue, a somewhat feeble-looking elderly woman pulled the door open. "May I help you, young man?" It was quite evident that the aged woman had been crying, for her eyes had that red, weepy look and she had a tissue somewhat wadded up in her right hand.

"Are you Miss Krenshaw?" inquired Nolan.

"Yes, I am. Is anything wrong, sir?"

Offering his identification, the agent performed his prepared monologue in hopes of calming the seemingly distraught spinster. "Ma'am, I'm Jet Jericho, a field agent for the State Bureau of Investigation. Please do not be alarmed, you are not in any trouble. I am simply seeking your assistance with some information on what you experienced last Thursday morning."

"Why, goodness alive! Wait here just a second, Mr. Jericho!" Without warning, Miss Krenshaw spun around and trotted gingerly down the hallway and out of sight. A befuddled agent now stood at the front door with no invitation to enter. But, after only a moment, the trotting senior came sprinting back down the hallway toward Nolan, waving a newspaper in one hand and carrying a pen in the other hand.

"Mr. Jericho, I can't believe you're on my porch. Why, you're famous all around our county—and I'll bet the state, as well. I've had this article about you in my stack of important newspaper articles under my coffee table—you know, with President Kennedy getting shot and news like that. This is the article from winter of 1967 when you solved those terrible ol' cotton gin slayings. See? Here's a picture of you standing next to Sheriff Niblock after you solved the killings. You'll never know the peace of mind you brought back to all us citizens in Icy Springs."

"Well, ma'am, although I appreciate your praise, I promise you that it's most unnecessary. I truly was honored to set things right and was very much humbled at all the accolades."

"Oh, posh! You're just being modest, but that's the way true heroes act, I suppose. I'm sorry I didn't recognize you at first. You see, my eyes are still hazy from all my weepin' over Pastor Paul. Anyway, Mr. Jericho, may I have your autograph?"

"I'm obliged, Miss Krenshaw." Gently taking the pen from his admirer, Jericho propped the article against the door facing and signed his name just above his picture. *To a wonderful citizen! My compliments! Jet Jericho.* He handed the paper back to the blushing spinster.

"Oh, mercy! Please forgive my manners, Mr. Jericho. Please, do come on in! We'll sit in the piano parlor." With the agent following Miss Krenshaw, they headed into a room at the end of the hallway. Upon entering the room, the spinster walked straight to the coffee table and tucked the newspaper carefully back in its spot within her prized history archives.

"Please rest your feet, Mr. Jericho."

"Right now, I'm admiring that plush-looking, cloth-backed rocking chair, ma'am."

"By all means, Mr. Jericho, rock to your soul's content. And, while you're sitting there, you are going to be trying a piece of my famous extra-moist Devil's food cake—I insist! Most people around here say Satan himself would find it too decadent."

"Well, Miss Krenshaw, I appreciate it, but . . ."

"Oh, hush, Mr. Jericho, I won't take no for an answer!"

"But Miss Krenshaw, Sheriff Niblock's taking me to supper tonight . . ."

"I don't care, Mr. Jericho. You've simply got to put my cake to your mouth. It has won a blue ribbon in the county fair every year I've entered it— first place, no less!"

"And, uh, how many years would that be, dear lady?"

"Let's see, *hmm* . . ." Mrs. Krenshaw closed her eyes, as if deriving the total was placing a severe strain on her internal calculator. "Umm . . . forty-two! Yes, that's it! I've won first place for forty-two years, ever since 1930! I'm thinkin' about retiring though. I suppose when I reach fifty or sixty straight years in a row, I might let some of these young girls around here stand a chance of winning."

"Mighty magnanimous of you, Miss Krenshaw. Okay, okay, if you insist! As much as my appetite is going to suffer at dinner, bring it on. I'll take you up on it."

"You won't regret it, Mr. Jericho." As the spinster headed toward the kitchen with sprite-like energy, Nolan could still hear her repetitiously assuring him. "No sir, fella, you won't regret it. You won't regret it *at all*!"

In her absence, the agent suddenly noticed the tick-tock of the antique clock on the mantle above the fireplace. Previously cloaked by Miss Krenshaw's hubbub about her cake, the clock's rhythmic heartbeat now served as a metronome providing a pulse to regulate Nolan's rocking. There were two homemade quilts blessing the back of a not-so-comfortable-looking couch, and on the walls were some ancient-looking photographs of ancient-looking relatives in some dime store frames. However, the centerpiece of the room was an old upright piano against the one wall which held no photos. The keyboard lid was flipped open, and Nolan found the hue of the extremely yellowed keys quite fascinating. *I'll bet that piano has had millions of notes played on it through the years.*

Buzzing back into the room, Miss Krenshaw confronted Jericho with the biggest piece of chocolate cake he had ever witnessed; he doubted he could ever finish it in one sitting.

"Here you go, son! Now, you take that fork and fill your mouth full. Then, I dare you to tell me that ain't no prize-winning Devil's food cake, first place at the county fair no less!" By now, Jericho had already concluded it was simpler just to obey Miss Krenshaw rather than buck her, so he quietly speared a moist, creamy corner of the imposing wedge and placed it in his mouth.

The agent's face suddenly froze with a look of serenity, his eyes nearly crossed in a state of bliss. It was indeed the rarest of expressions on Jericho's face, one that only Cat was able to induce during their more provocative moments together. He maintained that certain facial configuration for a few seconds while slowly massaging the inside of his mouth with the insanely delicious cake. Nolan practically moaned as the indescribable treat saturated his mouth. "*Mmmmmmmmmm . . . mmmmmmmmmm.*" Although all good things must come to an end, he tried to delay the moist, creamy concoction sliding down his throat until his taste buds had been slapped silly. "*Mmmmmmmmmm . . . mmmmmmmmmm.*"

"My God, woman!—Oh, I beg your pardon! I mean, Miss Krenshaw, dear lady, how did you come about perfecting a masterpiece like this? That's the best cake I've ever tasted, easily the best on the planet!"

"You do agree that Satan himself would find it too decadent, don't you now?"

"It's beyond decadent, Miss Krenshaw. How did you create this work of edible art?"

"Well, Mr. Jericho, a lady's got to have her secrets!"

Miss Krenshaw was gleaming with pride at her hero's obvious, uncontainable pleasure with her cake.

"Wow! Don't let this secret go with you to the grave, ma'am. You need to leave this for the world to enjoy." Jericho launched into another forkful and continued the orgasmic cycle of consumption, for now it was all about the cake and him! Satan would simply have to share on this day! *Mmmmmmmmmm . . . mmmmmmmmmm.*"

After five minutes had passed, Miss Krenshaw took the now-empty plate from Nolan and placed it on a small table. "Can I get you another piece, Mr. Jericho?"

"NO! Oops, again I beg your pardon, Miss Krenshaw. I mean, no, thank you, ma'am. I honestly couldn't survive another onslaught of the ecstasy you just dished up. My heart just couldn't take it!"

Smiling with an I-told-you-so grin, the satisfied spinster reached out unexpectedly and grabbed Nolan's left hand. "Why, I should have seen this sooner, Mr. Jericho!"

"Should have seen what, Miss Krenshaw?"

"Why, your hands, sir, your hands! You have classic piano playin' hands. I'll bet you easily have a reach of an octave-and-a-third, maybe even an octave-and-a-fourth."

"I take it that's a good thing?"

"Oh, yes, Mr. Jericho. You could play most anything Franz Liszt wrote with hands like that!"

"Once again, I take it that's a good thing?"

"Oh, Mr. Jericho, now you're just trying to poke fun with me. You know that Franz Liszt was one of the greatest, yes, he was!"

"Interesting. Well, now, I need to get to the reason I came to see you . . ."

"Mr. Jericho, would you be interested in a piano lesson while you're here?—only fifty cents?"

"No, thank you, Miss Krenshaw. I'm afraid I'm a better cake eater than I am a musician."

"Oh, come now, it would be a sin to waste those great hands. What about it?—only fifty cents?"

"Again, no, thank you. Miss Krenshaw. I really need to ask you some questions now."

"I know, sir, I know. I guess this old soul's just trying to delay the inevitable—you know, dredging up that horrible moment last Thursday morning."

"I totally understand, ma'am. Now, Sheriff Niblock told me that you've been the pianist for Pastor Paul's church for years."

"Yes sir, I have." Miss Krenshaw's whole demeanor suddenly changed and she started to weep. "Yes, I was the pianist there long before Pastor Paul started preaching at the church. I guess I've been the pianist there for around fifty-two years, ever since I was around twenty-two years old."

At this point, she began crying more profusely. Nolan half-stood from his rocking chair and extended his arm toward the tissue box on top of the piano. Retracting his arm and handing several tissues to Miss Krenshaw, he continued, "I know this will be hard, but could you tell me about Thursday morning to the best of your memory?"

"Well, Mr. Jericho, I was on my way to Monksville to see the doctor at ten 'til seven that morning. I had some pains with my sciatica acting up."

"What time was your doctor's appointment?"

Miss Krenshaw sighed and took a deep breath. "My appointments are always at eight-thirty."

"So, you left that early in the morning for a doctor's appointment? I mean, it doesn't really take *that* long to get to Monksville from here."

"Well, I'm such a particular sort, Mr. Jericho. I have my persnickety ways of doing things. Anytime I go to my doctor in Monksville, I leave extra, extra early to avoid people on the road on their way to work, and—even though my old chariot hasn't ever broke down—I always have the fear it could. So, I just leave extra, extra early. I don't want to miss that doctor's appointment—have to tend to my sciatica, you know."

"Good enough, ma'am, I understand. So, what did you see or experience Thursday morning?"

"Well, when I was passing the church, I looked toward it like I always do, and there he was! At first, I wasn't quite sure my old eyes were serving me right, but there was no mistake. It was our beloved preacher bound to the top of the steeple." Miss Krenshaw ceased talking and took in a sizable gulp of air between sobs. Nolan patted her hand gently and gave her a second to regroup.

"Then what, ma'am?"

"Well, I panicked and grew numb. I can't remember my actions clearly at that point, but I know I ran into the ditch out of hysteria. I got out of the car and ran to Miss Eden's porch—she's the neighbor next door to the church. Anyway, I banged and banged on her door with my fists. I was also hollerin' and pitchin' a fit. She finally came to the door. I told her she simply had to come with me and see the horrible sight I was seein'. Just as we were starting toward the church, Burley Rankin pulled up. He said he saw my car in the ditch and thought I was in jeopardy. He then said that when he got out of the car to check on me, he saw Pastor Paul's body on the steeple. Miss Eden, Burley, and I walked closer to the church. Then, Mr. Jericho, we saw what we saw! Oh, God rest Pastor Paul's soul, we saw what we saw!"

"Do you know why Burley happened to be going by so early in the morning?"

"He said he was on his way to Sharpton to get some parts for his business or something."

"Yes, ma'am, that agrees with what I've heard from other sources. Miss Krenshaw, living not too far from the church, did you hear or see anything unusual early Thursday morning? Anything that seemed out of the ordinary?"

"No, sir . . . and I'm a *real* fidgety type. If a dog howls at night or a cricket chirps out of tune, I get all bothered. But, I guess I slept okay that night, especially considering how badly my sciatica had been kicking up. Even when I was up at five-thirty that morning getting ready to go, I didn't notice anything strange."

"Fair enough. Now think clearly, Miss Krenshaw. Close your eyes, breathe deeply, and clear your thoughts. Can you think of anybody in this world who had anything against the Reverend? Anybody that might have had a reason to harm him? Anybody with any kind of argument against him?"

Miss Krenshaw sat back in her chair and followed Jericho's suggestions. Approximately twenty seconds after closing her eyes and breathing deeply, she eased forward in her chair with reopened eyes and began to speak with a tired, cracking voice. "No, sir, Mr. Jericho, nobody—nobody on God's green Earth can I imagine wanting to kill that wonderful man."

"Very well, ma'am. Miss Krenshaw, I guess I've bothered you long enough. Thank you so much for your time and trouble."

"Oh, no trouble at all, Mr. Jericho. Like I said, you're a hero to the people of this village. I'm praying you can come through for us again, Mr. Jericho. I hope you can catch the evil person that killed Revered Christmas!"

"So do I, Miss Krenshaw, so do I."

"Mr. Jericho, do you want some Devil's food cake for the road?"

"Well, Miss Krenshaw, as enticing as that sounds, I'd best refrain from that temptation. After all, I need to keep a clear head in this investigation, and your prize-winning cake tends to take a man's head and cloud it up pretty good. When I had your cake in my mouth a few moments ago, it was hard to keep my thoughts on the task at hand."

"I understand your plight, Mr. Jericho. Are you sure you don't want a piano lesson before you go?"

"Yes, ma'am, I'm sure. I'm on my way to pay a visit to your neighbor, Bud Holly."

"Well! Don't expect much out of that long-haired, worthless vagabond. He doesn't amount to much. When he's not littering the highway with his presence, I don't know what he does with his time!"

"Well, uh, I'll be on my way, ma'am. Thanks again for—"

"Mr. Jericho, I'm just about to watch an afternoon rerun of *The Mary Tyler Moore Show*. It's the one where news anchorman Ted Baxter falls in love with the daughter of Chuckles the Clown."

"I'm, uh, afraid I'm not that well-acquainted with *The Mary Tyler Moore Show*."

"No better time than the present! Would you like to wet your feet on the show and see a good episode right now?"

"I'm afraid I'll have to pass on that opportunity this time around. Anyway, thanks for your hospitality, Miss Krenshaw!"

"You're welcome. Are you positive you don't want a piano lesson?"

"Once again, no, thanks, ma'am."

"Fifty cents?"

"No, ma'am. But have a good day, Miss Krenshaw."

CHAPTER 13

The Fall of the Sloppy Joe Empire

So far today on this fast-fading Monday, I've questioned three people— four, counting my impromptu chat with Doc. And all I've ended up with is a belly full of Devil's food cake—but a damn good cake at that! At this point, Jericho had nothing even resembling a solid lead, although Doc had echoed Walt's assessment regarding the bitterness of Paul's brother and his tendency to shut Paul out of his life. It wasn't much to go on, but at least it was a thread of something. The agent was intelligent enough to realize that the chance of digging up any useful information from Bud Holly was a shot in a million. However, since Holly lived only a half-mile from the church and spent much of his time either walking on the highway or standing by it, there was the slimmest of chances that he witnessed something unusual the morning Pastor Paul's body was discovered.

Making a right turn out of Miss Krenshaw's drive, Nolan headed in the opposite direction of Doc's Store and the church. He cruised a quarter-mile from the spinster's house to the base of the holler and came to a dead stop on the highway across from a private entrance to his left. Pulling onto the virtually unnoticeable gravel drive from this direction involved performing a 180-degree *u*-turn and immediately descending a sharp, bumpy decline into . . . *where*? Nolan had passed the driveway many times coming through Icy Springs, and his line of vision had never permitted any details of the private drive past its entrance from Highway 64. Running parallel to the highway, the hidden driveway closely hugged the steep bank stretching from the highway's edge. The driveway was not the only real estate hidden from view. According to Walt's description, Holly's house was completely camouflaged by thick vegetation in the ravine at the bottom of the drive.

After completing the necessitated *u*-turn maneuver, Jericho slowly and cautiously headed his prized Sting Ray downward. Erosion and time had played havoc with the drive, for there were deep, tire-sized ruts which could easily swallow one of Polly's wheels. Highway 64 had now disappeared out of sight, although lying atop the steep bank beside him. Jericho stared with a little trepidation at the oncoming tunnel of vegetation halfway down the "driveway to Hell," a density of foliage cloaking Holly's house so thoroughly that the residence was imperceptible from the highway. Darkness swallowed the Sting Ray as the sunlight beaming through Polly's windows was strangled by the overtaking leaves and vines, now rendering it a shadowy landscape. *Well, here goes nothing. It's hard to believe I'm finally going to meet this odd joker I always see walking along the highway—if he's home, that is.*

The vegetation now engulfing Jericho could easily serve as a botanist's playground. There were thin brush, thick brush, vertical vines, horizontal vines, and trees of all heights, shapes, and sorts. An immense blanket of kudzu seemed to be draped scattershot across the trees, as if someone had haphazardly cast a net without any attempt at an even distribution of coverage. The world within this vegetation zone seemed so out of place for a location in North Carolina only an hour from Charlotte. To the somewhat disoriented agent, he could easily have been in the middle of the Amazon, with a huge anaconda about to slither across the hood of his car at any moment. It was not completely dark, but the hard-working sunlight was so filtered by the vegetative canopy that its beams were reduced comparatively to the anemic rays of a flashlight with nearly comatose batteries.

As the agent's pupils slowly adjusted to the dramatic change from bright to dim lighting, he blinked several times rapidly to make sure his eyes weren't playing tricks on him. In amazement, the agent let his Sting Ray roll to a gentle stop. He leaned forward to the right of the steering wheel and moved his chin toward the dashboard to gaze through the windshield.

Wow! And, double-wow! This is where expensive cars go when they die! Indeed, what Nolan seemed to be staring at was a small cemetery of high-line automobiles. *Incredible! Simply incredible! There's a Lamborghini 350 GT—1964, I do believe! . . . There's a 1962 Ferrari 365! . . . And there is the 1963 cherry-red Jaguar E-Type convertible I've dreamed of owning! Better not tell Anna about the Jag, Polly. Anna would be jealous! And, heavens to Henry Ford, there is a blue convertible Lotus Elan—1965, if I'm not incorrect.*

Nolan suddenly drew back in a mixture of disgust and horror at the realization that he was viewing a high-priced morgue for lovely, classically crafted vehicles. Yes, evidently Bud Holly was once wealthy enough to dabble in collecting supercars. The agent knew that possession of any one of these cars would have satisfied the dreams of so many poor saps and wannabes desiring a place within the elite realm of car owner royalty, himself included. And right here sat a Lamborghini, a Ferrari, a Jaguar, and a Lotus Elan swallowed by weeds—here, in the middle of Icy Springs, a virtual "Hooterville" in the world of luxury cars. *Vines growing in and out of them, no less, their tires rotting away, no chance they will ever start again! What a waste! What a tragic waste!* Jericho lamented.

Prying his attention slowly and painfully away from the expensive boy-toy stuff that dreams are made of, Nolan fixed his eyes on a structure standing at the core of the immense botanical wonderland. He eased the blue Sting Ray forward about another fifteen feet to a relative clearing, which seemed to offer a path toward the building, presumably Holly's house. Putting the car in park and turning the ignition key, he cautiously exited the car while still experiencing that creepy anaconda-about-to-drop-out-of-the-trees feeling one gets in the middle of a jungle.

Walking toward the small, one-story, wooden house, Nolan glanced from his left to his right in rapid-fire alternations, as if he were in a Vietnam jungle waiting for snipers to ambush him. It was just *too* serene in such a lush place; surely there was some kind of danger lurking. Reaching the front door of the house, he knocked on the glass of the door five times firmly, producing loud reverberations throughout the structure. Immediately, the unmistakable yapping barks of Chihuahuas filled the air.

Ruh-ruh-ruh-ruh-ruh-ruh-ruh. He knew the sounds of "rat dogs" well, as his father used to refer to the nervous little beasts. About fifteen seconds after the knocks, the agent shouted "Hello, Bud Holly! Are you inside, Mr. Holly?"

Ruh-ruh-ruh-ruh-ruh-ruh-ruh. The dogs continued announcing his presence, but no humans could be heard.

Okay, let's give it one more try. Simultaneously, Nolan tried knocking firmly while yelling "Mr. Holly! Are you home, Bud Holly?"

Ruh-ruh-ruh-ruh-ruh-ruh-ruh. The agent then heard some bumping and thumping as if someone inside had come to life and was up to something. Then, almost immediately, the irritating barks of the Chihuahuas were silenced as if the dogs had been perhaps temporarily put away behind a closed door on the other side of the house. The thumps and bumps began once again and became progressively louder until a shadow appeared behind the glass of the door. Hollering through the door, a voice inquired, "Who is it? I don't usually get any visitors 'round here. Who are you?"

"Agent Jericho, Mr. Holly! I'm with the State Bureau of Investigation!"

Through the door, Nolan could hear some mumbling and the lock being unchained and noticed the knob start shaking. "Yeah, I'm Bud Holly! Don't want no trouble with the law!" said a scruffy, long-haired, long-bearded man in unkempt clothes, as he opened the door and now stood in the agent's presence.

Even though Jericho had often seen the offbeat man walking along the highway with his binoculars, it was always at a distance, from his car, and at so many miles per hour. The agent once told someone that it's always interesting seeing a familiar person up close for the first time, for certain previously masked subtleties come to light. It was certainly the case in this instance: Nolan was somewhat taken aback by the degree to which Mr. Holly's face was pitted and scarred, as if the man had been through some really hard times.

"Mr. Holly, I'm Jet Jericho, a field agent for the State Bureau of Investigation. Please do not be alarmed, you are not in any trouble. I am simply seeking your assistance with some information on what you could have possibly seen or heard last Thursday morning." Having held out his identification, Nolan now felt at liberty to withdraw it.

"I know what you're talking about, agent—Pastor Paul's murder. Didn't see anything, didn't hear anything. Don't live close enough to the church."

"Oh, I realize that, Mr. Holly. No, I don't figure you were anywhere near the crime scene at all. I just think your memories of that early morning could possibly be of real value in helping me with this investigation."

Immediately, the scruffy man's demeanor did a "180," as if someone had said to him, "You are now the most important man in the eyes of North Carolina!" True, Holly was most likely relieved when Jericho had implied that he was not being considered a suspect. After all, since the disheveled man supposedly hadn't been messing around the church, he was thankful the agent wasn't insinuating that he could have been. Therefore, the agent had definitely started off on the right foot with Holly on that point. However, there was another angle in the agent's approach that was the trump card in winning over the scruffy resident's total cooperation. If rumors of Holly's tremendous fall from being a top dog to becoming a has-been were true, the down-on-his-luck man simply needed to feel he was useful once again in a particular situation to at least *somebody*.

"Agent, sorry about my rudeness. It's just that I'm not used to visitors. You wanna come in?"

"Thank you, Mr. Holly. I would indeed appreciate that for a few minutes."

As Jericho entered what he deduced was the living room of the house, he could readily see that Holly was living in abject poverty. Trash was strewn about the floor, and there were brown stains on the floor and walls, presumably from a roof in need of new shingles. A dilapidated lounge chair and sofa, both with torn upholstery and exposed springs, occupied most of the floor space, and—something the agent had never seen in any other house—the walls were covered with license plates! As Jericho looked all around, he could see most, perhaps all, of the fifty states. He spotted a few of the U.S. territories, such as Puerto Rico, Guam, and the U.S. Virgin Islands. There were even some Canadian provinces in the bunch, such as Quebec, Ontario, and British Columbia.

Holly pointed to his lounge chair with a proud gesture, as if the king of the house were offering his throne to a royal guest. Jericho was nervous about sitting in the chair with its exposed springs staring menacingly at his expensive, tailor-made suit. However, he wished not to insult his host and carefully took root in the chair, attempting somewhat awkwardly to position himself so as to avoid the thread-thirsty coils. Holly sat on the sofa, opposite the agent.

"Well, Mr. Holly, I heard your guard dogs through the door. Is it five or six Chihuahuas, sir?" Jericho was actually joking with the man a little, figuring there were really three or four Chihuahuas.

"Actually, only two, agent. I call 'em Dow and Jones—you know, after the stock market."

"Clever, Mr. Holly, clever. . . I've heard that you have done some wheeling and dealing on Wall Street in your time. Is that true, sir?"

"Yes sir, agent, very much so." Suddenly straightening his posture to that of a little dignity, Holly stated, "I rang the opening bell of the stock market on an occasion or two."

"Wow, Mr. Holly! You don't say!"

"I sure did, sir. I had millions of dollars at one point in my miserable life. I had two luxury apartments, one in New York City and one in London."

"That's what I hear, Mr. Holly. I've even heard you owned a small island in the Virgin Islands near St. Croix."

"Not true, agent, the island was actually off the coast of St. Thomas."

"I stand corrected, sir. Impressive! And, I noticed those really cool cars on my way in. What's the deal with those? I mean, something evidently happened to your finances. I imagine that liquidating those cars could have perhaps brought you a hundred grand or more."

"I love my cars, agent. When a man loses everything, he's got to have at least something to hang on to. I hid 'em down here in Icy Springs out of view from my creditors."

"I appreciate you being so candid with me, Mr. Holly." Jericho sensed that the former tycoon was being about as open as he could with the agent's questions, which was a good thing. The misfortunate soul had such a story to tell and, sadly, no one was ever around to listen to it. "Mr. Holly, if you don't find this rude of me to ask, just how did you lose your fortune?"

"Well, I guess I was younger and more full of foolishness at the time. Sloppy Joes, agent, sloppy Joes! That's how I lost my money!"

"Uh, sloppy Joes, sir?"

"Yeah, sloppy Joes. You see, agent, I had this cockamamie idea that I could add millions to my bank account by creating a unique chain of restaurants-— fast-food, I guess you'd call it, sort of like those *McDonald's* restaurants that seem to be sprouting up all over the place."

"And your brainstorm was that these restaurants would be serving sloppy Joes, I take it?"

"Yes, agent, and sloppy Joes only, plus a few side items likes French fries and onion rings. My chain, called 'Sloppy Heaven,' had a unique twist to it. Although we served no other entrees than sloppy Joes, we offered a rich variety of sloppy Joes for the customer to choose from. There were huge pots in our kitchens with different recipes. One pot had the ol' familiar, everyday sloppy Joe mix while another pot had sloppy Joe with Velveeta cheese melted in it, cheesy to say the least."

"Hmm, doesn't sound bad at all, Mr. Holly!" responded the cheese-loving agent. "No, sir, not bad at all!"

"Oh, it was delicious, agent. We also had another pot with chopped barbecue mixed in with the sloppy Joe, while yet another pot had super-spicy sloppy Joe—you know, chili pepper to light your insides up a little."

"Wow, sir, I can't fathom how your idea failed. It seems like people would have flocked in droves to your restaurants."

"Yeah, that's sure what I thought they would do—damnedest thing, huh? I figured people would go stark-ravin' mad over it. I guess the problem was that people didn't want to go out and spend their money on something the wife could easily throw together at home."

"I'm so sorry that it didn't pan out, sir. *I* would definitely have stopped at Sloppy Heaven if I had come upon one. I don't remember seeing one, though. Where did you establish them?"

"Well, that was perhaps another problem. I expanded them rapidly from outer New York City throughout New England. I threw the restaurants up faster than kids building sand castles, sinking all my money in 'em because I was sure I had a winning combination that would multiply my fortune ten times over. I did hardly any test marketing and insisted on ignoring demographics. I fired too many people that knew what they were talking about. My Sloppy Heaven turned into 'Sloppy Hell.' Those Yankees! They wouldn't know good food if it came up and gave 'em a blowjob!"

Amused by the frank and unique jab at the eating habits of Northerners, Jericho smiled and leaned back in the chair, only to feel a slight jab in his back from a free-agent spring. *Ouch!* The agent's concern immediately shifted to the well-being of his expensive suit jacket. Nolan sat upright again, attempting to regain his composure. "Well, Mr. Holly, the world will unfortunately never know what it missed with your great sloppy Joes."

"No, agent, indeed they will not!"

"Mr. Holly, I've seen you walking along the highway on occasion with your binoculars looking at the back of passing automobiles. Seeing your fascinating license plate collection on the walls, I deduce that you perhaps enjoy license plate watching along the road—sort of, I guess, like some people who spend their time looking at birds."

"Yes sir, love 'em! License plates each have a story to tell. No matter how rich or poor, young or old, meek or powerful a person might be, everyone has to have a license plate to have the right for access to our highways. You like my collection, huh, agent?"

"Quite impressive, sir."

"Yeah, it is—and, you're only seeing a portion of my plates. Got 'em on every wall all through the house."

Jericho suddenly recalled Sheriff Niblock mentioning complaints every now and then about license plates disappearing throughout the county, particularly down at the campground around Byers Lake. "Uh, Mr. Holly, how have you obtained the plates in your massive collection?"

Mr. Holly started fidgeting somewhat with his fingers, twirling and twisting the stuffing jutting through the holes in the upholstery of his sofa. "Oh, agent, I come about 'em here and there. Yeah, anybody can pick up a license plate here and there."

"So, I'm sure I could safely say you obtained all your plates legally, huh, Mr. Holly?"

"Let's put it this way, agent, I can safely say I have never obtained a license plate off of a moving vehicle."

Jericho smiled a little, for Holly's qualification of a vehicle as "moving" was somewhat amusing. The agent then sensed the need to immediately shift the focus of the conversation back to Holly's love for observing plates instead of dwelling on the manner in which he obtained them. Jericho knew he had to keep the haggard former tycoon cooperative in a relaxed, unthreatening discussion. "Uh, Mr. Holly, I've noticed a lot of cool license plates from all over the U.S. down at Byers Lake around the campground. Do you like to go license plate watching down there with your binoculars?"

"Oh, yes indeed, agent! I go license plate watching down at Byers Lake all the time—great place to spot a license plate!"

I'll bet so, Mr. Holly—that is, along with unscrewing it from the back of an unsuspecting camper's vehicle. At this point, Jericho realized that time was fleeting and he needed to get to the business of what Holly might have witnessed concerning the scene at the church.

"Mr. Holly, I really need to know if you saw or heard anything unusual along the highway late Wednesday evening or early Thursday morning last week before the ruckus started over the discovery of Pastor Paul's body."

"No, sir! Didn't hear a thing and didn't see a thing out of the ordinary."

"Were you perhaps out and about early Thursday morning along the highway?"

"Well, agent, there's a good chance I was. I have a bad habit of waking up at four-thirty in the morning when the semis are going by. Those eighteen-wheelers sure can roar through on a quiet morning. So, I go up to the road sometimes and just stand there, watching the plates go by. However, there are not too many cars on the road until on up toward six-thirty or seven o'clock."

Suddenly, Jericho realized he had been throwing darts all around the bull's eye, but not on it. Instead of wasting his time quizzing Holly about how his collection had grown, he should be asking if the man had seen an unusual plate around the crime scene. "Mr. Holly, if you can, sir, think deeply one more time back to early Thursday morning. Did you see anything unusual that morning?"

"Once again, agent, nothing out of the ordinary that I can recall."

"What about an unusual license plate, Mr. Holly?"

"Well, uh, I . . . hey, wait a minute! I did see a car with a license plate from South Carolina at around five-thirty that morning. I'm sure by now you must trust my keen eye for license plates."

"Yes, sir, I do. Can you tell me from what direction the car from South Carolina was coming?"

"Oh, it came from the direction of the church—you know, from the Monksville direction heading toward Sharpton."

A South Carolina plate coming from the direction of the church at five-thirty in the morning. Now, that's what I wanted to hear! That's something I definitely can pursue! "Mr. Holly, when I asked you the first time or two if you saw anything out of the ordinary, why didn't you mention the South Carolina plate?

"Well, agent, most license plates aren't unusual to me at all, and a South Carolina plate passing through Icy Springs is not really that out of the ordinary. But, I suppose if I had really thought about it differently the first couple times you asked, I guess a South Carolina plate on a car passing through at that time of the morning might be considered a little unusual. As I said, not many cars pass through that early in the morning—now semis, yes. You'll see a semi here and there with a South Carolina plate pass by real early in the morning, but a *car* with a South Carolina plate early in the morning could be considered a might odd."

"Mr. Holly, do you at remember at all whether the headlights of the car with the South Carolina arced out of the church's drive? . . . you know, as if the car was pulling out of the church's drive onto the highway?"

"Honestly, I don't remember seeing that at all, agent. It could have come out of the church drive, I suppose. The church is a good half-mile up the road and, after all, it *is* over the crest of the hill. While I suppose it's possible for me to see headlights coming out of the church drive, I'm not sure about that particular car on that particular morning. I might have been looking in the other direction at the time being. All I know is a car with a South Carolina plate passed right by me heading toward Sharpton."

"Mr. Holly, were you able to discern the make and model of the car with the South Carolina plate?"

"Didn't notice at all, agent. Car enthusiasts, like I *used* to be, study cars, while license plate enthusiasts dwell on license plates. I guess you can tell how my interests have changed over the years by the shape my cars are in. Honestly, sir, when a license plate rolls by these days, it could be attached to a Chinese rickshaw or a steam roller and I wouldn't notice the make or model of the vehicle."

"Very well, Mr. Holly. I know what you're getting at, sir. As the old saying goes, 'You're so busy watching the squirrel in the tree you don't even see the alligator at your feet.'"

"Bingo, agent! Exactly!"

"One more question, sir, and it's the most obvious question at this point, I'm sure. Did you get the license number of the vehicle?"

"No, sir, I'm sorry that I didn't. Some license plate watchers are number-oriented, but I'm not. I'm only interested in where the plates are from and the design of the plates. I just don't have the photographic memory for numbers."

"I understand, sir. Mr. Holly, you are without a doubt a most interesting fellow. It was an extreme pleasure to meet you. You've been of great assistance to me, to the SBI, and to the community of Icy Springs. I'll wave to you in the future when I pass you walking along the highway. I wish you some good license plate, uh, watching around Icy Springs and down by Byers Lake."

"Thank you, agent. It was my honor to be of help to you!"

Both men stood simultaneously and shook hands. At Jericho walked toward the door, he rubbed the back of his trouser legs lightly to check for any dangling threads which might have fallen victim to the lounge chair springs. Relieved at the lack of collateral damage to his suit, he headed out the door toward his car. Unexpectedly, Holly kept following behind the agent, escorting Nolan to his car. The former tycoon went immediately to the back of the Sting Ray and looked puzzled.

"Uh, agent, although I know from your credentials that you're on the level, every government employee I've ever seen from Raleigh has a permanent yellow tag on his vehicle. Your tag is that of a private citizen. What gives?"

"Long story, Mr. Holly. Let's just say I have some peculiar habits which give the director of my department a major headache. He would love nothing more than for me to get with the program and drive one of our state's amusement park bumper cars with a yellow plate. But as for me, Mr. Holly, I'm a big car enthusiast at this point in my life. As you said earlier, 'a man has to have at least something to hang on to'."

CHAPTER 14

The Great Beaver Junction Chicken Fight

"Dang it," muttered Walt as he maneuvered his Ford Bronco in the darkness on the narrow two-lane back road toward Beaver Junction. "Hear that, Jet? Hear that missing in the engine? This old bucket-o'-bolts shouldn't be sputtering like that, seeing as I just had a tune-up. Anyway, glad you got out of that suit for supper, Jet. You look a lot more comfortable in your t-shirt and sports jacket."

"Yeah, I'm quite relaxed, and the little cat-nap I took this afternoon didn't hurt, either."

"Well, fella, it's good you rested up. You're gonna need all your senses to fully savor the great meal ahead of you."

"I must say you've definitely piqued my curiosity, Sheriff. I figured that while I was in the area, we'd be going to Stag and Doe down at Cinnamon Grove for some of their oh-so-succulent, fall-off-the-bone barbecued ribs. But then you also know how much I enjoy Rick's Barbeque & Grill in Salliston. I mean, for a place that professes to specialize in barbecue, ol' Rick sure makes a mean plate of spaghetti—better than any Italian place I've ever been to."

"I heartily agree, Jet—meatiest sauce you'll ever find, for sure. And that Rick sure is a character, collecting all that racing memorabilia. You oughta see his place now; it's starting to become quite the local attraction. But, naah, I wanted to take you to a place I'm sure you've never sampled. —Dad blame it, Jet, there it goes again! Did ya notice that sputtering?"

"Yeah, Walt—it's there, all right. Anyway, what makes this chicken place we're going to so spectacular? I'm not really that big on poultry."

"Oh, you can't imagine what's in store for you, Jet. It's mind-blowing chicken like I've never had anywhere else."

"That good, huh?"

"Oh, yeah! You see, a black fellow by the name of Keaton runs the place. He has a sauce that's like something alien from another planet. It's not like

104

anything you can find anywhere else on God's green Earth. People come from all over and gladly torture themselves with his radioactive dip."

"Most intriguing, buddy, I'm certainly game! It's been a long day at the office."

"I swear, Jet, there it goes again. That missing in the engine is about to drive me crazy, I mean, this Bronco's done me pretty well, so far. But it shouldn't be running this rough because it just had a tune-up and the spark plugs checked out fine. Any ideas?"

"Well, Walt, I'll bet it's something right under the gas cap."

"What are you talking about, Jet? What d'ya mean, 'under the gas cap'?"

"Actually, it's a deficiency that's easy to remedy. All you have to do is unscrew the gas cap and move your Bronco to a junk heap somewhere. Then, pull a Chevrolet Blazer right up under the gas cap and screw the cap on. From there on, you shouldn't have any problems with your vehicle running inefficiently."

Walt looked at Jet with an I-ought-to-kill-ya-for-that grin on his face. "Jet, sometimes you can really be a smartass."

"Hey, I'm telling you, Walt, it truly is what you've got just under the gas cap, honest! Don't knock it 'til you've tried it."

"All right, agent, I get it. You certainly haven't changed in your bias against Fords, have you?! By the way, what did you get accomplished in your 'day at the office'?"

"Well, Sheriff, I did manage to see Miss Eden, Burley Rankin, Doc Lassiter, Miss Krenshaw, and Bud Holly, in that order. Man, I was certainly reminded how this village definitely has its share of, shall I say, *eccentric* personalities? They definitely don't use a cookie cutter at the hospital nurseries in this county, do they?"

"Nope, this county's full of characters. So let me guess—you heard the mating call of the Brazilian tree frog?"

"Geesh, Walt, Doc asked me the same thing. Anyway, the answer is 'no'. I have no idea how a horny Brazilian tree frog sounds, for I dodged that bullet just in time!"

"Okay then, agent. What exactly *did* your finely honed investigative skills come up with?"

"Well, Walt, I had come up completely empty until Miss Krenshaw filled my belly full of Devil's food cake."

"You lucky dog, you!"

"Tell me about it. Anyway, good ol' Doc replicated the information you shared with me earlier about Paul and his brother. You and Doc seem to be totally in sync on your mutual perception of Ron's estrangement from Paul. I came up with nothing at all from Eden, Rankin, and Krenshaw, other than the fact that their individual recollections of discovering Paul's body were in total agreement. However, ol' Bud Holly just might have come through with the one payout I needed. He gave me a lead that further justifies the plans I had on the burner for tomorrow—you know, of paying a visit each to Ron and Mary Christmas."

"Sounds great! But, wait a minute! When I talked to Holly, he swore he saw nothing unusual that morning, nothing at all! What'd you find out from him that I didn't?"

"First off, Walt, where did you question Holly? I'm betting you didn't go to his house, did you?"

"No. In fact, I can't say I've ever actually seen his house in my adulthood. I vaguely remember seeing it from the road when I was a small fry, but that was before all the vines and kudzu and stuff overtook his property. Only the electric company's meter reader goes down there; he's the one that told me about all the fancy cars sittin' around. Nah, Jet, never went to his house. I pulled up to him as he was standing by the highway and chatted with him on the side of the road."

"Well, Sheriff, I can tell you that a visit to Bud Holly's house is quite an experience. He not only spends his time watching license plates, he collects them like crazy. They are on every wall in his house from what I could tell."

"Where'd he get 'em all?"

"I'll, uh, leave that between your deputies and Mr. Holly—but go easy on the poor ol' guy, Walt. Try to give him a little discretion—perhaps, let's say, some diplomatic immunity? After all, he was kind enough to provide us a lead."

"Well, I can maybe wink a blind eye in his direction."

"Hey, I'm not telling you how to do your job!" said a smiling Jet. "Anyway, the big newsflash Holly gave me was that he saw a car with a South Carolina license plate go by his place coming from the direction of the church at five-thirty in the morning."

"That's not a bad lead!" agreed Walt. Then, a slightly perturbed expression can across his face. "But why didn't he tell *me* that, Jet?"

"Well, Walt, you probably did what I did at first and cast a rather broad line when you went fishing for information. However, upon seeing the license plates all along the wall and realizing the magnitude of the obsession Holly has with them, it hit me just *how big* this guy has it for license plates. That's also when I remembered Ron Christmas being from South Carolina, so I simply cast my line a little shallower by getting Holly talking about license plates. All of a sudden, his powers of recollecting dramatically improved and he coughed up the bit about the South Carolina plate."

"Great work, Jet. Surely he got the number on the plate, didn't he?"
"No. Unfortunately, Holly claims he's not a 'numbers' person like some license plate nuts, that he just looks at the design of the plate and where it's from."

"Did he manage to cough up the make and model of the car? No, wait Jet! Let me guess—"

"He only noticed the license plate!" droned both men simultaneously in an "It figures!" tone of voice.

"Yeah, Walt, he barely even noticed that the plate was on a car rather than a semi. But, hey, it is a generous lead in the rather sparse field of clues in which we're operating at the moment. It definitely validates my inclination to chat with Ron tomorrow and dig up more dirt on him—if any is there, that is."

"That's a definite, Jet, considering that Paul and Ron had a terrible relationship, with Ron not even attending his brother's funeral. Mix that in with the South Carolina license plate being spotted coming from the direction of the church early the morning Paul's body was discovered and the pack of Kool cigarettes found at the crime scene with the South Carolina tax stamp, then I'd say Ron needs a good talkin' to."

"He sure does, Sheriff. I mean, right now all we've got is circumstantial evidence of the loosest kind. But who knows? Perhaps I can spook ol' Ron enough into coughing up some good info—that is, of course, *if* he did it."

"Ah, gotcha, Jet! You once told me that the act of simply questioning a suspect can serve as a catalyst of events speeding up an investigation and possibly lead to an arrest."

"Right, Walt! If Ron's innocent, fine! I mean, I might make him a little nervous with my questioning, but he'll remain clear if nothing else incriminating materializes. But if he's guilty, that's another story. I've found that those who are pursued often become irrational and paranoid, thinking their pursuer has more on them than they actually do. And, out of desperation, the guilty often resort to stupid acts. They either attempt to cover their tracks by trying to get rid of any incriminating elements or attempt to eliminate the pursuer and possibly anyone else having incriminating evidence. And, that's the part ol' Fowler always warns me of—that of painting a bull's eye on myself."

"You may be right, my good buddy, so be careful. I didn't call you down here to get you killed." At that moment, Walt breathed deeply as a big smile crossed his face. "Well, here we are, Jet. Boy, are you in for a treat!"

"You have me salivating like a dog now, Sheriff!" retorted Jericho. The Bronco pulled into a red dirt drive semi-circling a gloomy, windowless cinder block building sorely in need of painting. About the size of a church fellowship hall, the building sported a homemade sign identifying the restaurant as *Keaton's Fine Chicken Parlor*. Underneath the crooked hand-painted letters of the restaurant's name was a smaller hand-painted slogan: "Your stomach will find our chicken to be poultry in motion." *Boy, this place is about as homespun and quaint as a place can get!* mused Jericho to himself.

For a hole-in-the-wall sitting out in the middle of nowhere, the restaurant was evidently not a well-kept secret. There was a line of people extending from the door of the building approximately ten feet into the parking lot. Nolan glanced around and noticed that there was no rhyme or reason to the establishment's parking. Cars were parked both parallel and perpendicular to the building, as well as diagonally and in all the in-between angles. "Hey, Walt," inquired Jet, "how come I've never heard of this place?"

Walt grinned and slyly responded "Well, Agent Jericho, I guess you just need to get out more often!" The sheriff allowed a second of silence for that ironic little comment to settle in Jericho's mind before continuing. "You know, Jet, it's great to finally have a one-up on you restaurant-wise, buddy! Now, I hate to ask this of you, but we need to leave our guns in the Bronco—Keaton's house rules. He doesn't allow firearms in his place, even if your name is John Wayne."

The waiting line gave a new definition to the word "slow", as Mr. Keaton seemed to practice his own unique non-system of processing food orders and collecting the money. The lawmen's place in line finally reached its first milestone, the front door, and Jericho was greeted by a guest book on a small stand just inside the doorway. Finding the registry to be an additional quaint calling card that one didn't encounter at just any restaurant, the again-stagnant line enabled the agent to starting flipping through the orange-stained pages of the large book, the orange stains presumably being barbecue sauce.

"Enjoyed the chicken, most unique."—The Merrimans, Juneau, Alaska

"Wow! Toxic heaven! Your sauce is killer."—Fred, Muncie, Indiana

"You've done it again, bravo!"—John and Marcie Drake, Eastport, Maine

"Is there any way you can ship this incredible tasty bird to our home in Southern Cal?"—The Pettigrews, San Diego, California

"Man," exclaimed a somewhat amazed Jericho, "people really come here from all nooks and crannies, don't they?"

"Well, Jet, the Pope hasn't been here just yet. I think the Vatican officials are afraid the barbecue sauce might ruin his fancy robe and hat!"

"You fool!" chuckled Jericho. As the line neared the counter, he continued assessing the environment of the restaurant along with its clientele. There were farmer-looking guys in overalls in one booth, with attorney- or doctor-looking types wearing suits and scrubs in an adjacent booth. As the agent took in the full view of the dining room, he concluded that the business drew quite a cross-section of society.

The signs on the walls suddenly diverted Jericho's attention from the customers. Written on the back of cardboard flats and posted along the walls were a litany of rules. Evidently, Mr. Keaton expected his customers to mind their manners at all times.

"No profanity!"

"Do not bring firearms inside the building!"

"A two-beer limit per customer!"

"*Cash only!*"

"*No cutting line! If ordering seconds, back of the line!!*"

"Goodness, Walt! Ol' Man Keaton means business, doesn't he?" inferred Jericho, gesturing toward several of the rules.

"Yeah, buddy. At this place, you'd better stay in line in more ways than one!"

As the two men eased up to the counter, the burley old black fellow on the other side barked out "Good to see ya, Sheriff! What'll it be, gents?"

"Howdy, Mr. Keaton, this is Agent Jet Jericho from Raleigh, and it's his first visit to the Chicken Parlor."

Seeming unimpressed, the rugged-looking owner nevertheless responded, "Hope it's not your last visit here, agent!"

"What d'ya want, Jet?," asked Walt.

"Sheriff, you order for both of us. I trust your judgment!"

"Mr. Keaton," continued Walt, "give us each a half chicken dipped extra hot, plus a side of mac and cheese and a side of baked beans. —And, oh yeah, I about forgot: two beers apiece. Is Old Milwaukee okay, Jet?"

"Sure!" responded a thirsty Jericho, by this time not so discriminatory concerning the choice of brew.

"That'll be all, Mr. Keaton. Put away your wallet, Jet. This one's on me, I owe ya!"

"Hey, whatever you say, Sheriff. I always try to accommodate a fellow lawman!" retorted Jericho, placing his wallet back in his pocket. "But, just for the record, Sheriff, you owe me nothing and you never did!"

Mr. Keaton held his orange-stained hands out and took a ten-dollar bill from the Sheriff. He ducked momentarily behind a wall between the counter and the kitchen, then reappeared with a little change and a small ticket. "Your number is 77, Sheriff!"

After grabbing their beers from the counter and securing a booth in a far corner of the adjoining dining room, the sheriff leaned back against his seat to await the "call of the bird" over the restaurant's P.A. system. Taking in a cool, refreshing first sip, Walt lightly pounded his fist on the table and winked at his friend. "Ahhh! That hits the spot, Jet!"

"Sure does, partner, it sure does! Tell me, ol' chicken expert, what makes the chicken here draw such a crowd?"

"Well, Jet, it's a secret process that only ol' Mr. Keaton knows about. I've heard he keeps the recipe for the barbecue sauce locked up in a safe. He's supposedly been offered a half-million dollars for the recipe, but he swears he'll go to his grave before anybody else gets it. I guess it's one of those if-he-tells-ya-he'd-have-to-kill-ya type of things." Jericho nodded his head somewhat while taking in the information, and each man swallowed another dose of beer before Walt continued.

"Anyway, in phase one, they deep fry the chicken until the skin of the bird crackles and snaps to the touch, yet the inner meat of the chicken is extremely tender. If you order the chicken mild, they dip it in a vat of their special dip once; if you order it hot, they dip it twice; if you get it extra hot, like I ordered it for us, they dip it three times; and, if they just plain don't like you for some reason, they'll dip it more than three times just to see you suffer."

"What do you think is in the sauce, Walt?"

"Well, I speculate lots of chili pepper. However, there is a secret ingredient that gives the sauce its kick and makes the recipe the closely guarded pot of gold that it is. You'll see what I mean. The sauce is frankly uh-mazing! It burns the lips upon contact, yet the inside of the mouth doesn't seem to feel the wrath. The flavor of the moist meat bathed in that volcanic dip is to die for! Better keep the beer handy, though, 'cause the ol' lips will keep a-burnin' throughout the meal."

"Wow! You've certainly got me cranked up for this masochistic meal, you tempter you!"

"One warning though, Jet—it's one of the sloppiest meals you'll ever eat. The sauce is real sticky and, even if you attempt to use a fork, the sauce will work its way up your fingers like the goo-thing in that movie, *The Blob*. Whatever you do, friend, don't rub your eyes, even if they itch. I've seen the toughest of men reduced to sniveling, helpless zombies staggering around the dining room with swollen eyes hollering 'Help me! I'm blind, I'm blind!!'"

"Thanks for the advice!"

"And wait 'til you try their mac 'n' cheese—the best I've ever had! Mr. Keaton's young niece makes it, and she must use a pound of lard in every servin'. Heaaa-vy?! Man, that stuff is heavy! You could soak a dozen pancakes in water and drop 'em on the floor, and they wouldn't make a bigger splat than a single servin' of her macaroni and cheese."

Switching the topic, Walt suddenly adopted a more serious look on his face. "Jet, while we're waitin' on our meal, I've got something I thought I'd share with you. I'm, uh, really considering giving Dreama her walkin' papers. I mean, enough's enough! I've thought a lot about what you said and I guess, well, I've had about all I can stand of Dreama myself. It's just that I've never fired anybody before. That's gonna be sort of hard for me to do."

"Well, ol' friend, you have to be logical about the whole situation and understand that the advantages of letting her go would by far outweigh the advantages of retaining her. I mean, Walt, not everyone is cut out to be a pre-school teacher as she once attempted or she would still be a pre-school teacher, right? Following the same suit, not everyone is cut out to be in law enforcement or you wouldn't be wrestling inside with this whole matter as you have. You can't retain somebody in a position of responsibility solely because you fear he or she might not find his or her own way out in the work world. I'm sure

Dreama will find her way some day, maybe as a . . . hmm . . . pole dancer or something?"

At that point, Walt about choked on his beer in a fit of strangulation similar to that experienced by Deputy Sanford during breakfast. Jericho always knew how to target the sheriff's funny bone with a well-aimed missile of a quip, and this time the zinger had definitely hit its mark dead zero. Still laughing a little while wiping his chin free of beer with his napkin, Walt shook his head at the agent. "Pole dancing, huh?"

"Uh-huh. Well, Walt, who knows?"

Pulling a slip of paper out of his pocket, Sheriff Niblock took on a slightly more professional demeanor. "Here ya go, Jet?"

"What's this?"

"Call me psychic, but I knew for sure you'd be heading to South Carolina tomorrow and I wanted you feeling all prepared. I had Maness contact the Sheriff's Department in Lexington County around Columbia. He found out that Ron Christmas now lives somewhere near Pelion, a little squirt of a place, maybe, I dunno, twenty miles outside of Columbia? Turns out that Ron lives on the family homestead, a farm at Pelion where Ron and Paul grew up. I guess the place is now solely Ron's, perhaps another motive for offing his brother? Anyway, I went through Pelion once. If you sneeze, you'll miss it. The town, if you want to call it that, is known for its statue of a giant peanut on a pole alongside Highway 302. Now, Jet, before you get that 'tourist feeling' and start packing your camera, the peanut is, uh, six feet tall at best. Anyway, the Christmas homestead is off a secondary road intersecting with 302. It's all provided in the directions. Ron's phone number is on there, too."

"Thanks, Walt!"

"No, thank you, doubly—make that triply! After all, remember, you're the one that's trying to help me restore life back to normal in Icy Springs. Like I said, I'd ride with you in a heartbeat to Columbia tomorrow if I wasn't involved in that idiotic court case."

"Don't sweat it, Walt. It's probably for the best if just a lone knight shows up. I mean, yeah, I do want to shake Ron up a little if there's some guilt there to agitate. I aim to intimidate him into making the next move, if he is prone to do so. But if the entire cavalry rode in, he might totally run for the hills and disappear entirely—I mean, there's nothing that guarantees he won't do that anyway. What I'm hoping for is that one man showing up might just delude him into thinking he can, let's say, manage an emerging crisis or attempt some damage control. In other words, maybe he will have the balls to attempt plucking the thorn out of his side and dispensing with it—that thorn, of course, being little ol' me."

"Gutsy plan, Jet. I'm sure you SBI guys have trouble buying life insurance. Anyway, you'll also notice on that paper that Maness got the directions from the Spartanburg County Sheriff's Office for visiting Mary Christmas. She's been moved from a retirement village to a full nursing facility named Elderly Acres, believe it or not! In fact, Paul actually had her address and phone number on the desk in his study. He called her every other day and visited her when he could, for he and his mother were actually very close. And just to remind you, Mary's practically blind and can only walk with some help. Elderly Acres is located on Highway 29 just outside Spartanburg—the city, that is, not the county."

"Thanks, Walt, consider me briefed!"

"Hey, let's change the subject, Jet. I tell ya, I wouldn't mind seeing that Cat person from Raleigh again. I enjoyed meeting her back in '67. She was really quite an intelligent, beautiful young lady, making me wish I had someone like her on my force instead of Dreama, but, oh well. Anyway, it would be great to see Miss Cat again sometime down the road."

"Well, partner, here you are in the process of torturing me with incinerating barbecue sauce while here *I* am a true-to-life genie about to grant your wish. You should think a little better of your genie, Sheriff!"

"What d'ya mean, Jet?"

"Merry Christmas, Sheriff! Your wish is hereby granted. Cat's coming down from Raleigh. Fowler told me when I talked to him this morning that he would mail 'er out Wednesday morning. I'm, uh, sort of looking forward to seeing her myself."

"Praise be, it'll be great to see that little filly!"

"Yeah, I'm sure, but how jealous will Sarah get?"

"Oh, Sarah and I have a sparkling marriage, and she won't have any problems with Cat being around. Besides, Sarah always has my gun loaded and ready for action," he added with a wink.

"Yeah," replied Jericho as he smiled with his slanted eyes nearly closed. "I've seen her handy work at protecting her turf."

"Hey, just call me Turf Niblock!"

"You clown! But, I know what you mean about jealous women. Cat will be ready to scratch out Dreama's eyes." *Oops! Damn! No one at this point, not even Walt, is supposed to know about Cat and me!*

Looking confused and scratching the side of his head, Walt slightly stuttered while trying to process what Jericho had just said. "Uh—"

"NUMBER 77!"

Suddenly, a blank look came across the Sheriff's face with the announcement of the waiting chicken, serving as an eraser and wiping his mind clear of all present thoughts. Like one of Pavlov's dogs, Walt began salivating at the ring of the bell. "Hey, Jet, chicken's up! I'll be right back with it."

As the sheriff departed momentarily, Jericho began admonishing himself. *Whew! That was close. Jericho, you ignoramus! Don't let your guard down,*

112

even with Walt. Your job—and Cat's—depends on you keeping your relationship as closely guarded a secret as the recipe for Keaton's sauce. Don't slip up again!!

Upon his return to the table, Walt acted as if he was presenting a man scheduled for execution with his last meal. Setting Nolan's plate ever so carefully in front of him as if it contained nitroglycerin, the sheriff didn't take his eyes off the agent as he waited for his friend to take the first bite. Feeling a little self-conscious, Nolan thought of the stare Cat always shot his way during the emotional climax of a movie they were watching. *What am I supposed to do, cry or orgasm or something?*

Nolan speared a forkful of the tender chicken and lifted it to his mouth. As the chicken grazed his lips upon entry, a ring of fire ensued, as if he had dared to kiss the sun. As the succulent chicken made friends with the interior of his mouth, the agent was amazed that something outlining such a burning sensation on the rim his mouth could establish such a state of epicurean harmony inside his mouth. With his taste buds free of the flame seizing his lips, the chicken seemed to melt into nothingness on his tongue as it simultaneously burst into an indescribable flavor.

"*Mmmmmmmmm!* Walt! God, Walt! *Mmmmmmmmm!* This is—*mmmmmmmmmm!*" The agent was at a loss for words.

"See! What'd I tell ya, Jet? Is that not the best chicken—let's see, how is it you would put it?—Is that not the greatest chicken on the planet?"

"*Mmmmmmmmmm!* It's outrageous, Walt—indescribably tasty on the inside and radioactive, just like you said, on the outside. Man, Keaton needs to bottle this sauce. He could become a billionaire! This stuff is orange gold!"

"He did begin bottling it just recently, Jet. I think he keeps a supply under his counter up front." As Walt began to savor his half-bird, he excitedly chatted with his mouth full. "And, wait, Jet, you ain't reached the best part yet!"

"*Mmmmmmmmmm!* What do you mean, 'ain't reached the best part'? I couldn't stand anything better than this!"

"Jet, you won't believe this. But in about ten minutes, you will get a little jittery. You'll actually get the shakes and have the irrepressible desire to order another half, as if you're addicted to it. Honest Injun, Jet, I swear on an entire chicken coop! It's the weirdest feeling. I don't know what ol' man Keaton puts in his sauce, but surely it can't be legal."

"The devil you say! You're pulling my leg on that one, partner."

"Just wait and see, Jet. You keep swallowing that bird and *just . . . you . . . wait . . . and . . . see.*"

And sure enough, Walt was on the level. Around a dozen minutes into the meal, Nolan felt a strange tingling throughout his body. His hands became a little shaky, causing him to fumble clumsily when grasping for his second bottle of beer and, as Walt had predicted, he suddenly possessed a ravenous appetite for more of the stuff. "Walt, you were right, buddy. There's something wicked in that sauce."

"Now you see what I mean, don't ya, Jet? I mean, Keaton's sauce has to have the same type of magic stuff in it that tribes in certain parts of the world consume in order to temporarily enter the spiritual realm. You've heard of that type of stuff, haven't you? I mean, this sauce has to be something like the Beatles got a hold of right before they wrote some of their later stuff."

"I don't know about any of that, my friend, but I do thank you immensely for treating me to this meal. It is truly a culinary experience unlike any I've ever had." Walt sat there beaming as if he had just helped deliver a newborn baby. The fact that he had introduced his friend, a man he respected to no end, to such a unique and memorable meal filled him with an immense degree of pride.

"Wow!" said Jericho as the two lawmen sat literally holding their stomachs. "I feel like I almost need to light up a cigarette after that pleasure, and I don't even smoke!"

"I know what you mean, Jet. It's the best pleasure a man can have in the absence of a woman. I don't know of anyone who wouldn't give their approval of this meal."

"A cardiologist, perhaps?"

With that wise-acre comment, both men laughed a little and took their last sips of beer. Suddenly, a loud voice rang out through the dining room all the way from the adjoining section housing the ordering counter. "I said, Old Man, I want another beer each for me and my brothers, and I want 'em NOW!" The obnoxious tone of the terse command caused several diners in the restaurant to gasp while others looked straight down at their plates, either out of embarrassment or being frightened into minding their own business.

Another voice shouted, "You heard Monk, Old Man. Choke us up three more beers, pronto!"

"Well, for one thing, you sorry jackasses," shot back Mr. Keaton's powerful voice, "you're breaking two of my rules. You're not gettin' in the back of the line for seconds like everyone else is supposed to and, even if you were gettin' in the back of the line, you'd be waitin' for somethin' you're not supposed to have more of anyway. You're not getting any more beer tonight, fellas, you're at your two-beer limit! So, pack up your shitty attitudes and take your ugly asses off of my premises!"

"Aw, man," said Walt, shaking his head. "That's the Hendrix brothers— Monk, Darrell, and Billy Ray. I didn't notice those clowns eatin' in here. Trouble follows those goons wherever they go. Of all the times for me to be in my civvies with no badge on and my gun out in the Bronco—just *great*!"

By now, you could hear a pin drop, and there was not a diner flinching a muscle in the whole establishment as the racket continued. "Old man, I think you got a definite hearin' problem, but I think me and my brothers got somethin' that'll cure that!"

Allowed a diagonal line of visibility from their booth, Walt and Jet stared intensely across the dining room toward the ordering counter, wondering what would happen next. The spokesperson for the brothers, the grizzly-looking bearded one named Monk, suddenly pulled a hunting knife out of a sheath attached to his belt. The patrons in line waiting to order instinctively backed up in fear, almost pinning themselves against the wall.

"Dammit!" said Mr. Keaton. "I knew I should-a changed the 'no firearms' rule on the wall to 'no weapons *period*.' I guess 'no firearms' was a little too vague for you dumb bastards."

"Why you sorry—" muttered Monk, lunging toward the counter as fast as lightning. Grabbing Mr. Keaton by the collar and holding the knife to his throat, he put his face about four inches from Keaton's, with the two men staring fiercely into each other's eyes. Darrell, dressed in camouflage and the shortest of the brothers, looked over toward Billy Ray, the lankiest brother not quite filling out his plaid shirt and jeans. Each of the two raised their fists in battle position awaiting their next orders from "General" Monk.

Without looking away from Keaton, Monk relayed the next orders to his two "lieutenants." "Darrell, Billy Ray, what say you just git on back there behind the counter and git us about, oh, say, three beers apiece. You screwed up, Keaton. A few minutes ago, all I wanted wuz another beer apiece for me and my two brothers. But now, let's say we just take triple that amount right now as a little payback for the time and trouble you caused us."

Having been quiet during the proceedings, Walt knew it was past time for some action by the law. He turned back toward Jet, but Jet wasn't there. The lean, stealthy agent had draped his sports jacket over the back of the booth and was already heading across the dining room toward the tense scene. Walt immediately stood up and began following, but Nolan looked back at the Sheriff and held the palm of his left hand vertically toward his friend, moving it in sort of a "back off" gesture. Mouthing *It's okay, I'll be fine* to Walt, Jericho walked on into the ordering area and planted his feet between Darrell on his left and Billy Ray on his right.

"Well, well, well . . ." uttered Monk in a mocking manner. Training his eyes on Nolan, he kept his firm clamp on Keaton's collar and pressed the knife even harder to his captive's neck. "Who do we have here? Or, should I say, *what* do we have here? I've never seen a man, if that's what you are, that looks like you. What are you? A chink? A spic? Or, are you a nip? Huh, you from Japan, *Boy*? You know, with your dark skin, you could pass for a nig—"

Interrupting Monk's ignorant parade of verbal manure, Nolan held both of his palms vertically in the air and looked into Monk's eyes with a fixed, cold glare. With his voice sounding equally cold in its fearless tone, the agent's words proceeded in a calm, deliberate fashion as if originating from a machine. "Who am I, you ask? As to who I am, my friends call me 'Jet'—therefore, you may not. As to what I am, you may call me an eradicator. I pull out weeds by their roots. You and your brothers are nothing but weeds in the eyes of these people."

As he heard those icy words coming out of the unflinching, perfectly proportioned man in the black t-shirt and black pants, Monk gulped and relaxed his grip slightly on Keaton's collar. Snatching himself away from Monk's grip, the husky black man reached out quickly, grabbing Monk's knife-wielding hand with his right hand and slapping a choking grasp around the neck of the brainless bully with his left arm.

With their fists still raised for action, Darrell and Billy Ray were utterly surprised at the sight of Mr. Keaton suddenly restraining Monk. The two distracted brothers briefly glanced away from the agent, allowing Nolan to lash out with a sharp thrust from his straightened left arm. As the back of the agent's stone-hard fist met Darrell's face, the clueless man's head shot backward from the blow with a loud pop. Simultaneously, Jericho's right leg was already extending outward and upward in a rapid motion in Billy Ray's direction. The heel of Jericho's foot planted itself solidly against the lanky man's chin and his head popped backward just as his brother's had. Both attacks had actually been executed in the time span of less than one second, the agent having treated the thrusts as a single motion rather than two separate moves.

Retracting his limbs at lightning speed, Jericho now stood perfectly straight, with the two unconscious brothers lying on their backs at his feet, Darrell on the left and Billy Ray on the right. Neither man ever truly knew what—or who—had hit him.

Startled and desperate, Monk managed to jerk his right hand away from Keaton's grasp and thrust the tip of his knife into the left arm of his restrainer. Keaton shot back in pain, immediately pressing his right palm against the wound on his arm.

With his attention now placed fully on Jericho, Monk extended both arms toward the agent while still tightly clutching the knife in his right hand. "All right, Mr. Magician. You seem to come out of nowhere, holdin' your hands up to me as if castin' some spell, sayin' some spooky words, and then, before I know it, my brothers are sleepin' on the ground. Tricks are over, now. It's just you, me, and this knife."

With that grand speech out of the way, Monk lunged forward with his right arm. Totally focused on Monk's motion, Jericho leaned to the right of the knife's trajectory while simultaneously swinging his left forearm upward in a swift, straightened position. The agent's blocking motion met the soft, fleshy portion of Monk's forearm in a perpendicular, painful collision—painful for Monk that is, causing the rowdy man to lose his grip on the knife.

As the knife fell towards the floor and with Monk's front torso fully exposed, Nolan initiated five rapid-fire machine gun thrusts of alternating fists into Monk's solar plexus—*left, right, left, right, left*. Similarly to his conquest of Darrell and Billy Ray, the entire five-moves-in-one motion occurred in less than a second.

The expression on Monk's face did not change. As the agent backed off, Monk stood facing him, completely still for the next five seconds. Then, the rugged man's body toppled forward to the floor; the goon had blacked out from both the pain and the momentary lack of air in his body.

Upon the instant Monk's body met the floor, the entire restaurant erupted into cheering and applause. Still nursing his left arm, Mr. Keaton laughed boisterously. "Man, son, now that was an ass-kickin' to top all ass-kickin's. You put all three of those boys out like a light, and in only a few seconds. They has been botherin' people for years, but I do believe their botherin' days has come to an end. Thank you again . . . uh, what was it, son?"

" Jet, sir. I'm proud for you to call me Jet. All of my friends do!"

Turning to his niece, Keaton shouted "Did you see that? Man, I never saw anything like that, and I never will again. I mean that was *one . . . royal . . . pure-t . . . ass . . . kickin'*."

A crowd of both diners and diners-in-waiting began crowding around Nolan, congratulating him with accolades like "Great job, fella!" and "Man, where'd ya learn that stuff?" Walt bulldozed his way through the mob and took charge, as if he were the manager of a prize-fighting champion. "All right, folks, show's over for the night. This has been a Jet Jericho production!"

As the crowd began to disperse, Keaton turned to his niece. "Hey, darlin', mind the counter for a few minutes and let me see off our special guests."

Jericho was reaching down toward the lifeless bodies of the brothers when Keaton hollered, "Don't worry with them, Jet. I got some guys in the back who were just about to take out the trash anyway. They can haul this garbage away with it." Nolan faced Mr. Keaton, then bowed his head politely and silently.

"Sheriff," clamored Mr. Keaton, "you bring this dude back anytime, and supper will be on me! Jet, for the cleanin' up you did tonight in my humble establishment, is there anything that I can do for ya?"

"Well, Mr. Keaton," Nolan replied shyly, "I normally ask nothing in return for helping others. I am always honored to be in a position to help others. However, would you mind parting with a couple of bottles of your barbecue sauce?"

As the Bronco headed back in the darkness of late night toward Icy Springs, both men had satisfied looks on their faces to accompany their full stomachs. Walt was the first to break the silence between the two tired men. "Hey, Jet, got a question for ya. . . Now, it's not like you needed my help anyway, but why did you back me off tonight from assisting you with the Hendrix brothers?"

"Well, friend, I meant no insult to you at all. I hope I didn't hurt your feelings. It's just that we had left our guns in your Bronco, and we really didn't have the space in that small area to have an out-and-out brawl. I thought innocent people might get hurt, so I just felt it wiser to go ahead and take 'em down and be done with it."

"Makes sense. And there's one more thing I've always wanted to ask you, Jet. I've seen several of those Chinese chop-socky movies in the past few years. In these movies, the guy beating up everybody is always carryin' on, just a-screamin' and a-hollerin'—you know, stuff like 'hieee-yaaa' and 'waaa-chaaa' and such. I've noticed you never utter a sound when open up a can of whoop-ass on anybody. Why don't you make those sounds, Jet?"

"Well, Walt, all individuals are unique, as all situations requiring force are unique. There's not really a set manual on how one properly goes about kicking somebody's tail in any given situation. Some people use the 'hieee-yaaa' stuff, as you call it, to strike fear in the hearts of their opponents, sort of like a war cry or something. With the Hendrix brothers tonight, I really didn't aim to give them any time to be scared before I took them out of commission."

"Jet, I swear, you are too much, buddy. And I mean, *toooo* much!"

CHAPTER 15

Sting Rays, Sock Monkeys, Sand Castles, and Shetland Ponies

It was not long 'til dusk, and cruising the sand-sprayed avenue along the seashore of Sunset Beach in his red convertible was a blessed break from the investigation of Pastor Paul's murder. As he neared the sign saying "*Pavement Ends*," Jericho could see his blue Sting Ray up ahead, parked along the side of the road. *I see Cat beat me here and, of course, she's nowhere to be seen. Well, I guess a little game of Cat-and-Mouse is now in session.*

The agent carefully maneuvered his prized Anna around the barricade, proceeding among the small dunes festooned with sea oats swaying in the ocean breeze. Anna's engine switched from her normally gentle purr to more of a slightly straining roar as tires fought for some traction in the soft, white sand. After nearly a half-mile of driving on God's handy work, Jericho pulled up to the edge of a small inlet with gently flowing water about ten inches deep. He was on the brink of the mainland and crossing the inlet would place him on Bird Island, a small chunk of land on the North Carolina/South Carolina border. *Let's see, now . . . Take it easy, agent. Lots of people cross this inlet in their vehicles. The secret is to cross back over to the mainland before the tide rises high enough to make passage risky, so you won't have long, Jericho.*

Holding his breath, the agent ever so slowly and steadily edged Anna through the water as if he were progressing through a mine field. *C'mon, baby, you can make it! And don't worry, when we get back home, I'll wash off all that nasty ol' salt water. You'll never rust on my watch, no, ma'am!*

Nolan sighed with relief as his Sting Ray emerged from the waters of the inlet onto Bird Island. He eased Anna up about forty more feet and put the red convertible in park, turning the ignition key. He opened the door and stood up straight, looking ever so lean and handsome in his black tuxedo. Stretching his arms and taking in a full breath of the ocean breeze, he laid the single rose he was carrying on the windshield, resting atop the wiper. The waves washing against the island's beach provided an almost hypnotic roar in the distance. The fast-fading sun dispersed different splashes of color all around, distorted by reflections within fugitive pools of shallow water randomly strewn about the shore. The prevalent hue of the landscape was a golden-brown, as the sun was fighting to remain above the western horizon.

"CAT!" Listening intensely, Nolan waited about ten seconds. He then cupped his hands over his mouth to form a natural megaphone and tried again. "C-A-A-A-T!" he yelled out against the breeze with a little more of an extended call of desperation. *Okay, Cat! The mouse is here. You can quit toying with me. Come out, come out, wherever you are. . .*

In the far distance, the agent suddenly spotted a wide-looking something— no, make that someone—moving slowly along the beach in his direction, but he couldn't quite discern exactly who it was. With nothing else to do at the moment, Jericho started walking in the direction of the unknown. As the someone moved closer, it blurred a little before gradually separating into two figures. *Hmm, it appears to be a person wearing a lot of white, leading a big dog on a leash. No, wait—it's a woman in a wedding dress! And, that's no dog she's leading—it's a pony! A miniature pony, no less!*

As the two opposing loners strolling on the beach narrowed the distance between them a little more, Nolan's mouth flew open. "CAT! Why, it's Cat! What the—?" Immediately, the agent tore into a rapid sprint and met the woman in white, clutching her arms firmly with his tense hands. After looking her in the eyes to make sure the figure he was holding wasn't an illusion, Nolan reached out and kissed her. "Cat, I was calling for you at the inlet. Why are you standing here in a white wedding gown in the middle of Bird Island?"

"Well, Agent Nolan Jericho, I might ask why are you standing here wearing a tuxedo!"

"I, uh . . . I don't know." Nolan suddenly looked down at the sand in confusion. "Just why are we here, Cat? And why dressed up like this? I have no idea what's goin' on here." The puzzled agent then glanced downwards at the albino Shetland pony, a creature as white as the driven snow. Anchored to the pony was a small saddle and sitting in the saddle was, of all things, a sock monkey!

"Cat, what gives with the runt horse and the stuffed monkey? Cat, just what in the hell is going on?"

"Don't ask me, Mr. Tuxedo Man. You're hosting this party!"

Suddenly, Jericho sensed a darkness forming in the small space between their feet. As he backed up farther, the darkness began to take shape on the grainy beach. "*My Lord,*" whispered Nolan, as the eerie silhouette emerged into clarity. Between Cat and Jericho was now a shadow of a steeple, accompanied by the form of a robed man. The Shetland pony inched up to the shaded outline, putting its nose to the dark edge. Immediately, the animal jerked back, pulling viciously at the leash casually held by Cat. The leash slid through the surprised woman's fingers, with the pony breaking free and trotting off as fast as Shetland ponies are allowed by nature to do. Nolan and Cat stared with their mouths open as the pony's form grew smaller in the horizon. It was the strangest of sights, the sock monkey being carried away with its back toward them, bobbing up and down in the saddle while fading from sight.

Looking downward, the couple noticed the shadow of the steeple slowing expanding, creeping menacingly toward them. Of why it was menacing, Nolan was unsure. All he knew was that his instincts told him it was time to flee. "Cat, run! Don't ask me why! But run with me, NOW!"

Reaching across the shadow, Nolan took Cat's hand and pulled her through the wedge of darkness. As she dissected the shadow, Cat exclaimed "God, it's so cold, like ice or—"

"Just run, Cat. I can't explain it. I don't know why, but we gotta get out of here!"

Running as fast as possible in tux and wedding dress, the couple reached Nolan's Sting Ray waiting faithfully near the inlet. "Get in!" he shouted firmly.

For some unexplainable reason, Cat delayed her response to Nolan's command and glanced behind her. As she gasped in awe, there it was: a giant sand castle! It instantly appeared only twenty feet behind them on the path they had just trodden, the elaborate sandy edifice at least thirty feet tall. As if under a hypnotic spell, Cat's eyes glazed over. *"Wow!"* she whispered in a mystified voice, as she starting slowly walking toward the castle. "It's so amazing, so pretty!" uttered the entranced woman.

"Cat, what are you doing? It's a trap! CAT!" As Nolan watched in horror, the entire castle suddenly collapsed with Cat standing in the crosshairs of its avalanche. With the sloppy, muddy quagmire of earth engulfing her, Cat instantly disappeared in its wake.

"CAT! Oh, God! CAT!" Nolan ran to the edge of the gurgling bog and furiously started plowing through the wet sand with his hands. "CAT! Can you hear me? CAT! . . . CAT!!"

From within the moist tomb of mud, Nolan heard Cat's muted voice pleading, *"Nolan . . . Nolan . . . help . . . I'm . . . dying . . . "*

CHAPTER 16

Rattling the Cage a Little. . .

"CAT!" Agent Jericho shot up in horror from his pillow, rapidly inhaling and exhaling frantic puffs of air. His body was drenched in sweat, although Room #5 at the Chat & Nibble maintained the extremely cool air-conditioning in which he slept so well. Nolan looked around the room, which was coated in its customary neon illumination. Sitting still in bed with his knees drawn back toward his chest, the agent momentarily wrapped both arms around his legs and let his kneecaps serve as a resting point for his forehead while his breathing returned to normal. Thankfully, reality edged back into his consciousness as the agent sifted through his whirlpool mind.

Man, helluva dream! Worst dream ever! I mean, really, sock monkeys? Shetland ponies? Giant sand castles? I mean, I love Cat and I enjoy Bird Island whenever I can manage to get there. But, that was the STUPIDEST collection of thoughts any one human could ever put together.

Looking toward the foot of the bed, Nolan fixed his eyes upon the case of twenty-four twelve-ounce bottles of barbecue sauce sitting across the room on the dresser, a gift bestowed upon him by a grateful Mr. Keaton after the agent's solicitous hint for a bottle or two. *That's it! The chicken! The chicken caused my nightmare! Boy, Walt was right! The Beatles HAD to have gotten into that sauce during the late sixties. Man! I need to have Ed Williams back in Raleigh take a shot at analyzing the chemistry behind this stuff. I tell ya, I sure am glad Keaton gave me a case of it!*

Agent Jericho knew he had another long day ahead of him. There would not be as much questioning as yesterday, but more driving would be involved. After showering and putting on his dark gray suit, Nolan pursued an early breakfast in the Chat & Nibble Café just long enough to incense Lora the waitress with his lack of reciprocal flirtation.

It was much hotter today, far more characteristic of July than the perfect weather experienced over the weekend. Jericho preferred to savor Polly's air conditioning in lieu of open windows as he headed on the long ride toward

Columbia. Although nearing lunchtime as he breezed through Columbia, the agent had already decided he would streamline the day by skipping lunch and taking in an early supper. *Yeah! Get on down the road, Polly, my dear! Let's shove on through Columbia and look for Pelion. It's time to locate Ron Christmas and rattle his cage a little.*

Not too far down Highway 302, Nolan spotted the landmark of all landmarks: Pelion's "giant" peanut! Nolan could imagine Cat sitting beside him, remarking sarcastically, *"Landmark of landmarks? Yehroit!"* Looking at the peanut, the agent scrolled his eyes suspiciously from top to bottom, then bottom to top. *I'm not even sure that the peanut is six feet tall—more like four feet maybe? Well, anyway, I'm in Pelion. Now, according to the directions provided by Deputy Maness, State Secondary Road 246 should be close by.*

After finding the road and turning left, Nolan drove about two miles before coming to a mailbox on the right having the provided address. *Finally! Okay, Ron, I do hope you're home 'cause it's time to meet you and see what you're all about.* According to what Walt had heard, Ron was always in between work since losing his fortune, going from one menial job to another. Nolan was crossing his fingers that Ron would be here, as he had been so fortunate yesterday to catch everyone at the right time and place for questioning. In some ways, the agent had established a potential Catch-22 with his long drive to visit Ron. Nolan did not really want to sit and wait forever for Ron to arrive in the event that he was not home, nor did he wish to double back to Pelion this evening all the way from Spartanburg for a second attempt at interviewing Ron after visiting Mary. However, Jericho's standard procedure in questioning a suspect was *not* to set up the interview. The agent felt that giving a suspect a heads-up by scheduling a visit could potentially contaminate the investigation. In other words, he liked to rattle the suspect somewhat by surprising him on his doorstep, thereby eliminating time for any naughty or misleading preparation.

The homestead, about a half-mile off the road, was accessed by a crude dirt drive which reminded the agent somewhat of the trail to Bud Holly's house. Cursed by deep ruts begging for some creative driving, the track wove its way between two fields fully clothed in high weeds and thistle plants blooming in the heat of summer. Any fence remaining along the perimeter was beyond salvation. The haggard appearance of the fields gave Nolan the immediate impression of this place as a has-been farm, with any days of prosperity long gone.

As the drive exited its narrow passage between the two fields, a large circular clearing of land unveiled to Nolan his idea of how a homestead on a typical Southern farm should appear. There was the two-story wooden house with its quintessential rural tin roof. A large porch highlighted the front of the house, with the tin roof of the porch sloping upwards to the wall just underneath several second-story windows. Across the circular clearing from the house was a very large A-frame barn, also sporting a tin roof. Both the house and the barn appeared to be in adequate shape, with their roofs relatively free of rust, and the exterior walls of each indicating that a paint job would be forthcoming not far down the road. Of the two structures, the only items crying out for immediate attention were several loose boards on the barn, with one board entirely missing. In addition to the house and the barn, there were five other outbuildings sprinkled around the clearing, ranging in size from the largest, which Nolan interpreted to be a chicken coop, to smaller sheds and storage buildings.

Parked midway between the house and the barn, facing the direction toward the main highway, was a light blue Ford Galaxie. *A Ford Galaxie—hmm, a FORD! That's a strike against him already; I'm ready to hang him!* As Nolan eased Polly to a stop in the center of the clearing, he noticed that the front door of the house was open, with only the screen door keeping the flies at bay. Stepping out of his Sting Ray, Nolan was almost paralyzed by the deafening silence filling the air. In his mind, a farm homestead was supposed to be racked by *moos* and *clucks* and *quacks* and *cockadoodledoos.* But here there was nothing but absolute quiet! It appeared that Ron definitely wasn't re-envisioning the property as a working farm at the moment.

Jericho walked up to the screen door of the house and rapped on its wooden frame. Again, there was nothing, no sound at all . . . no television, no radio, no washing machine . . . nothing! The agent pulled gently on the screen door. Discovering it wasn't latched, he cracked the door open about four inches and hollered inside, as if shouting through the screen might perhaps be ineffective with the wire mesh barricading the sound or something.

"Hello! Anybody home? Ron Christmas? Hello!" He waited about thirty seconds, but the call summoned no one. Nolan decided to not make another attempt, realizing the property was so silent that there was no way Ron could be in the house and not hear him, unless he was playing possum.

Quietly shutting the screen door, the agent decided that perhaps Ron could be doing some chores in the barn that were not quite audible enough for the agent to detect. Since July was up to her old tricks today, he jogged across the clearing to the barn with little vigor to avoid working up a sweat in his gray suit. The long crossbar anchoring the barn's two huge swinging doors was firmly in place. Nolan propped his hands on the crossbar and leaned forward slightly, pressing his right ear against the warm wood of the doors. Then, with his ear halfway-invading the slim, lengthy crack between the doors, he remained still for fifteen seconds . . . nothing.

Feeling strangely paranoid and looking around, Nolan carefully lifted the crossbar allowing the two doors to swing slowly forward from their own weight. Once the doors came to rest, Jericho walked slowly into the dusty barn, with hay strewn across the ground and straws hanging over the edges of the barn's loft. Deciding he would feel less paranoid in the open, Nolan positioned himself in the center of the barn and revolved slowly in a complete circle while surveying the barn from floor to roof. On the right side of the barn were several wooden compartments which the agent estimated to be stalls of some sort. *I assume these are for horses. Jet, ol' fella, sometimes it's tough not being a country boy when you're trying to figure out your head from your fanny in the middle of the good ol' South.*

Jericho began strolling down the side of the stalls, glancing into each one. A startling sight in the center stall brought him to a dead halt—red hay! No doubt about it, some of the hay in the middle stall was red, *blood* red! Nolan tugged gently on the stall's chest-high swinging gate, pulling it outward. He walked slowly into the compartment, pushing against the gate slightly as it closed in order to keep it from slamming shut. Looking down at the red hay, Nolan stooped into a crouching position and used the second and third fingers of his left hand to swipe up some of the "blood." The agent rubbed the red gooey liquid between his two fingers to experience its texture, then somewhat hesitantly lifted the reddened fingers to the ridges of his nostrils and inhaled. *PAINT! Nothing but red paint! Whew! Definitely good for Ron Christmas, I suppose. For a second, I thought I was on to something big, but . . . PAINT!*

"OKAY, WHOEVER YOU ARE!" shot out a voice behind him. "I don't know who you are, but this is private property! So take it easy, stranger, mighty easy! Now, TURN AROUND and let me see your face!"

Remaining in his crouched position, Nolan swiveled his body around, allowing the man possessing the voice to see the agent's face. The face belonging to the voice was that of Ron Christmas. Of that, Nolan was sure. After all, Jericho had met Paul Christmas on several occasions and had Paul's image firmly imprinted in his mind and, since Ron and Paul had been identical twins, this guy was definitely Ron! With a fierce-looking face, Ron was holding a pitchfork with its prongs pointed toward the agent. The tips of the tines hovered a mere six inches from Nolan's face. Straining slightly as he held the long pitchfork several inches above the closed gate from outside the stable, Ron attempted to steady its lengthy handle so he could jab effectively at any second.

"I don't recognize you, stranger. Identify yourself or prepare to be full of some holes."

"Hold on, cowboy! I'm an agent of the SBI. Ron Christmas, I know who you are, and I've driven a good distance to see you."

"You have, have you? How do I know you're what you say you are?" The handle of his pitchfork was shaking quite a bit, perhaps indicating that the agent's revelation regarding his line of business had struck a nerve in Ron.

"Easy there, Ron, I'm reaching for my wallet and—"

"Stop right there, stranger! I'm not *that* trusting. In fact, right now I've got an itchy trigger-finger with this pitchfork. Ya know, come to think of it, it doesn't matter how official you are. You were caught with your pants down trespassing on my property. As I see it, the law around here will be right sympathetic if I was scared enough to be a little hasty in shoving this fork clear through a trespasser. Ya know, the *more* I *really* think about it, the next time you take a drink you will be springing leaks all over."

Nolan knew by the nervousness and desperation in Ron's voice that the man was about to do something rash, so now was the best time to act. Still held at pitchfork-point in his crouched position, Nolan pivoted on his left foot while his right leg suddenly thrust forward like a flash toward the gate. As his knife-edged right foot smacked the gate with a loud crack, the gate instantaneously shot into Ron's slightly flexed kneecaps.

"Ohhh, Christ, you bast—" Ron couldn't finish his exclamation due to the intense pain, which simultaneously caused him to loosen his grip on the pitchfork handle. To his credit, the pain of smashed kneecaps did not make Ron entirely drop the pitchfork, as the handle fell to a resting position on top of the gate. With Ron having lost his monopoly on his grip, Nolan quickly reached up with his right hand and firmly grabbed the middle tine among the prongs to keep Ron from lifting the fork's handle back off the gate. Jericho stood up while holding the middle tine and swung his stiffened left arm around in a swift semi-circle, chopping the handle of the pitchfork in two with the knife-edged side of his left hand. The agent now held the prongs of the pitchfork in his hands attached to approximately eighteen inches of the split handle.

"Jesus, mercy! Man, why did you have to do that?" asked Ron, leaning over partially and staggering with some baby steps. He glanced at the three feet of split handle he was left holding while looking at the remainder of the pitchfork now in Jericho's hands. Furious, Ron slammed the partial handle to the ground. But it rebounded immediately, popping him smack on his right knee.

"Yee-ooww! Dammit!"

"Temper, temper, Mr. Christmas. . ." chided Jericho.

"I give up, mister! I give up! What do you want?" said a mighty sore Ron, huffing and puffing while rubbing his bruised kneecaps and confronting his equally-bruised ego.

"I want information—information, Mr. Christmas! You could have saved yourself a lot of grief if you'd just been a little more cooperative. All I wanted to do was ask you a few questions. I hollered through the door into your house and heard nothing. Then, I came over here to the barn looking for you. While I was 'snooping', as you perceived it, I noticed some red liquid on the hay that looked like blood."

"So you did! Well, it's paint as I guess you figured out for yourself. Look!" Ron took his right hand off his aching knee and pointed with his index finger up toward the loft right above the red hay at the same spot Nolan would have naturally checked next had he not been interrupted by the threat of Ron's pitchfork. Surrounding a crack between two boards of the stable's ceiling was a smudge of red. "The loft in this barn hasn't been used for hay in years, so I use it for storage. This morning, I was putting some paint cans up there for the time being and, as you can see by the spilt paint, I never was the most graceful pup of the litter."

"I do see. Oh, uh, here's the rest of your pitchfork, Mr. Christmas."

"Much obliged," said Ron in a slightly sarcastic tone as he took the remaining portion of pitchfork from the agent and tossed it to the side. "Okay, then, let's go inside the house and you can ask your questions. You go first, Mr., uh—what did you say your name was?"

"Actually, I didn't," responded Jericho, holding out his identification. "I'm Agent Jet Jericho of the SBI."

"Jet, huh?" Ron grunted before adopting a quizzical look. "Hey, wait a minute, *North* Carolina? When you said a few moments ago you were SBI, I thought you were an agent from out of Columbia. Aren't you a little out of your jurisdiction, Agent?"

"Not really, sir. We agents cross state lines from time to time to do a little investigating. But, I'll have to admit that—until a few minutes ago—I'd never had cause for any action in South Carolina. Anyway, I'm here to ask you about your brother's death—and that, sir, *is* a North Carolina matter. In fact, it's also a personal matter, as I had the pleasure of meeting with Paul on several occasions."

"Oh, really? Well, anyway, let's go inside. You first, agent—"

"Oh, no! After you, sir, I insist!" Jericho still didn't trust Ron as far as he could throw him, and he was not about to offer a chance to the aching man of retaliation from behind.

As Jericho followed the slightly taller, staggering man across the clearing toward the house, he mulled over what had just occurred in the barn. *It's just like I told Walt: if Ron had simply played it cool, guilty or not, I probably would have already thanked him for his time and been on my way out of here. But instead, I think I just struck some gold!* Nolan knew Ron had to have been panicky and thinking irrationally to initiate such a threat in the barn, especially after the agent had identified himself as being with the SBI.

The agent felt that his practice of conducting unannounced visits had just been soundly reaffirmed, and he now found himself shifting away from any nagging "iffy-ness" concerning his suspect's guilt. Thanks to Ron's nervous behavior, Jericho was now settling into a far more aggressive mode of thinking. *Okay, there's a great chance he's the guy. Now, how do I catch him?* The agent always relished this shift of thinking from doubt to assuredness, referring to it as the "golden switch." His instincts were rarely wrong when he homed in for the kill on a particular suspect. So, from this point on with Ron, it would be a matter of wise pacing, alert observation, and trying to collect more good information. And visiting Mary this evening in Spartanburg still did not seem a bad idea at the moment.

As he entered through the screen door, Nolan was somewhat surprised at how sparsely furnished the house was. There was little furniture, no television, and no bookshelves in the living room—just a couch, a lamp, and a couple of chairs. It was somewhat dark also, with the light fixture on the ceiling holding four exposed bulbs of which only two were lit. The room had the musty smell of an old house, possibly generated by the ancient-looking wallpaper, which was yellowing in some places and flaking off in others.

Ron continued walking on into the kitchen while Jericho stopped, leaning against the doorway between the living room and the kitchen. "Would you like some ice water or tea?"

"No, thank you, Mr. Christmas. I'm quite fine, thank you." At this point, Nolan was as thirsty as a man stranded in the desert, but he was still nervous about what could be going on in Ron's mind. *No thank you definitely, Ron Christmas. A little drug or poison in the drink and a grave in a secluded field out in the middle of a nowhere called Pelion, and they wouldn't be finding this agent's body til sometime in the 23rd century.*

As Nolan visually scanned the kitchen, a fascinating sight brought his eyes to an abrupt stop: an open carton of Kool cigarettes sitting on top of the refrigerator! *Well, what do you know? Kool cigarettes, huh? Hmm . . . as Alice in Wonderland said, "Curiouser and curiouser." A mere coincidence that a package of the same brand was at the crime scene? Perhaps, perhaps not. Okay, Jericho, let's keep on rattling ol' Ron's cage a little. Keep your eyes focused on that carton. Ron needs to see you see the carton. Let's see how he acts.*

After filling a plastic bag about half-full of ice, Ron spun around from the counter and noticed that Jericho was staring at the top of the fridge. Nolan didn't glance away from the carton as one would normally be inclined to do. Instead, he kept his eyes trained on the carton and intentionally formed a contemplative expression on his face, as if something were bothering him. *Don't say anything about the cigarettes just yet. Pacing, ol' boy—you'll play that trump card a little later.*

Ron's voice suddenly had a minute quiver in it. "Uh, go make yourself comfortable. . . I'll, uh, be right with you, agent."

Good, Jericho. Fishy's on the line. Don't reel him in too early, give him a little squirming room. Nolan turned his body around slowly while still keeping his eyes unsubtly trained on the carton. Then, he turned his head and proceeded into the living room.

Having no rocking chair as an option, Jericho accepted the sofa as the most inviting furniture at the moment. With his internal radar still on alert, Jericho sat in the middle of the sofa with his right leg crossed over his left.

Carrying the half-packed plastic bag of ice into the living room, Ron groaned as he sat in a plain wooden chair opposite the couch. "Man, my knees will be sore for two or three weeks thanks to your slick little maneuver back at the stable."

"Sorry about that, chief!" offered Nolan in an unapologetic manner.

"Oh, I see you've watched *Get Smart*, too, huh?"

"Yes, sir. they don't get any funnier than Don Adams."

"Okay, agent—I'm tired, so fire away! How can I possibly enlighten you as to my brother's death?"

Inhaling deeply, Nolan prepared to launch the serious tone of voice he usually employed when questioning someone he suspected of wrongdoing. Cat and Agent James always called it his "Confucius voice" because it sounded so emotionless and rational in its monotone quality. Jericho had always been baffled by his friends stereotyping the tone as Oriental. Instead, the agent liked to think of the tone as having more of a "Mr. Spock" quality.

"Well, for one thing, Ron, we missed you at the funeral."

"Oh, is it a law now in North Carolina that a man has to attend his brother's funeral?"

"No, sir, it's not a law—but, it does tell me that a man and his brother might possibly have had some issues with each other."

"Well, agent, you just might be reaching a little far for the gold ring on that one. I don't know that I can say I had any big issues against my brother, for we were just two completely different men. Paul was a goody-goody preacher boy who had a lot of people around him swallowing the goods he peddled so well from his pulpit. Paul was so happy being married to God, he didn't need anybody else to share life with. Me, on the other hand, I once loved an incredible woman to a higher degree than you or anyone else on this Earth will ever have the pleasure of doing. And I worked my tail off day and night to have the best lifestyle for her and myself. But, my wife and my fortune both disappeared like a will o' the wisp, as if God were punishing me for something. It was as if I were a child accused of not appreciating my toys and suddenly had all of them taken from me and sold . . . or given away . . . or something, when the actual truth was that my wife and the life we enjoyed together meant everything to me. I had it all one minute, and then it was all gone the next! So, agent, you asked me—did I have an issue with my brother? I don't know, you tell me! But, I will tell you I do have a real issue with his God. Yes, sir, agent, you're looking at a real angry man, a dog who has been kicked and kicked to the point of feeling vicious inside. Oh, I want to lash out all right, at anyone who gives me the slightest reason!"

"It appears to me that you've deduced, Mr. Christmas, that I did my research and am clued in a little as to your background. Indeed, I have been informed of your losses, both of your wife and of your fortune. Can you enlighten me further about the losses, other than the fact you're upset with God?"

"Not much to tell there either, agent. I had it all; I lost it all. Regarding my wife: I met Linda Fairbanks in high school and we got married the summer we graduated. She stuck by me as I clawed my way to the top of the business world. We didn't relax much, neither of us being the travel-around-the-world type, but we did enjoy boating on Lake Murray out from Columbia. We had a lakefront vacation home with a private dock—you know, all the bells and whistles. It happened on one of those nice early summer evenings seven years ago, the kind of night with a gentle breeze, a clear sky, and a bright moon. We were partying with some friends, anchored out in the middle of the lake, just a-drinking and a-chatting away while listening to some music. Neither one of us were bad alcoholics. Neither of us drank on a daily basis. When we worked, we worked hard. When we partied, we partied hard. Linda loved sangria, and on a night like that with no driving involved, she couldn't drink enough of the stuff. Anyway, the couple we were with saw her fall over the side of the boat, probably having tripped on an empty bottle rolling around on the deck. And that was the last time I saw her until her body washed up days later. You can check the records if you don't believe me."

"No problem there, sir. What about your assets?"

"Well, agent, what can I tell you? Investments are fickle, and it's definitely not a game for boys. I'm not meaning to blame Linda's death on me losing all my assets, but something about her being taken from my life did sort of kill the part of me inside that was confident—you know, the part of me that could make confident, aggressive decisions on trading. Again, what can I say? It is what it is. I once was rich and now I'm broke."

"In what type of things did you invest?"

"Oh, mostly European and Asian commodities. I made an absolute killing on an investment in Taiwan."

"Did you ever buy any stock in sloppy Joes?"

"I beg your pardon, agent?"

"Oh, nothing. I was thinking of another investor, I suppose. Now, you've got quite a homestead here with a pretty fair amount of acreage. How many acres, sir?"

"Around two hundred."

"I assume that the property here either was or is in your parents' names?"

"*Is*, agent! The property is in my mother's name. Dad died a decade ago."

"Who are the beneficiaries, sir?"

"Well, it was to be split between Paul and me, and I know where you're goin' with this, agent. It doesn't take a rocket scientist to draw the conclusion that I would now become the sole inheritor at my mother's passing, thus providing the motive for me to have killed Paul."

"No, sir, it surely doesn't take a genius to come up with that theory."

"Agent, the conclusion you maybe haven't drawn is that Paul had no use whatsoever for this land or the money it could possibly bring if liquidated. Again, he had a full little life down in his little perfect world of Icy Springs, and surely you can easily conclude that suddenly becoming the sole inheritor of this property wouldn't exactly transform me into a happy-go-lucky, free-hearted, wheeler-dealer."

Touché, Ron Christmas, touché! Yeah, Paul would have no use at all for this relic of a farm in the middle of South Carolina. Icy Springs was indeed his world. And, Ron, you are indeed a sordid-looking soul at this point, broken by ill fate and definitely lacking the confidence and charisma you supposedly once had. However, there is also such a thing as good acting.

"Ron, it's time to answer a basic question for me. Where were you last Wednesday and Thursday when your brother was murdered and tied to the steeple?"

"I suppose that's a fair question, agent. And if absence of a verifiable alibi is grounds for arrest, then take me on in. I'm guilty! Actually, I wasn't anywhere near Icy Springs, but I really have nobody I can enlist in my defense to tell you that I wasn't in Icy Springs. I've been here on this farm for a solid two weeks, piddling around and trying to fix the property up a little. I haven't made any calls and I haven't had any calls, other than the Sheriff's Department of Lexington County notifying me that Paul was found dead and offering me the time and location of his funeral."

"You're saying that you haven't been to the grocery store or anywhere?"

"No, I'm the veritable town hermit of Pelion. I've done quite fine with my stockpile of canned spaghetti, pork and beans, chips, and other simple foods. It doesn't take much at this point in my life to keep me alive."

"What about work? Surely, you have to bring in some income."

"Agent, surely you can reason that I have very little overhead here. The house and land are paid for. There's just me, myself, and I to feed—and, as you should deduce, there's not much expense there. No gas is needed, since I'm hardly on the go anymore. I'm on a well, so there's no water bill. You see how much power I use, if you'll notice the two bulbs above you that aren't burning. You don't see a TV on or hear a radio blaring away, do you? So, I barely have a power bill at all. I have a phone bill, but I'm thinking about having the phone disconnected."

"So, I take it then that you don't have steady work?"

"Well, let's say I'm constantly between jobs. I do some occasional odds and ends for some farmers around here when I need money—you know, fence mending, ditch digging, and other low-paying stints. When school's in session the rest of the year, I do a little substitute teaching when they are really, really desperate for a sub and I am really, really desperate for the money. I hate that job though, 'cause you have to interact with so many people, like kids and teachers, and you have to act like you're enjoying it. Anyway, I haven't had any payin' work at all in the last two months."

Okay, Mr. Christmas. I'll quit probing at the moment, trying to determine whether you were here last week or at Icy Springs. Like you said, I can't haul you in right now for not being able to vouch that you were on your farm. But, Ron, being a hermit certainly makes it convenient to commit a murder, doesn't it? "Well, Mr. Christmas—conveniently for you at the time being, I don't have any sources saying you weren't here on your property."

"Precisely, agent. Look, sir, let's call a truce. You evidently liked my brother. I've never heard of anybody saying that they didn't. I can tell that you think very little of me, and I've known very few people that thought well of me. It was always that way growing up, all through elementary school, high school, college, and real life. Paul had the magic of attracting people while I had the curse of repelling them. That's why Linda was such a blessing to me. She loved me, something that few people took the effort to do. That's why her death pretty much sealed my fate as a loner in this world. I never was a 'people person' to begin with, and now . . . well, let's just say I've come to terms with the fact that loneliness is my lot in life."

All right, Ron. Enough's enough! I've soaked and soaked in your pity party for the last ten minutes. Now, it's time to drop the bomb. Let's see what you've got to say about the little matter of the Kool cigarette carton on your fridge.

"Mr. Christmas, I think that's about all I need for the moment. However, there is one more thing I've noticed and would like to ask you about. You know, sir, I don't really smell any smoke in this house—cigarette smoke, that is."

"Sir, there is no reason you should, for I don't smoke. I'm proud to say that I have been off of the coffin nails for about a year now."

"Have you now? Wow! That's to be commended. I never smoke 'em myself, but, I suppose I have my share of habits that wouldn't be bad to surrender, providing I had the will power, that is. So you were a big smoker in your day, I take it?"

"Oh, yeah, agent, a big-time smoker. I probably went through two packs on a slow day."

"Well, Mr. Christmas, giving up that degree of chain smoking is most impressive, especially considering you are in a phase of your life when you seem to be most lonely and depressed. I understand that your brother also smoked, contradictory to the wishes of his congregation, and that he fought the habit up until his death. A friend of mine said that Paul really wanted to quit, but he never could seem to find the will or success that you apparently have achieved."

"Well, you know what they say, agent: 'The acorn doesn't fall far from the tree.' When a child is brought up in an environment in which a particular habit is modeled, the child will take on that habit. Dad smoked like a chimney until the day he died. Smoking was his undoing, the cancer finally finishing him off. Yes, Paul and I certainly grew up to be like our ol' man in that department. In that one habit, at least, Paul and I had something in common."

"I suppose so. Oh, yes—there is one interesting thing I need to let you in on, Ron. As a matter of fact, I found a package of Kool cigarettes near Paul's body at the crime scene."

"That's most interesting, agent. Any fingerprints—or do you check for fingerprints on things like that?"

"Oh, it can be done. However, to answer your question, we haven't turned up any prints on the package yet."

"Bad for you that you haven't, agent. If you had, you probably could have verified that they were Paul's. Unless he switched over the years, Paul smoked Kool, just like Dad and me. You know the old sayin': 'The acorn doesn't—'"

"—Yeah, yeah . . . 'fall far from the tree'. So you're saying that you also smoke Kool cigarettes, I take it?"

"*Smoked*, agent—remember, smoked! Yes, I indeed did smoke the brand until I gave 'em up."

"Which seems to be true, Mr. Christmas. Once again, I haven't smelled any smoke in the house. And, I honestly don't smell any on you at the moment, like I do on the clothes of most people who smoke. For example, I hate to ride in the car with Agent Engelbretsen, a colleague of mine. *Phew!* I won't let him ride in either one of my personal cars because he stinks 'em up so bad. Do you realize that the last time I ever let him ride with me, I had to use half a bottle of 'Newborn Baby' air freshener to get rid of Engelbretsen's cigarette odor?"

At that point, Ron was getting extremely restless and looking quite perturbed. "Agent, all of this is most, uh, interesting. I suppose that some people might even find that quaint little story mildly entertaining. Do you mind cluing me in as to where this line of questioning is heading?"

"Well, sir, I need you to clear up one thing for me, and I promise you that I'm outta here."

"What's that, agent?"

"Well, when you were packing your ice bag, I noticed an open carton of Kool cigarettes on top of your refrigerator with some packages still in the carton."

"I, uh, don't doubt you did, sir. As I, uh, said earlier, I smoked the Kool brand just like Dad and Paul—but, as I also told you, I kicked the habit and have not touched them in the last year. I didn't mean to throw such a clever, mind-bending curve ball toward your investigation, agent, but it's just that I have never gotten around to discarding the deadly things yet."

"Fair enough, and I do believe you when you say you haven't been smoking, sir. I truly don't detect one iota of it on your clothing and don't sense it in the house. It just struck me as odd that you gave up the habit a year ago and still had a carton of cigarettes lingering on top of your refrigerator."

"Agent, as I said, I haven't gotten around to throwing them away. But, if truth be known, it's possible that I might subconsciously have the need to keep the things around to remind me that there has been at least one thing in my life lately I've been able to conquer, at least one area in which I've not been a complete loser. And, you know what they say: 'Remain mindful of your temptations and the Devil can't take you by surprise.'"

"Perhaps so, Mr. Christmas, perhaps so. Uh, would you mind if I have a look at the carton, Mr. Christmas?"

"Yes, sir, I would mind that greatly. You might come in here manhandling me and chopping up my farm tools in half, but I'll be damned if I'm going to let you violate my basic legal rights. SBI or not, you're touching nothing on this property without a proper search warrant."

"Understood, sir, understood most clearly." *Oh, I understand, Ron Christmas. I understand clearly that you indeed seem to have much to hide..*

"Okay, agent, what's next on your agenda in the investigation? Who's the next person on your list to harass?"

"Well, if you must know, I'm on my way to Spartanburg to have a chat with 'yo' mama'."

Dead silence! Ron Christmas suddenly looked like a person who had just got off an amusement park ride that was a little on the rough side. Normally, it wasn't anybody's business except Fowler's who was next on Jericho's agenda. However, Jericho thought the tidbit about questioning Ron's mother would make for a final good opportunity at shaking up the man. The silence after Nolan's revelation began to turn downright awkward. It was as if Ron was not only trying to calculate the many reactions he could display concerning the agent's intent to question his mother, but was also attempting to predict the array of suspicions that any of his reactions might generate. Nolan could sense that Ron's mind was on overdrive. It definitely appeared that Jericho's intention to visit Mary Christmas had thrown Ron for a loop because—after all of the well-worded, grand speeches about losing everything he had . . . about everyone loving Paul . . . about being a loner . . . and about giving up smoking—Ron Christmas was at a total loss for words.

"Well, sir," said Jericho in breaking the silence, "thank you for answering my questions. At this point, I'm sure we'll be in touch sometime in the future. I will have the department issue you a check to cover the cost of a new pitchfork."

"While you're at it, agent, see if they'll write me a check for two knee replacements."

CHAPTER 17

Agent a-Plenty!

Jericho's least favorite time of the day in the summer was from around one o'clock to three o'clock, during the peak of the afternoon sun. Finding this particularly hot July day to be no exception, the agent had the air conditioning in his Sting Ray cranked to the max as he proceeded northerly on Highway 176 toward Spartanburg. He had found his meeting with Ron a most enlightening venture, perhaps even fruitful.

The hungry agent arrived at about a quarter to five in the city limits of Spartanburg. Having bypassed lunch in Columbia, his nagging appetite was sending continual messages to his head that the time had come to do something about the emptiness in his belly. In all truthfulness, Jericho had craftily planned the location where he would eat supper before he had left Icy Springs for Columbia. *Man, I have to say that it is past time to eat! So hang on, stomach. . .*

As the blue Sting Ray cruised along over the hot asphalt, Nolan looked down the avenue with anticipation. The horizon ahead had some slight road mirage of shimmering and wavering due to the gas fumes of city traffic dancing within the July heat. Nevertheless, the oasis he was seeking soon came clearly into view. Beside the street, a tall sign, shaped like a lighthouse, materialized. Featured on the sign was a piercing arrow proudly displaying the name of the dining establishment, with the arrow pointing toward a colorful building adorned with numerous banners. Just before reaching the sign, Nolan maneuvered his Sting Ray into the parking lot as commanded by the arrow. Agent Jericho had arrived at one of his favorite places in the Carolinas: The Beacon Drive-In!

All right, agent, time for a well-earned treat! I'm back at the Beacon, home of the best cheeseburger on the planet! Walking energetically up the steps toward the building, the agent was confronted by a vagrant at the door holding up a sign: *Need Money, Pleaze!* Digging into his pocket, Nolan pulled out a quarter and handed it to the bum.

135

"Thank you, kind sir!" responded the beggar as he nodded to Jericho.

The agent reciprocated with a polite bow of his head. "No problem. Have a good day." As Nolan entered the establishment's circus-like atmosphere, the flurry of activity was still as spellbinding now as it had been on his first visit to the Beacon. Cooks and servers were scurrying around like inhabitants of an ant farm, passing items to each other, flipping patties, tearing open packages, applying condiments, filling drinking glasses, and sweating. Standing on top of an aluminum counter was a man holding up a garden hose to a large tank. In the process of mixing a monstrous quantity of sweet tea, he was racing against the demand of customers to replenish the brew for which the Beacon had achieved world-wide fame.

Overriding all the ongoing hubbub was the ringmaster of the circus within the Beacon, the "Call It Guy." Orchestrating all customer orders, the Call It Guy had rapidly achieved celebrity status around the region. Customers were simply amazed not only by his ability to accurately holler orders over to the preparation counter but also by the quirky lingo he wailed out, a lingo peppered with entertaining vocal inflections. Even if Jericho wasn't the least bit hungry, he contended that the Beacon would be worth a stop just to hear the Call It Guy "do his thang."

When visiting the Beacon, a diner was not wise to walk up to the Call It Guy unprepared and start casually perusing the menu without a preference in mind. A diner committing that unwritten infraction would immediately receive the Call It Guy's verbal heave-ho. It happened to be that one of the Call It Guy's biggest functions was to keep the extensive line of impatient customers moving and, to do this, he would holler out "CALL IT!" as soon as a customer approached him. Upon the customer relinquishing his order, the Call It Guy would immediately shout "WALK IT!" Now, to a typical Southerner, perhaps unacquainted with the Beacon's traditions, this way of doing business could easily be interpreted as rude treatment or callousness that most Southerners had long characterized as typical of Yankee behavior. However, those having been indoctrinated to the Beacon's customs—"Beaconized," you might say—found being yelled at by the Call It Guy to "CALL IT!" and "WALK IT!" the equivalent of going to Yankee stadium and being hit by a ball fouled from the tip of Babe Ruth's bat. But, novelty and amusement aside, a customer had really better be ready to "CALL IT!" and "WALK IT!" when in the Call It Guy's presence, in lieu of just standing there like a statue out of blank-minded indecision.

Nolan stood to the side where he watched the circus and listened to the Call It Guy for about ten minutes. As usual, the agent was mesmerized by the Call It Guy's performance, a routine that hungry diners often considered the best free dinner show in the world. When ready to order, Jericho didn't need to resort to the menu posted above the ordering line. He knew what he wanted. Therefore, he had his battle plan ready for the Call It Guy.

After taking his place in line, it seemed like no time had passed at all until he was face to face with the ringmaster. "CALL IT!" barked the master of ceremonies.

"I'll have the Cheeseburger a-Plenty, and fix mine with chili, mustard, ketchup, and onions. Thanks."

"WALK IT!" After being commanded tersely to leave the ringmaster's presence, Jericho proceeded down the line as he listened to his order being shouted in the Call It Guy's unique, almost other-worldly dialect. The agent never could adequately describe the Call It Guy's system of communicating to Cat, nor could he explain to her how in the world the Call It Guy's co-workers could interpret his specialized language without ever screwing up an order. Nolan would merely end up saying, "Cat, one day I'm going to take you to that crazy place where you won't believe your ears or your taste buds. You've got to experience this place for yourself, for my words could never do it justice."

Carrying a loaded-down tray, Jericho chose a seat tucked in the corner of one of the quieter dining rooms. He took a sip of the refreshing sweet tea. The agent wasn't generally a fan of tea, but seeing as the Beacon's tea was among the best in the world, who was he to refuse it? As he surveyed the culinary task before him, Nolan remembered the crazy comment that he himself had uttered to Walt the other night at Keaton's about a cardiologist not issuing approval of the meal. The burgers at the Beacon were large enough without any sides, but he had ordered Cheeseburger a-*Plenty*. When a customer ordered his or her sandwich "a-Plenty" style at the Beacon, this meant that the massive sandwich would be virtually hidden beneath a pile of French fries and onion rings rising roughly seven to eight inches above the plate. Although Nolan thought the Beacon's onion rings were among the best he had ever eaten, he realized that the smothered plate was indeed a cesspool of cholesterol—a cardiologist's nightmare, so-to-speak. *You know, Cat's right. I guess I can't blame her at times for being aggravated at my ability to maintain a battle-ready physique after continually ingesting so much garbage. I need to put a little more stock into what Cat's trying to tell me about my diet. Yeah, I really do need to do that. Someday, that is. . .*

Hmmmmmmmm . . . It had been many moons since Jericho had tasted the Beacon's savory burgers, fries, and onion rings. The agent always practiced a certain strategy when attacking the Cheeseburger a-Plenty. First, he would alternate bites of fries and onion rings dipped in ketchup until he uncovered the sandwich. Then, once the burger was delivered from its womb of fries and rings, he would incorporate bites of burger into a cyclical pattern of burger-fries-rings, burger-fries-rings. About halfway through the meal, things would always take an ugly turn when the agent's casual dining experience would rapidly transform into a contest between his desire to finish off the plate and his stomach's incapacity to accommodate more food. Granted, it was a very tasty contest, but an uncomfortably challenging event, which would leave Jericho miserable for an hour or two.

Boy, I am sure glad I didn't participate in this gorge-a-thon before I visited Ron Christmas. I would have been so sluggish that I would have ended up with pitchfork holes in me for sure. It wouldn't have been a pretty sight at all. I'm going to have to sit here for several minutes and let some of the greasy delight I just swallowed settle in just a little bit.

While giving his digestive system a chance to come to terms with the inner lube job resulting from an avalanche of grease, Nolan sat back and did a little people-watchin'. He had noticed a somewhat tall, slim man with glasses going around from table to table and wiping each off with a rag. As the agent was recuperating from the meal, he decided to put his eavesdropping skills to good use, and he listened quietly as an older couple engaged the young table cleaner in some incidental conversation. From what Nolan could ascertain, the young man was a school teacher working a part-time job at the Beacon for extra income.

Nolan sat for another few minutes before realizing that time was slipping away, and he needed to get on out to Elderly Acres to visit Mary Christmas. Without saying anything, he glanced over at the young teacher cleaning the tables and he quietly took a five-dollar bill out of his wallet, discreetly placing the money on the table. Cat had commented several times on Jericho's unusual sympathy toward educators. Trying not to draw attention to himself, Nolan stood quietly and started walking away.

"Excuse me, sir—!" said the young man. "I don't mean to hold you up. But as I was wiping off the tables, I noticed you left five dollars behind."

"I, uh, did that purposefully, Mister . . . uh—"

"Richard, please call me Richard. But, sir, tips are not encouraged at the Beacon. I am paid on a scale of wages."

"Go ahead and take it, fella—it's on me."

"Well, sir, it is a most gracious tip, nearly what I will make here this whole evening at minimum wage. Do you mind telling me your name and, uh, why you did this?"

"Well, my name is unimportant. However, I will tell you that I am in law enforcement. Trust me, Richard, I do not make much at all myself and five dollars is also fair sum of money for me. But I am most honored to leave it."

"Thank you, sir. But I have to ask you again, *why* are you leaving me this, uh, *tip*?"

"Well, you see, it's like this: My mother was a teacher, and when she taught in her homeland of Japan, she was revered greatly by her society. She was as revered in her native country as any athlete, actor, physician, or attorney.

You see, Richard, an educator is regarded by some societies as one of the most crucial and important contributors toward a society's future. However, when she came to the United States, her status as an educator plummeted to that of a short-order cook or a guy who follows an elephant in the circus with a shovel. Whereas in Japan she commanded great respect, my mother encountered much disrespect in this country from students . . . from parents . . . and from the community at large, particularly from state legislators. The lawmakers of her state continually denied her and her colleagues pay raises and cut funding for their programs. Legislators continually cheated her and her colleagues out of thousands of hard-earned dollars through salary freezes while, ironically, having the audacity to feather their own nests by voting themselves a pay raise and increasing their own retirement pensions."

"Well, mister . . . I certainly can't argue with that. The teachers in our state continually experience shabby treatment by our politicians."

"It's like that in many states, Richard, but for some reason, it seems like it is impossible for the average citizen to imagine how poorly teachers are treated. However, I realize the monumental task you have before you. My mother, you, and other educators have been the political scapegoats for so many social issues that are not your fault, being blamed at every turn for problems you did not create. While bringing home shamefully inadequate paychecks, you've had to spend a significant portion of your own income on learning materials for your students. And—let me guess—you're not working this part-time job so you can go on a relaxing vacation with your family this summer, are you?"

"No, sir. I'm working this job just to be able to buy some clothes at the thrift store for my kids and some supplies for my students this fall."

"And, let me also guess, you probably have loans left over from your college education that prepared you to be a teacher, loans that you cannot seem to get paid off."

"Yes, sir. I'll be paying on these loans for at least the next fifteen years."

"Case closed, Richard! Here you are with a college education and working a part-time job in order to clothe your family, buy materials for your classroom, and pay off your college loans—and all the while, professional athletes in this country receive far more compensation within a month than a great teacher makes in a lifetime. Sadly, my mother used to teach in a school with a roof that leaked every time it rained, and her school was situated less than half a mile from a race track that cost millions of dollars to build."

"Wow! You really know how to put things in perspective, mister!"

"Yeah, Richard, I've been told that by others. At any rate, I know that teachers are required to undergo collegiate study and professional training equivalent to that of doctors and attorneys and that teaching involves equally high expectations and levels of stress in comparison to other white-collar professions. However, teaching salaries around our country often fall below that of garbage collectors, sewage plant operators, and undertakers. Think of it this way, Richard: our society values the services of those tending to its garbage, its sewage, and its deceased more than it does the services of those educating its children. Sickening, isn't it?"

"It is, sir, and extremely disheartening . . ."

"Well, Richard, it all boils down to the priorities of our society. I'll let you in on a little secret: as I entered the restaurant, I only gave a quarter to the vagabond outside because I am unaware of his personal situation or how much he really needs the money. But I do know your situation, and I realize my five dollars certainly won't pay off your loans or enable you to quit your night job. Anyway, Richard, please take the money to supplement your selflessness as a teacher in such an unappreciative society. Accept it as a slight gesture of gratitude from a citizen who is terribly ashamed of the abuse and lack of support you continually endure at the hands of wrong-headed, irresponsible, and corrupt lawmakers. With that five dollars, maybe you can take your children to the movies or to the amusement park or some other outing that is considered a luxury for an educator. I only ask that you take the money realizing that there are some of us out there aware of how horribly educators are abused and taken for granted by this country. Know that we praise you for rising high above the clueless ones who constantly try to keep you down."

"Thank you, sir . . ." Nearly in tears, the young man walked away from Jericho and resumed wiping tables, but with a warm smile forming on his face.

Jericho walked out of the Beacon with great pride that he had acted upon one of his convictions. He didn't fully understand his soft spot for educators, other than knowing it had been created by witnessing the unprofessional treatment of his mother. All of that aside, one thing was for sure: today, at least, he had brightened the afternoon of one underpaid educator named Richard. Easing back into the seat of his blue Sting Ray, Nolan thought about what his father used to say: "Try to maintain a positive balance in your daily account of deeds." *I guess I achieved a break-even balance for today: I just uplifted one man's professional esteem not long after having smashed one man's kneecaps, an even balance thus far!*

As Polly rolled gracefully along Spartanburg's Main Street, Jericho made sure he remained on Highway 29 North once the Main Street signs ceased. The directions provided by Deputy Maness indicated that Elderly Acres was only about two miles outside of the city limits on the right side of the road, about one-third of a mile before a big auto body shop and salvage yard on the right. He estimated that he should be arriving at an opportune time—right after supper and before the old lady's bed-time.

Pulling into the nursing home parking lot, Jericho started getting that weird, unsettled feeling in his stomach that many visitors often experience at facilities for infirmed citizens. Caught off guard by his own ill-at-ease reaction, the agent was somewhat disappointed in himself for being affected so. *Come on, Mr. Seventh Degree Black Belt! Come on, Mr. Champion of the Underdog! What is wrong with you? You've never been squeamish about death or disability. Why are you feeling so antsy all of a sudden?* After analyzing the matter, he rationalized that his squeamishness was perhaps due to the fact that he could not remember ever having the occasion to visit such an establishment.

As he entered the building, he noticed an odor to which he was unaccustomed. Although the place had a decorative enough atmosphere and appeared to be spic-and-span from a sanitary standpoint, it had the hint of a smell one might associate with dirty diapers. Distracting him momentarily, the odor gradually became less pronounced as Nolan's olfactory system adapted to it. Quietly approaching the reception desk, Jericho cleared his throat to address the lady positioned behind the desk. "Excuse me—Ms. Atwater, is it?" the agent softly inquired after peering quickly at her name tag. "Would you please direct me to the living quarters of Mrs. Mary Christmas?"

Busy jotting down something in a book, the receptionist had yet to look up at the inquiring agent. She did hear his question, however, and her accommodating reply nearly floored the worldly agent. "I shall help you gladly, sir!" replied Ms. Atwater in the most genteel manner. To a man having become accustomed to Southern drawls in the heart of the Carolinas, the woman's British accent seemed as out of place as a bottle of fine wine in a barbecue joint. Putting down her pen, the stylish receptionist's equilibrium was equally up-ended, as the transplanted Brit was apparently unaccustomed to a man of Jericho's cosmopolitan appearance and dapper apparel in the heart of the Carolinas. The woman was quite taken aback—well, jolted actually—and she temporarily misplaced her European elegance. "My dear, you certainly are a looker, aren't you?"

"Um, I beg your pardon, ma'am?"

"A looker! You know, a gazer? Someone pleasant to, uh, feast one's eyes upon?"

"Uh, I thank you for the compliment, ma'am. Would you kindly point me to the room of Mary Christmas? I would be most appreciative, Ms. Atwater."

"Oh, it's Addison, dear, but anyone of familiarity refers to me as 'Addy'. Dearie, I'll do you much better than pointing you to her room. It shall be my privilege to escort you there personally."

Nolan thought the Cockney manner in which she pronounced "dearie" was quite cute. But, considering the direction in which this unscripted interplay with Addy seemed to be headed, he knew it wouldn't be prudent to transmit his opinion that anything about her was cute. Feeling that her banter was becoming more playful with each passing phrase, the agent wished it not to become overtly risqué. Therefore, he deemed it necessary to tone things down quite a bit with a more business-like demeanor.

"Ma'am, I am most appreciative of you merely pointing me to her room. After all, I'm hesitant to pull you away from your primary duties as receptionist—you know, greeting people, answering the telephone, and such."

"Oh, posh! Dearie, it would be no trouble it all to see you to her room personally. Unfortunately for our residents, people do not visit much past six of the clock. I suppose that, for most guests, visiting equates to merely stopping by—you know, something to check off the list on the way home from one's work, like gathering some grocery items or going to the post office. Anyway, I'll take you there personally, and maybe I'll have the privilege of assessing the level of your appreciation, perhaps?"

The agent cleared his throat and avoided making eye contact with Ms. Atwater at this point. In a lower, more stoic voice, he responded, "I would be obliged, ma'am."

Walking down the long hallway of the facility, Addy continued lobbing her aggressive tendencies in Nolan's direction. "Well, 'tis a shame that you are privy to my name and I haven't been accorded the reciprocal pleasure, Mister uh . . . ?"

"Jericho, ma'am, Jet Jericho."

"Jericho, is it now? And *Jet*! What a charming name! Mr. Jericho, if you don't mind my asking, what is your sign?"

"Uh, ma'am, I beg your pardon?"

"Oh, you know, sign—as in your sign of the horoscope? I figure you to be a Leo, for you look like you could be a take-charge, bossy type of man when put in the right situation with, uh, a lady of submission such as myself?"

"Well, Ms. Atwater, I'm sorry to disappoint you. No Leo here. I was born on May 4th, so I'm a Taurus."

"Oh, well now, that means you can be quite possessive and, uh, self-indulgent with your, shall we say, *pursuits*?"

"No, actually my lady friend back in Raleigh says I make the perfect Taurus in that I am so full of bull."

"Clever wench, I'm sure she is," Ms. Atwater mumbled with a sound of disappointment. "Oh, well, Mr. Jericho . . . here we are. Just knock on the door when ready. You enjoy your visit with Mrs. Christmas. We all think the world of her, for she's a feisty, quite funny old dame. Anyway, 'twas a pleasure meeting you."

"And you also, Ms. Atwater," replied Nolan sincerely as his escort spun around in an aristocratic manner. Although she had pushed the limits of his comfort zone initially, the refined receptionist had redeemed herself somewhat by finalizing their brief encounter with a classy parting. At least, he hadn't had to haul out the ol' Newborn Baby-scented air freshener—good thing, too, as it was back in its proper storage place inside of Polly, he reflected as he knocked.

"Come on in!" snapped an energetic voice responding to the knocks. As Nolan eased the door open, the voice continued. "I'm not exactly in the process of taking off my evening gown!"

Wow! She does sound feisty! As Nolan entered the room, he saw a little lady with tufts of gray hair, sitting in a wheelchair positioned between the foot of her bed and the room's window. The agent's eyes were immediately drawn to the tiny woman's most unique feature, the eye patch on her left eye.

"Mrs. Christmas, I am Agent—"

"Let me guess!" interrupted Mrs. Christmas. "You're another damn casket salesman who has come a-callin'. Well, you're too late, my son was buried two days ago up in North Carolina."

"No ma'am, I am not a person of that nature," Jericho quickly responded in the hope of settling her down. "I am Agent Jet Jericho of the State Bureau of Investigation—the State Bureau of Investigation in *North* Carolina." At this point, the agent offered his identification in full view.

"Oh, put that away. If it was phony, I wouldn't know the difference. Sorry 'bout the 'casket salesman' remark. You wouldn't believe how those ambulance chasers come out of the woodwork like cockroaches when the child of a parent dies—or vice versa, I'm sure. Well, Mr. Agent Man, I can take another shot as to why you're here. I'm bettin' you want to ask me questions about my dear Paul."

Jericho sat down in the only chair in the room available for visitors. He proceeded to look Mrs. Christmas straight in the eye—the right eye, of course. "Ma'am, to be precise, I want to learn some information from you about both your sons. I would like for you to share your perceptions of their relationship through the years—you know, what the boys were like growing up and other items of information."

"Hmmph, Ron also, huh? Surely you don't think he had anything to do with Paul's death, do you?"

"Well, ma'am, let me just say that nobody's arresting anybody right now and just leave it at that."

"Hmm. Fair enough, Mr. Agent Man. You know, you're the first lawman of any kind who has bothered to talk with me, other than some officer man who called one day to tell me about Paul's pending funeral. Yeah, you heard me right—*called!* The powers that be didn't even have the decency to come and tell me in person."

"I'm terribly sorry, Mrs. Christmas . . ."

Silence is sometimes a blessing, sometimes awkward. At this moment, Jericho fell into an uncomfortable speechlessness at being unable to reactivate the conversation with any words seemingly appropriate. So overwhelming was the pathos conveyed by the sight of the wheelchair-bound little woman wearing an eye patch . . . a woman exiled by society to a facility where its castaways wait for the eventual codas of their lives . . . and a woman having just lost a treasured son. Nolan rarely experienced such a primal rawness of despair and loneliness within his gut, rendering him numb inside, an emotional numbness temporarily incapacitating his thought processes. However, the feisty Mrs. Christmas soon put an end to all this pity nonsense.

"Well, Mr. Agent Man, I know one thing—you didn't come here *not* to talk!"

"Uh, no ma'am, that I didn't. I'm sorry, I just lost my train of thought for a second."

"No, Mr. Agent Man, I know what track your train was on! Among other things, I'll gamble that this eye patch has thrown you for a loop!"

"Ma'am, you definitely do cut to the chase, and you make it exceedingly difficult for a man struggling for an ounce of discretion in your presence to exhibit any degree of tact. So, here goes nothing. Yes, Mrs. Christmas, I have indeed heard that you had only a remainder of your eyesight. But, until now, I had no idea that half of your vision had been wrenched from you. I apologize for having stared, but a man can't help but wonder about the 'how's and 'when's associated with someone else's suffering. Perhaps a terrible accident?"

"There you go! Now that's better, Mr. Agent Man! Now, the cards are on the table. And, thank you for your attempts at sensitivity. Most people look at me as if I am supposed to suddenly say 'Aargh! Ahoy there, matey!' It's as if they think I lost my left eye in the Everglades fighting crocodiles."

"Okay, Mrs. Christmas—by now, you must surely realize that you have my curiosity at full tilt. Just how in the world did you lose your left eye?!"

"Thought you'd never ask, Mr. Agent Man! I can tell you it wasn't a farming accident, even though I lived on a farm. I lost it when the atomic bomb exploded!"

"Well, that explains it—I, uh, WHAT? Did I hear you correctly? An atomic bomb?" Upon Mary's startling revelation, Jericho's squint-prone eyes flew open wider than the time Cat said she thought her period was way too late— which, thankfully, it hadn't been. "Now wait just a minute, Mrs. C., either I didn't hear you correctly or you're playing me for the biggest fool in town. You surely don't intend for me to believe you lost your eye due to the explosion of an atomic bomb!"

"That's exactly what I do intend, Mr. Agent Man! I lost my eye on March 11, 1958, when the U.S. Air Force dropped an atomic bomb from the sky on the outskirts of Florence, South Carolina. They say it was an accident, of course, but it still happened! After all, it was in all the newspapers around the state."

"You're not pulling my leg after all! Mrs. C., if I may call you that, I do slightly recall something about a military craft accidentally releasing an atomic bomb over South Carolina. Yeah, it's all coming back to me—I think it was over a little community just outside of Florence. I have a colleague who is a complete nut about weird events and trivia. He's always driving the rest of us bananas with some of the most obscure tidbits of information. Anyway, I do remember him going on about the 'great South Carolina nuclear attack' of the late fifties."

"Yep! Just as I said, March 11, 1958, some time right after four o'clock in the afternoon. And the community the bomb landed in was Mars Bluff, just several miles east of Florence. The crater is still there. If you don't believe me, go check it out. Boy, what an explosion that was!"

"Yeah, I'll bet it was!"

"It was indeed, Mr. Agent Man! That big blast sent a mushroom cloud way up in the air. It completely messed up a local family's home and did some damage to a local church. In fact, a guy was driving along on Highway 301 in his car and was several miles away from the blast, but they say the blast completely spun his car around."

"You don't say?"

"Oh, I do say, Mr. Agent Man. Luckily, no one was killed by the blast, or at least that's what the government claimed. The newspapers said there were several reasons nobody was killed, such as the ground being real marshy and absorbing the blast. There was some poppycock about the bomb not being fully activated or something, causing the bomb not to do a full nucular blast on impact. Yep, officials came up with several reasons for no one being killed, except for God's intervention. Of course, the government didn't give God any credit for the lives that were spared."

Although partially amused by the little lady's pronunciation of the word "nuclear," Jericho was nevertheless held spellbound by the woman's recounting of the event, captive to every word. "Wow! Incredible, Mrs. C.! But wait a minute, what were *you* doing in Mars Bluff? I thought you lived on the farm in Pelion until after your husband died. Florence and Columbia are quite far apart."

"Yes, I did live in Pelion, Mr. Agent Man. But what you don't know is that I often went for a week here and there to visit my favorite cousin who lived between Mars Bluff and Florence. My husband would tell me, 'Mary, just go and have a good time with Jenna for a few days. The farm'll be here when you get back. I can manage.' The hidden agenda was probably so he could fool around a little. Anyway, he'd drop me off at the bus station in Columbia, and Jenna and Buddy would pick me up at the bus station in Florence. I really enjoyed my vacations spent with Jenna and her family—that is, until the bomb dropped, of course. It exploded fourteen years ago, and I was sixty-two years old at the time. That sure was somethin' scary, I tell you!"

"I'll bet it was! So, Mrs. C., how'd you get caught in the blast?"

"Well, Jenna loved to walk! She claimed that one time she walked all the way from Florence to Darlington. I really don't know about that, but that woman was one walking fool! Anyway, she would talk me into walking up and down Highway 301. On that fateful afternoon of March 11th, we happened to be walking on the side of Highway 301. We were passing right near the place where the bomb hit, right when it dropped! I can tell you, you've never heard a scary sound until you've heard the sound of a bomb whistling as it's falling, just like in the war movies. I tell you, Mr. Agent Man, I got sort of an inkling of how the Japanese people must have felt when the atomic bombs were falling toward their cities."

"What about the injury to your eye, Mrs. C.?"

"Yeah, what about the injury to my eye! Just like the government downplayed the whole incident and underpaid the family whose home was destroyed, I guarantee you that the loss of my left eye was not headline news at the time. When the blast happened, Jenna and I were shaken off our feet and thrown to the ground. Jenna got a bucketful of dirt sprinkled on her while I received a seven-inch long portion of a tree limb shot like a missile into my eye."

"Did you receive any compensation at all from the government for the loss of your eye?"

"That family wasn't paid much at all for the damage to their home, but I guess what they received was a lot more than the big zero sum of dollars I received for losing my eye."

"None at all, huh, Mrs. C.?"

"None at all, young man! The government claimed there was no actual proof that the tree limb being projected was a result of the atomic blast. I guess it was one of those goblins that live up there on the moon constantly trying to spear us Earth people with tree limbs."

"Well, Mrs. C., you are definitely a living testimony to perseverance and good living. You are definitely something!"

"Why, thank you, Mr. Agent Man! Yep, you don't run into a person like me just anywhere in this ol' United States who can say that he or she survived a nucular blast."

"Okay, Mrs. C. Now, for the reason I came to see you, and that is to see if you can help me with any information which might assist me in solving the murder of your beloved son."

Starting to tear up a little, Mrs. Christmas grabbed a tissue off of the wall shelf adjacent to her wheelchair. "I'll do everything I can, Mr. Agent Man. Paul didn't deserve to die the way he did or as young as he did."

With Mrs. Christmas choked up, Nolan patted her left hand and rubbed it gently. "Just let me know when you're ready for me to begin my questions, ma'am," the agent suggested in a soft, patient tone of voice. After fifteen seconds or so, the little lady nodded to the comforting lawman, confirming her readiness.

"First of all, Mrs. C., allow me to cut to the chase and get the most obvious question out of the way first. Do you know of anyone with whom Paul had any kind of trouble? Anyone that might have wished to harm Paul for any reason?"

"Oh, no! No one at all, Mr. Agent Man. I can't think of why anybody would want to hurt my Paul. He did *so* much good in the world. He lived by God's word and was willing to die by God's word."

"Nobody from his childhood or his years as a teenager?"

"No, nobody. Growing up, Paul was as popular as a boy could be. Everybody wanted to play with Paul . . . go to movies with Paul . . . go to dances with Paul. That boy was the ultimate 'people person' if ever there was one."

"If you don't mind, let's talk for a few minutes about the relationship between Ron and Paul. How close were they while growing up?"

"Oh, when they were young'uns, they were as close as you would imagine typical twins being, almost inseparable. If one was out in the yard playing, so was the other. If one was watching the television, so was the other. It could be sort of strange at times, you know, regarding the typical behaviors of twins. If one had an illness, the other would also catch it. If one didn't feel like going to school, neither did the other."

"Okay, Mrs. C., what about as they got older?"

"Well, you know the old saying: 'All good things must come to an end.' Although they had been close in their youth, the differences between each boy became more pronounced in high school. You know yourself how friends from childhood typically grow apart during high school and college. I just attribute it to the way people change and find themselves. They finally emerge from the cocoon and, as adults, become individuals with different interests, talents, and beliefs, just as God intended. So to answer your question, Mr. Agent Man, yes! My boys grew further apart in high school and, by the time each was ready for college, they had virtually nothing in common."

"How so, Mrs. C.?"

"Well, with Paul being the 'people person' of the two, he was always into participating in organizations and helping others. You would never see Paul involved in any self-serving venture or worried about getting ahead in the world. I always sensed that, as a youth, Paul believed deep-down he was put on this planet to serve others. So, if there had been such a thing in high school as voting for 'Most Likely to Enter the Ministry,' the senior class would have elected Paul. He was born to be God's soldier, day in and day out."

"Okay, so what about Ron?"

"Well, that boy was certainly a horse of a different color in comparison to his brother. In high school, perhaps a little sooner, Ron started becoming more of a loner and always kept to himself. He didn't seem to enjoy socializing at all. I guess there's no better way to put it, but he just plain and simple did not seem to like people. Now, Ron did have a good work ethic, no doubt. As a teenager, he wasn't lazy by any means. But, whereas Paul would be off spending his time with some organization raising money and doing work for charities like low-income housing, Ron would be mowing yards, cleaning gutters, and other jobs—you know, jobs in which he could keep to himself while making money. He would squirrel away the money for the future. One time he told me he was saving up money so he could have things that others couldn't, things that he had been denied, having come up in a farming household.

"Well, Mr. Agent Man, now you have it! That was the big difference between Paul and Ron. Paul always felt so blessed no matter how little he had, and Ron always felt he was being denied no matter how much he had. In other words, Paul always viewed the cup as half-full while Ron always saw the cup as half-empty."

"Mrs. C., can you tell me anything about Ron's marriage and the loss of his fortune?"

"Wow, you have been shaking all the grapes off the grapevine, haven't you? Yes, Mr. Agent Man, interesting twists of fate there, particularly regarding the appearance of Linda Fairbanks in the lives of the boys."

"Did you say 'boys'—uh, plural? Linda was Ron's wife, am I right? What did she have to do with Paul?"

"Oh, Linda became Ron's wife. But, she had moved to the boys' high school during their sophomore year. Both boys seemed to care about her friendship quite a bit. From their sophomore year right up toward graduation, people used to laugh—and almost be amazed, frankly—about how the three of them could maintain such a civil arrangement regarding their dates and so forth. Sometimes, Linda and Ron would go out together; sometimes, it would be Linda and Paul going somewhere. And still at other times, all three of them would go to the movies together or a concert or something. One of my friends at church used to call it 'lop-sided dating,' being that there was two boys and one girl. It reached a point that I secretly feared they might be having one of those menatroys . . . uh, mirage-atroy . . . uh—"

"Do you mean *ménage à trois*, Mrs. C.?"

"That's it, Mr. Agent Man, that's it. I always had trouble saying those French words."

"Now, what you've told me is interesting, ma'am, but contradictory. I thought Ron was such a loner, but yet he ends up marrying Linda. And on top of that, if Ron had his eyes set on Linda, how did he tolerate Paul going out with her? I'm so confused—help!"

"Well, it all may sound complicated, Mr. Agent Man, but yet I think it's quite simple. Although I told you that Ron didn't like people and was a loner, he loved Linda to no end. She was really the only person outside the family that Ron ever loved. Paul really cared for Linda as a friend, but I don't think he ever thought of her as more than a close friend. You see, he was already feeling a tug to the ministry in high school. Not that ministers can't be married, but Paul told me one time while in college that spending a life doing God's work was going to demand so much of his time. He said it was hard to see himself becoming a family man, and I think he felt that it might not be fair to a future wife or kids to spend so little time with them. At any rate, I really don't think Ron ever perceived Paul as a threat or a contender for Linda's affection on account of Paul's declarations about his future profession."

"So, in the long run, how did Linda end up with Ron?"

"Initially, I believe Linda enjoyed the company of both boys from a friendship standpoint. But I'm sure those little ol' settle-down-and-have-a-family hormones started plaguing Linda around the beginning of her senior year. She started going on outings with Paul much less frequently and upped the ante on Ron, dating him more often. You see, Mr. Agent Man, while I'm not saying that Linda Fairbanks was a complete gold-digger, she was pragmatic and liked lots of pretty things. Also, she was definitely no future preacher's wife. She was born to play the part of a spoiled socialite. In other words, it didn't take a rocket scientist to see that Ron's desire to conquer the world would be more attractive to a worldly Linda looking forward to a lifetime of worldly things."

"Makes sense, Mrs. C. What about Linda's death and Ron losing his fortune?"

"Mr. Agent Man, I won't ever claim that Linda deserved to die or that Ron deserved to lose all the material things he thought made him so happy. But, I do believe that there comes a time when we all have to lie in the beds we make for ourselves. In other words, Paul's faith is eternal and he was able to carry it with him to the grave and beyond. But, worldly things come and go. Linda liked to drink and party, and eventually—that is, in 1965—these things became her undoing. Ron placed every fiber of his devotion into Linda and his material possessions, and neither pleasure was guaranteed for any length of time. Ron gambled and he lost, and that was his fate. You might say that since he didn't put his faith in God like his brother did, Ron's fate was in the stars . . . and stars eventually burn out and fall."

Jericho whimsically imagined how Ms. Atwater, the zodiac-oriented British receptionist, might interpret Mrs. C.'s last comment about stars determining one's fate. At this point, Jericho was getting tired, therefore he felt Mrs. Christmas might also be experiencing fatigue. It was time to wrap things up. "Mrs. C., in your opinion, is your son Ron bitter about his fate—about the turn of the cards he's experienced?"

"Oh, definitely! Yes, definitely, Mr. Agent Man. He had a shallow soul to begin with, and when everything collapsed, his soul was useless in helping him cope with his losses. Yes, he's bitter all right!"

"Uh, Mrs. C., did, uh, Paul smoke?"

"Yes, sir, that was one bad habit he inherited from his father. Paul told me on an occasion or two that he was trying to quit, but I don't know if he ever kicked the habit or not."

"What about Ron?"

"I don't know about Ron, for he never mentioned anything about it. I'm sure I've smelled it on him occasionally, but neither boy ever really smoked in front of me. They knew I sure didn't approve of the filthy habit and would kick up some sand at the sight of it."

"One more question, Mrs. C., then I'll let you turn in for the evening. This is what it all comes down to, ma'am: do you think there is any possibility that Ron, in all his bitterness, killed his brother?"

"Oh, no! Mr. Agent Man, no! That I positively do not think at all! Ron is guilty of being a pitiful soul and having had poor judgment. But I can't imagine Ron being that jealous of his brother. I can't possibly imagine Ron wishing to kill Paul! How could you imagine Ron wishing to kill his twin brother merely out of sheer jealousy or bitterness?"

"That's the problem with my line of work, Mrs. C. I'm paid to have a big imagination. Anyway, you really have provided me with much information to assist my investigation. I have a much greater depth of understanding now that you and I have talked. I know this wasn't easy, but I thank you."

"Please just find out who killed my son, Mr. Agent Man, will you?"

"I'll do my best, ma'am." Winking at her, Jericho added, "That is, unless somebody drops an atomic bomb on me."

"Hey! It can happen, Mr. Agent Man. I'm living proof that it can happen!"

CHAPTER 18

Railroad Death Trap

As he settled into Polly and reached for the ignition to start her up for the long trip back to Icy Springs, Jericho reflected on his interview with Mary Christmas. *"Please just find out who killed my son, Mr. Agent Man, will you?"* The thought suddenly struck him that, if he were right in his suspicions about Ron and he could prove it, Mary would ultimately have lost both her sons. *How sad: she survives an atomic blast but loses her whole family. She's strong, that one, but this . . . Is she strong enough for this?*

Pulling out of Elderly Acres, Nolan headed his car northerly on Highway 29. He intended on going up the road a little piece toward the town of Cowpens and, *via* a side road, cutting on over to the relatively new stretch of Interstate 85 which would carry him on toward Charlotte. The highway seemed relatively clear at this time of the day, a prime time for some evening cruising. The next few miles for the agent seemed rather happy-go-lucky, but his joyride was soon unexpectedly interrupted. As he glanced downward at the instrument panel, he noticed a nearly empty fuel gauge. *Sorry, Polly, ol' gal. I was so busy earlier looking after my appetite, getting all "Beaconized," I never considered that you might be getting hungry also—I sure hope I can find a filling station on 29 that's still open at this time of the day. . .*

The agent cruised on along the highway, starting to feel a little apprehensive on Polly's behalf—and his, of course. The needle on her gauge was sitting practically on its "E." His red Anna was always willing to run another twenty miles on fumes, but Polly would leave Jericho stranded in a heartbeat once her needle grazed the "E." The nervous agent started scanning the relatively deserted highway a little more feverishly, hoping the road ahead would offer the traveler's providence he was now seeking but certainly didn't deserve.

Nolan breathed a deep sigh of relief and sent a little thank-you to the Lord as a Phillips 66 station on the horizon rolled out the red carpet in spite of his

151

carelessness—and, looky-there: a pickup truck was just pulling out of the station, so it was still open for business. *Okay, Polly, soup's on!* Gratefully pulling up to a gas tank and shutting off the engine, Jericho rolled down his window and shouted with exuberance to the approaching attendant, "Fill 'er up, sir! And fill 'er belly to the brim!"

The agent stepped inside the filling station to use the rest room and sip on a Nehi grape for a few minutes. Although eating at the Beacon was always a great experience, the food also always left Nolan with a greasy aftertaste that demanded the intervention of a sweet, tasty soda. Man and car satisfied, Jericho settled up for the fuel and the drink and once more headed up 29 North, back to Charlotte. It would not be long before dusk and, although he loved that time of the evening, the tired agent wished to be on the interstate before darkness enveloped him. Yawning widely as he approached a curve, he encountered a caution sign on his right, alerting him to a narrow underpass with low clearance, thirteen feet six inches. *Okay, truck drivers, this caution is definitely for you, not me.* Rounding the curve, Nolan could see, several hundred feet ahead, one of those low-lying concrete railroad bridges. Jericho always marveled at how these flimsy-looking structures could support the weight of a freight train, and he was usually happy if good timing placed him going under these structures with no train overhead.

Approaching the bridge, Jericho noticed a dirt road on the left side of the highway with an interesting sign: *No Entrance! Maintenance Drive, Southern Railway.* The drive disappeared into a wooded area located up toward the railroad tracks extending from the bridge. If Agent Jericho had been super-observant on this particular evening, he might have noticed the faint wisp of dust in the air left as a result of a car having sped up the maintenance drive into the woods a minute or so earlier. Nothing caught his attention, however, for the dust had nearly dissipated. By the same token, the agent had also not noticed a light-blue Ford Galaxie pulling out from the body shop and salvage yard near Elderly Acres as he walked to his Sting Ray in the rest home parking lot, the unobserved car having been camouflaged among a sea of discarded cars. *And,* if Nolan hadn't been so consumed with replenishing his empty fuel tank back at the service station, he just might have spotted that same light-blue car—having preceded the agent from the salvage yard by roughly three-quarters of a mile— pulling off on the side of the road momentarily, about a half-mile beyond the filling station and waiting. Yes, *just maybe* the travel-weary agent would have noticed any of these peculiar circumstances, but he hadn't.

However, as he approached the railroad bridge, Nolan *did* spot a suspicious sight: an oddly-garbed figure was sitting on one rail of the train track, dangling his feet just over the right lane of the highway. Straining his eyes for clarity, the agent detected that the individual was cloaked in a raincoat and wearing a baseball cap and sunglasses. Immediately, Jericho's instincts for self-preservation propelled him into a quick analysis of the scene. *What's this joker doing sitting there above the road? And what's the deal with the raincoat on this hot July day?*

Within the blink of an eye, Jericho's attempt at rationalizing the unexplained turned into one of those surreal moments when time suddenly passes in slow motion, one of those moments when the tempo of one's mind supersedes any physical reactions one can muster up. The mystery person on the bridge casually reached behind and, securing a rather chunky object, instantaneously lobbed it toward the highway below.

Whoa, what's he—? Oh, shit!

Jericho's instincts immediately overrode his thoughts as what appeared to be a concrete block zeroed in on his Sting Ray. The block seemed to float surreally in the air, as if manipulated by the strings of a puppeteer, but in reality bore the approach of a guided missile. Its trajectory lent itself dead on target toward the driver's side of Polly's windshield. The agent gritted his teeth and maintained his grip firmly on the wheel. Veering to the right would have meant certain death, as the concrete abutment of the bridge hugged the edge of the narrow highway. With his mind racing at the speed of light, Jericho popped his seat belt loose and flung his body toward the passenger seat. As he fell, he relaxed his grip on the wheel so that the momentum of pitching himself downward would not have him jerking the wheel to the right and into the abutment. The Sting Ray suddenly veered to the left, slightly misaligning the path of the driver's seat with the approach of the concrete block.

CRASH!!!!

The block's destiny was fulfilled as the glass of Polly's windshield exploded violently. The concrete missile ricocheted off the dashboard, grazing the edge of Nolan's upper left arm. Remaining cool as the storm of glass blew over him, the agent miraculously managed to reassert his grip on the wheel with his left hand, despite the pain in his arm from the ricocheting block. After skimming off his left arm, the unforgiving block soared onward in its path between the two front seats, bouncing with a thud against the upper edge of the rear seat and proceeding to crash through the rear window.

Still lying in the passenger seat and having no visibility of the highway, the agent had instinctively estimated the slight degree to which he needed to pull the steering wheel back toward the right after impact to avoid ramming into the left side of the bridge. Jerking his body back up into an upright position, Jericho found himself now traveling in the center of the highway, having managed to realign Polly as well as humanly possible while driving blind.

Beeepp! Beeepp!

The shocked agent was now staring face-to-face with an oncoming pickup truck having high side boards on its back, the kind of outfit that owners use to haul an excessive load of produce or something. Having barely dodged threat number one, Jericho once again took evasive action by jerking Polly to the right. After narrowly missing the old truck, the agent slammed on his brakes as his Sting Ray slid off the right side of the road.

The battle-scarred car rammed into a hedgerow at about thirty miles per hour and came to a dead halt. Physically stunned, Nolan shook it off and tried to open his left door. It didn't budge, as it was pinned shut by a stubborn pair of bushes. His bruised left arm wouldn't allow him the luxury of applying much force to the door, so the agent crawled over the passenger seat and secured his exit through the passenger door. He darted onto the highway, holding his left upper arm with his right hand, then trotted toward the bridge. The pickup truck, a green Chevrolet hauling watermelons, had come to a stop on the other side of the bridge. A large, gray-haired man wearing overalls and sporting a white beard stepped out of the truck.

Appearing free of anger, the concerned man hollered out something to Nolan. However, the agent did not respond, as he was already bolting up the steep bank on the right side of the highway stretching toward the top of the bridge. Once reaching the track, Jericho looked toward the center of the bridge where the strangely attired assassin-to-be had sat. Seeing nothing, he glanced in each direction. The horizon was clear of vegetation on the other side of the bridge, with nowhere to hide. Nolan logically chose to sprint to his right along the track, heading toward the wooded area. About fifty yards down the track, he spotted the end of the maintenance drive owned by Southern Railway, the same dead-end access road he had passed earlier, extending from Highway 29 to the track. Mysteriously enough, there was now smoke billowing between the end of the access drive and the edge of the track.

Reaching the area where the dirt drive looped around at the tracks, Nolan saw a heaped mass burning on the ground beside the track. He approached the pile, puzzled, grabbed a nearby stick and poked curiously at the flaming debris. Shifting the burning material, the agent lifted the remnants of a crumpled-up raincoat. From what he could tell, the smoldering rim of a baseball cap sat on the edge of the fire. Jericho could smell the gasoline with which the articles had been hurriedly doused to assure incineration. Tossing aside the stick with a disgusted look, he caught the flash of something lying in the red dirt of the dry, dusty turnaround: a *coin!* Although Jericho considered himself a well-traveled man of the world, the coin was unlike any he had ever seen. It bore no words on it but possessed most unusual markings.

All along the maintenance drive toward the highway, dust was hovering in the air like the vaporous trail of a comet. Whoever had tried to kill Jericho had made a hasty retreat down the dirt road and was now headed in the direction of Spartanburg. The disappointed agent walked back along the railroad track and eased down the bank, re-appearing on the highway.

The old owner of the watermelon truck walked out from under the bridge. "I tell ya, young man, I just went to your car. I only lost two watermelons when I had to swerve around you, but it appears you lost a might more in the process. What in the blue blazes happened here?"

"Sir, did you see a car pulling out of the access drive on the other side of the bridge heading toward Spartanburg?"

"Well, sorta . . ."

"What do you mean by 'sorta', sir?"

"Son, it all happened so fast. First, you nearly plowed into me, and then I looked back and saw you running up the road. I hopped out of the truck and ran to help you. Just after you climbed up the bank to the train track, I did see a car disappearing in the distance. It was a blue car of some kind. That's all I can tell you, young fella. Again, would you mind telling me what in blazes went on here?"

"Well, sir, it appears that someone wanted me dead. They were sitting on top of the bridge and chucked a concrete block toward me as I was approaching. I'm definitely not too happy about the damage to my car. Dammit!—" Nolan looked at his left upper arm for the first time since the attack. "And," continued the frustrated agent, "I'm not too happy about the torn sleeve of my suit. This particular dark gray suit is, naturally, the most expensive item of clothing I possess."

"Young fella, you're lucky you didn't lose your head. I don't see how you managed not to get yourself killed."

"Truthfully, sir, it took some mighty fancy driving on my part—along with a little bit of luck—to be standing here talking to you. If you had come along two or three seconds earlier, we might both be playing a harp right now looking down on a fiery crash still burning under the bridge. I'm truly thankful you weren't any closer than you were. Either we would have crashed head on or I would have had to let the concrete block take my head off. Either prospect would have been mighty gloomy at the moment."

"Well, the Man upstairs looks after us. He sure did in that case."

"Yes, sir, that He did!" At that point, Jericho retrieved his identification and exposed it to the man. "Sir, my name is Jet Jericho. I'm an agent for the State Bureau of Investigation in, uh, *North* Carolina, and I was just sort of . . . passing through. Since it appears you were on your way into Spartanburg, would you mind giving me a ride?"

"I'd be glad to, young man. Where are you wanting to go?"

"Hmm . . . To tell you the truth, I don't know. I know I need to get to a payphone. But first, let me ask you about the possibility of having my car towed. What about that big body shop and salvage place on up the road next to Elderly Acres?

"Oh, that's Bobby Bartlett's garage. Let me tell you, young man, he is a wizard at repairing cars. He can take a car that looks like a beat-up old jalopy and make it look brand new. You can't go wrong with him!"

"Do you think he's still open?"

"No, but he does emergency calls—you know, overnight tows and such. He'd come out here and pull your car back in, and he and his crew would probably start working on it first thing in the morning."

"Then, I must impose upon you, Mister, uh—"

"Applebee, young fella, but you can just call me Lonny!"

"Well, uh, Lonny, would you be so obliging as to drop me off at the garage for five or ten minutes? I would like to meet Mr. Bartlett and arrange for him to tow in my car and, more than likely, repair it—that is, if he is as good as you say he is. I'll certainly take your recommendation seriously on that matter. Lonny, if you wouldn't mind, I would then appreciate you taking me to the bus station in downtown Spartanburg—that is, if it's not too much of an imposition."

"I wouldn't mind at all, young man. They say you meet some of your best friends in an accident where you nearly kill each other. Consider me a new friend. I'll be glad to do it. Actually, the bus station is only about six blocks out of the way from where I was going—I'm taking all these watermelons to the market this evening to set up for the Farmer's Market tomorrow. It'll be no problem at all!"

"Thank you so much, Lonny. I'll be much indebted to you."

"Yessiree Bob, Spartanburg has a huge produce market on the fourth Wednesday of every month in the summer. My watermelons give me a lot of summer income. As a matter of fact, I'll be sellin' some of my melons this comin' Saturday morning at a big market outside of Columbia. I'm sort of known around these parts for my juicy melons. Would you like to buy one off of me?"

The last thing in the world Jericho really wanted at this time was a watermelon, no matter how juicy. However, the agent also felt mighty guilty for nearly killing Mr. Applebee and destroying two of the old man's melons while trying to swerve around him. Since he had caused the farmer trouble and was now bumming a ride from him, then one watermelon it would be! "I would love one, sir, but I wouldn't have the slightest idea how to go about picking out a good one."

"They're all good, young fella. But here, come on over! I'll pick you out a prize of a melon, and then we'll hit the road!"

It was now nearly dark, and lightning bugs were flittering all along the landscape, seeming to illuminate the highway. Jericho began seething as he glanced toward his prized blue Sting Ray, his sweet Polly now paralyzed along the side of the road and engulfed by the hedgerow. *Okay, Ron Christmas, maybe it is still possible that you're not the culprit, but I'm sure you are! Right now, I'm quite pissed off, and I'll get you!* The angry agent shook his head as he turned away from Polly and started following Mr. Applebee. *Yeah, that's a bad hand he's dealt me, a bad hand indeed!*

◆ ◆ ◆ ◆ ◆

The stop at Bobby Bartlett's garage provided some relative comfort, for Mr. Bartlett seemed to be the kind of creature who lives and breathes his work. Living next door to his body shop, the "car doctor" stepped over briskly from his house and seemed eager to get about the business of towing Polly to his garage and surveying her damage. While at the garage, Nolan was able to peep at some of the patients currently under the surgeon's knife, and was reassured that Mr. Bartlett's body work appeared to be of top-notch quality. The how and when of the agent getting back later to Spartanburg to pick up Polly after her repairs was another issue, an issue that would have to wait. For now, the agent's primary concerns were getting to the bus station and arranging a trip back to Charlotte from Spartanburg. Walt once mentioned that out-of-town buses only served Sharpton during the daytime, which meant a long taxi ride back from Charlotte to the Chat & Nibble. On top of all that, the weary agent had to check in with Fowler. Oh, it was going to be a very *long* night indeed!

◆ ◆ ◆ ◆ ◆

Standing at the bus station cradling his "prize" melon, Jericho was appreciative of the fact that his near-fatal collision had been with a wonderful Samaritan named Lonny Applebee. After all, he could have still been at the bridge trying to thumb a ride. There was little hubbub in the Spartanburg bus station now that darkness had fallen, making it feel more like a mausoleum, with a couple of zombies manning the ticket windows.

Okay, the die is cast, and here I be! I guess I'm destined to sit at the Spartanburg bus station until the middle of the night. Well, time to report to the head honcho. As Nolan staggered to the pay phone, he mulled over the always dependable correlation between the lateness of an hour and the grumpiness of Director Fowler.

Luckily, Jericho caught Fowler just as he had finished adding some new stamps to his stamp collection. The director seemed especially jovial due to his recent acquisition of a rare find from China. The tenor of the conversation flowed smoothly as the agent recounted the chilly reception offered by Ron Christmas in Pelion and the enlightening visit with mother Mary in Spartanburg. It was the episode at the railroad bridge involving the attempt on Jericho's life where Fowler seemed to become a little derailed; however, when the agent assured Fowler that he was merely "banged up and bruised a little," the director seemed to settle down somewhat.

This seemed as good a time as any for Jericho to probe Fowler for his special request. "Sir, uh, you know how agents and other employees are provided workman's comp in case of an injury occurring while on duty. Sir, is there any kind of, uh, insurance for my Sting Ray, being that it was injured in the line of duty?"

"Now, Jet, we've been through this dance before. Ya know that all our agents have the prerogative to requisition a state vehicle for their assignments. I've tried time and time again to get ya to drive the state cars. After all, damage to them is covered. But, ya always insist on taking your private cars, which I can't really stop ya from doing. Ya know that when ya drive your own car, I can pay ya the state rate toward mileage, but I can't—and I repeat: I CAN'T—pay for any damage to your private vehicle. The state insurance won't cover that."

"Oh, well, it didn't hurt to try. . ."

"So, Jet, what's your next move?"

"Sir, I'm going to have the strange coin left behind by my would-be assassin at the bridge checked out. Also, I think I'll see if Sheriff Niblock can contact the Sheriff's Department of Lexington County around Columbia. I would like to acquire a search warrant. Perhaps Sheriff Niblock and me can pay a little visit to Ron and really have a look around—that is, of course, with the two of us being escorted by law enforcement officials from Lexington County."

"Of course! Jet, I guess I was not thinking at all when I permitted ya to cross the state line by yourself, for you were totally out of your jurisdiction. And, if somebody had gotten hurt or killed, then God help us. We were damn lucky! You just make sure that, if Niblock agrees with your plan, the two of ya act totally within the jurisdiction of the law and that the two of ya are indeed accompanied by others who can act within jurisdiction. Remember, you are a state agent, not a Federal marshal!"

"Got it, sir! Uh, sir, do you know when—" Jericho had begun to ask a question of Fowler, but his burly boss cut him short.

"Oh, Jericho, there is one more thing. If ya need any assistance from me beyond your intention of the search warrant, I can probably pull off more than ya think I can. My old army buddy is actually the head of the South Carolina Bureau of Investigation. I haven't talked to him for quite a while, but I could probably clear a lot of things through him that would circumvent your limitations. If I had thought of it yesterday, I would have given him a call to see if he could have offered ya any assistance today. But, that's water under the bridge."

"Thank you, sir, I'll keep your army buddy in mind. But for now, I think that Walt and I might be able to take our next step in South Carolina with the assistance of law enforcement at the county level."

"Okay, but you boy scouts know that I'm always here for you guys. I just can't fix your cars for ya when you're too damn stubborn to follow normal procedures. —Oh, yeah, Jet, it seemed like ya were about to ask me something a few seconds ago before I interrupted ya."

"Yes, sir. What time tomorrow do you think you'll mail Cat out to me? I've got some things I'd like to run through her, I mean, uh, *by* her. I think she'll greatly expand my capabilities in Icy Springs."

"Hold your horses, Jet. I'll have her out to Icy Springs by around two o'clock tomorrow afternoon. She's coming by the office tomorrow morning to finish a couple of secretarial matters, then she'll be heading on down that way."

Jericho knew he had to be extremely crafty with the following request, for he didn't want Fowler drawing any inconvenient conclusions—inconvenient, that is, for the undercover relationship between Cat and him. "Sir, I have one favor to ask of you, something that I need you to have Cat do for me tomorrow."

"Go ahead, agent, shoot!"

"Director, would you mind asking Cat if she would drive down in my red convertible Sting Ray tomorrow? I would appreciate having that car for the remainder of the assignment."

"Oh brother, you really do need to go to the school for slow learners, don't ya, Jericho? Did ya not learn a thing from what just happened today with your other car? Was there some part of my lecture which seemed a little too abstract for ya? Huh, agent?"

"Well, sir, it's just that I absolutely hate driving those cracker boxes on wheels that are offered to the agents. They're, uh, Fords of all things!"

"Aw right, aw right already! Jeesh, you'll never learn, Jet. Have it your way, agent! Cat'll drive your car down to ya tomorrow, and then maybe you'll have the opportunity to flip it over, too, and be several thousand more dollars in the hole. Maybe, just maybe, when ya have destroyed your whole damn armada, you will come crawling to me and begging me to drive one of our cracker boxes on wheels!"

"That wouldn't be likely, uh, sir. . ."

"Anyway, agent, how can Cat get the key to your car?"

"Well, uh, sir, she has a key to my apartment. Would you have her stop by my apartment and get the key to my car?"

"What, Jet? Why does she have a—"

"—well, you see, sir, it's like this: You know how we agents are always on field assignments which can last for several days or more? Well, Cat, uh—you see, she waters my plants. Yes, sir, when I'm out of town, I can always count on that gal to stop by and water my plants."

"PLANTS! You've never mentioned anything about having any plants to me."

"No sir, I guess I haven't. I suppose I'm an agent of many mysteries. Anyway, I appreciate ol' Cat. If it wasn't for her, for heaven's sake, my prized proboscis would be wilting away right now as we're speaking."

Upon those words leaving his mouth, Jericho knew he had just blundered. *Jericho, you idiot! That's not the word! There's no such plant as a proboscis. A proboscis is a long nose! You should have said "hibiscus," you moron. You are so cool in every situation except, of course, when it comes to Cat. Well, genius, the jig may be up!*

"Jericho, something doesn't sound right here. What about when Cat's out of town? Why happens to your plants then if you're not around?"

"Well, sir, Cat has her older sister stop by the house and water them for me."

"Oh, okay. I guess I understand what you're saying. A man does have to look after his stuff and, from what I've heard, it's hard to keep a proboscis alive. A man sure wouldn't want a wilted proboscis, would he?."

"No, sir. He definitely wouldn't. Yes, I'll have to hand it to Cat, she really knows how to keep a man's proboscis from wilting. She keeps my proboscis looking quite perky, among other things of mine."

"Okay, Jericho, it's my bedtime! Where do I tell Cat that the key to your car is?"

"Uh, it's in the kitchen drawer that's closest to the refrigerator. Tell Cat just to come straight to the Chat & Nibble."

"Okay, agent, will do. Good night."

"Good night, sir, sleep tight." Upon hanging up, Jericho drew in a deep breath. *Phew! I guess that went okay. He sounds like he's about as big a flower expert as I am.*

The clumsy conversation with Fowler about the key would have been completely averted if Jericho had been willing to call Cat directly. Oh, how he longed to hear her voice! But, with such a long distance separating them, he really didn't want to tell her at this late hour about his brush with death, his smashed-up Sting Ray, and his banged-up arm. Cat would worry and not sleep a bit. Even worse, she might tear out toward Spartanburg in the middle of the night in hopes of finding the bus station before the bus departed to Charlotte. Not that Jericho wasn't chomping at the bit to see Cat, but he didn't want her doing anything rash that could be dangerous or leave her extremely exhausted. No, it was the prudent thing for Cat to keep on schedule and arrive worry-free and rested in Icy Springs tomorrow afternoon around two o'clock. Besides, he really wanted his red convertible. If he had called Cat and asked her to drive

Anna to Icy Springs, Fowler would have been extremely suspicious of the fact that Cat didn't requisition one of the company cars and had driven his. No, believe it or not, lining things up through Fowler was probably the sanest move to make. Maybe . . .

Sitting back on the bench, the agent looked around the empty bus station and sighed. *Man, it's going to be a LONG wait here on this bench until two o'clock, and this sure is one lonely place at this time of the night. Nobody here but just me—well, make that just me and my watermelon.*

CHAPTER 19

When a Cat Meets a Dobermann . . .

Jericho rolled over as the piercing morning light managed to pry itself around the edges of the curtains and smack him in the face. He stretched his shoulders and groaned, becoming slowly aware of the air conditioner's musical hum. Glancing toward the dresser, his droopy eyes gradually achieved focus on his cherished case of barbecue sauce, with a watermelon now sitting beside it. He felt refreshed and ready to tackle the day despite the nagging throb in his left arm, compliments of the concrete block. But first, he wanted to inform Cat of yesterday's events and prep her on how to respond to Fowler.

Managing to flop over to his stomach, Nolan was instantly stung by the time indicated on the clock. *What?! Ten o'clock?! No way! I swear, I guess I was so tired when I got in at 5:00 this morning that I forgot to set the damn thing. Well, forget prepping Cat! She has already met with Fowler and is probably getting ready to pull out pretty soon. I have a nagging feeling that I will have a lot of explaining to do when Cat arrives, and if Cat didn't dodge the bullets with which I unwittingly armed our director, both of us might have a lot of explaining to do to Fowler when we get back to Raleigh.*

Rolling over once again, Jericho lay on his back with his aching arm feeling some relief in the cool sheets of the chilly room. *What IS IT about Cat that turns me into such a mindless idiot?! I mean, I'm highly regarded by all the guys at the Bureau for my ability to be calm and collected in virtually any situation. Put five, six, or seven thugs around me, and I can methodically take them out in thirty to forty-five seconds without getting the least bit excited or breaking a sweat. That is, of course, unless they are armed. Then, it might take me a good minute or so to neutralize them. So, just what is it about Cat? Why is it that when I get into any situation involving Cat, my usually dependable logic is totally paralyzed? Why is it that I can't sensibly rationalize any issues involving Cat? It seems that when I deal with Cat, I'm stuck emotionally in some time-continuum . . . that, in essence, I behave impulsively, like a total idiot! I mean, taking her out to eat in public for all Raleigh to see, and now telling Fowler that Cat has a key to my apartment! What is wrong with me? What has Cat done to the inside of my head?*

Temporarily placing his anxieties on hold, Jericho decided it was time to check in with Walt and apprise him of yesterday's events. Jericho knew that his trusty partner was probably chomping at the bit to know what had transpired in Pelion. After only one ring of the telephone, the patient-but-eager sheriff answered with an air of forced nonchalance. "Hello, Sheriff Niblock speaking—"

"Morning, Walt. You sure sound like you're up and at it already."

"Morning, Sunshine! I was beginning to wonder if I was going to have to form a posse and head to South Carolina. You must have gotten in pretty late."

"Yeah, Walt, you might say that. Hey, how did things come out in that domestic dispute case you attended?"

"Well, we waited and waited at the courthouse, but the husband never showed up. Later on we found out that he had run away with his wife's mother."

"Hmm—very, uh, backwoods, wouldn't you say?"

"Yeah, it sure was, Jet. The funny thing is that the husband and wife are both in their sixties, so there's no telling how old her mother is—in her eighties? Nineties? Who knows?"

"Yeah, Walt, way, way in the back of the woods, my friend!"

"I'm telling you, Jet, *Love, American Style* happens within all age groups, doesn't it?"

"Yeah, I suppose it does."

"Okay, buddy, I've rattled on enough about the twisted little affairs here in Peyton Place. Don't keep me in suspense, Jet: what the hell happened yesterday down south of the border?"

Walt was all ears as Jet meticulously recounted the day's events, from Ron's pitchfork-pronged reception to the odd meeting with Mary Christmas to the calamity at the railroad bridge. At the conclusion of what most listeners would dismiss as a "tall tale," there were a few seconds of silence as if the usually gabby sheriff was trying to soak it all in.

"Man, Jet—Sorry to hear about your prize Ray. I know you love that car," Walt consoled, as if a friend or beloved pet of his friend had been injured. "So, what do you have planned for today?"

"Well, since I have no car at the moment, I suppose I'll grab a little rest."

"Hey, Jet, I could come by and pick you up—won't be any trouble at all."

"Thanks, but maybe a little later. Just give me a little time and a hot shower, and I'll feel up to joining the living."

"No problem, Jet. Talk to you later."

Jericho lay back on the bed, determined to find a little more sleep, but daylight had already bulldozed too harsh a path into his consciousness. After flailing about on the bed like a fish out of water for a half-hour, he decided to take an extremely hot shower followed by a cold rinse. The near-scalding water served as the perfect stimulant for the sleep-deprived agent and, upon exiting the shower, he once again felt invincible enough to take on the outside world.

Since he would not be interviewing anybody today, he decided to dress "Jet-casual": black shoes, black pants, black polo shirt, and black sports jacket—and, oh yes, a subtle splash of Cat's favorite cologne under his chin. Jet Jericho was ready for this nice, sunny Wednesday!

Although he still had the no-car dilemma to solve, Nolan decided this would be a good time to walk down to the motel office and make sure they were still holding Room #4 for Cat. Since the two rooms were adjacent, Cat would be snuggling up with him at night. However, for appearances' sake, Fowler would need to see charges for two rooms listed on reimbursement requests from the Icy Springs assignment. Opening his door to the warm, inviting beams of sun, Jericho's jaunt to the motel office was temporarily placed on hold by a curious sight, for parked just outside his room was a patrol car, with a red bow on the front edge of the hood and a typed note attached:

Jet, I'm off to check on an airplane lying upside down on Highway 64 down below the school. I thought you might go stir-crazy without some wheels. So here you go, courtesy of Deputy Maness! Sorry that it's a Ford. Get over it! Don't smash her up, because I'd have a lot of explaining to do to my higher-ups. Anyway, the keys will be waiting for you with the clerk in the motel lobby.

Nolan cracked his first near-smile of the day. *Wow, a car appearing like magic while I'm in the shower—now, that's what I call service! That goofball! Walt sure knows how to play the gracious host.* And sure enough, the generous sheriff had known just what the agent needed. After all, Walt was evidently going to be tied up this morning supervising some incident involving an airplane. And seeing that it would be several hours until Cat arrived, there was some time to kill.

As tempting as it was to see what was up with the airplane, Jericho decided to head in the other direction. Even though the airplane was a potentially interesting spectacle that surely didn't happen in Icy Springs every day, the agent sensed he needed to give Walt a little space to exert his abilities to command. It would be inappropriate to rush to the sheriff's side every time an emergency arose—that is, unless his friend summoned him. And, even though his friend had left a Ford—Nolan hated the way the things felt as they accelerated—he grudgingly admitted that there were probably not a whole lot of options available to Walt and was grateful for the mobility. It sure beat watching re-runs of *Andy Griffith* in the motel room.

◆ ◆ ◆ ◆ ◆

It had been a while since Jericho had traveled on Broad Street in Sharpton. It was a perfect example of "Main Street, U.S.A.," and the agent always enjoyed cruising along the unique storefronts in the picturesque town—the Heal Your Sole Shoe Repair, The Playhouse Movie Theatre, The Buck Stops Here Taxidermy, The Gem Dandy Jewelry Store, Sweet Temptations Bakery, The Pill Peddler Pharmacy, and so on. Nolan always felt a hard-to-explain sense of peace passing by these small-town businesses. And he liked the way that the town square at the intersection of Broad Street and Center Street featured the huge town clock gracing the top of the city hall, a building designed in the clean lines of Palladian architecture.

Jericho glanced respectfully at the town clock as he initiated a right turn signal and subsequently proceeded down the somewhat hilly Center Street. The Ford patrol car found itself soon parked outside the Star Pharmacy—well, to be more precise, the Star Pharmacy Grill, an annex to the huge drug store located in the Forest Heights Shopping Center. It was lunchtime, and the hungry agent had ended up at this specific location for a cheeseburger! Introduced to the site by Walt, the part-SBI agent/part-beef connoisseur had not yet bestowed the title of "Best Cheeseburger on the Planet" to the Starr Pharmacy Grill, but their version of the charcoal-grilled treasure was definitely in the running.

After satisfactorily fueling his body, Jericho still had about ninety minutes to kill before Cat's arrival. The restless agent decided that, for once, he would park along a Broad Street storefront and mess around a little. *I think that, at least for the next hour, my purpose will be to have no purpose.*

Peeking in the window of Sweet Temptations, Jericho was quite fascinated by the alluring assortment of delectables available for the enlargement of all waists. There were cakes and pastries of all shapes and sizes—Frisbee-sized cinnamon buns, cupcakes topped with all colors of icing, cookies of all flavors, cheese straws, and pies with jiggling mounds of meringue atop. Definitely, Sweet Temptations was a stylish crack house for sugar junkies. After staring through the glass for the better part of two minutes, Nolan decided that walking inside the place would indeed tempt him to engage in one indulgence too many—besides, after partaking of Miss Krenshaw's Devil's food cake the other day, any other efforts in the confectionery world would most likely pale by comparison.

Easing over to the next store window, the agent suddenly gulped as he realized where he was: The Gem Dandy Jewelry Store. While looking through the window at all the glass cases filled with rings, necklaces, and bracelets, a cold feeling suddenly grabbed the pit of Jericho's stomach. It seemed to be the kind of flu-ish feeling one gets when a bug or virus invades the body and attempts to take root, the sort of feverish sensation that makes one feel warm outside while the inside seems chilly.

Acting only on instinct, with no forethought whatsoever, Nolan entered the jewelry store, the rational part of his mind sending frantic questions to the part that seemed to be in control of the body. *What the hell am I doing? What could I possibly be looking for in this—hey! Would you look at that!*

Nolan came to a halt at the establishment's premiere showcase, the glass case positioned strategically in the exact center of the store. Already baffled by his irresistible urge to enter The Gem Dandy, the agent was now truly confounded by the magnetic attraction pulling his eyes toward the diamond rings inside the showcase. *Okay, agent, why in the world are you—wow! Look at that baby sparkle! That sure would look great on Cat's finger! Man, I tell you, that is one classy bauble!*

Suddenly, the flu-ish feeling super-intensified within Jericho. His insides now felt like ice. *No way! Jericho, you dummy! What do you think you are you doing, you sap? Remember what you told yourself earlier, that you never think clearly when it comes to Cat. Sharpton is not the time and the place for anything like this. Get a grip, Mr. Calm and Collected!*

While Nolan's eyes remained transfixed on the beautiful gem adorning its golden mount, he began breathing methodically—four short breaths in . . . and four short breaths out. After thirty seconds of continuing the breathing pattern with his eyes closed, the flu-ish feeling passed. *Okay, agent, case closed! Your insanity came, your insanity went! There'll always be plenty of time in the future to launch this crazy marriage-stuff with Cat. Yeah, Jericho, no ring today, buddy! Thank goodness! Regarding your feelings for Cat, for once logic has conquered!*

"May I help you, sir?" inquired the proprietor as he approached the confident agent.

◆ ◆ ◆ ◆ ◆

Driving back toward Icy Springs, Jericho peeked over at the little square box sitting in the middle of the seat on the passenger side of the patrol car. It was such an ordinary box, not at all like the elaborate packaging one would expect to house something like a $1,200 diamond ring. *Boy, Cat'll love this little surprise. And, it's time! I mean, it's been time! I love that cat-loving nutcase and she loves me. So, to hell with Fowler and the department and the rest of the bunch. If we lose our jobs, then I guess Cat and I can move to somewhere like Chicago. We could open up a private detective agency or something. We'll call it "The Bloodhound and the Cat." Yeah, that's what we'll do. So, to the devil with the SBI; we'll survive without 'em. But, the big question for now is: When and where do I ask her to marry me?*

Pulling back into Room #5's parking space at the Chat & Nibble, Nolan looked at his watch. *Hmm, one-thirty! Cat ought to be here pretty soon. I suppose I'd better get on inside and find a secure hiding place for my expensive little surprise.*

Inside the nicely chilled room, the agent looked all over for the best place to store his valuable commodity. If he just had his car, he could simply stash it under the extra tire in the trunk or some compartment of the vehicle. Since that was not an option, Nolan had to find a trustworthy spot somewhere in the room, a real trustworthy spot since Cat would also be using the room. Finding that certain spot would not be an easy task since Cat might be staying around the motel some while he was out investigating, further complicating the scenario because Cat was so damn NOSY! She had a homing instinct unlike that of any other creature Nolan had ever encountered. He couldn't hide it in one of the drawers of the room's little kitchenette. Cat would go through everything when preparing a snack just to see what-all the place had to offer. He was afraid to hide it in his suitcase or among any of his clothing items, for Cat tended to peruse his wardrobe and his toiletries. It was doubtful that the reason Cat surveyed the agent's belongings was merely to pick out something for her man to wear, for she fully knew the options in that department were limited. After all, the choices were either "Jet-casual" black or his suits. Nolan had figured out by now that Cat had either a strong territorial instinct to take inventory of all things regarding "man of Cat" or a suspicious tendency to ensure that his belongings were free of any trace of "all females non-Cat."

Jericho started sweating as his options for hiding the ring continued to dwindle. He couldn't even resort to the old stash-the-loot-under-the-mattress trick. As a general rule, Cat's ultra-sensitive body always detected even the tiniest lump a mattress had to offer. *Okay, Jericho, you're running out of time. There's got to be somewhere in this place that—*

Wait a minute! Nolan suddenly paused as he stared pensively at the dresser. *Aha! Got it!* Suddenly, the agent darted into the kitchenette area and, rifling through the drawers like a madman, pulled out a sharp knife. Flinging open the cabinet doors above the sink, he immediately zoned in on an open box of plastic sandwich bags. Going back to the dresser with the knife and a plastic bag, the surgeon immediately placed his hands on the patient and proceeded to operate, cutting a three-inch by three-inch square in the green rind of his prize-winning, plump watermelon. Using the knife as a wedge, the agent carefully pried out the dripping section and held it over the exposed core of the melon.

He waited for about half a minute until the drops had nearly subsided and then took a quick bite of the juicy sinews. *Mmm, man, that's good! I guess ol' Lonny Applebee knows a thing or two about raising melons after all. Now, let's see if this works . . .*

Nolan fitted the extracted slice back into the melon, sealing the hole. Grabbing a tissue, he wiped beads of juice from the seams along the cut square's perimeter. *Perfect: unless you're really looking for it, you don't notice where the melon has been cut. I think this'll work.. . .*

Taking the ring box out of his pocket, the crafty agent dropped it into the plastic sandwich bag and sealed the bag. Once again prying the square out of the watermelon, he then stuffed the bag into the melon and returned the slice to its proper place. *Jericho, ol' boy, you're a genius! Cat hates watermelon; I remember her saying so. She won't have any reason to pick up the melon and inspect it—I mean, a watermelon's a watermelon. Once again, agent, you've generated a quick and handy solution off the cuff!*

Jericho returned to the kitchenette with the watermelon, opened the door of the refrigerator and placed the melon on the lower shelf, turning it so that the portal to the treasure inside was facing the back of the refrigerator, even though the cut section didn't call attention to itself, and angling the cut section slightly upward, to prevent any unwanted leakage of juice, which might possibly arouse Cat's curiosity.

As Nolan closed the door to the fridge, he heard a car door slam just outside his room. *CAT!* Trotting by the bed, he peered through the blinds and spied his beloved Anna, his gorgeous red convertible Sting Ray, sitting in front of Room #4 next to his loaner, the patrol car. Throwing open the door to his room, he stepped outside into the brightness of the sun and smiled as he took a good look at Cat, now standing beside Anna. She was decked out in sort of a cowgirl outfit: brown cowboy hat, Western-style white shirt with short sleeves, tight blue jeans, and brown suede boots.

"Man, Cat, I would say it's a quite hot today to be wearing that, but I think it might be more appropriate to say that you look quite hot in what you're wearing. I missed you!"

She flipped her hat backwards off her head, and its strap allowed the headpiece to rest perfectly against her shoulder blades while sandwiching her beautiful, flowing hair. "I missed you, too. But, cowboy, you've got *a lot* of explaining to do."

"Yeah, yeah, I know. I'll clue you in on everything." Going up to Cat, he reached out to her and gently placed his hands on her forearms. She suddenly burst forth from his loose grasp and wrapped her arms tightly around his body, arms and all.

"Owww!" reacted Nolan, pulling away, with his left arm throbbing.

"Hmm, I stand corrected, cowboy. I think you've got a *helluva* lot of explaining to do."

"Sorry, darling, that was not an indication on my part of any lack of glee in seeing you. I had, uh, a little accident."

"Uh-huh, I'll bet it was a 'little' accident. So tell me, why was I blindsided by Fowler this morning? Why didn't you call me?"

"Well, I couldn't. I, uh, didn't get back to my motel room until after five o'clock this morning."

"Okay . . . so, once again, let me say that you *really, really,* have a lot of explaining to do."

Nolan reached into the car's back seat to grab Cat's suitcase but dropped it and froze at the sight of the other object on the seat, which had been obscured by her suitcase. It was a stuffed animal, the kind of thing Cat enjoyed collecting and the kind of thing to which the agent normally paid little attention. This one was different, however, and it sent a chill rippling through Jericho's body, for sitting in the back seat staring at him was a stuffed, white Shetland pony.

"Hey, Tiger, what's wrong with you all of a sudden?"

"Sorry, Cat, I had a terrible nightmare the other night, one in which you were wearing a wedding dress and I was in a tux."

"Well, thanks a lot, Mr. Cold Feet. That's certainly gives me a lot of hope for our future."

"No, no, I don't mean *that*. That wasn't the scary part."

"Okay, I'm all ears."

"Well, it was a crazy dream actually, nothing that really made any sense. But, in the strangest of sights, you happened to be walking toward me on the beach with, of all things, a white Shetland pony beside you. Man, what a weird coincidence! Where'd you get the pony?"

"Well, babe, where I got it wasn't so weird. When Fowler had me run some papers out to Agent James in Fayetteville, I stopped at one of those little gypsy-like portable amusement parks—you know, the type that puts a few rides and games up overnight in the parking lot of a shopping center and then is gone a week later. Anyway, you know what a sucker I am for the games. I won my little white Shetty throwing those stupid plastic rings around the tops of pop bottles. I don't have to get rid of him, do I?"

"Nah, Cat, he's fine. It just rattled me a second because of the dream."

"Let's see, now, you and me walking on a beach toward each other. Correct me if I'm wrong, but that still doesn't seem to qualify as a nightmare, at least in my book."

"Well, normally a beach dream with you in it would be a dream of ecstasy I wouldn't want to wake up from, except this one ended with you being buried beneath tons of sand from the collapsed wall of a giant sand castle, and I couldn't dig you out."

"I tell you, Tiger, Sigmund Freud could make examining your head a lifelong ambition. Anyway, don't let any dreams about me rattle you, 'cause I can keep you off balance enough in reality. I promise that you won't get rid of me as easily as falling prey to a giant sand castle. Now, let's get back to what we were discussing about you having a lot, and I mean *a lot,* of explaining to do."

"Okay, but first, let's get out of the sun. I'm very impressed that you tracked me down and deduced to park in front of Room #4, seeing that I even neglected to tell you the motel where I would be staying. How did you figure out where I was?"

"Fowler told me—you told him where you were, remember?"

"Oh, that's right," replied Nolan, slightly embarrassed.

"Anyway, who are you kidding, Nolan!? Even if Fowler hadn't told me, how many lodging options are there around Icy Springs? And, you stay at the Chat & Nibble in Room #5 every time you come here to go hunting with Walt. It doesn't take a genius, you know, although the patrol car did throw me a little."

"I suppose it did. Anyway, Kitten, we'll take your stuff into Room #4 just for, uh, storage purposes." As Nolan grabbed Cat's suitcase, she reached into the back seat and got her stuffed white Shetland pony. Then, she reached into the front seat and grabbed her six-pack of Canada Dry ginger ale.

Nolan tossed Cat's suitcase onto Room #4's bed and Cat left her Shetland pony sitting on top of it. The pair then started walking over to Nolan's unit with Cat carrying her soda, prompting him to feel a little squeamish. "Why didn't you put your ginger ale in the fridge in your room?" he nervously asked.

"I'll put it in your fridge, Ding-Dong," Cat responded. "I mean, I'm probably going to be spending the majority of my time over here, am I not?"

"You bet, darlin'. Uh, just place your soda on the top shelf of the fridge. I've got a watermelon on the bottom shelf."

Passing by the large case of barbecue sauce on the dresser, Cat glanced at Nolan with a suspicious look. "Hmm, a year's supply of barbecue sauce on your dresser and a watermelon in the fridge. This is getting more interesting every minute. Who all did you screw?—a farmer's daughter or the daughter of a guy who owns a barbecue restaurant? . . . or both?"

"Oh, Cat, quit being ridiculous!"

"Well, you haven't started your explanation yet . . ."

After placing the ginger ale in the refrigerator, Cat and Nolan sat on the edge of the bed. For the next fifteen minutes, the agent recounted his pitchfork-pronged welcome by Ron Christmas in Pelion, his visit to Mary Christmas, and his near-fatal encounter with the cement block thrown from the train bridge. Cat listened to the whole shebang, from the agent getting a ride with Lonny Applebee and having to store his beloved Polly in Bobby Bartlett's garage to the bus ride from Spartanburg to Charlotte and the taxi ride from Charlotte to his motel room.

Cat still had a quizzical look on her face. "Uh, so what about the barbecue sauce?"

"Well, I actually acquired that in a restaurant Walt took me to the night before I left for Columbia. The owner was grateful that I beat up three guys makin' a scene, and I asked him for some. I've got some plans for some of it . . ."

"Okay, Tiger, now for the big explaining! WHY didn't you call me from Spartanburg? Or when you arrived back at your room early this morning? Why didn't you clue me in?"

"Well, I was afraid that you'd tear out of Raleigh in the middle of the night, and I didn't want you driving by yourself all night. Besides, I thought Fowler might find it suspicious if you came running out to assist me without a company car. My upper arm and the rest of me were okay, I promise you, but I just felt it better that I keep you on schedule, free of worry and exhaustion. I meant to call you this morning right before you went to the office, but I guess I was so exhausted that I forgot to set the alarm clock and overslept. What happened in Fowler's office?"

"Well, as usual, he didn't tell me a darn thing about what you'd been up to. He didn't mention you had wrecked or I would have worried to death, so I guess it's good I didn't hear it from Fowler. I don't know if I could have restrained myself from reacting too emotionally to the news in front of him. He just said that you wanted me to drive your red convertible to you here in Icy Springs. He told me that you told him I had a key to your place because I water your plants anytime you are away. What is the deal with that? You wouldn't know a plant if it cross-pollinated with you!"

"Well, I had to come up with something. I mean, I couldn't have Fowler thinking you had access to my apartment without a decent reason!"

"Why the need for a reason? Why couldn't I just drive out in the normal company car that all our other agents use?"

With his eyebrows furrowed and his mouth wide open, Nolan glared at Cat in disbelief. "Cat, you've got to be kidding? Navigate in those molasses-mobiles? Arrgh!"

"It wouldn't have killed you. The great Jet Jericho doesn't always have to parade around like James Bond and bedazzle the women in his sports cars and his expensive suits!"

"Oh, Cat . . ."

"Don't 'Oh, Cat' me! If you would have at least contacted me, I could have brought out your car to you without Fowler being in the loop and him now knowing I have a key to your place."

"No, that wouldn't have worked. Give me *some* credit, Cat, at least I thought *that* much through. I promise you that Fowler would have grilled you later about why you didn't requisition a company car."

Cat's perturbed look suddenly turned into a worried look. "Well, Nolan, you just don't think. Yeah, I know you are so cool under pressure and can save the world and all that. But, when it comes to me, you go completely bananas. You act so impulsively without any rhyme or reason."

Jericho's thoughts flashed to the purchase from The Gem Dandy Jewelry Store stashed inside the watermelon chilling in the refrigerator, and he nodded in agreement. "Yeah, tell me about it. I know exactly what you mean."

"Oh, Nolan, I love you. Even though I seem to turn you into a complete idiot, I really do love you." She reached out and grabbed his head, placing it against her chest and holding him tightly.

"Same here, Cat," responded the tired agent. "I love you, too. I don't know why I react so impulsively. Like I've said, it's almost as if I'm daring the SBI and the rest of the world to keep us from being together. It's like I'm being subconsciously defiant, just wanting to get this being-caught-being-together thing over with. I'm tired of hiding for the sake of holding onto a job that offers meager payment to begin with. I mean, I put my life on the line for this state and, in return, its government tells me I can't be with the woman I love. Is that the way you want to spend the rest of our lives, Cat? Sneaking around together after hours just to steal a prohibited embrace? And walking on egg shells at the office, merely exchanging polite good mornings in the office while handing each other papers? Is that the way you want it?"

Cat released her grasp on the agent's head, allowing him to sit back up and look her in the eyes. "You know that I don't wish that for us, Tiger. But I don't know what's right anymore, for I'm as confused as you are. Just hang in there, and we'll eventually figure out something, I'm sure we will. We just have to be patient and stay cool about things."

"Speaking of cool, I know I left you unarmed and vulnerable in your meeting with Fowler? How did it go overall? Do you think he suspected anything?"

"No, not really. I mean, as usual, he did most of the talking and I just listened. Of course, I *was* surprised that he knew about me having the key to your apartment, but I held my composure as he mentioned watering your plants. I think that—for right now, anyway—Fowler's still clueless."

"I hope so. Again, I'm sorry about that bit of silliness on my part."

"That's okay, Tiger. I think sometimes that's one of the many reasons I'm attracted to you. I love it when you're vulnerable and screw up. I don't want to marry Superman. I suppose I've always fancied myself as more of a Clark Kent woman."

"Well then, come here Lois Lane. I don't believe we've yet properly kissed." Jericho gently placed his right hand on the back of Cat's head and eased his lips toward hers. The kiss was a moist, tender kiss settling into one of those comfortable this-isn't-going-to-end-in-sex kisses. It wasn't a gesture leading to "something bigger," for it *was* the something big, a kiss full of love and assurance.

"Mmm!" purred Cat at the kiss's conclusion. "Wow, Tiger, you certainly know how to get this cowgirl primed to ride the big bull."

"Same here, cowgirl—and right now, I seem to have quite a saddle horn up and going, waiting just for you. However, that will have to wait, for it's time to hit the dusty trail and take this patrol car back to the Sheriff's Office. I'm sure Walt's back by now."

"Okay, if we must, Trigger . . ."

"Again, thanks for handling everything so well with Fowler this morning."

"No problem. I will warn you though: as I was leaving the office, Fowler mentioned something about going to a greenhouse. He said he had been messing around so much with his stamp collection, that he was feeling guilty about neglecting his wife. So, he's planning to buy her a 'proboscis,' like the one you mentioned. I wonder what he'll think when he is told that he's attempting to purchase a snout of some kind."

"Well, cowgirl, that might be when you and I need to head for the hills and get out of Dodge!" Cat looked at the agent for a second with a smirk. She then let out a tiny snicker, prompting both of them to crack up.

◆ ◆ ◆ ◆ ◆

Arriving at the Sheriff's office, Nolan parked the patrol car and quickly hopped out. He waited as Cat pulled up and parked his red Sting Ray, quickly opening the door for her. As they entered the office, activating the tinkling bell over the door, the pair simultaneously let out a soft "*Ahh . . .*" when the air conditioning of the little building hit them in the face.

"Wow, Walt! I've meant to tell you that your air conditioning is as good as the Chat & Nibble's!"

"Yeah, Jet, I gotta have it on during these hot days. Be right with you, buddy—just doing a little paperwork in the heat of the day and gotta fill in this one line . . . Okaaaay, there we go!" Partially standing upwards, he came around the partition in a slightly bent position, still trying to work out the kinks in his back from sitting at his desk. Suddenly, he straightened up with a vigorous snap. "Why, Miss Cat! Lord have mercy, it's good to see you again. You certainly are a prize filly to behold after such as long absence. You're really looking good, young lady!"

"I sure am, ain't I, Sheriff!" responded Cat, without missing a beat. Upon that silly little retort, both Walt and Jericho laughed as Cat smiled seductively in an obviously joking manner.

"Okay, Walt, what's this about the upside-down airplane on Highway 64 near the school? I thought you said things were always slow around here and that nothing interesting usually happened in Icy Springs."

"Well, I stand corrected. Between the murder of Reverend Paul last week and the plane crash this morning, I'm starting to think differently. It seems that the pilot of a little Cessna airplane was flying above Icy Springs when he ran out of gas. Mr. Switzer was lining up some push mowers just outside his hardware store when he heard the sputtin'. He looked up and saw the plane circling around. Anyway, according to the pilot, he thought initially about landing in the Pages' cow pasture. But the lower he got, the more inviting the highway seemed. He didn't see any cars in either direction, so he tried to land it safely on the road. He almost made it, but it was a little rougher than he thought it would be. His plane flipped over and he landed upside-down in front of the Dagenharts' house next to the school. Man! If school had been in session, the kids would have gotten a kick out of the bus driver having to maneuver around the upside-down plane. I'm surprised you didn't come down to see it, Jet!"

"Oh, as interesting as it all sounded, I thought I would just stay out of your way, buddy."

"You wouldn't have bothered me a bit, Jet. You would have gotten a kick out of the giant anteater."

"Uh, giant anteater?" inquired a puzzled Cat, with Jet exhibiting an equally mystified gaze.

"Yeah, Miss Cat, a giant anteater. Seems that the man had actually committed a crime. He had stolen the creature from the Knoxville Zoo in Tennessee and was flying it to a private buyer. Thank goodness, the odd looking creature wasn't harmed. There's a funny story about it, though—"

"Wait a minute, Walt," interrupted Jericho. "Are you implying that so far there's been nothing funny about this story?"

"Oh, you ain't heard nothing yet, Jet. Seems the man had a jar full of big ol' African fire ants for the anteater to occasionally snack on. Well, when the plane crashed, the jar was smashed to pieces and all the ants ran amuck. The pilot couldn't get out of the plane fast enough and the anteater couldn't slurp 'em up fast enough, so some of the little varmints went up the pilot's pants. Jet, when I arrived on the scene, it was chaos! My goodness, you've never beheld such a scene as one with a man dancing around and jumping up and down with fire ants in his pants. Until this morning, I never truly understood the serious implications behind the old expression 'ants in your pants,' but, boy, I do now!"

"Okay, I give, Walt," followed Jericho with his hands up in a position of surrender. "As usual, you're right. That was indeed the funny part of the story."

"Yeah, it sure was. The biggest headache I had in this whole affair was arranging for pest control experts to arrive on the scene. You know, I didn't want Icy Springs to become the African fire ant capital of the South. To change the subject, Jet, I've thought a lot about what happened to you yesterday in South Carolina. What are you going to do from here?"

"Well, I've got two ideas: one is a little shocker strategy; the other is the good old-fashioned search warrant I mentioned to you on the phone. From the way Ron Christmas acted yesterday, he's definitely an A-lister now as far as suspects go. After the attempt on my life at the bridge, I'm convinced he's the guy—that is, being that he is the only person other than you, your deputies, and Fowler that knew I was going to be in the Spartanburg area. We definitely have enough reasonable suspicion to merit a search warrant, don't you think?"

"Definitely, Jet."

"Walt, do you think you can work with the Sheriff's Department of Lexington County in procuring a search warrant for us? I would like for you and me to pay a little visit to Ron's tomorrow. Can you go?"

"Sure thing, Jet. I'm through with court business for a while, and nothing else seems to be happening other than one little thing I've got to check on this afternoon."

"Well, let me know if you have any trouble arranging the search warrant at the local level. Fowler said that he could also pull some strings. It seems an old army buddy of his is the head of the SBI in South Carolina—quite handy, to say the least."

"Sure is, Jet. Nah, the search warrant should be a piece of cake."

Reaching into his pocket, Jericho pulled out the coin souvenir left behind near the train tracks at the trestle incident. "And while I'm at it, Walt or Cat, have either of you ever seen a coin like this?"

"No, Agent Jericho, I haven't," responded Cat in her business-like manner of concealing her relationship with the agent. "It sure is interesting, though. Look at the unusual markings on it."

"Yeah," replied Walt, scratching the back of his head a little, "looks definitely like a foreign coin of some kind."

"Yeah, that's what I'm thinking, Walt," agreed Jericho. "I tell ya, Cat, hang on to this coin. I may send you somewhere to an expert to have it checked out. Walt, does anybody know anything about coins in Sharpton or Monksville?"

"No, there was a coin shop in Sharpton, but it's long gone. The owner died several years ago. I'm bettin' the nearest coin expert these days would be somewhere in Charlotte or Winston-Salem."

"Hmm, okay. Anyway, hang on to the coin for right now, Cat. I would really like for you to accompany Walt and me to South Carolina tomorrow."

Walt's face lit up with delight. "Yee-haw, Jet, I didn't know our trip to South Carolina was going to be a pleasure trip. Why, you just made my day! Miss Cat here will certainly brighten up those long miles to Columbia."

"Don't get too excited, buddy," replied Jet. "It's still all business. Besides, Sarah wouldn't want you *too* happy to have a young female along for the ride. But of course, silly me! I forget that Sarah's probably used to that with Dreama around."

Suddenly a stone-cold trance came across Cat's face. "Dreama?" she quietly asked.

"Yeah, Miss Cat, Dreama is a new deputy on my force. However, she is probably not going to be with us much longer." Upon that pronouncement, the sheriff glanced over toward Nolan and winked slightly to remind the agent of their talk at Keaton's Chicken Parlor about dismissing Dreama.

"Anyway," said Nolan, "Let's all get some good rest this evening for the trip tomorrow."

"Sounds good to me, Jet. Hey, while we're at it, what was the little shocking strategy you were talking about earlier concerning Ron Christmas?"

"Oh, yeah! Walt, you probably have Ron's phone number sitting right on your desk, don't you?—you know, from the information Deputy Maness dug up?"

"Sure do, Jet, what about it?"

"Well . . ." continued the agent, "I think I'll give Ron a quick little call. Nothing will chill a man's soul more than to hear from the ghost of a man he supposedly killed the day before."

Grinning widely, the Sheriff nodded in agreement. "Damn right, Jet! Man, I love the way you toy with your prey. I sure learn a lot from you every time you're in town. Miss Cat, is he always this quick on his feet and in control of everything?"

Looking over at the agent, Cat had that *Yehroit!* look on her face as she was nodding in polite agreement with the Sheriff. The meeting with Fowler this morning was still sticking in her craw. In her mind at least, Jet Jericho was not always quite so cool and in control. "Yeah, he's a slick one, all right," Cat offered sarcastically while looking over at Nolan. "A real Johnny on the spot."

"Come on over to my desk, you two!" said Walt enthusiastically. "I've got to hear this for myself." As they went around the partition, Walt reached toward the corner of his desk. "Here ya go, Jet. Here's the number and there's the phone! I'll put it on the speaker mode so Cat and I can listen."

After dialing the number, Jericho waited while the phone rang eight times. In the middle of the ninth ring, a voice hesitantly answered with a rather faint "Uh, hello . . . ?"

"Yes, by any chance, is this Ron Christmas speaking?"

There was a least three seconds of silence. "Yeah, it is. Who's calling? I, uh, don't get many callers. I like my peace."

"Ron, this is Agent Jericho—you know, we met in your barn yesterday. I just wanted to thank you for the visit. You were most informative. By the way, how are the knees?"

After five seconds of silence, Ron responded with a noticeably shakier voice. "Uh, they'll do. No problem, agent. I hope you got enough information from me that we're square and you needn't trouble coming back."

"Oh, we're square. I doubt I'll being seeing you anymore, at least for the time being." Looking over at Cat and Walt, Jericho held the phone away from his mouth and whispered to them, *"At least for today, that is!"* Putting the phone back to his mouth, the agent continued. "Yeah, Ron, we're good for now. Hey, I did go and talk to your mama like I said I would. She's quite a lady and also very informative. I learned a whole bunch that I didn't know previously, so I don't think I'll have to bother her again, either."

Another four seconds of silence intervened. "Well, uh, agent, that's good, I suppose. The less you have to talk to either of us, the better off we are, right?"

"Right, Ron. Well, I'd better get on my way. I got in real late last night here in Icy Springs. I'll have to confess to you, sir, as I was leaving Spartanburg last night, I felt almost, uh, stoned! You know how lonely it can be when you're on the road. Sometimes, it's all a person can do to keep his car on the road. But, I'm back here all safe and sound. At any rate, I just wanted to thank you for the hospitality. Have a great evening!"

Yet another four seconds of silence reigned. "Okay, uh, agent—I'm glad you didn't have any trouble getting back. Good luck in finding my brother's murderer. Goodbye." And he hung up.

Upon hearing the dial tone, Walt started laughing out loud. "Boy, Jet, you were right. You'd think ol' Ron had just heard from the ghost of Caesar! He sounded scared to death. And I loved the subtle way you wove in the stuff about the accident at the bridge, definitely one of your trademark psychological tricks—you know, some of that 'I'm-just-letting-you-know-that-I-know-you-know' stuff."

"Yeah, Walt, sometimes it's the things we refrain from saying that actually say the most, that play the most havoc on the minds of those we encounter. The trembling in his voice conveyed a lot of guilt to me, as did his hesitancy in answering each question. The cogs in his mind were definitely spinning at many rpm's, trying to maintain damage control. He's guilty, all right. And, he knows that I fully know he's guilty, and he knows it by *my* choice. This was the perfect example of a cat-and-mouse ploy."

"It surely was, Agent Jericho," commented Cat. "But how does that fit in with the search of his property tomorrow?"

"Well, Cat, nervous people do stupid things. I don't think at all he'll suspect I'm coming back so soon per what I said to him just now. However, I've made him nervous enough that he might try to sweep a little dirt under the carpet in the next several days. And, if he's in the process of doing it at the moment we knock on his door, then so be it!—all the better for us, wouldn't you say?"

"Yeah, Jet, so be it!" echoed Walt. "Well, you two, I need to attend to that little task I hinted about earlier. Believe it or not, there is a black bear that has wandered down from the Brushy Mountains into Sharpton. It seems he's stuck sitting in a tree on the campus of Mitchner Community College."

"Darn, Walt! I was in Sharpton earlier today until about one o'clock, but I didn't witness any wackiness transpiring."

"Yeah, I guess you missed Gentle Ben's entrance into town by about an hour. A student saw him crawling up into the tree around two-thirty. Evidently the poor bear's terrified."

"Mercy, Sheriff," exclaimed Cat. "Between giant anteaters, African fire ants, and black bears, this county is turning into Wild Kingdom."

"Sure is, Missy! What a weird, weird time we're having. I mean, you've got Paul's death, the plane crash, and animals on the loose. Jet, would you say that Icy Springs might be becoming one of those strange regions of Earth, like that Bermuda Triangle where all those boats and planes have disappeared?"

"Oh, Icy Springs is definitely a strange little place, Walt, but not due to any of the circumstances we've experienced in the last week. I can tell you one thing for sure: Paul's death was caused by a deranged human mind, not an unnatural or paranormal force of some kind. Anyway, Walt, I'm surprised you've been sitting so calmly doing paperwork with a bear on the loose in your county."

"Well, I was just taking a thirty-minute sit-down break after coming back from the airplane scene. I had already radioed for Deputy Hodges to go to the campus with a tranquilizer gun. One shot, and Smokey should be going beddy-bye up in the tree. I'm just anxious to wander over and see what kind of progress Hodges had made. Wanna come with me?"

"Well, Walt, I know I'm beginning to sound like a broken record, but as interesting as that sounds, I think Cat and I will head on back to our rooms at the Chat & Nibble. I'm sure Cat is tired from traveling all the way from Raleigh, and I'm still feeling the effects from yesterday's activity. I'm also gonna try to catch Fowler before he leaves the office and let him know what we're up to tomorrow. Thanks, anyway, but Smokey's all yours!"

"Okey-dokey. You know me, Jet. I just wanted to offer. And while I'm thinking about it, count on me doing the driving tomorrow to Columbia so you two can rest on the way. I'll pick you up at the Chat & Nibble around ten a.m.," offered Niblock.

178

"It's a deal!" Jericho replied. Although he would much rather be driving his red convertible, the agent knew that letting Walt drive would allow his sore upper arm to recuperate a little more.

As the party of three exited the building, a patrol car suddenly pulled up beside Jericho's Sting Ray. Jericho looked at the figure slinking out of the car and dropped his chin against his chest. *Oh, Lord! Dreama! Man, was my timing off in this instance! One more minute, just one single flyin'-flippin' minute, and Cat and I would have been out of here. Damn!*

"Oh, there's Deputy Dobermann," said Walt. "I've had her up on Highway 150 in the northern part of the county checking out a possible burglary." Walking toward Dreama, Walt put on his sunglasses while addressing her. "Well, Deputy, what about it?"

"Not anything really, Sheriff. A rock thrown by the neighbor's lawn mower had shattered the couple's sliding glass door and the wife couldn't find her diamond necklace. So, they prematurely concluded that they had been burgled. On my way up there, the husband found the rock under the sofa and figured things out. While I was there, his spouse found her necklace at the last place she had left it. Anyway, after wasting my time and the county's gas, they sent me on my way with a brief apology."

Jericho happened to glance over at Cat during Dreama's report and was shocked to find his lover transfixed on Dreama with a wickedly contemptuous glare, an austere expression of an intensity that Cat had never exhibited. *Whoa! What in the world is wrong with Cat? She looks like she hates Dreama. I know Cat can be jealous, but I haven't yet mentioned Dreama's free hands under the breakfast table Monday morning. Why, she looks like she could strangle Dreama!*

"Thanks, Dreama," responded Walt. "Sorry you went all the way up to Union Hill on a wild goose chase. The way those people sounded, you would have thought they were missing everything but the kitchen sink. Whoops! Sorry, everybody, attending to business made me forget my manners. Dreama, I know you and Jet have met each other. Cat, this is Deputy Dreama Dobermann. Deputy, this is Jet's assistant from Raleigh, Miss Catherine, uh, Marshall."

With her eyes still eerily transfixed on Dreama in a zombie-like stare, Cat robotically clarified Walt's introduction with an emotionless, "Cat, they call me Cat!"

Having been preoccupied with filling Walt in on the "burglary" and then tossing a quick seductive glance toward Jet, Dreama's eyes now locked onto Cat's face for the first time upon hearing her voice. Looking for a second like she had seen an apparition of some kind, Dreama quickly adopted Cat's demeanor and facial expression with the same emotionless stare. Without an ounce of inflection in her voice, Dreama droned out, "Pleasure to meet you . . ."

Mimicking the same somber tone, Cat followed with, "Likewise, I'm sure."

For the next thirty *long* seconds, it was as if Jericho and Walt had been banished to another dimension. The two females appeared not cognizant of male presence at all. Neither Cat nor Dreama shifted her eyes away from the other, each totally maintaining her focus with a dagger-throwing stare. During this spooky mutual transfixation, each female slowly walked around the other in an approximate semi-circle without daring to look away. The entire half-minute-long event resembled a battle ritual one might witness between two chiefs of different tribes in a *National Geographic* special.

With his mouth closed and practically speaking through his teeth, Walt whispered, "*Jet, what in the hell is going on here? Have these two met before? Or is this just what two pretty, single women do when they meet?*"

"*You got me, buddy*," whispered Jericho in similar fashion. "*I've never seen Cat act like this before. I'd hate to see what's going on inside their minds right now! Walt, do you get the feeling we're at the O.K. Corral?*"

"*Big-time, Jet, big-time! Only worse . . .*"

Breaking the seemingly eternal silence, Dreama looked directly at Jet. "Where'd you dig up Annie Oakley? I thought the cowgirl look went out a century ago!"

"Dreama!! That was rude!" reprimanded Sheriff Niblock.

"That's okay, Sheriff," interjected Cat. "I always take anything with a grain of salt when it's uttered by a window mannequin from Boobs-R-Us!"

"Whoa-ho-ho, ladies!" interceded a now nervous Jericho. "Tell ya what, Walt. We'll see ya tomorrow at ten. I think it's time for us to head on out. You go on and check on your bear in the tree."

"Yeah, good idea, fella. My weatherman never called for the stormy weather that's happenin' right here. Dreama, you get on inside the office. You and me are gonna have a little talk later—maybe today, if I get back in time from checking on the bear."

"Sure thing, Sheriff!" chanted Dreama as she swung her hips around toward the building and opened the door. Before entering the office, she turned around and leaned against the door frame in a seductive pose. "'Bye now, Jet. I really enjoyed having breakfast next to you the other morning!" With that, the shapely deputy looked at Cat with a smirk and disappeared inside the building.

After Dreama was out of sight, Cat shot a lethal stare toward Jet. If Cat had been the Starship Enterprise at that moment, the speechless agent would have been obliterated by photon torpedoes. "Uh, get in the car, Cat. See ya tomorrow, Walt."

"Sure thing, Jet. . ."

CHAPTER 20

Bear Catching

The ride back to the motel was extremely awkward, to say the least. Cat seemed to still be in her fuming mode, and Jericho knew enough not to pour any water on a grease fire. As they pulled up in front of Room #5, the agent finally decided to fire the first shot. "Okay, talk! What's it all about?"

"I am not in the mood to talk right now, thank you very much!" She folded her arms defiantly as the two remained seated in the convertible.

"Well, Cat, that meeting back there between you and Deputy Dobermann had all the subtlety of an interview between two rival professional wrestlers before a big match. Don't you think you owe me an explanation?"

"Well, Mr. Snuggle-Up-At-Breakfast, I might request the same of you, mightn't I?"

"Oh, *that*! Lord, Cat, you have to know what Dreama's like. Walt can tell you that she's a promiscuous flirt, and he's about to fire her because of it. I didn't have breakfast with her alone. She, Walt, and Deputy Sanborn all met me for breakfast in the motel café on Monday morning. I didn't even know she was coming, and I definitely didn't want her sitting beside me. At any rate, I was in the middle of telling her that I had a significant other back in Raleigh—you! But I was interrupted while I was telling her, and I don't know if she got the message."

"Well, Rhett, I would say that, judging by the way Scarlett ended up leaning on the door frame staring at you wistfully, I don't think she got the message!" Nolan and Cat then made deep eye contact with each other for the first time since arriving at the Sheriff's Office. He raised his eyebrows slightly and she let out a little giggle . . . and upon that, they both started chuckling. The agent threw his right arm around Cat and pulled her tightly against him with the cheeks of their faces touching.

"I'm sorry, Nolan. I didn't mean to take it all out on you. I do feel your continual faithfulness even though I may constantly hiss around other women like some jealous hellcat."

"Works both ways, darlin'. I feel equally possessive at times, like some ram ready to butt heads with any other male ram strutting around you. Anyway, I do assure you that Dreama nauseated me from the beginning with her, shall we say, assertive personality. There's nothing about her that attracts me in the least."

"Well, that's good to hear, Tiger, 'cause you need to remember that this Cat's got claws! And you described Dreama as assertive, did you? Let me simplify things a little. She's a slut, a two-bit hussy."

"Uh, Cat, aren't those two terms mutually inclusive?"

"Sure, Tiger, they're redundant all right. However, I find it much safer to use them both in describing Dreama just in case the two words don't quite mean the same thing. I sure don't want any bad meaning being overlooked by just using one of the terms."

"Oh, Cat, you're such as nutcase! Anyway, I guess I can safely conclude that you and Dreama have encountered each other in the past. Care to share on that?"

"No, Nolan. Not right now. Perhaps later. Let's just go inside good ol' Room #5 and, uh, get more comfortable."

"You got it, Cat-Woman! Before we do that though, I'll get that quick call to Fowler out of the way."

◆ ◆ ◆ ◆ ◆

After lying in bed and holding each other for several hours in the chilled motel room, Jericho got up. "Where are you goin', Tiger?" asked Cat.

"I'll be right back. There's something I want to try." Cat enjoyed the warmth underneath the covers while watching with curiosity as Nolan walked toward the dresser. With his back toward her, she heard what sounded like the top of a box being ripped open. Turning around, the agent proudly walked toward her carrying a twelve-ounce bottle of Keaton's barbecue sauce. "Wait 'til you get a load of this stuff!"

Lying back down, he unscrewed the lid to the bottle, plugged his index finger inside the top, and tilted the bottle slightly. He retracted his index finger, which was now coated with the orange, spicy-hot juice. With a naughty look, the agent smeared the sauce across the top of his chest as if he were finger-painting. He repeated the entire sequence several times until his chest had quite a few brush strokes across it. "Okay, Cat, sample a little of this sauce."

"You're a fool, you know. I don't even care for most barbecue sauces when they are on pork, so what makes you think that—" Suddenly, there were no more words as her lips became busy mopping up the colorful liquid off the skin of Nolan's chest. "*Mmm*! Tiger, what is this stuff? Wow, it's got a slight burning sensation on the lips that's hard to describe. Pour out a little more of that junk!"

"Your wish is my command, O Cat!"

◆ ◆ ◆ ◆ ◆

At around eight o'clock the next morning, the bright sunlight illuminated the blinds just enough to awaken Jericho. He sat up with his back against the headboard and gently nudged Cat, but that did not awaken her. Her leaned over in her direction and put his lips about three inches from her head. He blew lightly into her ear and she yawned widely, opening her eyes.

"Good morning, Kitty Cat."

"Morning, Tiger, what time is it?"

"Oh, it's just after eight. I thought we'd cuddle up for about fifteen minutes and then get ready. We'll have breakfast at the motel café at around nine o'clock. We should be through in time to brush our teeth before Walt picks us up."

Cat moved her body right next to Nolan's and cuddled up in his arms as both were now propped against the headboard. Staring at the half-empty bottle of Keaton's sauce on the nightstand, a big smile of satisfaction came across the agent's face as he reminisced about Cat's antics the night before. Suddenly, Nolan began laughing with a silly chuckle and couldn't stop.

"What's up with you, silly?" asked the confused lady. "Has your foot fallen asleep or something?"

"No, I can't tell you with a straight face. You'll have to see for yourself. Go look in the mirror of the dresser."

Cat's curiosity was in overdrive. Hopping out of bed with sudden energy, she went over and gazed in the mirror. Turning around to Jericho, she once again had that photon torpedoes look in her eyes, for standing before Nolan was an orange-tinted Cat whose face would make any circus clown proud. Not only was there a dark orange ring around her mouth, an orange film was painted all over her face from cheek to cheek and running from her neck to her forehead.

"Let me say this, Mr. Have-Hot-Sauce-Will-Travel: if this stuff does not come off of my face with some mild-to-moderate scrubbing, then my scrubbing with be the last sounds you will ever hear! The next junk I'll be scrubbing off my face will be your blood."

After issuing that proclamation, Cat reached down beside the dresser and grabbed one of the agent's expensive dress shoes. With the aplomb of a baseball pitcher, she fired the shoe at Nolan. Still leaning against the headboard, he slid down as rapidly as his arched body would allow. The shoe slapped the top of the headboard with a violent smack at roughly thirty miles an hour, right at the spot where the Jericho's head had just rested. *"Whew!!"* sounded the agent with a great sigh of relief. Peeking back up at the headboard, he noticed a black scuff mark on the headboard where the heel of the shoe had made contact.

Rolling out of bed, Nolan got on his knees and put his head down upon the cool sheets. "Lord, I don't ask much, but please——I ask you, *please*—make it so that crap comes off Cat's face with a minimum of effort. Thank you for listening. Amen."

In about fifteen minutes, the bathroom door flung open and Cat reappeared. "Buddy, you owe your life to a luffa sponge and some Ivory soap. If that hadn't worked, you'd be gasping for air at this very moment. So, come here and kiss me good morning, you crazy fool!"

After they kissed, Nolan continued hugging Cat with a tremendous squeeze. *That Cat—there is <u>never</u> a dull moment with her. I don't know from minute to minute if she's going to make love to me or decapitate me. But, I sure am enjoying the rollercoaster ride.*

◆ ◆ ◆ ◆ ◆

Cat looked cute in her light blue skirt and pink blouse, walking beside the dapper-looking Jericho in his dark blue suit as they made their way down the long porch to the café. Upon entering the café, the agent pointed to a booth along the back wall. "Cat, this isn't Raleigh, and Walt's not going to be here until ten. So, let's sit all snuggly on the same side of the booth for once. I don't think we'll draw any unwanted attention."

As they sat with their hands clasped together, Jericho exclaimed, "Man, it's Thursday, isn't it? It's exactly a week ago that Paul was murdered. Seems like longer than that, given some of the things that have happened."

"I'm just glad you've survived 'em so far," shot back Cat. "You do manage to draw trouble right to you, just like a magnet."

"Well, Cat, I like to think of myself more as a flytrap."

"Oh, fiddlesticks! Sometimes I wonder who the fly is, the person you're chasing or you!"

"Excuse me, please. . ." Two hands suddenly appeared, setting water down in front of the lovebirds. Looking more pissed off than ever, Lora the waitress instructed them in a monotone, "Let me know when you are ready to order."

"Cat, let me introduce you. This is Lora the waitress, and she's a daily dose of sunshine in this establishment. Lora, this is Catherine Marshall, in from Raleigh."

"Yeah, I figured. Just let me know when you're ready to order."

"I think we're ready," Nolan replied. After taking their orders, Lora slumped off toward the kitchen with the enthusiasm of a clam.

Cat then closed her eyes. Making an interesting waving motion with her hands as if she were rubbing a crystal ball, she began speaking with a mystical-sounding voice. "Oh, Agent of Agents, Madame Cat knows all that has transpired. The first day this waitress served you, she came on to you. You humored her flirtatiousness for a couple of minutes. But you ultimately kept her at bay, evidently disappointing her by telling her about a significant other back in Raleigh."

"Man, Cat, you're good with this female psychology stuff."

Dropping the gypsy routine, Cat fired a deadpan look at the agent. "I know, and it'll serve you well to remember that!"

"Tell me, just how did you know all of that from just a thirty second interaction with Lora? I mean, she could have been just another tired and grouchy early-morning waitress."

"Well, O Master Detective, it's actually a complex composite of behavior. It's stuff like posture, physical gestures, expressions of the eyes, inflections of the voice—you know, subtle stuff."

"Amazing!"

"Not really, Tiger. Remember, there are basic differences between men and women that are inherent from early childhood. You remember the Barbie doll and G.I. Joe study that a bunch of eggheads from some university did, don't you?"

"Yeah, sure, Cat—You know, come to think of it, I do. That's the one where researchers gave some young girls G.I. Joes to play with while giving some young boys Barbie dolls to play with, right?"

"Uh-huh, but you remember what happened, don't you?"

"Yeah, vaguely. Wasn't it that boys still acted like boys and girls still acted like girls?"

"Bingo, Tiger! In the girls' sandbox, the G.I. Joes were talking to each other about how it felt to be in a war and about how they were tired of having the same ol' matching camouflage outfits from day to day. However, in the boys' sandbox, the Barbie dolls were decapitating each other."

"Uh, Cat," Nolan interrupted, "do you mean much like you nearly did to me with my own shoe a little while ago?"

"May I continue, *puh-lease?* Anyway, the boys had the Barbie dolls decapitating each other and being run over by Tonka trucks and other idiotic stuff. In other words, the boys' sandbox was going to hell in a hand basket."

"So, Cat, I guess what you're saying in your own demented way is that males spend their time physically trying to manipulate the world outside of people while females go about emotionally trying to manipulate the world inside of people."

"Yeah, Tiger, kind of. Basically, men worry about what they and other people are doing. Women worry about what they and other people are thinking or how they are feeling, and that's how I knew exactly what had happened between you and Lora the waitress. You see, I've spoken the language of women my whole life. After a while, a woman becomes an expert at knowing what is going on inside another woman's mind. But I have to admit, I sometimes have trouble reading a man's mind. It seems most of their brains are a blank slate."

"Ha, ha, ha!" intoned Nolan sarcastically. "I didn't realize I was eating breakfast with Joan Rivers." Upon that, Lora the waitress reappeared to deposit Cat's breakfast in front of the two armchair psychologists. While setting Cat's plate down, Lora stared at her momentarily. Cat sensed Lora was looking at her, but when she glanced upwards, the waitress turned her head. "Yes, Lora," exclaimed Cat dramatically. "I'm the woman from Raleigh who keeps this good-looking hunk of man unavailable."

"I was afraid of that," muttered Lora as she lumbered away. The incensed waitress continued to grumble all the way back to the kitchen.

"See there! What did I tell you? I answered the question she was pondering while she was staring at me."

"Amazing, Cat! When we get married, remind me to never introduce you to my mistress."

"Ha, ha, ha!" retaliated Cat. "So now I'm dining with Johnny Carson!"

"Uh, Cat, while I'm thinking about it, are you possibly in the mood to tell me what the deal is with you and Dreama?"

"Okay, I guess so. But remember, you asked for it!"

"Fair enough . . ."

"Well, Tiger, for one thing, I just plain don't like Dreama. Let me put it in terms you can understand, in Beacon Drive-In terms! . . . Uh, let's see . . . she's Boobs a-Plenty with Brains a-None."

"Honestly, Cat, that was nothing I didn't already know."

"Well then, stop the presses! I've got a newsflash for you that your clever-but-cute little ol' intellect probably hasn't figured out yet. Yeah, Dreama's a slut all right! . . . a hussy, well that's a given! . . . a floozy, certainly! . . . a tramp, by all means! . . . and, unfortunately . . . she's my sister!"

For the first time in his life, Jericho practically pulled a "Deputy Sanford," almost choking as the lawman had Monday morning when Dreama ordered the Polish sausage. Barely keeping his drink in his mouth, Nolan stood up and coughed a time or two, and then moved to the opposite side of the booth so he could converse more easily face-to-face with Cat during this serious moment.

"Told ya!" warbled Cat in a mischievous little singing voice. "You asked for it!"

"Wow, the eyes! That explains the eyes! I noticed when I met Dreama that her eyes had that somewhat exotic or Oriental look, like your eyes do—you know, the quality I refer to as slightly asymmetrical. Even though I swear to you here and now that I wasn't attracted to Dreama, I will have to say that I did find her eyes slightly attractive, and I guess it was because I was seeing your eyes in hers. Sorta weird, huh?"

"*PUH-lease*!! Don't you ever say again that you see anything about me in her, or I'll make sure your shoe connects to that noggin of yours the next time I hurl it."

"But wait a minute, darlin', Dreama can't be your sister. The whole time I've known you, you've only talked about the one sister you have that is eight years older than you. You said your mother ran away when you were two years old and that your father never re-married. So, how—"

"Okay, just slow down, and give me a second to explain!"

"Sorry. I'll try to keep my mouth shut, Cat."

"Don't worry about it, babe. I'd be blown away by all this if I were in your shoes. You see, Dreama's my half-sister. Mother became pregnant by a Sgt. Dobermann, who was some soldier passing through Raleigh who she met when I was about a year-and-a-half old. He was a Marine, based at Camp Lejeune in Jacksonville. Anyway, to get down to brass tacks, Mother was a lot like Dreama. She was a slut who was very attractive and she received loads of attention from men. Any and every jerk she came across who was willing to give her something more than just the time of day was an automatic one-night stand."

"Just curious, Cat—since you and Dreama have similar eye features and you say your mother was attractive—did your mother's eyes have that asymmetrical thing going on that I find so mesmerizing in you? And, don't ask me why I'm asking that. I'm not really sure that I know why."

"Don't worry, Tiger, no question is a stupid question between us. You'll always have a safe harbor with me. I mean, there's got to be total honesty on both sides, right? Anyway, to answer your question about Mother's eyes: I would say no, not really—or, at least, I don't think her eyes had what you call that 'asymmetrical quality.' I suppose the only thing quirky about Mother's eyes were that they could only focus on the part of a man's anatomy below his waistline. She was cock-eyed, I guess you might say."

"Man, Cat! I really had no idea you had that much burden on you in your childhood. I'm sorry, baby!"

"Well, Tiger, although I appreciate your love, you can ixnay the ity-pay. My older sister looked after Father and me just fine, and she taught us to live better than ever without Mother. The sad thing about it was that Father was willing to let Mother stay, even though she was pregnant with another man's baby, all just because Father's belief in family was so strong. What was even sadder was that, after Mother gave the three of us up so she could move to Jacksonville with Sgt. Dobermann and her demonic bun-in-the-oven, Mr. Military Hero sent them out on the street not long after Dreama was born. From what I understand, Mother continued whoring around from man to man to man, and I assure you that is definitely a case where the apple doesn't fall far from the tree. That's where Dreama gets her promiscuity."

"Did you ever see your mother again? And how did you come to dislike Dreama so much?"

"No, I never saw Mother again because I never wanted to, and I don't regret it one iota. However, Dreama came to live with Father and me twice in Raleigh, once for about half a year when she was fourteen and another time for about three months when she was nearly seventeen. My half-sister was like an alien in the serene world that Father and I finally shared—no, make that the serene world that Father and I had painstakingly carved out for ourselves. But then came Dreama, and with her there was constant partying, excessive drinking, and inviting sleazy men to hang around. That's right: not boys, men! It was such a painful time for Father, even though Dreama was not his child. We finally told her it was time to leave and that neither of us ever wished to see her again. So, until yesterday at the Sheriff's Office, I hadn't seen Dreama again since Father and I ejected her."

When Cat ceased talking, all Nolan could utter was "Boy, oh boy! Whew!" He stood up and moved back over to Cat's side of the booth, sitting down beside her and leaning his head over against hers. "I really love ya, Cat. I can't tell you how much my admiration and my appreciation for you grows by leaps and bounds every day."

"Well, you can show that appreciation by just keeping all of the Dreamas of the world from ruining our relationship. Now, you'd better not tell Walt or any of the guys at Raleigh about my relationship to Dreama—for now, that knowledge is for your ears only, got it?"

"Sure, Cat, sure. Uh, let's eat before our breakfast gets really cold."

With that, Nolan reached over and gave Cat the most tender of kisses. When he pulled away, they both happened to glance across the dining room and noticed that Lora the waitress was leaning against the soda machine watching them. She gently raised the index finger of her right hand to her mouth and poked it in and out several times to signify a gesture of gagging.

◆ ◆ ◆ ◆ ◆

"Are you ready, Cat?" Nolan called as he knocked on the door to Room #4. "Walt's here. Didn't you hear his horn?"

"Yeah, just about finished—" came Cat's muffled voice through the door. "Hold on!"

Cat emerged from the room, Nolan opened the back door of the Ford Bronco for her, and she slid in. Then he hopped in the front seat with Walt. Just as the two had felt it best that Cat be brushing her teeth and tending to other necessities in her own room solely for appearances' sake, so they also realized that the two of them should not ride in the back together on the way to Columbia. After all, if Cat's relationship to Nolan was merely that of a go-fer and field secretary, then this was the manner in which two SBI employees would normally ride.

Walt's smile was as exuberant as ever. "Morning, Miss Cat! Morning, Jet!" bellowed the sheriff as the two of them took their places in his vehicle. "Looks like it gonna be a good day for a daytrip. Still hot, though! Hey, Miss Cat, I don't mean to mind a lady's cosmetics, but you've got a tiny orange smudge of some kind on your right cheekbone."

Cat snatched out her compact like King Kong grabbing Fay Wray. Flipping open the mirror, she isolated the spot and immediately commenced to scrubbing it off. "Thank you, Sheriff, the lighting is not so great in those motel rooms, you know." She then fired yet another photon torpedo glance toward Nolan, as if to say, "Thanks again for the hot sauce, you moron!"

"Man, Walt, Cat and I ate breakfast together in the motel café this morning, and even I didn't notice that little smudge," said Nolan.

"Well, Jet, the prettier the young lady, the better my vision is!—of course, meaning that respectfully to you, Miss Cat . . ."

"Better be careful, Sheriff," Nolan responded slyly. "You do remember, don't you? . . . Sarah? . . . the shotgun? You'd better behave on this trip or Sarah will have you mounted on the wall of your den!"

"Hey, Jet, you know how much I love Sarah. I'm still up to my rear end in puppy love with her, but even a chained dog has to bark a little now and then."

Upon that comment, Cat started laughing to beat the band. Jericho was quite amused also, but for some reason, his thoughts quickly zoomed back to the ring in the watermelon. With a more reflective look on his face, the agent glanced sideways at his friend Walt and noted the joy on the sheriff's face. *Walt talks about being a chained dog, but he always appears to be the King of Mirth and Merriment. He just seems so at peace inside while I often wrestle with such a loneliness I can't quite explain. However, Cat always makes the loneliness go away when she's around, much like Sarah does for Walt, I suppose. I think I'm dead on target with my plans for proposing to Cat. But where? And when?*

"Hello, Earth to Jet! Earth to Jet! Come in!"

"Huh? What? Oh, uh, sorry, Walt. I was just thinking . . . uh . . . about an upcoming meeting. There's a proposal I'm in the process of putting together."

"Huh? What proposal?" asked Cat. "Fowler's not got any meetings on the calendar for the agents until the end of August."

"Forget it. Sorry I zoned out on you two."

"That's okay, fella," replied Walt. "You just scared me for a second. You're usually more alert that a naked man wrapped in barbed wire and stuffed in a phone booth with ten porcupines."

"Man, Walt, that would be rather alert!" said Jericho, bearing a grin prompted by Walt's weird analogy.

"Well, anyway," continued the sheriff, "I was about to ask you something around the time you checked into Pancake Valley for a few seconds. Passing through Charlotte, we could stop at the South 21 Drive-In for lunch. They're really famous for their fish sandwiches with tartar sauce."

"Yuck," replied Jericho without hesitation. "Why would people eat slimy creatures that swim through water when they could feast off of large, meaty, mooing animals that lumber brainlessly through pastures? The idea of eating fish is disgusting to me."

"Well," chirped Cat in an annoyed tone, "this whole conversation is disgusting to me!"

Ignoring her comment, the sheriff finally directed his unasked question to Jericho. "Jet, South 21 is also well known for their burgers. Would you like to grab a cheeseburger while we're going by there anyway?"

"Walt, ol' buddy, ol' pal, WOULD I!!"

In the back seat, Cat had begun to somewhat unconvincingly bang her head against the door, in an effort to convey her feelings about the lunch plans. "Oh, for Pete's sake, Cat!" exclaimed Nolan as he caught the tail end of her performance. "Cut the drama. You don't have the right kind of agent sitting here to critique those theatrics!"

Cat straightened back up. "You'll have to pardon my sudden loss of sanity, Sheriff. But, it's just that every time I'm out in the field with our beef-eating agent here, it's cheeseburger, cheeseburger, cheeseburger, cheeseburger! I declare, Sheriff, this man has never heard of the word 'salad.' Tell us, Agent Jericho, just how many places have you stopped at for a cheeseburger within the last week, from last Friday to today's lunch? And be honest!"

"Okay, Miss Marshall, no problem at all! There were just one or two places, I assure you. Let's see, Miss Smartie, there was Char-Grill for lunch last Friday, Johnson's in Siler City on Saturday, and, uh, The Beacon Drive-In on Tuesday. I suppose you could count the Starr Pharmacy Grill yesterday in Sharpton, and I guess one might include the South 21 Drive-In in Charlotte to which we're heading. Okay, okay, Cat—you win! Five burger places in the last week instead of one or two. Are you happy now?!!"

"Gosh, you two argue more than Sarah and me! You'd think that you two were a couple or something," noted Walt with unintentional irony. "I guess what they say is true. People do begin to act like spouses after working together for so long. So, you two cut it out!"

"Yes, sir, Sheriff," responded Cat and Nolan in sync, with each offering a salute.

"Ya see? Ya see? You're still thinking just alike. Cut it out, you two! Oh, I about forgot: I need to stop in at Ireland Memorial Hospital in Sharpton for a few minutes before we proceed to Columbia and check on Deputy Hodges. Hope you don't mind, Jet."

"No, I don't mind. Aw, man! I meant to ask you about the bear incident, Walt, but my cheeseburger-hating accomplice in the back momentarily distracted me. Isn't Hodges the one you sent to handle the bear situation? What happened?"

"Well, it all had a mighty weird outcome, one that's left my department looking not so good. I'm surprised you haven't seen it on television yet."

"I can't speak for Cat, but I didn't turn on the TV last night or this morning."

"I didn't either," responded Cat, following Nolan's cautious lead on the need for the appearance to have had separate sleeping arrangements.

"Well," continued Walt, "I spent all last night and early this morning on the phone doing some damage control with the county commissioners. They are fit to be tied! They are afraid our county is going to become the laughing-stock of our state, and they just might be right. That's why I appear so happy right now. I guess it's what they call denial. I suppose I'm glad just to be getting out of town for the day."

"WALT! For the love of—*what happened*!" Nolan firmly demanded with an impatient curiosity.

"Well, Jet, I'm glad that Hodges is okay, but right now I feel like killing him. Anyway, as you know, I had him take the tranquilizer gun to the college. All the dope had to do was shoot Gentle Ben with a dart, and when the ursine snoozer fell out of the tree, they would simply load him up and haul him back up to the Brushy Mountains, where the rascal would wake up in the woods with nothing but one heck of a hangover."

"Okay, Walt, so . . .?" prompted Jericho.

"So, I ask you—if you shot a bear in a tree with a tranquilizer dart, would you walk directly underneath him when he fell asleep?"

"I suppose a good answer to insert here would be *'no'*?" suggested Cat.

"To most intelligent humans, yes, ma'am. But it seems that after he fired the dart, Hodges thought that maybe he only grazed ol' Smokey because the bear was twitchin' and jerkin' a little and wasn't fallin' out of the tree. So, the Einstein of my force walked over to have a look-see and, before you know it, Hodges was flat on the ground with the ass of a five hundred-pound black bear covering his head."

"Poor fellow, was he hurt badly?" asked a concerned Cat.

"Let's see, there was a broken collarbone, three broken ribs, a broken right arm, and a real bad gash on the side of his face. The doctors are still checking out his back to make sure his spine is okay. Hodges was definitely a victim of the laws of physics, specifically the law of gravity. Anyway, he'll live, at least until I kill him. But for a while, I'm going to be short one deputy. Right now, they are running footage of Hodge's accident constantly during the newsbreaks of every local station. It's like a comedy, with the newscasters cracking up every time they introduce the clip. I've heard they're even beginning to show it in some foreign countries like Belgium. It's making me look like the head of the Keystone Cops. I tell ya, you two, it's been bad for me recently, what with Paul's murder, Dreama's antics, and now the bear incident. I'm gonna lose my job yet."

"No, you're not, buddy," said Jericho in his most consoling tone. "We're gonna catch Paul's killer and you'll be at the top of the charts again, I promise."

"Thanks, Jet, your confidence always has a way of making a cheeseburger taste better. I think my heart will be fully in our little stop at South 21."

"Oh, brother!" muttered Cat while rolling her eyes.

CHAPTER 21

Back in the Land of the Giant Peanut

Escorted by a patrol car from the Sheriff's Department of Lexington County, Walt turned his Bronco into the dirt drive leading into the Christmas homestead. "You know, Jet, you were right. Pelion's giant peanut isn't so giant after all. It wasn't near as big as I remembered it bein'."

"I told you, Walt. Time has a way of exaggerating the memory. Suffice it to say, it's still a big goober."

"And me without my camera!" chimed in Cat. "What a lost opportunity!"

"Why, Miss Cat," Walt said smiling, "if I didn't know any better, I would say there was a little sarcasm in that comment."

"Sheriff, I think you're getting to the point you can read Miss Marshall like a book," observed Jericho wryly.

"Hmm, just call me woman-literate, Jet. Hey, whad'ya bet ol' Ron is gonna be quite surprised to see us pullin' up?"

"Well, Walt, that's just what I'm counting on. Thanks for arranging the search warrant."

"No problem. These guys in South Carolina are really efficient. They can arrange stuff like that in the blink of an eye. Hey, I see Ron's Ford Galaxie parked between the barn and the house, so he ought to be home."

"Good deal," responded Jericho. "Walt, I want to fine-tooth-comb this property. If you would, you and the fellas in the other car search the barn, the chicken coop, and the other sheds and storage buildings. I also want his car searched thoroughly, as if you thought he was a drug czar from South America. I'll take the search warrant with me. I think that Cat and I will chat with Ron a little bit and search the house."

"You got it, Jet," said Walt as his Bronco rolled to a halt. As if synchronized, the doors on both vehicles flung open at once. Walt immediately walked over to Sheriff Gordon West and his two deputies. After chatting with

West for a few seconds, Walt started walking back toward Jericho with an envelope in his hand.

"Here you go, buddy," said Walt as he handed Jericho the search warrant. "Here's the ticket that will get you into any Ron Christmas production."

"Thanks. And Walt, be sure to check the loft in the barn thoroughly. Watch out and don't get any paint on you."

"Will do, partner!" acknowledged Walt energetically.

"Okay, Cat, time to go in. You've never actually been in on the search part of an investigation, have you?" asked Nolan.

"No, Tiger," responded Cat out of Walt's earshot, "but it's sort of exciting."

"Cool enough. So, you're not nervous?"

"Sort of, but not much. At least, I don't guess I am."

"Don't worry, Cat. Just let me do all the talking. I'll keep you right by my side. I don't think Ron will try anything with the cavalry here today. Besides, I think he found me to be quite enough on a one-on-one basis the other day."

Cat tugged gently on Jericho's sleeve, prompting him to halt just as he was about to step up on the porch. "What, Cat? What is it?"

"I'm just curious, Nolan. You've never asked me to accompany you on a search before. I'm truly not serving any purpose today. I could just have easily been in Charlotte today checking on your strange little coin. You've just acted *so* strange lately, and it's hard to put my finger on it. You zone out occasionally, and you don't seem to think some things through clearly. What's goin' on with you?"

"Nothing, Cat. Does everything have to be so black and white with you?"

"No, Nolan . . . with me, no. But with you, yes. Everything's always been black and white in that analytical mind of yours."

"Don't worry, Cat. I promise that nothing's the matter. Maybe the Icy Springs murders always creep me out a little more or something, I dunno. Anyway, I guess I asked you to come with me today because, uh, maybe I just wanted you by my side. I dunno."

"Hmm, well that was clear as mud," muttered Cat.

"Come on! Time to knock on the door." As Nolan balled his knuckles up into a fist and raised it to the screen door, the inside door suddenly opened.

"I was wondering when you were ever going to come in," stated Ron. "I saw your circus caravan pull up while I was reading. I glanced out the window and saw the two of you talking at my porch steps. What were you doing? Counting the boards on my porch? Making sure I haven't replaced a board because perhaps I'd used the original to bash my brother's head in?"

"Well, Ron, that's a idea. I might check on that while I'm here today. However, I was just telling Miss Marshall that I thought I left something in the car. Oh, and right here it is—a handy-dandy little search warrant! And don't worry yourself over whether it's within my jurisdiction on this round—save your knees. Mind if we come in and just have a little look around the place?"

"You may 'can' the search warrant, agent, and you may 'can' the cute one-liners. I'm already tired of your company, so let's just get this over with. I thought I was an informative enough host the other day."

"Well, I must say that I do learn something each time you and I get together. I learned a lot down at the bridge in Spartanburg."

"I don't know what you're talking about, agent!" responded Ron in an insistent tone.

"Miss Marshall," started Jericho in a wry tone as he turned toward Cat. "Correct me if I'm wrong, but isn't there an old saying that goes something like 'People who live in glass houses shouldn't throw concrete blocks'?'"

"I don't know, Mr. Jericho," countered Cat, playing along. "I think the one I've heard is 'People who throw concrete blocks have the shortest memories.'"

"Ahh, I think you're right, Miss Marshall!" agreed Jericho, his voice still conveying a somewhat tongue-in-cheek tone. "Concrete blocks do have a way of destroying brain cells. I damn near learned that Tuesday evening myself."

"I don't know what kind of performance you two are putting on here," insisted Ron. "But it's from a show I find very tiresome. Now, are you going to search my place or not?"

"Patience, Ron, we didn't mean to make you nervous. And, I'm sorry I didn't introduce you. This is my assistant, Catherine Marshall."

"Your state's SBI must have a good budget if they can afford to provide you agents with assistants!"

"Oh, we get by. Would you care to escort us around?" asked Jericho.

"Frankly, no, I wouldn't. I'm going to sit here and finish reading my book."

"Ah, yes, I see you're reading *Moby Dick*," noted Jericho as he spied the book lying on Ron's couch. "A story about a man on an obsessive hunt. I love those kind of stories Ron—you know, the suspenseful building toward a climax with an exciting conclusion. I would have to say that *Moby Dick* sort of parallels my hunt for the killer of your brother. Perhaps you could think of me as being sort of like the, uh, Captain Ahab of Icy Springs, you know? Do you think I fit the part of an obsessive hunter, Ron?"

"You fit the part of a pest. Get on about your business and be on your way, and don't steal anything! I want you out of here within a half-hour."

"That's magnanimous of you sir, but unnecessary, considering our warrant doesn't really specify a time limit on the search. However, we'll do our best. Cat, let's go into the kitchen first," ordered Jericho, without missing a beat. He was indeed glad Ron chose to sit on his couch and read. The agent was really starting to hate the man, and the bastard would at least be out of the way while Cat and he searched the rest of the house. There wasn't anything to search for in the sparsely furnished living room anyway. Jericho could visually detect nothing of any interest there. However, the kitchen was another matter. Nolan was extremely anxious to see the top of Ron's refrigerator. As Nolan and Cat walked into the kitchen, his eyes locked immediately upon the refrigerator.

"Damn, they're gone!" whispered Nolan. *"He's moved 'em already!"*

Cat immediately moved her body alongside the bothered agent. *"What's wrong?"* she whispered back.

"The jackass has moved them!"

"Moved what?" inquired Cat.

"The carton of Kool cigarettes on the fridge. I saw 'em the other day—and, thanks to me, he knows that I saw 'em. I just wanted to check out the tax stamps on the packages."

"What next?"

"Let's search the fridge, the cupboard, the cabinets, and the drawers thoroughly. Then, we'll move to his downstairs bedroom and bathroom. After that, we go upstairs."

After turning up nothing on the entire first floor, Nolan and Cat started walking up the stairs. True to his word, Ron remained on the couch reading *Moby Dick*, not seeming to pay his visitors any attention. Halfway up the stairs, Nolan looked down toward Ron. *Man, he seems totally relaxed—or, at least, he wants it to appear to us that he is.*

After searching several rooms upstairs, Nolan and Cat walked into the upstairs bedroom. On the dresser was a framed picture of a pretty woman, signed with the words *"To Ron. I love you, Linda."* The agent became almost paralyzed as he spied a figure on the dresser sitting across from the photograph. What he saw before him was the stuff bad dreams are made of. It was, of all things, a sock monkey!

"Tiger, what's wrong!" whispered Cat. *"You look like death warmed over. What is it?"*

"The sock monkey—" answered Nolan.

"What about it?" asked Cat. *"I'm sure it's housebroken, and it probably doesn't have rabies. I don't think Little Tiny Monkey's gonna hurt Big Bad Agent!"*

"It's not the monkey itself, Cat. It was in the dream I had the other night of you being killed by a giant, collapsing sand castle. It was on the saddle of the Shetland pony."

"Let me in on a little secret, Tiger. Just how much LSD did you take or how many gasoline fumes did you inhale before having that dream? You truly did have a bizarre ol' time during that sleep."

"Yeah, I sure did. Anyway, sorry about being creeped out by the monkey. Let's get back to the business at hand."

Being more furnished than any other room, the upstairs bedroom was apparently the bedroom in the house where Ron slept and perhaps where he spent most of his time. It took a little longer than the kitchen to search, but still not that long at all, considering that Ron had few belongings. And, as with every other room in the house—nothing!

"Hey, Cat, we're turning up zilch. I think it may be time to play a little dirty."

"What do you mean?" asked a confused Cat.

"Watch! It'll be our little secret!"

With a somewhat sneaky expression, Nolan reached into the pocket of his suit and pulled out the mysterious coin! As Cat watched with high interest, Nolan bent down and firmly wedged the coin between a crack in the floorboards. "Hey, Ron!" shouted Nolan. "Can you come up here a minute, sir?"

As the pair heard Ron trudging up the stairs, they could also hear grumbling accompanying his footsteps. He appeared with his book in his hand and leaned on the doorframe. "Yeah, what do you want? There's surely nothing up here of any interest!"

"You're right, Ron. Once again, you seem pretty clean. I just wanted to know where you got the sock monkey. Miss Marshall here collects them." As Nolan glanced in Cat's direction, he noticed the sudden amused expression on her face, as in *Really, agent? I like sock monkeys?*

"You called me upstairs for that? Why didn't you ask me that on your way out? I dunno, I got it for Linda at a store somewhere—in Ohio, I think, just before she died."

"Oh, okay. Sorry to have bothered you, Ron. I wasn't thinking. It's just that one doesn't see sock monkeys every day, and Miss Marshall was too timid to ask you."

"Yeah, yeah, I understand. Sorry I grouched at you. I think I'll just go ahead and lie down on the bed up here. The two of you can see yourself out. I told you that you wouldn't find anything interesting."

"So you did, sir," responded Jericho. "Yes, it's time we were on our way. Thank you for your hospitality."

"Yeah, sure. And make sure that bunch of clowns snooping around my property outside leaves with you," replied Ron with an irritated tone.

"Sure thing, sir. Hey! Hold on, wait a second! Miss Marshall, take a look at this! Why didn't I notice this before?" Leaning over, Jericho pried the coin he had planted out from between the floorboards and pretended to study it for the first time. "Have a gander, Miss Marshall," said the agent as he handed her the coin.

"Wow, sir, I can't say I've ever seen anything like it," Cat replied on cue. By now, Ron was sweating a little and craning his neck out as far as he could to catch a glimpse of the coin.

"Oh, I'm sorry, Ron. How rude of me!" exclaimed the agent. He held the coin out in plain view for Ron to see. "Is this *your* coin?"

"I've, uh, never seen the thing," replied a nervous-sounding Ron. "You've got to remember, agent. This house was the family homestead for decades. It could have been here for years."

"Yeah, quite possibly," agreed Jericho. "Uh, would you mind if I take it with me and have it examined? I promise that—worth anything or not—you'll get it back. You have a witness here with the presence of Miss Marshall. She can vouch for you that I said I would return it."

At that point, Ron had quite a look of consternation on his face. "Uh, sure. I guess so, agent. Yeah, take it with you. It doesn't belong to me."

"Thanks, Ron. Oh, if you need anything from us or think of anything—and I mean *anything*—that might help our investigation, please don't hesitate to give me a call. I'm staying in Icy Springs for the rest of the week. You can reach me by calling the Sheriff's Department there. Here's the number—"

"Okay, sure thing, agent."

After everyone met back at Walt's Bronco, Sheriff West and his deputies bid their adieus and left in their patrol car. "Those are some nice ol' guys, Jet," shared Walt, "but we didn't find a thing. All there was in the barn that was the least bit unusual was some spilled paint and pieces of the pitchfork you said you smashed up. The other buildings contained nothing except old feathers, moldy feed half-eaten by rats, and other artifacts from when this place operated as a farm. But, nothing at all, Jet. Sorry."

"That's okay, Walt. Cat and I didn't find anything, either. Ron had gotten rid of the Kool cigarettes on the fridge."

"*Hmm*, that's interesting, Jet. Do you really think it's because of the tax stamps? Or do you think you merely reminded him the other day that they were on top of the fridge and he needed to simply get rid of them?"

"I don't know, Walt. I really would have liked to have seen that carton. I might have overplayed my hand the other day using the carton as a way to make Ron nervous. If I hadn't done that, they maybe would have still been on top of the fridge today. At any rate, I'm still mentally processing this business with the cigarettes. Ron is complex, being not what he seems. He's clever as a fox, but I still think he's guilty and I plan on outfoxing him."

Cat then decided to jump in on the debriefing. "Even though we didn't find anything in the house, our own Agent Jericho did a slick little maneuver with the mysterious coin, although, to be honest, I really don't know what it was all about. *Or*, for that matter, how legal his little charade was."

Smiling and leaning with his back against the Bronco, Jericho proceeded to explain. "Well, Walt, the slick trick Cat's talking about is that I wedged the coin between two floorboards and pretended to find it in front of Ron. I'm pretty sure it was him that dropped it in the dirt near the railroad bridge. So, I wanted to see how he would react to it, especially when I told him I would like to take it and have it examined. A man truly having nothing to hide—that is, a man having never seen the coin before—wouldn't find it that big of a deal that I had found it and that it piqued my curiosity enough to confiscate it."

"Oh, I see now what you were doing, Ti—I mean, uh, Agent Jericho." Quickly regaining her composure after her near slip-up, Cat continued. "You're right. Up until then, Ron had been cool as a cucumber—you know, talking about how much we were bothering him and how we would find nothing and how he wanted just to read. But, the minute that coin appeared, he was a nervous Nelly, to say the least!"

"Right, Cat, I really painted him in a corner on that one. I mean, if Ron had seen the coin before, he sure wouldn't want me finding it. But, I did find it, so to speak, so he was forced to act obliged for me to take it. After all, his whole ruse up to now has been that of being a guy with nothing to hide. Yet, with all this nothing-to-hide business, the carton of cigarettes was missing on top of the fridge today. Why get rid of them so soon after my last visit, with the cigarettes having sat there for so long after he had quit smoking? Then, as the *pièce de resistance*, Ron visually appeared to be all torn up inside about the appearance of the coin and my taking it."

"Boy, you really did play dirty with the coin trick," observed Cat.

"Yeah, but all's fair in love and war," suggested Nolan. "After all, the first one who played dirty in all of this was Ron—when he killed Paul."

"Well, Mr. Strategist, it appears your ploys are all getting under his skin," Cat stated emphatically. "And guess what, Sheriff—our strategizing agent here even told Ron that he is staying in Icy Springs for the rest of the week, that he could easily be reached through your department."

"Oh-oh!" said Walt. "Sounds like some more of that crazy stuff you do in setting yourself up as a bull's eye."

"Maybe, Walt, I dunno. I just know that I had to throw a little spice in the stew at this point, because the cat-and-mouse game we've had going on up until now is starting to get a little stale. I needed to keep Ron paranoid and thinking I know more than I actually do. And, I needed to have him thinking he might now have an opportunity to seize the advantage on me. I just didn't know how much longer I could keep the game going on Ron's turf. So, I've now issued him an invitation to our turf. I hope you don't mind me potentially setting up Icy Springs as a stage for our little drama."

"Of course not, Jet. If any action does happen down our way, maybe it will distract from all the media hoopla about prying my deputy out from under the rear end of a bear."

"Yeah, that could very well be an added bonus," admitted a smiling Jericho. "At any rate, whether Ron stays put here in Pelion or whether he brings his show to Icy Springs, I do want to keep tabs on him. If you don't mind, I would like to stop at a pay phone outside of Columbia and call Fowler before he leaves the office. Maybe he can arrange for his old acquaintance in

Columbia to send one of his agents out here to keep track of Ron's comings and goings. *Or*, quite possibly, Fowler might get permission from his buddy to send out one of our guys out from Raleigh. Either way, I just feel at this point we need to put a bell on that sneaky cat for the next few days. Ron's really restless right now. If he does head to Icy Springs, there's no reason why we shouldn't get a little advance warning, eh, Walt?

"None at all, Jet. Hey, before we hit the road, I've got to take a leak. Pardon me for the vulgarity of the situation, Miss Cat. I'm gonna ease back behind the chicken coop for a second and shake the dew off my lily, then we'll head on out."

"Okay, Walt, we certainly won't leave without you."

While Walt was gone to take care of business, Cat turned toward Nolan with an extremely concerned expression on her face. "Tiger, are you sure you know what you're doing? You think of yourself as Captain Ahab. But I can't help but think of you as the mouse in your, uh, cat-and-mouse game."

"Cat, I came so close the other day at the train bridge."

"You idiot, you came close all right! You came close to getting yourself killed."

"Don't you worry about your Tiger, baby. This tiger's still on the prowl, growling better than ever!"

"Well, just make sure you don't end up as a tiger-skin rug or a souvenir head on the wall of your quarry."

"You're crazy, Cat. You know that, don't you?"

After looking around to make sure Walt was still out of sight, Nolan leaned over and kissed Cat tenderly on the lips. During their kiss, a curtain opened slightly in an upstairs window of the house. The lovers ended their kiss with a very tight hug before climbing into the Bronco. Thereupon the curtain in the window slowly eased back into its closed position.

CHAPTER 22

The Proposal

"Dammit!" mumbled a visibly frustrated Jericho as he sat back down in the front seat of Walt's Bronco. "Sorry to keep you two waiting so long. Walt, thanks anyway for stopping at the payphone."

"You don't sound too happy," said Cat from the back seat, fully aware that she was stating the obvious. "Did Director Fowler chew you out or something?"

"No, actually he was quite cooperative. The reason it took so long was that he put me on hold while he contacted the South Carolina SBI director. His old friend said that he couldn't spare any men for the next couple of days because of something big going down with some smuggling on freighter ships in Charleston. However, he gave Fowler his full blessing to send any of our agents from Raleigh to do a stakeout, and Fowler said he would only mail out one at the time being."

"Well," remarked Walt, "one's better than none, isn't it?"

"Not if that one is Ortmann!" shot back Jericho, having enunciated the name with a perturbed tone. "If Fowler was only going to send one, John Ortmann is the worst guy he could have picked!"

"Oh, don't be silly. Now who's being dramatic? John's not that bad of an agent," countered Cat.

"What's wrong with the guy, Jet?" asked Walt.

"Well, Walt, you know how aggravated you are with Deputy Hodges right now?"

"Yeah, I suppose so, but what about it?"

"Let's see how tactfully I can put this, Walt. Agent Ortmann is the bear catcher of the North Carolina SBI."

"Agent Jericho, if I may say, I think you are being a little bit over the top." suggested Cat.

"Am I, Cat? Ortmann will probably go right up to Ron's door, knock on it, and say 'Excuse me, sir, I just wanted to make sure this is the Christmas residence before I hide my car inconspicuously and set up a stakeout'. I could see him doing just that. Sleeping Beauty would be better on a stakeout than Ortmann—at least, Sleeping Beauty would stand a better chance of staying awake. Cat, I think Ortmann has fallen asleep on every stakeout he's ever been on. He could have been assigned to keep an eye on the bombing of Nagasaki and slept through it."

"Just how do you guys keep awake on those long stakeouts, Jet?" inquired Walt, the topic having stimulated his interest.

"Well, Walt, we've got agents that are great at it—you know, a little caffeine . . . cracking the window slightly for ventilation . . . adjusting the car seat slightly to where it's not too comfortable . . . and then they're good to go. Many of them are able to catnap lightly if there is no other man to alternate shifts with. For some agents, all it takes is a rustling of weeds or the sound of a car engine in the distance to snap them back to full alertness. However, John Ortmann is not one of those men. But, whatcha gonna do? The boss is the boss, so Ortmann it is!"

"Just out of curiosity, is there anything Ortmann is good at?" asked Walt.

"Well, uh . . ." began Cat. "He, uh, *hmm* . . ."

Jericho then rescued Cat, who couldn't seem to pluck an answer out of the air. "Well, Ortmann can catch a bullet better than anyone in our department. He's been shot seven times in the last two years."

"*Okaaay* . . ." responded a slightly puzzled Walt. "Sounds like another Hodges, all right. Then why does the SBI keep Ortmann on the payroll? Why not give him his walking papers?"

"It's like this, Walt—" answered Jericho. "John is the fiancé of the daughter of the Lieutenant Governor."

"Oh, gotcha!" replied Walt. "I've heard nepotism pays well in Raleigh these days."

After stopping for a quick supper in Charlotte, the tired trio wasted no time in getting back to Icy Springs. As the Bronco pulled in at the Chat & Nibble at roughly ten o'clock, Walt let out a big yawn. "Well, good fella and pretty lady, we'll see you two tomorrow. Just come on to my office when you're all sufficiently rested up and we'll talk about which direction we need to head in next as far as our investigation. Good night, y'all."

"See you tomorrow, Walt. Good evening," offered Jericho as he opened the door for Cat to step out.

"Have a good night, Sheriff," echoed Cat.

The two lovers watched as the Bronco pulled back onto Highway 64 and headed toward the sheriff's home in Icy Springs. "Okay, Cat, he's out of sight.

Slip into something comfortable, but if you would, stay in your room—number four, that is—and I'll be right over."

"Okay, whatever you say. . ." responded an unsure Cat.

Once he entered his room, Nolan walked quickly to the fridge and opened the door nervously, relieved to find that the watermelon had not mysteriously vaporized during his absence. The agent gently lifted the chilled melon and set it on the counter beside the sink, and, grabbing a knife from the drawer, he efficiently pried the pre-cut section of rind upwards and tossed it in the trash can close by. Retrieving the plastic bag from the watermelon's interior and placing it on the counter, he then lifted the once-useful melon and positioned it in the right section of the sink for temporary storage with the gaping hole face-up. Snatching the bag once again, Nolan held it under the spigot over the left section of the sink and proceeded to rinse the juice of the fruit off the plastic. After drying and opening the bag, the methodical agent then extracted its valuable prize. He opened the ring box as if it were the Lost Ark, checking it just to make sure it was as it should be.

Having changed into a black t-shirt and black jogging shorts, the barefooted agent walked to the door of Cat's room with his right hand tucked slightly behind his back and the ring box cupped inconspicuously in his palm. Knocking on the door lightly, Nolan announced himself with a moderately dynamic voice, "May I come in, Lady Cat?"

The agent smiled upon hearing Cat's firm reply, "You may enter, Squire Tiger." Peering around and slowly opening the door, Nolan's mouth fell open slightly as he found Cat lounging on the bed wearing her black lace négligée, the one she had worn at her apartment the night her cats launched their assault against him.

"What's the matter, agent? Cat got your tongue?"

"Yeah, that and more," replied Jericho.

Walking up to the edge of the bed, the agent stood there silently for a few seconds. Having anticipated that her sex-starved man would have hopped right in as if she were having a bargain sale, Cat looked up at him with a furrowed brow and crossed her arms. "Well, what are you waiting for, an engraved invitation?" inquired the lace-donned lass.

"Well, Cat, I, uh . . ."

After a few more seconds of his stuttering and stammering, Cat's impatience reached its peak. "Tiger, WHAT IS IT? I mean, you're worrying me like crazy these days. You just seem to be having trouble formulating your thoughts around me, as if you were uncomfortable with me or I were a complete stranger or something. Come on, Tiger, sit right here on the edge of the bed beside me and get it out of your system. Are you having second thoughts about our relationship? Are you wanting more emotional distance between us or something?"

"Oh, Cat, no! Oh, my dearest one, on the contrary, you couldn't be farther from the truth," assured Jericho as he looked deeply into her eyes. Sitting down beside her and still maneuvering the ring box outside of Cat's visibility, he placed his left hand on her right knee. "Cat, uh, I guess the reason I've been acting so weird or un-cool around you lately has to do with the fact that I feel *so* comfortable with you. You stand right now as the best friend I've ever had. I'm definitely not wanting more space between us. I only yearn to be closer to you with the passing of every minute. Oh, sure! I'm having second thoughts about our relationship, all right, but I'm betting it's not the kind of second thoughts you evidently think I am having."

"Tiger, I will say one thing about you," exclaimed Cat while shaking her head as if trying to clear it. "You definitely are an enigma, like one of those Oriental puzzle boxes. Just when I think I'm on the verge of figuring you out, you can manage to get so cryptic on me. So, then, you're saying you *are* having doubts about our relationship."

"Careful with what you're hearing, Cat. I never used the word 'doubts'. I said that I am having second thoughts about our relationship."

"Okay, Mr. Academia. While you're acting as a tour guide on this wonderful excursion through the world of semantics, your precious Cat here is floating way out in a sea of cluelessness on a raft looking for any land in sight."

"Sorry, Cat. Okay, then, here we go. I'll try to be a little more to the point."

"That would be nice, Tiger. I sure can't wait for the chance to shout 'Land Ho!' when I finally understand what's going on with you."

"Fair enough! Yeah Cat, I'm having second thoughts about our relationship. I'm tired of being shackled by the world into keeping our love so discreet, like we're both on some covert operation or something. There are times I want to pull my hair out because of being denied the simplest of affectionate gestures, like reaching out to hold your hand or hug you goodbye."

"I feel the same way, Nolan—trust me, I do. But, we've talked about this before. You know we would both lose our—"

"—jobs. Yeah, yeah, Cat, I know. We might lose those jobs that pay us so handsomely," snapped Nolan sarcastically.

"Hey, you're the one with two Sting Rays and a closet full of silk suits," retorted Cat in a humorous tone, in an effort to calm down her lover a wee bit.

"That's not fair, Cat. You know I realize that the cars and the clothes absorb the better part of my salary. However, if there ever comes the time I truly want a house for a family to live in and a family to go in it, the handful of carrots dangled by working at the SBI won't be sufficient anymore in holding me hostage to employment as a field agent."

"Yeah, I do know what you mean there, Tiger. I can hardly afford my apartment."

"See, that's what I mean, Cat! That's why I've been having second thoughts about the status quo. Why don't we throw caution to the wind and consolidate our living arrangements? If we lived together, then two salaries would only be paying for one apartment."

"Yeah, Nolan, but there goes that vicious circle again. If we lived together, we'd lose our jobs and couldn't even afford one apartment between the two of us."

"So, we perhaps move somewhere else, like Chicago or something. I could maybe become a private eye, you know? We could open up a private detective agency, with you as my secretary and me as the guy who kills all the bad guys. I could call it—get this—'The Bloodhound and the Cat'!"

Cat held her lips together upon hearing the proposed name, as if fighting madly to contain outrageous laughter. "Well, I must admit, love, as exciting as that sounds on the exterior, I just don't know. I'm just not as nomadic by nature as you are. I've not got the gypsy in my blood that you possess."

"Well, what if we simply came out of hiding, relationship-wise, to see if Fowler would really have the guts to let us go. I mean, right now I'm seen as the home-run hitter of the department among the agency. And I just couldn't see the boss letting you go, either. I mean, you're the face that gets everybody's day started off right in the office. The agents are all really attached to you. Fowler wouldn't want the morale of his men to start to sink any. The function you serve is extremely important, Cat. It's the exact same reason that Walt made such a big mistake in hiring Dreama. He was simply trying to boost the morale of his department with a vivacious presence, but it backfired on him. Whereas you are so efficient and valuable to the department, Dreama is *so* incompetent."

"I suppose, Nolan. I know this is gonna sound creepy, but think about it this way. Although I consider myself unavailable to other men in *my* heart, the guys at the office don't think of me as unreachable. They see me as a single, beautiful female. I don't mean to sound egotistical on this issue, but I know how men think. And, you've said yourself that you hear all their dirty fantasies about me. I am useful in the office because I'm like a live wire. I keep the sexual tension resonating because each of those guys wonders in the back of his mind 'Is today gonna be my lucky day?' So, Nolan, what if that question was already answered for them? What if the other agents realized that any chance of scoring with me was a lost cause? That the great Jet Jericho had secured the brass ring, thus squashing their dreary little fantasies? Then, my friend, the stock on this big morale you say I create at the office would greatly plummet in value."

"*Hmm*. I, uh . . . *hmm* . . . Cat, uh . . . Good lord! I can't mount any kind of argument with you. You drive me crazy! You always think about three arguments ahead of me. Why can't you women dwell in the here-and-now once in a while instead of thinking three steps ahead of us guys?"

"If we women did dwell in the here-and-now instead of anticipating the future, we'd all end up with wet rear ends sitting on commodes with raised seats. We've got to exist in the future to make up for a present full of absent-minded men."

"Well then, okay. You win on that one, Cat. All I know is that no matter how well you anticipate the future, there is never one-hundred percent certainty as to how plans will play out. Remember what John Lennon once said—"

Gulping slightly and looking somewhat sadly into Nolan's eye, Cat summoned forth the quote. "Yeah, Tiger, I do remember: '*Life is what happens while you're busy making plans.*' He *was* on the money with that one, wasn't he, Nolan?"

"Yeah, Cat, he sure was! So, maybe that explains why I've been such a fruitcake lately. I see life passing us by and us doing nothing about it. Now, I'm not sure what spurred me on into a higher gear in resolving my restlessness. Perhaps it was the terrible dream I had the other night about your death and my powerlessness to do anything about it. Frankly, I don't know. All I do know is that I took a big step yesterday before you arrived in doing something about this restlessness and powerlessness and loneliness."

"Okay, Tiger, you seem to be finally getting to 'Land Ho!', which is not an easy thing for you, I might add."

"No, Cat, it's definitely not. Anyway, close your eyes. . ."

"Okay, but what—"

"Shut up, just close 'em!"

"Yes, sir!"

Seeing that Cat had followed his command, the nervous agent eased off the bed and turned to face her while kneeling on the floor. "Okay, Lady Cat, you may open your eyes!"

"O MY GOD! Oh, Nolan, you impulsive—OH, MY! It's so beautiful. It's the most gorgeous ring I've ever seen! But, how could you afford it? I can't begin to imagine how much it must have cost."

"And that's not for you to imagine, is it?"

"Tiger, you are amazing. I can never predict what you're going to do next. I guess that's one of the reasons I find spending time with you so special. There certainly never is a dull moment with Jet Jericho in the house."

"Well, Cat, the time has come to make it even more interesting."

"What do you mean?" asked Cat slyly, even though she knew where Nolan was headed.

"All right, ladies and gentlemen, we now pause for this special cut-to-the-chase moment," announced Nolan. Looking into her eyes intensely, the agent continued, "Miss Catherine Marshall, will you do me the extreme honor of becoming my wife? I promise to make you my past, my present, and my future . . . to love you eternally, infinitely, and unequivocally . . . to love you exclusively with my heart, my mind, my body, and my soul. What do you say to my request, Catherine? Will you accept my hand in marriage?"

With her eyes ever so watery, Cat glanced away for a few seconds and then looked back at Jericho. Then, focusing her eyes intensely on her lover, she began to speak, but no audible words were forthcoming. Clearing her throat slightly, she made a second attempt. "Nolan, love, I don't know what to say. I mean, you mean the world to me, and it's nearly impossible to imagine life without you. I can honestly say that, on more than one occasion, I've fantasized about being Mrs. Nolan Jericho. Trust me, it's the stuff that dreams are made of for most women—"

"Okay, Cat, now it's your turn to cut to the chase. Is it indeed the stuff that your dreams are made of? I just need to know, will you marry me? Yes or no?"

"Well, Nolan, I, uh . . . NO! I can't!"

At this moment, Nolan began visibly shaking. After staring at the floor for what seemed an eternity of silence, he looked back into Cat's eyes. "Now, it's you that needs to do some enlightening—for apparently, you have gone far beyond second thoughts about us being together. And you said I'm being cryptic! Who's being the puzzle box now, Cat?"

"I do so love you, Nolan, more than you could ever imagine!"

"Well, then start talking, Cat, 'cause right now I'm in a lot of pain. Trust me, in the world of law enforcement, I've been shot, stabbed, and run over by a car. I've nearly been crushed to death by a steamroller, and I've been bludgeoned by lead pipes and left for dead in an alley. But, never, and I repeat, *never* have I experienced the hurt I'm now feeling. So, TALK!"

"Tiger, it's hard to talk about. It's just that I'm, uh, well . . . I'm scared!"

"About what Cat? I'll always be able to protect you. I'm conditioned and trained to beat 9,999 out of every 10,000 people easily in hand-to-hand combat. I can beat the other one out of every 10,000, but it might take me a little effort to do so."

"No, silly, it doesn't have a thing to do with your ability to *physically* protect me. I certainly have no doubts in that department!"

"Well then, Cat, it must come down to the fear of not being able to provide for ourselves. You're afraid we'll lose our jobs and starve on the street, right? Darlin', I've already told you that with our knowledge, capabilities, and experience, we could set up our own business in a larger city somewhere."

"No, Nolan, you're still way off base. That's not what scares me, either."

"Well, Cat, as you're known for saying: I'm all ears!"

"I know, Tiger! I know that you so want to understand, and I do owe you that much. It's just that you're the best friend I've ever had, my everything. And, I've always been used to everything in my life disappearing on me.

Mother may have not been much of a mother, but she was my mother before going AWOL on our family. For a while, my sister became my salvation and my guiding light until the world beckoned her and sucked her away from my side. My blessed father became my best friend after Sis left—that is, until his pancreatic cancer left me alone once again. So, Nolan, how long, huh? You tell me. How long until you're there one day and gone the next? HOW LONG, dammit?!"

By now, Cat was beginning to sob uncontrollably. She reached down to her travel box of tissues on the nightstand and grabbed several in rapid-fire succession. As Nolan reached out and touched her arm, she turned her back to him. She struggled to talk between her tears. "I'm—*sob*—so sorry, Tiger. I'm just—*sob*—not used to having somebody of any permanence—*sob*—in my life. You'd be whisked away, too—*sob*—just like all the others. I know you would."

"Catherine, my dearest Catherine, please turn around and face me. Right now, please!"

"No!—*sob*—I can't, I'm such a mess right now."

"Oh, you're a mess all right, but the kind of mess a man can't get enough of. Baby, please face me—the Tiger commands you to!"

At that, Cat let out a little giggle drenched by the wetness of her teary face. She slowly turned around, looking down at the floor. Nolan put his right index finger under her chin and gently elevated her head until their eyes met. "Cat, I'm going nowhere. No man is going to take Nolan Jericho out of your life, and certainly no woman! This Tiger is here to stay, I promise you that."

His lover's red eyes now looked so tired as she appeared to be searching deep for the words to follow such a confident promise. Evidently exhausted from expressing what was in her heavy heart, Cat slowly lay her head on the agent's strong shoulders. It wasn't but a few seconds, however, until she began sobbing again.

"Nolan, I realize another man—*sob*—or woman wouldn't take you from my life. But I've seen—*sob*—through the years what happens in the marriages of others. I've seen how the strongest bond—*sob*—between the closest of friends can deteriorate over time. So, even though—*sob*—it's not another man or woman that would take you away from me—*sob*—how long will it take until the familiarity of a long marriage—*sob*—prompts you to take yourself away from me? How long—*sob*—until you go out for one of those not-so-mythical pack of cigarettes that—*sob*—always seem to keep men from coming home?"

Still embraced in a tight hug with her head upon his shoulders, Nolan dropped his voice to a gentle and soothing tone. "Oh, Cat, that won't happen. I assure you of that. You're too important to me. You're too *interesting* to me! I love you too much. We'll always be close, you and I."

Nolan's voice, soothing and calming, had diminished Cat's sobbing, and she shifted abruptly to a stubborn, almost angry tone. "Yeah, you say that now. But I know what happens down the road! I've seen it over and over in failed marriages—especially when kids are involved. The children end up getting hurt and feeling unloved. What was once a couple of sweet-talking lovers becomes a pair of bitter enemies to the end, wading through a never-ending swamp of desperation, separation, litigation—it never stops!"

At this point, Cat's frantic mind had gone into overdrive, and the lightning tempo of her voice shifted into a gear most would call babbling. Nolan hugged her tighter in an effort to calm her state of mind, but her accelerated stream of consciousness persisted. "Yeah, Nolan, it never stops. And, there's no fairness, no fairness at all. One party always gets the short end of the stick in divorce settlements, while alimony and child support often become mad money for the other party's extravagant spending. One party goes on expensive shopping sprees for the finest clothes, buys top-of-the-line luxury cars, goes on cruises, and travels to places like New York City to see expensive Broadway plays, while the other party has to shop for clothes at thrift stores, can't afford even the cheapest of vacations, can't afford to go to the movies, and is doomed to drive used vehicles in need of repairs that are never scheduled. Yeah, I've seen stuff like that happen when marriages end, and it's not fair. I'm afraid it would happen to us! I can just feel it!" Since Cat had speedily rattled off the whole litany of litigious inequities in one breath, she inhaled voraciously at the end of her monologue.

"*Shh!*" Nolan gently whispered. "Calm down, darling—say no more. Just put your head again my chest. That's right, feel my heartbeat and just relax. . . That's my girl, Cat. Just relax."

For better than three minutes, Jericho and his temporarily off-balanced lover stood firmly in each other's grasp. The quiet of the room seemed to Nolan a blessed counterpoint to the now silenced cacophony of distress Cat had unleashed.

"*I'm so tired,*" she whimpered feebly while still keeping her head anchored to his chest.

"It's okay, Kitten, we're here together and that's all that matters for the moment."

"Nolan, I really am sorry. Your proposal was so sweet, and I didn't mean to go off on you like that. You just had to have been in my shoes growing up in such a dysfunctional marriage. Even though I was only two, the tension was always there. Sis got Father and me through the worst of the storm, but we all still had to sift through years of debris and rubbish left behind as a consequence of Mother's actions."

"I'm really sorry you experienced that, Cat. Although my parents didn't display much emotion in my presence, they still had a strong union," recollected Nolan. "So, while I can't personally know the *extent* of the hurt you went through, I do feel great pain for *what* you went through."

"I'll be okay, Nolan, I'm a big girl. It's just that Mother was such a miserable, needy woman who was so unhappy with herself. She always needed new stuff around to keep her happy—you know, new cars, new clothes, new men. I think you get the picture. And then there was her tendency to drink alcohol excessively, which I'm sure I needn't go into. From what I understand, Mother had an extremely miserable childhood and felt unwanted by her own miserable, needy mother. You see, Nolan, I come from a long line of miserable women, women with whom unsuspecting men just happen to have the misfortune of crossing paths. Father was such a loving man, but Mother used him as a whipping post, constantly criticizing him and constantly crucifying him to cleanse her own soul of the pent-up anger and other demons within her—and all the poor soul ever wanted to do was to simply make her happy."

"Your mother did indeed sound like she had her share of problems. But Cat, why are her demons yours to inherit? Why do you have to be trapped in that legacy?"

"Nolan, it's hard to explain, but I just don't want to become my Mother. I have the fear of being *that* woman who relieves her frustrations by continually sighting a good-hearted man in her crosshairs and heartlessly blasting away. I don't want to gradually push you away from me emotionally until you decide I'm not who you thought I was, and then you have to pull the plug and leave me."

"Cat, for right now, I just want you to ponder over one important difference between you and the women preceding you. For me, the most dangerous enemy is an enemy of which I am completely unaware. Ninety-nine percent of the battle is knowing who, or what, the enemy is. In your case, you have a massive head start against overcoming your fears. As opposed to these other women, you not only know who or what the enemy is, you know *why* the enemy exists—the enemy being namely this fear within you. There is no way that you could become who your Mother was, for you are armed day to day with the knowledge and will-power allowing you to keep the evil genie bottled up. Don't get me wrong, the genie will always be there. But, there is no way that the great Cat Marshall can ever become subordinate to a ghost of the past, a ghost rendered so weak by your knowledge of its very existence."

"Nolan, I . . . I've never thought about it in that way. I'm . . . I . . . don't know what to say at this point."

"How about this, Cat? Let's take a rain check on the proposal for now, okay? I was perhaps a little premature. You're the only one for me, I assure you of that. To be honest, I have questioned myself on and off about my readiness to marry you, convincing myself at times that any second doubts were probably all on my side. But, seeing as you have your own demons to slay before you're ready, you need some time and space. And that's okay. I promise you. I am here to stay, and we have all the time in the world. We'll both battle our demons together, and we'll take on the world together."

"I do love you, Nolan Jericho. I hope you know that."

"Back at you, Cat-Lady! Now, I'm just gonna keep this ring in a secure place for the time being. I vow to you one thing, for sure—when you feel equipped to answer my wishes with a 'yes', my proposal will still be in effect. But, for right now, let's just go to bed and hold each other tight."

"Thank you, Tiger . . . for understanding, that is."

"Sure thing, Kitten." Nolan knew that Cat enjoyed him referring to her as "Kitten" from time to time, but in this case, it seemed so appropriate, as the agent had just been exposed to all of her vulnerability. "You do realize, don't you, that I actually want to get around to making love to you someday in that tantalizing little négligée. You look rather babe-o-licious in it!"

Her mind having returned to its normally crystal-clear state, Cat laughed and kissed Nolan on his cheek. He was now her hero more than ever, for maybe—just maybe—the agent would remain good to his word. For once, maybe she had found a partner in love that was in it for the long haul.

"Tell you what, Cat, let's go back to my room. I think I'll sleep much better in good ol' Room #5. But I know I'll sleep best with you in my arms."

Within several minutes, Cat was nestling in Nolan's arms as the couple prepared for a night's rest. Though his proposal had not come to fruition and the ring was carefully tucked away, the agent still felt on top of the world for some strange reason. Cat still insisted that she loved him, and tomorrow would bring yet another day of their togetherness. Nolan felt an unexplainable sense of confidence rising from all the chaos. Every moment spent with Cat seemed to equip him with more knowledge about what made her tick and of those things which threatened the ticking. *Patience, Jericho, patience. The complexity of Cat will continue to unveil itself. Before long, she won't hold anything back and all of her fears will be extinguished. Just give her that time and space you promised.*

After lying in bed wide-eyed for a few minutes, Nolan suddenly heard an eerie sound in the distance. Unless it was his imagination, it was a howling sound somewhat akin to that made by wolves. "Cat, did you hear that?" asked Nolan.

"Hear what?" she responded.

"A howling sound—hold on a minute!" Immediately, Nolan popped out of bed and turned off the air conditioning unit, filling the room with complete silence. "*Listen-—*" whispered the agent urgently.

Ah-woooo . . .!

"There is it, Cat. What is it? There aren't any wolves around here."

"I don't know, Tiger. Sounds to me like some wild dogs. I think maybe you've just hopped out of bed to the sound of two dogs humping in the night," said Cat, already weary of analyzing the noise.

"It's just a different sound than any I'm used to. Well, forget it!" With that, Nolan turned the air conditioner back on and settled back down into bed.

"Hey, Cat," uttered the agent once again in the darkness. "By the way, you wouldn't want two or three slices of watermelon for a late-night snack, would you?"

"Tiger, you know I hate watermelon!"

"Oh, yeah. I nearly forgot."

"Nearly forgot? It sounds to me like you did forget."

"Okay, Cat, so I forgot! A man's entitled to simply forget once in a while, isn't he?"

"He sure is, just as much as a woman is entitled to always be right!"

"Good grief! Anyway, sweet dreams, Cat."

"Sleep tight, Tiger. . ."

CHAPTER 23

The Call

The harsh ringing of the telephone was an unwelcome intrusion into the still of the night. Nolan slid his arm gently out from under his Sleeping Beauty, hoping her sheer exhaustion was allowing her to remain dormant through the noise. The clock beside the phone indicated 3:15 a.m. and, reaching groggily toward the phone, his mind raced to predict the identity of the caller—perhaps it was Ortmann, reporting that Ron had made his move.

"*Hello—?*" intoned the dazed agent in a half-whisper to avoid waking Cat.

"Hello, Nolan Jericho, it's been quite a lengthy period of time since we last talked."

That voice! I know that voice. Wait a minute, it's— With his mind pinpointing the caller's identity, Nolan snapped to full alertness and sudden curiosity. "*I would say it's been over a half-decade since I've heard your voice, Dr. Rob—that is, if that's still your code name. The last time you called me was when you bailed me out of that crazy mess in New York City by getting the mafia off my back and arranging the SBI job for me in Raleigh.*" Jericho looked down as Cat rolled over from her back onto her right side into a curled-up fetal position.

"Oh, I'm well aware of the actions I took on your behalf. If I hadn't intervened, you would have ended up as fish food in the Hudson River. You always did have an incredible talent for making the wrong people mad."

"*Tell me about it! And I'm well aware of how you saved my life. It's just the 'why's' that I don't understand. I guess I'll never understand why you came to my rescue and why you bothered re-locating this targeted man to a friendlier environment. At any rate, I'll always be grateful to you and would shake your hand if you would make yourself more than just a voice on the phone.*"

"Your gratitude is duly noted, Nolan Jericho, but draining you of appreciation is not why I've called you."

"*Okay, Dr. Rob. Then the ball's in your court.*"

213

"Actually, I've initiated contact with you for two reasons. First, to warn you: be careful in your current investigation, for things are not always as they appear. The man you're chasing is far past the brink of insanity. He'll do anything to stop you. So, watch your back and the back of the young lady with whom you are so enchanted."

Dr. Rob's blunt warning had the subtlety of a brick being tossed through a window. *Wait just a minute!* thought Nolan in a slight state of shock. *How in the hell does he know about Cat?* The agent cleared his throat as quietly as he could before continuing. *"Hold it right there, partner! You're hitting a little too close to home right now and you owe me an explanation. Just how, and what, do you know of any young lady, huh? Tell me! What is her name? I'm guessing that, for some weird reason, you are bluffing with me on that account."*

"I owe you no explanation, Nolan Jericho. I owe you nothing. And, I *never* bluff. Just watch your back and the back of Miss Marshall! Now, the second reason I've contacted you is that I have arranged for you to have a position with the CIA in Washington if you should accept it. The opportunity is sitting there waiting for you."

Cat suddenly mumbled something in her sleep. Looking at her peaceful body, Nolan reached down and lightly stroked her arm. *"Keep talking, Dr. Rob. You've got a captive audience."*

"Quite frankly, Nolan Jericho, you've become the biggest of all fish in the minor leagues of the SBI corps. Just think of me as one that has a lot of influence on the talent scouts, so to speak, from the major leagues. Right now, thanks to me, you have the attention of the top echelon of the CIA."

"So you're saying that you can just plop me down, right smack in the middle of the CIA and, having been knighted by higher-ups within the CIA, I will have earned my right to be there? So, I will be immediately accepted, huh? Don't you think that sounds a little too good to be true? Trust me, I know you have quite a bit of pull, for you've proven that. But re-locating me to Washington with the wave of a magic wand? I don't know about that."

"I understand your lack of faith, Nolan Jericho. But what you don't know is that for the next several years, Washington is going to be quite busy mopping up after a big mess the Nixon administration has just created. Let's just say that in the huge wake of a huge upcoming scandal, the likes of which the Presidency has never seen, a good many people at the top will be left with their pants down. And, while the town of Washington is figuratively burning, I'll be able to make off like a thief in the night amidst the chaos. My ability to enact change has never been more potent than it is now, and it will only grow stronger. So, yes! I can 'plop' you, as you put it, anywhere I damn well please—anywhere, that is, except the Presidency. I wouldn't think of doing that to you. I respect you too much."

"*Well, Dr. Rob, it's not that I'm unappreciative of your mysterious campaigning behind the scenes on my behalf. But frankly, I like my minor league position, as you put it, that you arranged for me in Raleigh. At any rate, I can't give you an answer this instant. Your offer is one I'll definitely have to mull over.*"

"Fair enough, Nolan Jericho. I can comply to a degree in extending the deadline for an answer. Just keep in mind, however, that this particular opportunity may not be there next week—or the next—as the political climate is shifting as we speak. I may eventually become, let us say, distracted by having to deal with other issues, perhaps even with governments other than our own."

"*Thank you for the extension. It will be a difficult decision as I really enjoy the company of my comrades in the SBI.*"

"Your comrades should be of little concern to you at the moment, Nolan Jericho. It is a strong likelihood that the future for you and your young enchantress will involve the two of you being dismissed from the SBI. So, your job satisfaction in Raleigh may be a moot point anyway."

"*Okay, that's it! I've already asked this once. How DO you know about the young lady?*" Although he tried to keep his voice to a whisper, he could hear himself growing louder.

Click.

Damn! thought Nolan as he carefully hung up the phone. *He always seems to have the upper hand! Just who is this guy? And why does he continue to play the role of my fairy godfather? I feel like I'm living my life on the screen of someone's television, as if I'm an actor in a melodramatic teleplay unknowingly performing for someone's perverse entertainment.*

"Tiger—" uttered Cat in a phlegm-obstructed voice brought on by deep sleep in a chilled room. "I guess I was just dreaming," speculated Cat while yawning. "I thought for a second I heard whispers, and it sounded like you were hanging up the phone."

Knowing that Cat had been sleeping well and had no awareness of the length of the call, Nolan decided to spare her the baggage of Dr. Rob's mysterious job offer for the time being. In fact, Cat knew nothing of Dr. Rob's existence, for elaboration on his mysterious benefactor would be sparse as best. At any rate, now was definitely not the time, for she had gone through enough emotional trauma earlier on regarding her fears of commitment to marriage. She simply didn't need any more drama to deal with at the moment.

"You didn't imagine things, darlin'. It was just a wrong number. At first I thought it might be Ortmann, but it wasn't. I was afraid the ringing of the phone might have awakened you. Anyway, that was me you heard whispering and I hung up the phone as gently as I could. Sorry, Kitten, you were sleeping so soundly. I hate that you were disturbed when you were sleeping so peacefully."

"That's okay, Tiger," Cat reassured through her yawn. "I'll be back out like a light before you know it. Just keep holding me, okay?"

"Sure thing, darlin'. Love ya."

"Love you, too . . ."

As he held his precious Sleeping Beauty once again, Nolan's eyes remain fixed on her beautiful face, bathed in a slight glow from the neon light invading the room. Not until she was fully asleep did the agent take his eyes from her. Staring at the ceiling, his thoughts immediately centered around Dr. Rob's offer to join the CIA in Washington. *Is this something I would want? Would Cat be willing to go with me? Is it a move to which she would be willing to make a commitment? Or, is Dr. Rob right? Is getting out of town something about which we both will have little choice? Is Fowler close to figuring things out? And would he dismiss us if he did put things together? So many questions, too many questions. I just wish I had some answers. Help! Anybody! Land Ho?*

Chapter 24

It's Not Nice to Fool Father Nature . . .

After Cat had made a mid-morning dash over to Room #4 to get ready, Nolan took a hot, hot shower—and it felt so good. For the first time since being tagged by the concrete block on Tuesday evening, his left upper arm seemed to be nearly free of the intensely pulsating soreness which had been plaguing him. There was just something about extremely hot water which seemed to serve as a miracle cure for the agent. Upon waking at 9:30, Cat had suggested a little frolic in the shower together, and normally Jericho would have been "all systems go!" with enthusiasm for a plan like that. But he felt it incumbent upon himself to warn Cat that this was just one of those days he simply had to up the Fahrenheit for his body's sake, and he knew that his lover could never begin to set foot in near-scalding water.

Although sex with Cat was the best physical sensation the agent had ever experienced, the extremely hot shower ran a close second. Actually, the hot shower probably tied in a dead heat with Miss Krenshaw's Devil's food cake and Mr. Keaton's hot sauce. Nonetheless, Nolan felt completely at one with his now-relaxed, totally soothed body. It was indeed a good day to wear his loose-fitting "Jet-casual" apparel of a black t-shirt, black pants, and a black sports jacket.

When he knocked on Cat's door, she bellowed, "Come on in, Tiger!" He was surprised to find the door unlocked, and, as he entered, he beheld his lady fair spritzing her favorite perfume. Looking svelte in a pair of tight designer jeans, a crisp, white seersucker over-blouse, cinched at the waist with a wide red belt, and suede boots, she blew a kiss to him from across the room.

"Better be careful there, hadn't you?" cautioned the agent in a tongue-in-cheek tone. "How did you know it was me rapping on your door?"

"Well, now, let me see, genius. You tell me, as you're about to hop in the shower at 9:45, that your shower should last roughly seventeen minutes. And after that, you would take roughly seven minutes to get dressed and should be at my room at roughly 10:09, 10:10 at the latest. Now, I realize you don't even begin to see the irony of using the word 'roughly' with precise measurements of time like 'seventeen minutes,' 'seven minutes,' and '10:09'—nevertheless, that's beside the point. Anyway, Mr. Precise, as I'm getting dressed, I hear knocking at my door. I look over at the clock on the nightstand and the time is 10:09. Now, I realize that I don't possess the brilliant powers of deduction that you exhibit, Nolan Jericho. But, just who the hell else would I speculate is knocking on my door at precisely 10:09? Oh, pardon me! I almost forgot: I meant '10:09, 10:10 at the latest'? Huh, Aristotle? I ask you, who else would be at my door at 10:09—Marlon Brando?"

By the time Cat's mock tirade had ended, Jericho had eased over to her and put his arms around her waist. He planted a passionately kiss squarely on her lips. As he pulled away, Cat's demeanor transformed into a near swoon. "Wow!" she exclaimed. "Thank God it wasn't Marlon Brando! I'd rather have a kiss like yours as opposed to a grapefruit being shoved in my face."

"Uh, Cat, I think perhaps you're thinking of James Cagney regarding the famous cinematic example of amusing things one can do with fruit."

"Yeah, that's right. Cagney shoved the grapefruit in the face of Mae West, I remember now."

"Uh, Cat, the somewhat-forgotten actress was a woman named Mae Clarke, not Mae West."

"All right, already! I'm hungry! It's way past time for breakfast, *you dirty rat*—" indicated Cat, with the poorest of Jimmy Cagney imitations as she strutted out the door.

"Oh, brother! I think I'll order some grapefruit this morning," mumbled Nolan as he pulled the door to her room closed.

The motel café seemed more crowded than usual, perhaps because it was a Friday. Fortunately, the pair were still able to secure a booth in the area which the agent preferred. Nolan always found himself gravitating to the sections of restaurants which were not in the central path of traffic. He didn't like being in the middle of the hubbub and, by sitting off to the side, he found he could maintain a richer assessment of all comers and goers.

"Oh, dear," sighed Nolan in feigned disappointment. "I don't see Lora the waitress. She must not be working this morning."

"How sad!" shot back Cat. "And I was just beginning to master the art of keeping my food down while watching her fawn all over you. There's definitely going to be little challenge toward eating my breakfast this morning!"

"Although you reek of jealousy, my love, I must say that I totally agree with you. I'm actually looking forward to savoring my food this morning without Lora's leers. Cat, take a look over there! Who's the goon?"

"I don't know, Tiger. If he's waiting on tables, he has got to be the biggest waiter I've ever seen!" responded Cat in amazement.

"Damn right! He reminds me of a Sherman tank!" said Nolan, trying to size up the object of their sudden curiosity. Standing at a table located diagonally across the room was a HUGE man holding a pen and a pad for taking orders. Every bit of six feet and eight inches tall, the waiter was definitely no basketball player. There was nothing slender about him. He was built like a brick wall—and all muscle, with not an ounce of fat.

"*How much would you estimate that moo-cow weighs?*" whispered Cat.

"*I don't know,*" responded Nolan with equal discretion. "*I would say three-hundred and fifty, maybe even four hundred pounds. All I know is, the only way they would allow that guy passage through Panama is if he used the Canal. He's built like an oil freighter.*"

"*Hold on there, Tiger, your description gets bigger as you go along. A few seconds ago he was only a Sherman tank. Nolan, look! What in the heck is he doing?*"

As the curious pair continued to eye the man-monster, the gigantic waiter, apparently in response to a request from a diner who had flagged him down, suddenly stood on one leg and started jumping up and down. Then, he slowly began turning his body in a circle while continuing to hop on the one leg. As he hopped and turned, the behemoth also extended his elbows in the mimicry of chicken, flapping his "wings" in an up-and-down motion. He quickly came to a stop and then began walking toward Nolan and Cat.

"*Oh dear, Tiger, here he comes. I think he's snapped. If he tries to kill us, how quickly can you take him down?*"

"*I'm studying on it, Cat. One lightning jab to the solar plexus should bring down Goliath.*"

"*Okay. Good luck, David. I'm closing my eyes. Let me know when you're done.*"

When the hulking juggernaut came to a halt at the table of the apprehensive pair, Nolan found he had to tilt his head all the way back to look the waiter in the face. "Can I take your order, sir? . . . ma'am?" boomed a gargantuan voice, well matching the body generating it.

"Uh, I think I'll have the Western omelet—that is, if you don't mind, sir?" responded Cat in an unsure voice, basically asking the waiter's permission to pursue her choice. "And, uh, some coffee with cream and sugar?"

"Very well, ma'am. And you, sir?"

"If you would, bring me a coffee, also with cream and sugar. And, I think I'll also have an omelet. However, I would like you to ask the cook to create a meat lover's omelet for me. I don't see one on the menu. Just have him dice up some ham, sausage, and crisp bacon strips, and add plenty of cheese. That would get my day started off right, good fellow!"

"Sure thing, little fella. I'll be right back with coffee in a few seconds."

As the juggernaut of a man lumbered off, the two immediately began re-assessing their situation. "He seems gentle enough," observed Cat. "I don't think you'll have to resort to bopping him in the solar flexus, uh, little fella."

"*Plexus,* Cat—solar plexus!" Nolan responded in correction. Ignoring her "little fella" jab, the agent continued. "No, he actually seems like a rather nice guy. I wonder if he'll do his chicken dance for us."

The man soon re-appeared at the table with two cups and a pitcher. His huge right hand gently caressed the pitcher, maneuvering it carefully enough to fill the cups without spilling a drop.

"There you go, folks, and the food should be right up."

Nolan took the lead. "Uh, sir, where is Lora today? She's the one who I've seen waiting tables all week."

"She works Sunday through Thursday. I'm a part-time worker on weekends."

"I'm dying of curiosity—after all, you're a rather, uh, stout fellow. What do you do the rest of the week?"

"I work quite a bit, having a wife and three kids. Monday through Thursday, I work part-time as a doughnut delivery man for Krispy Kreme Doughnuts—you know, those vans with the green colors you see going up and down the highway?"

"Certainly do," responded Cat. "I've always had the desire to hijack one."

"Well, I drive one of those. I deliver doughnuts to area grocery stores and restaurants. I don't really see my family much, due to my night job. At nights, I am a professional wrestler for a regional wrestling alliance based in Morganton known as the F.W.A., the Foothills Wrestling Alliance. I'm proud to say that I am the world champion."

"Wow! World champion, huh?" Nolan exclaimed. "You certainly look the part. What is your, uh, professional name."

"My real name is Rick Hunter. In the ring, I go by Rick 'Father Nature' Hunter."

"One more thing, Mr., uh, Nature," said Cat with a hesitant-sounding tone. "We couldn't help but notice the dance that you did at that guy's table over there. What was that all about?"

"Oh, that. For the last two Fridays, that guy has come in here and ordered our pancake special—you know, you pay for a full plate of pancakes and then get another plate of pancakes free. Unfortunately, this guy always takes advantage of the system. He thinks I'm dumb as a brick. After his second plate, he'll wait just long enough and order yet another plate. But he'll claim it's just his second, saying that I got mixed up. I have no proof that it is actually his third helping, and the cook's too busy to keep up with all the plates of pancakes he's sent out. So today, I did that little chicken dance in front of that pancake-stealing con artist, telling him that this is a little dance our staff now does when someone orders a free re-fill of pancakes. Now, I *dare* him to say he hasn't already ordered his re-fill and that I didn't stand there in front of him doing something as memorable as that."

"Clever, my man, clever!" noted Nolan with a grin. "I seriously doubt that he will attempt to, uh, beat the ol' pancake system today."

"Anyway, folks, nice talking to you—your breakfast should be ready by now."

As the mammoth walked away to retrieve the omelets, Nolan and Cat looked at each other while keeping their lips closed as tightly as possibly to avoid cracking up, but they were only half-successful.

Somewhat snickering, Cat shook her head in disbelief. "Why doesn't the restaurant owner just use an odd-colored plate or a plate with a number on it or something to keep track of pancake re-fills? Why doesn't Father Nature simply mark it down on his pad? I mean, come on—a chicken dance? You've got to be kidding!"

"Well, I must say, at least he came up with something that the customer couldn't argue with—or, for his own good, *shouldn't* argue with," remarked Nolan. "Cat, I declare, to me, it would take a mighty gutsy customer to try and pull a fast one on Father Nature. I'd be afraid that instead of cheating him out of a third order of pancakes, I'd end up *as* a pancake! That customer must be a daredevil. After all, it's not nice to fool Father Nature."

The pair of diners immediately silenced themselves as Father Nature re-appeared and set their plates down. "Have a nice day, folks. Let me know if you need anything."

"Thank you, sir," responded Nolan. "And you have a good day, also!"

"Well, I'll have to say," continued Cat when Father Nature had retreated, "whatever the food ends up tasting like, this was certainly a most interesting meal. It's not every day that one meets a part-time waiter/part-time doughnut delivery man/part-time world champion wrestler."

"No, he definitely is a character," agreed Nolan.

"Yeah, Tiger, but at least he didn't come on to you like Lora the waitress. That would have definitely been interesting, you sexy dynamo, you!"

"Cat, you are, without a doubt, a pure-t, one-hundred percent, certifiable lunatic!"

"I know, lover, I know. However, I must remind you: who was it that came up with the idea to hide an expensive diamond ring in a watermelon?" Cat asked with a grin while looking in the agent's eyes lovingly.

"Point taken," Nolan wryly observed. "You win. yet again!"

❖ ❖ ❖ ❖ ❖

Nolan was always in heaven riding along in his Sting Ray convertible with Cat in the passenger seat. It was a complete turn-on, as she looked *so* sexy with her long, flowing hair blowing wildly in the wind. He especially enjoyed the way her brown locks periodically teased her face and watching as she casually brushed them aside with the swipe of a hand. But these such excursions always ended exactly the same: out came the hair brush!

After pulling up at the Sheriff's Office and putting Anna in park, Nolan waited patiently as the Cat-Woman prepared herself for all comers using his rear-view mirror. Having perfected her hair and triple-checked for lipstick smudges, she sat back and glanced over at Nolan. "Are you ready?" asked Nolan in a somewhat smart-alecky tone.

"Well, it wouldn't take me so long if a sunny joyride for you wasn't whisking me along in a wind tunnel. I think you derive quite a bit of pleasure seeing me struggle over here in an effort to remain lookin' so damn good."

"Yeah, that you do!" reciprocated Nolan. "And sure enough, I do have much fun at your windblown expense. Okay, let's get in there and see if anything has happened, but I doubt it has. Walt was supposed to contact me at the motel if he heard anything about Ron Christmas."

"Just who is John Ortmann supposed to contact if Ron makes a move?" asked Cat.

"I'm sure that Fowler provided Ortmann with the number to the Sheriff's Office here and the number to the Chat & Nibble. I told the owner of the motel that I would be out for the remainder of the day, and I requested that he personally screen any calls. If Ortmann contacts the motel for any reason, the owner has been instructed to tell John that I'm out and to contact the Sheriff's Office. And, just for the sake of thoroughness, I asked the owner if he would also give the Sheriff's Office a quick ring himself to apprise us that Ortmann had called the motel. You see, I don't want anything at all falling through the cracks merely because Ortmann wasn't able to reach somebody."

"Understood," answered Cat.

After the bell on the door finished its annoying ringing, Nolan and Cat were surprised to find nobody in the office. "Anybody home?" called Nolan. "Walt?" hollered out the agent, pretty sure that no one was behind the partitions. It was *too* quiet.

Suddenly, the sound of a commode flushing shattered the silence; then came the sound of running water, followed by the snap of a paper towel being pulled from a dispenser. The door to a little room in the back opened and out came Walt. "Oh, hey, you two. Sorry, just taking care of some dirty business with this upset stomach."

"For a few seconds, we didn't know if anybody was home," said Nolan.

"Yeah, it's hard for me to hear that stupid bell when I'm, uh, engaged. Sanford's in Winston-Salem attending a training event in my place. The state feels it has to re-train law professionals every few years in making sure we know how to properly supervise school crosswalks. Every sheriff's department in the state is required to send a representative to the training. But, as typical with bureaucratic decisions, what doesn't make sense is that we have no school crosswalks in the rural parts of this county. Oh, there are a few crosswalks in Sharpton, but the city police handle those, being in their jurisdiction. Go figure!"

"I know, of course, that Hodges is still recuperating from his little bear episode," stated Nolan. "Where are Maness and Dobermann? Per chance, you haven't dismissed Dobermann yet, have you?"

"Well, Maness is assisting with a funeral procession on the other side of the county. Dobermann? No, I haven't had the emotional where-with-all to give her the ax just yet. So, I sent her on some menial busy-work kind of duties out and about. She's only working a few hours anyway this morning, as she has her weekly night patrol this evening. I figured after the way Miss Cat here and Dreama, uh, hit it off the other day, it would be best to avoid any catfights—if you'll pardon the pun, Miss Cat."

"Wise decision, Sheriff," agreed Jericho. "As they say, 'Hell hath no fury . . .' when it comes to the rage of women." The agent knew that Walt was dying inside to know what was up between Cat and Dreama. Nolan hated to keep his good friend in the dark, but he had promised Cat that he wouldn't let anyone else know for now that she and Dreama were half-sisters.

"Hey, you two, would you like to hear a good joke?"

"Sure, Walt," responded Jet politely as Cat shrugged her shoulders, perhaps indicating she wasn't sure of exactly what she was approving.

"Okay, it seems that Mother Superior was trying to spruce up the ol' convent. She called two nuns into her office and said, 'Listen, you two, I'm completely renovating my office during the next several days. I'm having everything changed, with new curtains, new furniture, new carpet, a paint job—you know, the works! I would like for you two to please paint the walls white today while I go into town for some supplies. The paint and equipment are over there in the corner.' After she left, one nun looked at the other and said, 'Hey, if we paint this office while clothed, we will get paint all over our habits, and then Mother Superior will pitch a fit. So, let's lock the doors and paint the office with our clothes off. We'll keep our clothes paint-free and no one will be the wiser.' The other nun said, 'Sounds good to me!' So, in the middle of their painting, they hear a knock at the door. Looking at each other nervously, one nun hollers out, 'Uh, who is it?' A voice on the other side of the door hollers back, 'Blind man!' The other nun says, 'Oh, it's a local beggar, one of the blind men who solicits money on our street. Open the door and hand him a few dollars. It won't matter since he can't see us.' The nun follows her colleague's suggestion and walks over to the door, flinging it wide open. The man at the door stares in amazement with his mouth dropped open wide. 'I'm, uh, the blind man. Where do you want me to hang these blinds?'"

At Walt's jolting punch line, Cat started giggling while Nolan cracked a slight smile. "*That* one was actually quite funny, Walt. Where did you hear it?" asked Nolan, with his smile now withdrawn.

"Aw, I heard it from Hamburger Sam," replied Walt.

"Uh, Hamburger Sam?" inquired Cat.

"Yeah, he lives over on Turkey Farm Road. His house is right at the top of Cigar Hill next to ol' Cigar Johnson's place," clarified the sheriff.

"Hey, Walt, while I'm thinking about it, I need to ask you something. Last night I could have sworn I heard wolves howling in the distance. Do you know what it could have been? Cat also heard it from, uh, her room."

"Yeah," acknowledged Cat. "But I told Marlon Perkins here that it was probably two dogs gettin' it on in the neighborhood."

"Well, you're both probably right—and, you're both probably wrong. Jet, you're right in that the sound was likely made by wild animals, and Miss Cat, you're probably not far off base in your assessment that there might have been some mating going on. However, I doubt the two of you heard wolves or wild dogs."

"What then, Walt?" asked Jericho with an extremely puzzled expression.

"Coyotes!" bluntly responded Walt.

"Coyotes!?" exclaimed Nolan and Cat simultaneously, as if neither could believe his or her ears.

"Yeah, coyotes," verified Walt with a somber expression on his face.

"But there aren't any coyotes in North Carolina. They aren't indigenous to this part of the country," argued Nolan from his knowledge of zoology and geography.

"Well, there's a story there, and it's slowly becoming a big problem around these parts. About three years ago, a rich doctor with way, way more money than sense imported some coyotes from Wyoming or Montana or somewhere. It seems that he wanted to begin a simulated ranch of some sort at the base of the foothills here in our county. Well, before any of us could do anything about it, the dum-dum accidentally allowed some of the coyotes to escape since he did not have them adequately contained. The varmints shouldn't have been brought to North Carolina to begin with. Now the coyotes are doing the two things that coyotes do best: breeding and eating anything they can get a hold of. Farmers are losing livestock and poultry, and villagers are losing family pets such as cats and dogs. The citizens are in an uproar over the doctor's ignorance and carelessness."

"Man! I never knew Icy Springs had coyotes running loose," replied the amazed agent.

"Yeah, sorry I neglected to mention it. You'd think I would have, seeing as we've been hunting together. Anyway, people are even a little nervous to let their kids swing in the back yard, especially as darkness comes on. So the next time you and me go hunting down at the old Yates place, we'd better keep our eyes out. It's no longer just deer and wild turkeys that are out there."

"Wow," responded Cat. "Who would have known that this sleepy little village had a problem with night predators?"

"Well, actually, it has had a problem with another night predator: specifically, one named Ron Christmas!" clarified Nolan. "So, getting back to the business at hand, I suppose you've heard nothing from anybody, eh, Walt? Nobody has called me at the motel."

"Nah, nada! It seems that, for the time being, all is quiet on the Western front."

Chapter 25

Railroad Death Trap #2

"Sheriff, I guess there's nothing to do at the moment but wait, not that I don't enjoy your vivacious company, of course," mused Jericho.

"Hold on there, partner! Actually, we can at least act on one thing. Do you still have that little coin in your pocket?" Walt asked.

"Yeah, I sure do—and thanks for remembering. I had just about forgotten that I wanted to have this coin checked out today by an expert."

"Well, it was a little slow this morning, so I had Maness look up a coin shop in Charlotte and call at around nine o'clock to see if the guy could meet with one of us today. Mr. Barber, the coin guy, said that Maness caught him just as he was walking out of his shop. He said he was on his way to a coin show over in Gastonia. However, being that tomorrow is Saturday, Mr. Barber said he would go ahead and drop off his new acquisitions at the shop this evening after supper, sometime in the area of 6:30 to 7:30. He said if someone wanted to meet him at the shop, he'd gladly answer any questions he could, seeing that the matter is as important as it is."

"Perfect! Thanks again, Walt, and pass on my gratitude to Deputy Maness. I'm thinking perhaps that, providing Ron appears to still be in hibernation by later this afternoon, I may ride with Cat to Charlotte to talk to Mr. Barber."

"Sounds logical," remarked Niblock.

The afternoon indeed seemed long, with no calls coming in and with no news or information to act upon. Although Nolan truly enjoyed time with his friend Walt and with Cat, of course, times like this almost drove him out of his mind. He just wasn't geared simply to wait . . . and wait . . . and wait. Jericho felt that he had adequately baited and tormented Ron to the point that surely the paranoid loner would also be going out of his mind sitting and waiting in that empty farmhouse. However, there was no word yet from Ortmann. Had the narcoleptic agent fallen asleep, giving Ron unchecked passage out of the homestead?

As the clock on the wall indicated 4:30, Nolan stretched and stood up. "Well, partner, I guess Cat and I had will head on down toward Charlotte. I don't want to miss Mr. Barber. Anyway, things with Ron are evidently at a standstill for today. Perhaps Mr. Barber can provide us with some useful info regarding the coin."

"Well," intervened Cat, "before we go, Agent Jericho, I need to make myself look presentable once again. Permit me go to the bathroom quickly and do some cosmetic surgery," she requested as she started digging through her purse.

"Oh, Miss Cat, you could be in a train wreck and you'd come out of it presentable!" quipped Walt.

"Thanks for the compliment, Sheriff," responded Cat. "But you know us women—hey, wait a minute! I can't find my hairbrush."

"It's out in the Sting Ray, Cat," said Nolan. "You laid it down beside the seat earlier when you were checking your makeup."

"Thanks, Agent Jericho. Sometimes, your powers of observation actually do come in quite handy," replied Cat. "Bear with me for a moment. I'll fetch my brush and go to the bathroom a second, then I'll be good to go."

As Cat walked outside with the bell above the door ringing away, Nolan looked over at his friend. "Women!" uttered the impatient agent. "You can't live with 'em—"

"—and you sure wouldn't want to live without 'em," finished Walt. "You know, Jet, I really envy you, being able to travel about with a lovely creature like that. They wouldn't even have to pay me to do that. I'd pay for that privilege, myself!"

"Well, being on the road's not all it's cracked up to be," responded Nolan. "But I will confess, Cat keeps things interesting. There's never a dull moment with her." Jericho smiled inwardly at the irony of what he had just said. If only Walt knew just how interesting things got between him and Cat.

Suddenly, the door burst open like blazes with the bell nearly coming loose from its wall attachment. "Guys, I think Ron has made his move. Take a look at this—" exclaimed an excited Cat as she held out a single piece of paper. "This was attached to the screen door. I didn't notice it going out, but saw it on my way back in."

"Holy crap, if that creature isn't a slick one!" said Walt as Jericho snatched the paper from Cat. "He must have parked a little ways up the road, snuck up to the door, and taped it on. I didn't hear a thing or see a shadow of any kind."

"I didn't either, Walt. He was stealthy, all right," noted Jericho as he was looking over the paper.

"Well, Jet, don't keep it to yourself. What is it?" asked Walt, about to explode with curiosity.

"It's a typed note—from Ron, I'm sure. It's not signed, of course. I'll just read it," informed Jericho.

"SO YOU WANT A KILLER, DO YOU?
AGENT JERICHO! I KNOW YOU'RE ANXIOUS TO CATCH THE KILLER OF PAUL CHRISTMAS. IF YOU WANT SOME INFORMATION WHICH WOULD ALLOW YOU TO SEIZE THE GUILTY PARTY, THEN MEET ME THIS EVENING AT 7:00 P.M. TAKE THE DIRT ROAD OFF OF HIGHWAY 70 TO THE TRAIN TRESTLE OVER THIRD FORK CREEK, SOUTH OF BEAVER JUNCTION. AND COME ALONE! IF I DETECT ANYBODY IN THE AREA OTHER THAN YOU, I WILL BE LONG GONE. THIS IS A ONE-TIME OFFER, AGENT JERICHO! DON'T DO ANYTHING STUPID!"

"Man!" said Walt in disbelief. "He even titled the note, but the note would have been more appropriately titled '*So You Want to Be Set Up Like a Clay Pigeon, Do You?*'"

"I agree, Walt," responded Nolan. "The narrative in this note was a little wordy. In my experience, notes from nervous informants are usually shorter—you know, more to the point and a little less fussy. This note reeks of a set-up—one might say, of a cat toying with his mouse before the kill. Ron is definitely as anxious to get rid of me as I am to catch him. Dammit! I knew Fowler made a mistake sending Ortmann to Pelion on a solo stakeout."

"I hope John's okay," uttered Cat.

"I do, too," echoed Jericho. "But Ortmann aside, I guess I *am* getting what I wanted in a timely fashion. It's just that it's a little more on Ron's terms than I had hoped it would be since Ortmann failed to tail him or, at least, warn us."

"Okay, my friend," interjected Walt. "I hope you don't think I'm going to let you go down to Third Fork Creek alone."

"Well, Walt, we may have no choice. Jeesh, just what is it with that lunatic and train overpasses? Tell me, what's the landscape like down in the area of the trestle?"

"The dirt road worms down from the highway through some very thick woods. Remember, Beaver Junction is across the county line, just out of my jurisdiction. Therefore, I don't patrol that area. But to the best of my memory, it seems like the dirt road comes out into a wide clearing, where it simply dead ends at the trestle. Yeah, that's it! The spot referenced in the note ends up in a big meadow or field of some sort."

"Man, Walt, that doesn't sound good at all. It sounds like plenty of woods in which a killer can camouflage himself and a wide-open field in which to shoot a sitting duck."

"Yep, that about sums it up. And that's why I strongly oppose you going alone."

"I know, friend, but this is perhaps our only remaining chance. I mean, if the cavalry rushes in, there's no telling exactly where Ron will be. Walt, he could be *so* well hidden that he would have plenty of headway to evacuate if an approaching posse scared him off. And I doubt if Ron will be willing to take any more chances like this. I'm sure he's on the verge of pulling up his stakes and fleeing to a place where we'll never find him. So far, he's been *mighty* obliging to hang around the Carolinas."

"Strangely enough, he has, hasn't he?" replied Cat.

"He sure has, Cat, and thankfully for us!" reaffirmed the agent. "But for how long? Walt, this may be my last chance to nail Ron—that is, while his egomania has him literally parading into his late brother's home turf and waving his self-confidence in our faces. If we had had more than just a two-hour notice, perhaps we might have mobilized enough men to shut down the area within a specified perimeter and flush him out, but that is not the case here, as time is ticking away. So, friends, I'm going by myself. Walt, do me a favor. I would like for you to alert the law enforcement agencies in this county and all surrounding counties to be on the lookout for a light blue Ford Galaxie. If they could set up dragnets on main routes and check the license of anybody driving a car of that make, model, and color, that would be great—but I want those dragnets *after* seven o'clock this evening, not before. If I fail to successfully capture Ron in the process of carrying out his, uh, plans, then I would certainly like for us to keep him from heading back into South Carolina. We've got to cage him while he's here, if possible."

"Will do, partner. Jet, you know that I rarely second guess you, but are you sure you know what you're doing?" asked Walt, with a concerned look on his face.

"Well, Walt, let's just say that it appears my best chance to catch Paul's killer is going to be when I've got him right where he wants me."

Cat was already going ballistic inside. Although she had a world of confidence in her man's abilities, she just knew that this was one of those events with the potential of taking Nolan out of her life. She could smell it coming! The man of her dreams proposes to her and, before she accepts, he's taken from her by a deranged killer, leaving her alone once again. It certainly would figure, wouldn't it! Her powerlessness to have any say in this matter made it all the more frustrating.

What was really awkward for Cat—*and* Nolan—was the fact that they had to keep their feelings for each other concealed in front of Walt. Cat's lips were pursed to scream "Don't go!" and Nolan's arms were flexed to reach out and comfort her anxiety. However, all that needed to be said had to be said with their eyes, which was nearly impossible.

"Agent Jericho," said Cat in a voice clumsily disguising her pleading. "I really prefer you to think your plan through, for nothing says that an SBI agent must set himself up as a sitting duck. I've never read that in any training manual distributed to our agents."

"Well, Miss Marshall," answered Nolan in strict formality, struggling to avoid unleashing his baser instincts of reaching out for her touch. "I don't put my life on the line for a hopeless cause. You are well aware of my marksmanship, and I have my gun sitting all comfy in its holster right under my jacket. No man's been able to take me out one-on-one yet, weapon or no weapon. I'm 99.99 percent sure that I'll be in your company and Walt's tomorrow."

"I'm well aware of your abilities, Agent Jericho, but, it's that point-zero-one percent chance of you not returning that has me concerned." Cat glanced toward Walt to ensure that the lawman was buying this exchange of dialogue in which she and Nolan were being forced to restrain feelings of such high emotional content. "I, uh, would hate to call Director Fowler with the news that he has lost one of his most efficient and effective agents. Losing you would be an incredible loss for the department—one which I'm sure the, uh, department would have much difficulty dealing with."

Jericho knew what she meant by "department"—after last night, he now well understood her fears of losing him. Oh, how he wished he could just grab her and kiss her again and again and whisper in her ear how he would come back this evening to her arms, come hell or high water. But, with Walt looking on, he couldn't. And now, he still had to tell Cat to do something that she would really rail against.

"Miss Marshall—uh, Cat, I still need you to go to Charlotte and check on that coin."

"Yehroit! You've got to be kidding!" shot back Cat. "And leave you when you're about to set yourself up as a shooting target for some insane jackass! You've simply got to be kidding, Ti—"

"—Please," interrupted the agent, sensing that Cat was losing her composure in front of the sheriff. "I really need you to follow my orders. That coin might give us the information we need to hang Ron. In other words, you going to Charlotte and meeting with Mr. Barber might ensure that my efforts this evening are not in vain. So please, Cat, go to Charlotte and find out about that coin. There's nothing you can do here but worry. When you get back from Charlotte, I'll meet you at the Chat & Nibble."

Still seething, Cat knew the stubborn ignoramus was right. There really was nothing she could do at this point but worry. "Okay, Agent Jericho, we'll do it your way. But, you'd better come back alive. I don't want the department having to deal with some bad news."

"Assured, Miss Marshall," said Jericho as he gave Cat a slight wink and nodded his head ever-so-slightly as if to say, "Hey, I'll be okay, Kitten." Turning to Walt, the agent once more put on his serious face. "Sheriff, I really don't want Cat going to Charlotte alone in her state of concern. Uh, would you mind asking one of your—".

As if on cue, the bell on the door suddenly rang with the arrival of Deputy Maness. "Hello, everybody. Hot out, isn't it?"

"Hi, Deputy Maness," Jericho said as the sweaty, muscular lawman sighed with relief upon hitting the refuge of cool air.

"Howdy, Agent Jericho, any closer to nabbing the reverend's killer?"

"I think we're getting close, Deputy, mighty close."

"Great! If you'll just give me the opportunity to choke the bastard for ten or fifteen seconds myself when you catch him, I sure would be grateful."

"Who knows, Deputy, you may just get that opportunity," smiled Jericho.

"Maness, was everything okay in that part of the county?"

"Oh, it was fine, Sheriff. The funeral procession was smooth. After that, I just patrolled the area for a while. The little old hen lady up near Linney's Mill sent us some eggs again like she does every time I stop by."

"That's nice of her, Maness. Just be sure to get them out of the heat, unless you're ready for some fried eggs after your car warms back up in a few minutes."

"Yes, sir, will do. I'll give half of 'em to you to take home to Sarah."

"Uh, Deputy—" said Walt, recalling his manners. "You remember Miss Marshall from Raleigh, don't you? Remember, she was out here with Agent Jericho back in '67."

"Well, how could I forget a lovely little heifer like her? Howdy, Miss Marshall, the sight of you sure adds a great deal of relief to the air conditioning on this sultry day."

"Why, thank you Deputy Maness. It's good to see you again, also," responded Cat with politeness.

"Uh, Maness, I know you get off work at five, but seeing as you're a bachelor and don't have a family to go home to, would you mind accompanying Miss Cat to Charlotte this evening? She needs to go see that coin expert for about fifteen minutes or less—you know, the guy you called earlier this morning. After that, you can both head on back to Icy Springs. What do you say, Deputy? I'll be glad to pay you overtime or I can give you comp time and you can come in at noon on Monday."

"Why, Sheriff, you make escorting this lovely little lass to Charlotte sound like some kind of chore, like slopping hogs or something. Why, Miss Cat, you would be a pleasure to escort anywhere! I'd be honored to escort you through a river full of piranhas." Cat smiled politely at his exuberant remark, while Nolan looked over the deputy's solar plexus, just in case it ever came to that.

"Great, Maness. Hopefully, though, the trip to Charlotte won't be quite that adventurous," replied Walt. "Well, I guess you two had better hit the road. With the Friday rush hour traffic, it'll take you the better part of an hour-and-a-half to get there. You still have the directions on your desk, don't you, Deputy?"

"Sure do, sir. Ma'am, I'll go out and be cooling the car back down. Come on out when you're ready."

"Thank you, Deputy. I'll be right out."

"Sure thing, ma'am," said the deputy as he tipped his hat slightly.

While Cat was in the bathroom brushing her hair and adjusting her makeup, Walt looked over at his friend as if he were awaiting approval for his quick decision to send Maness as Cat's escort to Charlotte. "Walt, uh, thanks. I appreciate the use of Maness to ensure Cat's safety."

"Think nothing of it, buddy," replied Walt. "Miss Cat will be in fine hands with Maness. He'd better mind his manners, though, with him being a lonely bachelor and all."

"Oh, have no worries there, my friend. Cat can take care of herself. If, by chance, the young fellow would happen to disregard his manners, Cat has claws. I, for one, certainly wouldn't want to tangle with her."

"Me neither," asserted Walt. "She looks like she could be a little hellcat if you got 'er wound up."

"You bet! At any rate, thanks, Walt. This'll definitely keep Cat busy and out of the way—you know, keeping her preoccupied keeps her from being such a worry-wart."

"I heard that!" exclaimed Cat, exiting from the bathroom. "Watch your mouth, Agent Jericho," she warned, "or next time my brush is misplaced, it might be found crammed up your—"

"—Point well taken, Miss Marshall!" interrupted the agent. "Sorry about the worry-wart comment, but I am glad you will be on a mission very useful toward our investigation instead of sitting here worrying about the, uh, department's potential loss."

"Sheriff," began Cat, "while I'm gone, please do your best to make sure nothing happens to Agent Jericho. He is our department's best."

"Will do, Miss Cat."

Making eye contact with Nolan, Cat walked toward him in an angle slightly obscuring her face from the sheriff's view. Extending her right hand, the tense young lady shook Nolan's hand firmly. "You keep yourself in one piece, Agent Jericho. I don't have time to assist Fowler in finding a replacement for you."

"Don't worry, Cat. Just be prepared to meet me this evening at the Chat & Nibble. I'll tell you what all happened."

With her face still turned away from Walt, Cat mouthed the words "*I love you.*" Nolan slightly squinted his Oriental eyes, as if conveying an "I love you, too" with his blink, and then nodded his head up and down slightly. He stood at the door and watched as Deputy Maness assisted her in taking her place in the passenger side of his patrol car. The agent watched the car pull out of the drive with a bittersweet feeling. Yes, he was elated that he and his quarry were slated to encounter each other on this hot summer evening, for he wanted to get the business of Paul's murder resolved once and for all. But, in a mood uncharacteristic for the usually confident Jericho, he couldn't shake the melancholy feeling he was experiencing that perhaps Cat was right. Perhaps, this was the day that an agent who once thought himself indestructible at the hands of others would be taken out of this world prematurely, that he would be taken away from Cat.

Perhaps this is the double-edged sword of what passion, of what intensely loving someone else, is all about. When you're alone, you really have nothing to lose. You live your life as if there is no tomorrow because if there's not, big deal! But when you love somebody as much as I love Cat, then suddenly the quantity of breaths you take means something. You're suddenly given a reason to stick around as long as you can, because someone else is also depending on you being there. Once you give someone else partial ownership of your life, you're not only accountable to yourself, you owe that other person as much of you as you can give them.

"Uh, Jet, are you okay?" asked Walt in one of his quietest tones.

"Yeah, Walt," replied Jericho as he turned around toward the sheriff. "She's quite a character, isn't she?"

"She sure is. When you told me the other day that Miss Cat would be coming back to town, I knew we were in for a grand ol' time. Well, what are you going to do for the next hour, Jet? Anything I can do for you?"

"Nah, Walt. If you will just write me down the directions to get to the Third Fork Creek trestle, that should be enough. How long will it take for me to get there?"

"Oh, fifteen minutes, twenty at most. It's not too awfully far from Keaton's Chicken Parlor."

"Okay. Well then, Sheriff, I do believe that some good things are destined to happen this evening. And please don't follow me to Third Fork Creek. You're a good friend, but I really don't want Ron panicking and running for the hills. For now, I think I'll go back to my motel room and make a call I've been needing to make. Why don't you go on home after you arrange our dragnets and spend some time with Sarah. I can reach you at home to let you know what happened as easily as I can call you here."

"Okay, Jet, but you promise you'll call? If I don't hear from you after dark, I'm gonna fly a fleet of helicopters in to get you!"

"Walt, I promise you. I'll tell you everything that happened." Smiling, the agent added "Scrap the helicopters, Sheriff. This isn't Vietnam, you know."

"Okay, buddy. But if it gets too late, I will come searching for you."

"If it makes you feel better, Walt, you have my full blessing on that one."

◆ ◆ ◆ ◆ ◆

As Nolan relaxed on the cool sheets of the motel room bed, he glanced at the clock on the nightstand. Seeing that the time was 6:10, the agent knew he only had ten or fifteen minutes to make his call, then it would be time to head on over toward Beaver Junction.

Sitting up, he dialed a number on the phone with a somewhat nervous hand. *It's been quite a while,* he thought. *I wonder if she's at home.*

The phone was picked up on the fifth ring. "Hello?"

"Hello! Xiaoling Ogawa?"

"Yes, this is Xiaoling speaking."

"Mother, this is Nolan. I don't think we have a great connection. I can hardly make out your voice."

"Nolan, I think that you are correct," responded the tiny voice, speaking a little louder. "I, too, can barely recognize your voice."

"Well, Mother, part of the reason my voice might not be so recognizable is the fact that I ashamedly haven't called you for two or three months."

"Two-and-a-half months, Nolan. That is how long it has been. Your mother misses your voice greatly."

"I'm sorry, Mother. My excuses are limited and poor at best. I get so wrapped up in my own life working with the SBI that I have been most neglectful. I mean no disrespect, but you also have the prerogative to call me at anytime."

"My son, I've been afraid that I would bother you. It is not logical for this isolated old woman to distract her productive young son from contributing to society and building his own life."

Mother, heavens above! Is that how you view yourself? As an illogical distraction? As an annoyance to this selfish son?

"Oh, Mother, it is I that am not worthy of your time and love. You never have to worry about intruding upon my life. I welcome your presence at any time."

"And I yours, my son. The distance between us, both in time and in space, is a challenging obstacle both physically and emotionally for this old woman."

"And for me also, Mother. I just wished to call and hear your voice. I wished to tell you of my great pride in you, for raising me to be such an independent and resourceful man and for all of the students you taught for many years to become productive, healthy adults. You will always be, in my eyes, a most remarkable woman."

"My son, I feel equal pride in my heart regarding you. I cherish your existence, and I only want what is best for you. I have a bit of wisdom I wish for you to consider, Nolan."

"What is it, Mother?"

"Life is more than the activities in which one engages; rather, life is about those with whom one engages in the activities. I fear that your late father and I spent so much time preparing for your future that we never let you savor your childhood or learn to cherish the importance of people around you. I hope you can learn from my mistake."

"Mother, uh, I love you dearly. Please accept my best wishes, and I shall not let so much time pass until we next speak with each other."

"And I shall do likewise, my son. You have my full love with you wherever you may be and in whatever you may do."

"Thank you, Mother. Goodbye."

"Goodbye, my son." And she hung up first.

Nolan sat on the bed as if he had just had the supreme emotional enema. His spirit felt *so* clean and relieved, as if a sword had been suddenly pulled from his heart. Nolan had been so nervous about leaving his mother in New York City back in the winter of '66 when he moved to Raleigh. When the mysterious voice-on-the-phone rescued him from a dire predicament, Nolan also feared for his mother's life. He literally begged her to come to Raleigh with him, but she was totally uninterested in moving away in her senior years from what she had always known as home. Dr. Rob promised that he would do his best to oversee her safety in New York City, but the mysterious voice said he could make no guarantee. Nolan always feared that those who were out to get him would eventually do so by going through his mother. Fortunately, that never seemed to materialize. Perhaps Dr. Rob was everything that he purported to be.

◆ ◆ ◆ ◆ ◆

Following Walt's directions, Nolan was savoring the warm breeze as he cruised along on Baker Mill Road in his red convertible—an unusually warm breeze, considering it was close to seven in the evening. *Wow! Life is good, Anna! Even though we're in the middle of the Piedmont, it feels like we're riding along Ocean Boulevard north of Myrtle Beach at Cherry Grove Beach or Ocean Drive Beach. It's feel just like we're cruising along the seaside, Anna!*

Once Jericho reached Highway 70 and turned right, it was only about two miles until he reached the unmarked dirt road on the right that he was supposed to take. Pulling onto the dusty, dead-end route, he let Anna roll along ever so slowly at around ten miles per hour. His adrenaline was beginning to accelerate, as it was nearly show time. Looking ahead, Nolan saw that the dirt road ran through a thick patch of woods, exactly as Walt had described. It reminded him of Burley Rankin's driveway, which had also involved driving on a dusty track through some woods; the big difference here being that the woods just ahead of him were much thicker than on the passage to Burley Rankin's garage.

As Nolan entered the wooded gateway, it was as if a solar eclipse had engulfed him. The sudden absence of sunlight dimmed the surrounding landscape immensely. The agent's nerves began testing him slightly, as there were just too many places along the road—too many trees to hide behind— from which he could easily be ambushed. *Yikes, Anna! Thank God you have the quietest engine of any Chevrolet I've ever known. At least I can still hear the sounds of birds and such in the woods. If there's any sudden rustling, perhaps I'll hear it. If you were a Ford, a train could run me over before I'd hear it coming!*

Nolan found himself gritting his teeth slightly in the deepest part of the woody passage. As he approached the very center of the woods, the dirt road came to a railroad crossing. Slowly crossing the track, the agent paused momentarily and looked each way for anyone or anything suspicious. Since a virtual tunnel had been carved out through the trees, allowing approaching trains clearance along the track, this was the part of the woods capable of readily exposing a trespasser. Not seeing any sign of life, Nolan eased his Sting Ray off the tracks, proceeding onward, then—

PE-YOWW!

"What the—? Who the—?" shouted Jericho as he rapidly ducked down in his seat. He quickly reached inside his jacket and retrieved his gun from its holster lightning-fast. *Okay, somebody just fired a rifle. They didn't hit me or Anna, I don't think. So keep your head, agent. Stay low! Now, check your perimeters in rhythm. Look to the left . . . look ahead . . . look in the rear view mirror . . . look to the right. Keep looking cyclically, keep your gun ready, and be ready to floor it if need be.*

Jericho remembered Walt talking about how people hunted all the time in the thickly wooded areas of the region around Icy Springs. As the shot had not hit him or Anna, perhaps it was some hunters in the distance having at it—after all, acoustics can play tricks on a person's ears. Perhaps the shot wasn't as close as he had thought; possibly having been amplified somewhat among the trees. At any rate, an encore shot did not seem to be forthcoming, much to his relief. If someone was trying to kill him while he was traveling through the woods, wouldn't they have simply unloaded all their ammo upon him in a hailstorm of bullets?

The dimness of the woody passage began to recede as the red Sting Ray neared the clearing up ahead. Nolan breathed a slight sigh of relief and decided to lay his gun down in the passenger seat for the time being, the weapon remaining in the realm of a quick grasp. As the agent came closer to the edge of the woods, he suddenly heard a flock of birds, followed by a loud, crackling sound. Looking sharply to his left, the agent could hardly believe his eyes. *My God, a tree!* He floored Anna's accelerator out of nothing but sheer instinct, and the red Sting Ray literally leaped forward. The falling tree roared downwards, snapping and popping limbs of neighboring trees in its descent. Thankfully, the convertible triumphed, as Anna cleared the tree's resting point by roughly six feet. Jericho slammed on the brakes, and Anna slid to a stop on the dusty trail. Immediately, the agent turned around in his seat, sitting up on his knees and looking fiercely into the area from which the fallen tree originated. He saw no one, no movement at all.

Okay, agent, you see no one at all. Perhaps the falling tree was a coincidence, but a mighty big coincidence it would be! I could back up to the tree to see if the trunk was sawed in two or if it had naturally rotted itself in two. But I need to get away from these woods, for I am a sitting duck around them. I guess I'll ease on down into the clearing and park near the trestle as the note instructed me to do.

Once again, Walt had been accurate in his description of the landscape, this time regarding the clearing. It was basically a huge, wide-open field or pasture dissected by the dirt road. As Nolan drove Anna on down the dusty cul-de-sac toward its end, he could see the moderately high trestle in the distance extending across Third Fork Creek. The agent's nerves kept his senses on full-alert as he neared the terminus of the road. He maintained his cyclical rhythm of surveillance, looking to the left . . . looking ahead . . . looking in the rear view mirror . . . and looking to the right.

Nolan came to a stop and glanced at the trestle, his eyes opening wide. There was something sitting on top of one rail of the track, right smack in the middle of the trestle. *What the hell is that? Hmm, it looks like I'll be hitting the ol' tracks again. Ron is definitely not subtle in his methods when it comes to baiting his prey. Yeah, I could play it safe and just sit here, scrunched down in my car. I mean, I sure can't drive out of here since the tree that nearly killed me is now blocking my exit. My only other option is to play along with Ron's game, see what it's all about, and get it over with—one way or the other.*

The curious agent eased himself out of the driver's seat and gently closed Anna's door. He started walking the hundred feet or so leading to the train track, all the while glancing back toward the woods to ensure no one was rushing him. Once he reached the train track, the agent, now sweating in the hot late evening sun, had roughly a hundred feet standing between him and the edge of the lengthy trestle. Centering himself on the track, Nolan began trudging toward the trestle. Adopting a flexible stride in order to plant his feet firmly on the railroad ties, the agent looked ahead as the little object on the right rail of the track continued to grow ever so slightly in size. Walking on the trestle proved to be a task allowing for little nonchalance. Looking downward, the agent noticed that the height of the trestle increased dramatically every few steps. As the trestle neared the edge of the wide creek flowing below, Nolan estimated the height of the structure to be roughly forty, maybe fifty feet above the water. Ever so carefully, he continued stepping widely from one tie to the other, for one misstep could mean death—and, if not death, possibly a lifetime as a quadriplegic anchored to a wheelchair.

While carefully maneuvering along the track, Jericho re-focused his attention on the object ahead. *Just what in the devil is that? It almost looks like a stuffed animal of some kind. It's really hard to tell with the sun shining in my eyes.* The agent tried squinting with his eyes nearly closed, but that did not help him to determine exactly what the surprise lying up ahead was.

As Jericho came within ten feet from the object, his eyes opened widely and he said out loud, "My God, what—!? A sock monkey!—just like the one sitting on the dresser in Ron's bedroom back at Pelion." Continuing to stare at the sock monkey, Nolan could tell that it had some smaller objects attached to its hands. *What the—? What in the world is the monkey holding?*

The agent knelt down to look at the surreal artificial simian and beheld one of the most bizarre sights he'd ever come across in his career as a law enforcer. No, it was not the goriest sight he had ever witnessed, nor was it the kind of thing that startles or repulses a person with a sudden, gut-wrenching jolt. Instead, it was the creepy little stuff of which childhood dreams are made, dreams of an ilk that can be filed away in the subconscious alongside evil clown faces, wicked dolls, and grotesque puppets coming to life, the sort of weirdness that slowly burns in one's soul, leaving behind a wrenching residue of tucked-away fears waiting to surface during an unplanned solitude.

Taped to the left paw of the monkey was a small, billfold-sized photo of Linda Fairbanks Christmas, Ron's deceased wife. Looking over to the right paw of the monkey, Nolan noticed a coin taped to it, the exact same kind of coin that Cat was probably questioning Mr. Barber about in Charlotte at this very minute. Jericho breathed deeply as he read the phrase written in red lipstick across the chest of the monkey: *DIE, SBI.*

"Okay, Ron Christmas, I've got you now," muttered the agent with the utmost intensity. "You've really left some unquestionable calling cards this time around. Now to find you and haul your sorry ass in to Walt."

PE-YOWW!

Nolan felt a sudden scratching sensation along the back of his neck. He reached his right hand quickly around to his neck and brought back reddened fingers before his eyes. *Blood! Thank God, it just grazed my skin! That was no hunter!*

Standing up straight, the agent quickly turned toward the woods in the distance through which he had driven earlier. Walking on the track emerging from the edge of the woods was a figure carrying a rifle with a scope on it. As with the sock monkey, the figure made for an eerie, downright spooky sight in Nolan's eyes. Juxtaposed against the picturesque backdrop of majestic woods bounded by pasture land, the approaching figure was wearing a hood with two eyeholes, *à la* Ku Klux Klan, except that it was a satiny purple and covered with glittery specks. The rest of the figure's body was clad in a black sweat suit. Now walking on the train track, the sparkly-hooded figure in black said nothing. He merely kept walking in the middle of the track toward the agent who was now pinned in at the center of the trestle.

Okay, agent, he's got his gun lowered. And you're the guy who's known as the crack shot of the SBI. So, get ready! Take a breath and stretch your fingers a little . . . and . . . NOW—! Reaching inside his jacket at lightning speed, Jericho drew his hand back in horror. *Oh, no! Oh, dear God! Tell me I didn't! Jericho, you IDIOT!*

Jericho's worst nightmare had come true. For the only time in his whole distinguished stint with the SBI, he had made the kind of blunder for which beginning agents are severely reprimanded. And worse yet, this was no training exercise or what-would-you-do scenario. This was reality, and the great Jericho had made a fatal blunder. He had no gun!

Immediately, his mind flashed to the passenger seat of his red convertible, upon which his gun now lay. Of course, it was still resting at the same spot where he had temporarily set it following the quick draw in response to the sound of gunfire in the woods. Unfortunately, the tree nearly crashing on his car had served as enough distraction for the agent to become momentarily absent-minded. And, it certainly hadn't helped any that, upon coming to a stop at the end of the dirt drive, he had exited the car instantly out of curiosity for the object sitting in the middle of the trestle.

Whatever reason any agent could possibly present to justify misplacing or neglecting his gun, it was all a moot point in a life-or-death situation where a gun was truly needed. For once, Cat's worst fears had a good chance of coming true, leaving her totally alone. For once, Xiaoling Ogawa's pride and joy might not be coming out of a bad situation alive, leaving her childless. For once, Jericho felt that the bad guy might actually come out the victor. And, in his line of business, all it took was that one "for once." *Well, hero, it looks like you've literally made yourself one of the bull's eyes which Fowler had warned you about becoming. Looks like your great fighting skills won't be worth squat in this situation, for you can't outrun a bullet. What'cha gonna do, hero?*

Sweating profusely, Nolan looked around. There was nowhere to run. If he tore off in the other direction on the trestle, he could easily be pegged by virtually any powerful rifle with a half-decent scope. At forty or fifty feet up, he couldn't lunge from the trestle because of the rocky terrain along the creek. He would break his legs or hip in the best of outcomes, and the result would be the same, ending up as a lame duck easily picked off by the killer through a clear shot from the trestle. He couldn't dive into the creek directly beneath him: it looked to be only twenty to thirty inches deep at best. A broken neck or paralyzed back would surely make an escape unlikely. *Nowhere to go! Okay, hero, think! What can you do? Bluff, maybe? Talk to him? Shake him up a little? Well, why not . . .*

As the sparkly-hooded figure in black approached the edge of the long trestle, Jericho began shouting. "Okay, Ron Christmas. I know it's you. In fact, the whole world does. Everyone knows how much you hated your brother. I know it was you that tried to kill me at Spartanburg. The local authorities and I now have enough evidence to put you away. Killing me won't stop that and it won't bring back your beloved Linda. Killing me will only increase the time you're locked away. So put down your rifle, Ron. It's all over but the cryin' and the weepin'. Lay it down, Ron, and we'll go in peacefully. Turn out the lights, the party's over. What do you say?"

Jericho watched intently for what seemed an eternity. As the agent stood straight and poised with both feet planted on a railroad tie and centered exactly between the two rails of the track, he glanced through the space between the ties at the water below. At that instant, Nolan began to experience a flashing of images in his mind: of an orange-faced Cat hurling a shoe at him; of his mother teaching in her classroom; of Agent James sitting on the grounds of the state capitol and painting his heart out; of Walt and him taking shots at a herd of deer on the old Yates place; of eating a Jack's cookie at Doc's Store while talking to Doc Lassiter; of Smokes kidding around with him at the Char-Grill back in Raleigh; of his father Roberto tucking him into bed as a young boy; and of holding Cat tightly as they lay in bed.

Having kept one eye planted on the hooded figure, Nolan began to sense that his impassionate argument with the gunman was futile, and he was right. Suddenly, while still standing at the edge of the trestle, the hooded figure quickly lifted the gun and took aim. As the gunman proceeded to sight his quarry through the scope of his rifle, he grunted out, "Huh? What the—" and lowered the firearm in bewilderment. Jericho had flat-out disappeared from sight!

Yeooouch! That sure didn't feel good! thought Jericho as he clung by his fingertips to the sharp, squared-off corners of the railroad ties. Unbeknownst to the gunman, Nolan had performed the only feat he could conjure up. Occurring literally during the blink of the gunman's eye as he was positioning his rifle, the agent had lifted his arms straight in the air and, pointing his toes downward and straightening his body like an arrow, had allowed his slender body to do a bombs-away drop in the narrow rectangular opening between the railroad tie he was standing on and the tie directly in front of him. As Jericho's arms had passed by the tie in front of him, he had miraculously reached out and locked onto the fleeting tie with his strong fingers. The incredibly powerful jolt rendered by jerking to a sudden stop in mid-flight on the splintery, knife-edged board had nearly torn the ligament of his already-tender upper arm and had sent needles of sharp pain throughout his straining fingers. So, out of the frying pan and into the fire! The dangling agent, now feeling much pain in his upper extremities, looked down at the shallow water below as a confused gunman began slowly maneuvering his way across the trestle.

"All right, Jericho!" hollered the gunman. "You can't 'clever' your way out of this one. You might as well show yourself." Having not yet spotted Jericho's slim fingers clinging to the railroad tie up ahead, the gunman carefully navigated the spaced boards as he mumbled to himself. "Damn idiot! If he did jump, the fool is surely dead. If he's not, then he will be."

Jericho's heart beat like a hummingbird as his fingers began slipping on his creosote-covered perch. As Jericho looked downward, he saw that there were two large rocks rising out of the water slightly to the right of a straight-down plunge. If he let go and hit either of those rocks, then the opera would indeed be over and the fat lady would indeed have sung.

Noted among his colleagues for its cool, analytical nature while under extreme pressure, Jericho's calculating mind suddenly kicked into gear. *Okay, agent, think! You know how those jokers do those high-dives in only one or two feet of water. They brace themselves and fall with their bodies as flat as possible. From way up high, the velocity of your fall pressing the mass of your body against the hard plane of the water's surface would have enough force to kill you. But from a lesser distance, the velocity of your fall wouldn't necessarily have enough force to crush you against the surface of the water, yet the hard plane of the water's surface would still decelerate the speed of your fall. So, agent, go for it! Do a belly buster and, for God's sake, miss those rocks. Oh, Lord! This is gonna hurt like hell!*

Jericho suddenly let go of the railroad tie, and his fingers immediately felt relief, but there was no time to celebrate. As his body plummeted downward, he straightened out his arms and legs in a position akin to that of skydivers in free-fall. The water seemed to shoot toward him like a bullet. *Lord, please help me through this!*

Spuhhhlaash!

The agent's body smashed violently against the wall of the water's surface, rapidly slammed almost to a halt, and then, in what the careening agent perceived to be a nearly simultaneous blow, crashed against the bottom of the creek bed. Even though the plane of the water's surface and Nolan's flattened body position had served to break his fall considerably, he nearly fell unconscious upon the crushing impact. His stomach stung beyond belief and he was literally seeing stars, but the dazed agent had the presence of mind to lift his head out of the water. Gagging and coughing out water, his breath nearly knocked out of him, Nolan began pulling his black sports jacket off. Having narrowly missed the two rocks jutting out of the water beside him, he quickly draped the jacket over one of them while trying to acquire a full breath.

Looking around, Nolan noticed a huge pile of brush, more than likely the remnants of flooding, clinging to one of the large pylons serving as a support beam for the trestle. He made his way through the water to the pylon and wedged his body underneath the brush so that he was camouflaged between the brush and the pylon. Attempting to keep his body completely submerged and hidden from view, Nolan pressed his nostrils against the cement base of the pylon, keeping them barely above the water.

After slowly treading the half-length of the trestle, the sparkly-hooded gunman stood near the center of the structure. He looked down at the black jacket surrounded by the water below, which was lying in a somewhat rounded position as if a body were doubled up beneath it. The mysterious assassin stood for a second as he stared at his handy work. Nolan glanced upward, with the view of his water-soaked eyes somewhat distorting the figure hovering above. Through the railroad ties above, he could make out that the blurry figure was still holding his rifle. He remained totally still, knowing that if the killer detected the slightest movement, he was a goner.

Sensing no movement from the deceptively spread out black jacket, the gunman muttered, "Dumb-ass. Taking the bullet would have been a lot less painful." He then reached down and retrieved the sock monkey with its picture of Linda and the mysterious coin.

Jericho waited another half-hour beneath the pile of brush, his body tucked against the pylon. Having managed to survive thus far after making such a fatal blunder in leaving his gun in the car, the agent was not about to do something stupid like coming out of hiding too soon. After all, the gunman might simply double back to the edge of the trestle and sit down for a while in case the agent had the gall to rise from the dead.

As darkness began to set in, Nolan pushed away from the support beam and wiped himself free of sticks, leaves, and other particles of the brush. He moved over toward the bank and, standing up at the creek's edge, began seeing stars, not of the astronomical kind but of the kind that professional boxers dread seeing. Not truly realizing how exhausted he was from the ordeal of escaping the gunman or how stunned his body remained from the fall, Nolan collapsed on the bank of the creek, lying on his back with his face toward the oncoming night sky.

Breathing laboriously, Nolan looked up at the sky as the moon began to shine. He kept staring upwards, fighting to stay awake. Once darkness had totally set in, the last thing the agent remembered seeing was the wisp of a falling star trailing across the horizon. As he could no longer keep his heavy eyes open, he heard the sound of howling in the distance, the sound of the wild coyotes.

CHAPTER 26

Catfight on a Hot Friday Night

Cat pulled the coin out of her purse mostly to ensure it was still there. "Hmm, Nolan certainly will find Mr. Barber's assessment quite interesting. Deputy, if you don't mind, just let me out in front of the motel's café."

"Here you go, ma'am. Good luck with everything. Have a good evening."

"Thank you, Deputy," said Cat gratefully as she stepped out of the patrol car. She had a headache-and-a-half, probably from worrying about her lover. *I do hope they have some aspirin at the restaurant counter since I don't have any Bayer left in my pocketbook.* The anxious lady walked hurriedly into the café, aiming to literally throw down the money, grab the aspirin, and get on around the corner of the restaurant to Room #5. *I'm sure he's okay, even though my man could fight the entire British army. I can't wait for him to tell me what happened.*

As she rounded the corner of the café and the row of units with Rooms #1 through #5 came into view, the nervous young lady immediately panicked, for there was no red convertible Sting Ray in sight. *Oh, no!* thought Cat as she broke into a sprint. *Please tell me he's hauling the jerk to jail or that he and Walt are tying some things up.*

Running along the rooms under the covered walkway, Cat noticed a patrol car parked somewhat inconspicuously alongside the woods jutting out from the edge of the motel. Although it sparked her interest for a millisecond, she had no time to analyze why the law enforcement vehicle might be sitting there. The only thing dominating Cat's mind at this instant was the well-being of Agent Nolan Jericho.

Feverishly applying the key to the lock of Room #5, Cat pushed on the door gently. She was dreading the sight of nothing-at-all probably awaiting her on the other side. *I pray to God there's at least a note on the bed or the nightstand. He's got to be with Walt!*

Cat stood in the doorway, swallowing deeply upon facing the dark room. A overly sensual voice suddenly emanated from the direction of the bed. "Come on in, Cutie. I thought I'd take a tiny pleasure break from my little ol' night patrol. But I promise, the pleasure you'll get from my body won't resemble anything tiny."

Still standing within the door frame, Cat felt her body tensing up as she began fuming at the recognizable voice. With her eyes now adjusting to the faintly lit room, Cat could see a deputy's uniform and gun belt slung over the back of a chair not far from the foot of the bed. Gritting her teeth and expanding her fingers slightly in the similar way a cat protracts its claws, the Cat-Woman now took one step into the room and turned to her right. Facing the head of the bed, Cat filled the dimness with an emotionless voice. "So, Deputy, does your night patrol involve, uh, undercover work as a call girl?"

The deputy in the bed, hearing the response in an obviously female voice, shot out an arm suddenly and activated the switch on the lamp. As the room became instantly illuminated, the figure in the bed yelled out in panic. "Catherine! What are you doing here?"

"Shouldn't you be answering that question, dear *half*-sister?" asked Cat of the startled Dreama, who was in the process of desperately pulling the thin bed sheets up over her unclothed form. "Honestly, Dreama, I don't know which part of you is the bigger, the *bore* or the *whore.*"

"Well, you're certainly one to talk, Catherine. I'm smart enough to know what's going on between you and Jet. I'm no dummy, you can see it for a country mile! *Cat*, is it? Now I know why men call you that, for I know a kept pussy when I see one! Who else would have a key to his room?"

"And how, may I ask, did *you* get in here, Dreama?—turn some tricks with the desk clerk for the key?"

"No, I was smart enough to use the master key that Sheriff Niblock has to all the local businesses, in case of emergencies, like my insatiable libido. I'm smart in a lot of ways, Cat, smart enough to get what I want and smart enough to know that Jet would like a go-round with me."

"Why, you immoral sack of social disease!" retorted Cat with steam in her eyes. "You're not smart enough to know the back end of a donkey if he's sitting on you. Well, on second thought, maybe you do know that! On that rare night when you've not suckered a two-legged jackass into the sack with you, you probably head to the nearest barnyard for some gratification."

"*Argggh!*" grunted Dreama with her fists clenched furiously. "Now I understand why Momma left you. Your personality stinks so much that a skunk dipped in horse shit couldn't stand your company!"

"How dare you bring up Mother!"

"Well, it's true! Momma wanted *me*, but *she never* wanted you, and you just can't deal with that because you're a two-bit loser!"

At that verbal jab, Cat let her claws relax somewhat. Putting her hands on her hips, a calm look suddenly came across her face as she stared toward Dreama with a blank expression. Having anticipated an explosion from Cat at her callous remarks involving their mother, Dreama began trembling a little at her half-sister's zombie-like demeanor. After around fifteen seconds, Dreama couldn't stand it anymore. "Uh, Catherine, what's going on in that mind of yours? Are you thinking about apologizing to me?"

Another seven long seconds passed by. Then, like an unanticipated strike of a lightning bolt, Cat reached down to the foot of the bed and grabbed the bottom of the sheet that Dreama was using for shelter. With the subtlety of a dozen sticks of dynamite and with a fury fueled by an adrenaline overload, Cat yanked the sheet toward herself. Clinging desperately to the sheet, Dreama went along helplessly for the ride to the foot of the bed. There Cat clamped her arms in a vise-like grip around Dreama's neck and yanked her nude half-sister completely off of the bed.

"You're—*gasp*—choking me," gurgled Dreama within the throes of Cat's headlock.

"Sorry, my oversight—" snapped Cat with a maniacal tone. "I understood clearly what you just said, which means you're still getting some air!" she remarked, furiously continuing to tighten her grip.

In desperation, Dreama lifted Cat up until her half-sister's feet were several inches off the floor. Losing balance, the two grunting women fell backwards onto the chair holding Dreama's uniform and gun belt. In their hyper-accelerated states of mind, neither woman flinched as the flimsy piece of furniture buckled under their combined weight. With the chair disassembled into several pieces and both women lying on the floor, Dreama reached over and grabbed a handful of Cat's brown hair, with Cat following suit.

"Owww! Ughhh!" The two struggling women continued to shout and grunt in pain as each refused to let go of the other's hair.

"Let go, you bitch!" commanded Dreama.

"Not on your sorry life!" shot back Cat.

Dreama suddenly remembered her gun in the belt now lying on the floor. Looking around, she spotted it about two feet from her shoulders. Letting go of Cat's hair with her left hand, she reached out to retrieve the waiting firearm. However, Cat, sensing what Dreama was up to, let go of Dreama's golden hair with her left hand and snatched Dreama's wrist just before the hopeful woman could grab the gun. With each of their right hands still pulling fiercely at hair, both women exerted as much energy as possible with their left hands. Literally engaged in an arm-wrestling match, Cat struggled desperately, trying to keep Dreama's hand from reaching the gun while Dreama tried to twist her wrist free from Cat's powerful grip. Since Cat's overextended position left her somewhat at a disadvantage, Dreama was able to mobilize the fingers in her left hand enough to crawl along the carpet inch-by-inch while dragging Cat's persistent left hand with it.

Dreama's fingers lay within an inch of the gun belt, and Cat's now sweaty grip—locked onto the wrist of an even-sweatier Dreama—slipped slightly, thus allowing Dreama's fingers to unsnap the holster. As Cat's grip slipped even more and slid further down Dreama's forearm, Dreama was able to slide her gun out of its holster.

With Dreama now holding the gun loosely in her left hand, Cat re-asserted her grip on Dreama's arm. Continuing to exert their maximum force while grunting heavily, the two female gladiators managed to sit up on the floor. At that point, Cat released Dreama's hair and shot her right hand straight towards her half-sister's left forearm in an effort to take possession of the gun. Following Cat's lead, Dreama released her right hand from Cat's hair and swung it around into a firm grip on Cat's left wrist.

Dreama pulled wildly at Cat's left wrist as Cat's left hand still firmly gripped Dreama's left wrist, her right hand gripping Dreama's forearm. The two sets of arms began waving wildly in the air, back and forth, within a pendulum of consolidated flesh. It was now virtually a contest of perseverance, with Dreama determined to get full control of the gun and Cat dead-set against Dreama doing so. Cat wanted to reach out and scratch Dreama's face, but she was afraid that releasing one of her hands from Dreama would open a window of opportunity for her half-sister to pull completely away.

While both women rocked back and forth on their bottoms, the pendulum of tangled limbs began to swing wider and wider. Suddenly, in mid-swing, Dreama's fingers let go of the gun and it flew in a perfect arc across the bed. As the gun landed perfectly square on a pillow, Dreama butted her head against the right cheek of Cat's face.

As the temporarily dazed Cat shook her head, Dreama hopped up and lunged toward the bed with her fingers falling about three inches short of the pillow. Just before she was about to reach for the gun once again, a tremendous tug by Cat on the nude woman's right ankle forced Dreama back off the bed, with Dreama now standing fully erect.

"You little harlot," snapped a nearly breathless Cat as the two women stood face-to-face. "What good would arresting me at gunpoint for supposedly assaulting you do while you're stark-naked? I'd like to hear your explanation for that."

"Who said I was gonna take you in?" retorted an equally breathless Dreama. "I'd be perfectly at peace shootin' ya."

Following that terse statement, Dreama's right hand immediately shot out like a cannonball and slapped Cat's left cheek with a loud pop. Cat's cheek immediately turned red, her entire face even redder. She let out a scream and threw her body forward. Using her shoulder as a battering ram against

Dreama's mid-section, Cat's knees landed on the carpet as Dreama toppled backwards from the contact. Dreama's rear end hit the carpet with a thud as the back of her head hit the door with a loud crack. Cat watched as Dreama slowly stood back up, using the door knob as a crutch. "Had enough, '*Half-Sis*'?" hissed Cat.

The two women again stood face-to-face, panting heavily. Looking into Cat's eyes, Dreama once again began her sharp needling. "Now, you see? You see what I mean? Momma had to leave you. You're so explosive and immature! Nobody can stand to live with you, Catherine!" Cat gritted her teeth tightly and clenched her fists.

The warm night air permeated the darkness outside the motel, and all was quiet in the vacant parking lot for a few seconds. Then, a few loud thumps could be heard from Room #5, though somewhat muted by the door. Suddenly, the door opened and out sailed Dreama's nude body about four feet in the air, with her arms flailing wildly. Cat's sweaty, exhausted figure appeared in the doorway as she made gestures with her hands simulating that of wiping her hands clean. Looking at her naked, nearly unconscious half-sister lying spread-eagle in the parking lot, Cat let out a grunt of victory. "Uh-huh!" she exclaimed, nodding her head up and down. "Never mess with cats, Dreama, you'll get clawed every time."

The victorious woman then turned on her heels and marched backed into the room while mumbling. "Call me explosive, will she? Call me immature, will she? Well, I just took her to college in a course called Messing with a Wildcat 101. Wonder how she liked the final exam I just gave 'er?"

Returning to the doorway, Cat left-handedly tossed Dreama's wadded-up deputy's uniform on the fallen woman's still-motionless body. "Here, do the world a favor, '*Half-Sis*.' Put these on as soon as possible!" A pair of black dress shoes then zoomed through the air, compliments of Cat's right hand, landing just beside Dreama's head.

Turning on her heels once again, Cat walked over to her pocketbook sitting on the floor at the corner of the bed. Picking up the bag and setting it on the nightstand, she sat down on the bed next to the pillow. She took out three pieces of Bazooka bubble gum from the pocketbook and proceeded to chuck the trio of pink chunks into her mouth. After chewing vigorously for around fifty seconds, she took the ball of gum out of her mouth and lifted the gun off of the pillow. She then held the gun barrel-up and plopped the moist wad of gum on top of the barrel. Retrieving a pencil from her pocketbook, she began stuffing the sticky gum down into the gun's shaft using the pencil as a tamping rod. Cat could hardly contain the wicked smile nearly prying her lips open as she began mumbling aloud once again. "Let's see you fire this gun, Dreama. It'll backfire and blow your brains out! Uh, correction, it'll blow that hollow head of yours off your shoulders."

Walking back to the door, Cat grinned as Dreama was now on her feet. The dazed deputy attempted to shake the cobwebs out of her head while cradling the wadded-up uniform in her arms just below her abdomen, partially covering her privates. "Don't forget your gun, Deputy," said Cat in a mocking voice. "I'm sure you're going to have some difficulty explaining to the sheriff why your gun barrel is filled with bubble gum." That said, Cat lobbed the gun in the air. Dreama snagged it with her right hand and pressed it against her uniform so she wouldn't drop anything.

Without saying a word, Dreama stuck out her tongue at Cat and turned in the direction of her patrol car, waiting at the edge of the woods. When Dreama had wobbled about halfway to the car, Cat hollered out, "Oh, one more thing, Dreama! That bubble gum in your gun barrel is the most satisfying blow job I've ever performed! Sorry *you* missed out on your chance to perform tonight, you one-woman red light district."

As the patrol car limped off humbly out of sight, Cat walked back into the room. Still quite worked up, she continued talking out loud to herself. "Well, that's the last time that walking-talking sperm bank will mess with me! And, I'll tell you one more thing! Even though I'm sure this little rendezvous in Room #5 was totally Dreama's idea, I know a certain Agent Nolan Jericho who had better assure me that he would have ejected that sour tart. He'd better show me he has no interest at all in that trampy little bit o' room service. He'd better—wait! Oh, my God! Nolan!"

Once again conscious of Jericho's no-show, Cat ran frantically over to her pocketbook sitting beside the pillow. Setting herself down on the bed, she swiftly took a folded-up piece of paper out of her purse and dialed the number on it as quickly as possible. When the ringing stopped, she didn't even wait for the other party to answer.

"Hello? Hello, Sheriff Niblock?"

"Yes! Miss Cat?"

"Sheriff, he hasn't come back yet. I just got back from Charlotte and his car's not here at the motel. Has he contacted you?"

"No, Cat, he hasn't. I was just about to—"

Cat interrupted Walt, her voice now quivering. "I'm afraid something has happened, Sheriff."

"Me too, Cat. I was just about to go down to Beaver Junction to check on our good buddy."

"Um, Sheriff?" whimpered Cat, as the rest of her question was strangled by emotion.

"Yes, Cat?"

"Walt, may I please go with you?"

There were a few seconds of silence, as if options were being weighed. "Sure, Cat, but promise me you'll stay in the car until I give you clearance to exit, understand?"

"Yes, Sheriff, I will. I promise!"

"Miss Cat, I'll be there in two shakes of a sheep's tail."

"Sheriff, how long is that in Raleigh time?"

"Five minutes!"

"Okay. Thank you, Sheriff!"

"Yeah, I'll be right there!"

◆ ◆ ◆ ◆ ◆

As the din of howls seemed to grow closer, Jericho slowly opened his eyes to the glowing moonlight. The exhausted agent strained to lift himself up, but for some reason, his legs wouldn't move. *What the—? I didn't land on my legs, nor did I break my back. What's wrong with me? Why can't I move my legs?*

The howls now sounded only half the distance they had been at just seconds ago. Suddenly, Jericho heard what seemed to be a chain saw in the distant woods which, of course, made no sense at this time of night. But, why question providence? After all, perhaps whoever was at work would possibly drive the coyotes away with the sound of the sawing.

As the sawing persisted, so did the crescendo of the howls. Jericho considered yelling for help, but he deemed it wise not to alert the coyotes to his location so quickly. *Patience, Jericho, patience. Maybe they'll find some other prey, a deer or rabbit or something, before they get to me.*

Suddenly, a growl came from just around one of the pylons near the bank at the trestle's edge. A pair of devilish-looking eyes seemed to glow in the dark as they moved closer to the agent. A deafening howl sprang out from the floating pair of eyes and, within fifteen to twenty seconds, three new sets of glowing eyes appeared in accompaniment. As the growls grew louder and the eyes drew closer, four shadowy forms began to appear. *Well, looks like the sawing didn't scare the coyotes away. It's all up to me and whatever resources I have at my disposal. Hmm, unfortunately, my resources appear to be none at all!*

Still not able to move his legs, Jericho sat up as straight as he could and looked around desperately for rocks, sticks, just anything he could use as a weapon. *Man, it'll be bad news if the number one agent in the SBI ends up as coyote excrement. Okay, Jericho, how are ya gonna get out of this one?*

Looking around, he found one rock within reach, a rock about the size of a walnut. Taking aim at the snarling, approaching forms, he unleashed the impromptu projectile with great speed. However, his attempt proved to be an exercise in futility, as the stone disappeared into the darkness and the dogs of night came closer. He might as well have hurled a Hershey's kiss at them.

Suddenly, the lead coyote lashed out and tore open the calf of his right leg with its razor-sharp teeth. *My God, the pain! Why does it hurt so much if my lower extremities are paralyzed?*

The coyote looked as if it was about to settle in for the kill, but, strangely enough, it backed off and stood still. As if following the cue of their leader, the other three coyotes froze in their tracks. After the passage of a few seconds, Jericho understood the reason behind this—a train! Apparently, a train was not too far distant from the trestle. The agent could hear the train blowing its horn at a road crossing several miles away. *Wow! That's a messenger from God, all right. If a train roaring across the trestle doesn't scare these vicious things away, nothing will.*

The next two minutes were very tense as the rumble of the train became more prominent and the coyotes remained motionless like statues, looking Jericho in the eyes. *Come on, train, come on! Hit that trestle with all the thunder you've got. Scare those bastards away from here.*

As the train neared the trestle, the coyotes began to blink more frequently. Re-positioning themselves, they appeared poised to leap outwards into the darkness. The roar grew almost deafening, but the beasts retained their newly adopted posture. As the sound of the train reached its climax midway across the trestle, the lead dog flinched slightly, continuing to hone his posture even further into evacuation mode. *Come on, you dogs of hell, run! Get out of here, now!*

After reaching its peak, the sound of the train began a steady decrescendo as the monster of the darkness roared off in the opposite direction. As the once-inspirational roar of salvation diminished into a whimper signifying hopelessness, the coyotes transformed their getaway pose back into the stalking mode they had momentarily abandoned. The lead dog now re-focused its concentration toward the helpless agent with renewed intensity. *Damn, I guess they are around trains so much in this area that they've become accustomed to them.*

Out of desperation, Jericho yelled out into the darkness. Maybe, just maybe, someone would hear him in time to rescue what was left of him—either that, or the lesser likelihood that his yells might scare off the animals. "HELP!! *AAIEE!!*" Looking in the faces of the evil beasts, he continued his banshee-like wailing. "HELP!! GET AWAY!!!" He even tried roaring, "*RRRAAARRR!!*"

With no help in sight and the unfazed coyotes in front of him, Jericho braced himself for the onset of carnage. The other three coyotes proceeded to line up beside the leader, who had resumed ripping at Nolan's calf, and the agent disappeared in a mass of fur, as the coyotes tore at his body in their feeding frenzy. It was so painful at first, but, before he knew it, he was slowly going to sleep and felt the pain no longer.

After what seemed like only a few seconds, Jericho was re-awakened slightly by the sweetest voice he'd ever heard. "Nolan! Nolan, are you okay?" the voice was crying out. As Jericho slowly opened his eyes, he found his head being cradled in Cat's arms.

"I suppose, Cat. At least, those beasts evidently didn't chew off my face," said the groggy agent while attempting to regain his bearings.

"Thank God! Huh? Who didn't chew off your face, Tiger?" asked his confused lover.

Another familiar voice suddenly came from beyond his feet. "Well, ol' buddy, when we saw you lying here from up on the edge of the trestle, we thought you were dead. Good to see you still alive and in one piece, Jet!" exclaimed Walt, as he set down the lantern he was carrying.

"One piece? But what about my body?—the bleeding? What about the coyotes?"

"What coyotes, Jet?" inquired Walt with a baffled look. "Miss Cat and I haven't seen any coyotes."

Jet instantly glanced down at his intact body, which was free of blood. Sitting up quickly, he continued surveying his body for a few seconds, but the only injuries he could detect to his skin were some scratches from hiding in the brush next to the pylon. "Sorry about the coyote-thing, you two. I guess it was just some hallucinating I did while semi-conscious. Thank you for bringing me back to reality with your, uh, first aid experience, Miss Marshall."

"No problem, Agent Jericho. You and your strange dreams! You might need to see a staff psychiatrist when we get back to Raleigh about your hallucinations."

"Yeah, I won't argue that point, Miss Marshall!" said Jet as he tested his legs by shaking them vigorously. "I also dreamed I couldn't move my legs and that I heard a power saw and a train crossing the trestle before the coyotes proceeded to chew me to pieces."

"Well, Jet, I can assure you that you did hear a train crossing the trestle, ol' buddy. And you also heard some sawing," said Walt, evidently not having quite processed the degree of concern Miss Cat had showed for the agent or the fact she had lovingly called him Nolan. "What you heard was the tree being sawed in two that was lying across the road near the train track. It was being cut so we could get your car out of here."

"Did Ron get snagged in any of the dragnets set up along the highways?" asked Jericho in an anxious voice.

"Unfortunately, no, we didn't get him," answered Walt.

"Damn, Walt, how can Ron be that slippery?—like an eel or something! Only a ghost could have gotten through the roadblocks I asked you to set up— that is, if he planned to head back to South Carolina, which I'm sure he did."

"I don't know, Jet. I really can't tell you, but he sure is a slick one, all right. Now, please inform Miss Cat and me: just how did you end up lying here on the ground?"

"Well, that sort of has an embarrassing little moment within it, embarrassing on my part, that is," offered the agent hesitantly.

"Okay, Agent Jericho, we're out in the middle of a big field next to a creek and we're all ears," said Cat in an ironic tone.

"All right, you two. Here goes, but keep in mind that there is one detail in the story that I'd have to kill anyone else after sharing it. I'll spare you two if, and only if, you promise not to tell anyone else."

"*Okaay . . .*" uttered Cat in a drawn-out response of cautious curiosity.

"I promise I won't say a word," stated Walt with utmost sincerity.

"Well, I ended up here because I forgot my gun. I, uh, left it lying on the passenger seat in my car."

"Let me check my ears, Agent," requested Cat with a degree of disbelief. "Did I hear you say that you forgot your gun?"

"Yeah, that's what I said. I forgot my gun," Jericho repeated while rolling his eyes.

"How in the world did you do that?" inquired Cat, quite taken aback.

"Well, it wasn't easy."

"I would bet not," affirmed Cat.

"Man!" exclaimed Walt. "The great Jet Jericho forgetting his gun! Why, that's like John Hancock forgetting his pen or Paul Bunyan forgetting his ax or Christopher Columbus forgetting his—"

"All right already, Walt!" interrupted Jericho with an agitated tone. "I think everybody here gets the point! Do you wanna hear the story or not?"

"Please continue, my friend," requested Walt in an apologetic tone. "Pardon my enthusiasm, but it truly has amazed me to see that you are human like the rest of us. And there's nothing wrong with that, Jet."

"Okay, then . . ." continued Jericho. "Riding in the woods, I heard a shot and grabbed my gun. I didn't detect anyone around, so I laid it on the passenger seat for quick access. The tree you found blocking the road nearly smashed Anna and me to kingdom come. Not wanting to remain a sitting duck on the edge of the woods, I floored Anna on down toward the trestle. I then saw something placed mysteriously—quite purposefully, to be exact—on the rail in the middle of the trestle. I hiked out to the middle of the trestle to check it out and, unfortunately, that's when I realized I didn't have my gun on me."

"What exactly alerted you that you were missing your gun?" asked Cat.

"The, uh, bullet that grazed the back of my neck. It's amazing how alert you become when something like that happens!" noted Jericho.

"A bullet hit you? Are you okay?" asked Cat loudly with obvious concern.

"Oh, I'm fine, Cat. It was nothing that came close to inconveniencing the, uh, department," quipped Jericho. "Just a scratch. Anyway, the shot was fired by Ron, who was wearing a purple hood as he came out of the woods. He had a rifle with a scope on it. When I went to draw my gun and take him out, that's when I discovered that I had left it in the car. Talk about a sitting duck! There is none better than an unarmed guy on a high train trestle."

"Pardon me, Jet, I'm not trying to play Devil's advocate here," interjected Walt. "But how can you be one-hundred percent sure that Ron was the would-be assassin in the hood?"

"Well, the item on the track I was examining when he took a potshot at me was the sock monkey Cat and I saw on his dresser when we searched his place yesterday. Mix in the fact that a picture of Linda Fairbanks Christmas was taped to one paw of the monkey and a coin identical to the one Cat took to Charlotte was taped to the other paw, and I'd say that Ron accommodated us in every way except leaving his baby pictures and a written confession. By the way, Cat, what did you find out in Charlotte?"

"Agent Jericho," she said. "Would you mind if we get out of here? What I found at the coin shop was quite interesting, and I'll be more than glad to share it a little later, but standing out here in the middle of the field near midnight is not my idea of a social gathering."

"You are so right, Miss Cat!" echoed Walt. "Anyway, Jet, my lantern is destined to run out of kerosene soon."

"All right, no problem with that," responded the agent as he stood up for the first time since passing out. He groaned as he moved very slowly and attempted to stretch his muscles.

"Are you okay, Jet?" asked Walt.

"Fine, Walt, just stiff as hell. I'm probably gonna be quite sore tomorrow."

Cat looked at Nolan with a sudden inquisitive stare. "By the way, agent. You didn't tell us how you escaped the gunman, that is, Ron Christmas. Nor did you tell us exactly why you were lying here on the creek bank."

"Oh, Cat, that was no problem, actually. I jumped," responded Jericho with in an extremely casual tone, as if the feat was nothing.

"You've got to be kidding!" barked Walt. "You leaped from the middle of the trestle? Why, pour me a gasoline cocktail and stick a firecracker up my butt! How did you keep from breaking your fool neck?"

"Well, no problem, actually," continued Jericho, speaking in the same tone of hocus-pocus nonchalance. "I simply aimed for the middle of the creek."

"The hell you say, Jet! That creek can't be much more than two feet deep. There's no way you dove into that without breaking your neck or back or *something*."

During the whole time Jericho had described his escape from Ron, Cat stared at him with her mouth totally agape. "Okay, quit jerking us around," said Cat impatiently. "What did you really do?"

"I jumped from the trestle, I told ya, but I guess you wouldn't say I actually dove into the creek. I did more of a belly flop, I think you would call it. I then hid in some brush against a pylon holding up the trestle until the gunman was satisfied that I didn't survive the fall. Anyway, I definitely have a newfound respect for those high-dive fellows that plunge into real shallow water."

"Jet, there's one thing you've got to think about, though," clarified Walt. "The guys that usually do those stunts have tubs for bellies and their flab smacks to a dead stop against the surface of the water. As lean as you are, I'm surprised that your nauseatingly slender body didn't slice right on through the creek bed and have you drilling for natural gas halfway to China!"

"Hmm, Walt, sometimes your mind scares me. Uh, by the way, you two, hang on for a minute while I wade through the creek and get my jacket. I used it as a decoy of sorts on one of the big rocks in the creek to fool Ron into thinking I was dead."

As Jet retrieved his coat, Walt continued to stare upwards at the trestle in amazement. "I tell ya, Miss Cat, nobody else would have managed to get out of that pickle."

"You're definitely right, Sheriff. Nobody could have done that but the great Jet Jericho." Cat looked at the slender agent wading back toward her, a wistful, melancholic expression on her face. Then she closed her eyes, as if partially in prayer. . .

"Okay, folks, let's get on outta here," said Jericho with a sudden tone of urgency. "By the way, Walt, is my car okay? Ron didn't take it or mess with it, did he?"

"Naw, once we get out of this ravine, you'll see your car in the moonlight. Ron didn't appear to have messed with it. However, we didn't really look your car over thoroughly when we discovered you weren't around. That's why we didn't notice your gun in the passenger seat. We just started combing the area and hollering out for you. Thanks to that bright moon, Cat noticed you lying on the creek bank from the edge of the trestle."

As the trio began the hike back to their cars, another question came across Jericho's mind. "Walt, one more thing: where did you get the power saw to cut the tree? And, if you and Cat were busy searching for me, who was sawing the tree?"

"Oh," began Walt, matching Jericho's hocus-pocus tone. "I threw the power saw in the back of the trunk before I left home. For all I knew, I thought I might find you pinned under a fallen limb or something, thick as these woods are—just a precaution on my part."

"Man! Quite an astute precaution, I must say! I'm impressed, Sheriff, and grateful."

"Why, I thank you, Jet! I was obliged to be of service," responded a proudly beaming Walt. "And, I know this doesn't come as a surprise to you, but when we came upon the tree, we found that it had definitely been sawed. Someone was trying to give you a mighty woodsy welcome."

"Yeah, you're right, Walt, no surprise there. Anyway, who did you get to cut up the tree?"

"Oh, I brought along Sarah. She's a hearty country woman, and I'm proud to say that she's as good with a power saw as she is with a shotgun. She said when she finished cutting up the tree, she'd wait for us in the car."

"Wow, Walt! Is there anything Sarah cannot do? I mean, she cooks, shoots, sews, and saws."

"Hmm . . . well . . . she can't drive worth a damn. She doesn't turn her head to look behind her or use the rear view mirror. She just backs up slowly until she feels something make contact with her bumper."

"Sorry I asked, Walt."

"No problem, Jet. I assume you and Cat are riding back in your convertible."

"Yeah, Walt, that fall took a lot out of me, so I think we'll get back to the motel and get a good night's sleep. I guess Ron will hold. After all, I'm sure he thinks he has taken me completely out of the picture. I want you and me to go back to Columbia one last time. We'll leave at eight o'clock tomorrow morning and bring our 'slippery eel' back to Icy Springs. With me exterminated and out of his way in his imagination, we should find him lounging on his couch finishing up *Moby Dick*. I'm not gonna check in with Fowler at this late hour, but I'll get a hold of him in the morning and request that he get clearance from his SBI buddy in Columbia for us to bring home the bacon, a sorry slab of foul pork named Ron Christmas."

"Sounds good, Jet. Ron is as now as good as a pig in a poke, in my opinion—or should I say the pokey?"

"Yeah," agreed Jericho, massaging his own sore shoulders with his hands as he walked. "It's definitely past time for that pig to roast!"

CHAPTER 27

Hey, Whad'ya Say We Blow the Roof Off This Joint?

Jericho opened the door to Room #5 and allowed Cat to enter first. "After you, Kitten. Whew! I'm glad I brought my six-pack of Bengay along on this assignment. Even as superbly conditioned as my body is, I'm going to be sore all over in the morning. I can already feel it coming— Hey, what the—?! It looks like a tornado hit in here!"

"Uh, yeah," muttered Cat in a nearly inaudible reply. "I guess I neglected to tell you about the little mess I made here this evening."

"What in the world happened, darlin'? Did Ron attempt to kill you, also? I mean, I figured he was busy enough with me. I don't know how he would have had time to—"

"Hold on, Tiger," interrupted Cat. "Ron had nothing to do with this. As far as we know, he still doesn't even know I exist, even after me accompanying you in searching his house yesterday."

"Then what happened, Cat. I've got to hear this one!" commented Nolan, raising his right eyebrow in a slightly sarcastic gesture.

"*Well*, would you be satisfied with my explanation if I said I was doing some, uh, house cleaning and threw out some unnecessary, filthy ol' trash?" asked Cat in a timid tone, betraying her assumption that the agent wouldn't buy her story.

"No. No, I wouldn't be satisfied with that answer," responded Nolan. "Try again, and this time, you might at least attempt an explanation that accounts for the chair in the corner that's in . . . let's see . . . uh, one, two, three, four, five— uh, five pieces. You realize Fowler's gonna wonder about a charge on our invoice from the motel for a chair. So, try again, please: explanation number two."

"Uh, would you believe termites?" asked the evasive woman, with her chin down and her eyes completely fixed on the floor.

"No. Now, explanation number three, if you please, and make sure this one is the right one," requested Nolan while looking straight into Cat's beautiful eyes.

"All right, all right! Well, it wasn't termites, but it definitely was a huge pest. And I appointed myself chief exterminator, so there!" asserted Cat, crossing her arms and moving her head in one defiant nod.

"Keep going, I detect that you're perhaps getting closer to telling me the truth."

"Well, I wasn't a happy camper and it was time to take care of business," continued Cat with her arms still crossed.

"Warmer . . . warmer . . ."

"It was time someone put her in her place; she's such as ass and it was all up to little ol' ass-kickin' me!" assured Cat as she uncrossed her arms and placed her hands on her hips.

"Warmer . . . warmer . . ."

"All right, all right, all right," responded Cat in rapid triplicate. Falling just short of snorting while exhaling, she looked at Nolan with fire in her eyes and half-shouted, "It was Dreama! That little pipsqueak of a porn queen. She was here in bed when I got back from Charlotte, waiting on you."

"Aw, man! I, uh—oh, my!" exclaimed Nolan with his eyes wide open. "Wait a minute, you said she was in bed waiting for me, so I assume that she had no clothes on. Please tell me the two of you didn't have a knock-down-drag-out with Dreama in the nude."

"Whoa there! You can just put a harness on that juvenile visualization of yours, Hugh Hefner. Stuff like you're trying to picture belongs in magazines hidden under the mattresses of high school boys. Save your fantasies for the one woman that's worth fantasizing about, and you're looking at 'er."

"Oh, mercy! I, uh, just thought of something," exclaimed Jet, with a somewhat worried look on his face. "Cat, what did you do with the body?"

"I'm *not that* impulsive, you ding-dong. However, I can't honestly say that killing her certainly didn't cross my mind. It actually would have made for a great public service. Anyway, to answer your silly question, no! I didn't kill 'er. Dreama got off rather easy, in my opinion. I sent her running back to her patrol car with her tail tucked between her legs, what was left of 'er sorry butt." Having given the Cliff Notes version of the event, Cat now smiled slyly, indicating satisfaction with herself.

"Whew! Thank God, I certainly don't have time this week to serve as a character witness at *your* murder trial," remarked Nolan in mock relief.

"All right, buddy, speakin' of character, *your* character isn't totally off the hook. You'd better convince me you knew nothing about this potential little rendezvous. I'm not a hundred percent sure that you didn't have plans to jump on the ol' *tramp*-oline."

"Oh, Kitten, retract those claws and simmer down. I told you the other day that I've only actually been close in proximity to Dreama just once, and that's when I involuntarily ended up sitting next to her at breakfast in the café with two other lawmen present. Now, look into my eyes," directed Jericho, lowering his voice into a much more serious tone and placing his fingers gently under Cat's chin. "Yes, she definitely has flirted with me, but I've reciprocated nothing. She has received nothing from me in return. You are the one for which I had a ring waiting in a watermelon, remember?"

About five seconds passed before Cat's tight-faced expression loosened into an apologetic smile. "Yeah, Nolan, I know, and I guess I knew it all along. I'm sorry about my jealousy and this, uh, trust stuff. I hate that I continually have you jump through my hoops, always asking you to verbally assure me of your faithfulness. I can tell you one thing, though, Dreama does bring out the absolute worst in me."

"Think nothing of it, Cat. You're so worth the hoop jumping. I definitely have my share of issues, and I also run into people here and there that manage to yank my chain. I can't assert a claim toward perfection any more than the next person."

"Nolan, you really don't have to make an impassioned argument convincing me of your imperfection——that is, considering the fact that several hours ago you ended up in the middle of a train trestle unarmed."

A loving smile crossed Nolan's face as he realized Cat had done it yet again. No other woman had the agent ever met who could so turn his own words against him, not out of ill will or resentment, but out of love. She simply had an amazing capacity to always find the humor, and even the irony, in his quirks. She could use words cunningly as a mirror to reflect his character flaws, and she had that impish way of going about it that made him love her so. No matter how you cut it, Cat was so utterly, indescribably sexy. As much as Jericho wished to pursue this mood, he suddenly remembered a bit of unfinished business.

"Hey, Cat, what about the coin? What did you find out from that Barber fellow in Charlotte?"

"Something sort of strange, Tiger: the coin's probably not as intriguing as you thought. It's what is known as a widow's mite."

"A widow's mite?!" responded Jericho, apparently somewhat in the dark.

"Yeah, babe, a widow's mite. Remember? It's something that's mentioned in a significant story of the Bible—you know, the part about the poor woman who gave most everything she had as an offering to God."

"I'm no coin expert. But if the coin I found was a widow's mite, wouldn't it be worth a king's ransom?"

"Well, Tiger, you'd better hold off any elective surgeries you had planned. The widow's mite you found was a replica."

"A replica?!" asked Jericho, his voice sounding confused and mixed with a tinge of agitation.

At that point, Cat handed the coin back to the agent. "Yeah, and that's the interesting part, Nolan. Mr. Barber said that coins like this one are a dime a dozen. He said you can easily buy a sack full of them in gift shops and other tourist traps."

"I'll be damned, a widow's mite! Anyway, thanks love. I've no doubt that what you've told me will probably come in handy down the road. Now, let's hit the hay. I am dead tired."

◆ ◆ ◆ ◆ ◆

The clock's alarm sounded as abrasive as a factory whistle at 6:30 a.m. Jericho eased his achy right arm out from under Cat and stretched it in slow motion along with his achy left arm.

"*Yowww . . . ohh,*" he whispered in muted agony, realizing just how sore his rib cage was from smashing against the creek bed in the fall from the trestle. *Man, I guess I should count my lucky stars that I'm able to feel anything this morning. I definitely flirted with the possibility of serious injury last night, if not death.*

"Morning, Tiger! You sound like you're hurting quite a bit—definitely not a good way to begin a Saturday, is it, sugar?"

"I tell ya, Cat, I feel like I've been dragged for ten miles behind a team of horses."

"Yeah, you did a number on yourself all right, jumping from that trestle yesterday. Why do you think I held off on the négligée last night? You can hardly handle me when you're in tip-top condition. I couldn't see further damaging a man still reeling from being wounded in the line of duty."

"Oh, Cat! I wasn't hurt that bad. For crying out loud, let me be the judge of how out-of-commission I am. The next time you're selecting your evening wear, why don't you spare me the 'sparin' me'?"

"Oh, don't cry over spilt milk, Tiger. Besides, you were practically asleep before your head hit your pillow."

"Yeah, I did bail out on you, didn't I?"

"Sure did, sleepy-head, but I'm sure you needed it for whatever might be facing you today."

"Aw, no need to worry, Kitten. After all, you're dealing with Superman here."

"Yeah, don't I know it. Every time you turn around, you're getting yourself waist-deep in Kryptonite."

"You never give up, do you? At any rate, I'll going to take a hot, hot shower to melt away some of this soreness. If you wanna join me in about ten minutes, I'll go easy on the hot water. Interested?"

After a slight hesitation, Cat relented. "I'm probably asking for trouble, but I'll give you the benefit of the doubt. But you'd better put a muzzle on the hot, or it'll be the last time I gamble on you roasting me." With a defiant smirk, she spun around and slid back underneath the covers.

Nolan showered for ten minutes in water hotter than his lady would have tolerated and, good to his word, turned the heat down considerably as Cat stepped in. They enjoyed the water together for fifteen minutes, then Nolan stepped out to let her do the extensive shampoo-and-conditioner routine on her long, flowing hair. With some of his soreness now relieved, he sat on the bed and stared at the chest of drawers. *Oh, what to wear?* Considering the likelihood that today could prove mighty active, the agent decided on "Jet-casual" once again—a black polo shirt with a black sports jacket and black pants.

After dressing, he sat back down on the bed and dialed the telephone. As the phone began ringing, the anxious agent literally crossed his fingers. *Okay, it's seven o'clock on the dot. I hate calling Fowler at home, especially on a Saturday, but I'll catch hell if I don't. I know he's wondering what been going on and, frankly, I'm dying to know if he's heard anything from Ortmann. I sure hope Fowler's early-birdin' it this morning at home like he does the rest of the week. C'mon, Fowler, pick up!*

A surly voice cut the seventh ring in half. "Hello, Fowler speakin'."

"Director, Jet Jericho here."

"Well, better late than never. What the hell's been happening down there?"

"First of all, Director, anything out of Ortmann?"

"No, Jet, nothing. It's getting to the point where he is as deficient in his tendencies to check in promptly as you are!"

"Well, either Ortmann went to sleep on the job *as* usual or—"

"Watch it, agent! I evaluate the performance of your peers, you don't!"

"Uh, sorry, Director, that was somewhat out of line on my part. Anyway, Ron Christmas somehow got past John and made an appearance in Icy Springs, dressed like a hooded figure straight out of a dime store novel."

"You sure it was him, Jet?"

"Yes sir, he flaunted some mighty incriminating clues, such as a stuffed monkey I had seen upstairs in his bedroom when we searched his house. The biggie, however, was that he had a picture of his late wife, Linda Fairbanks Christmas."

"Okay, so may I assume he in custody?"

"No, sir. He is not," Jericho mumbled.

"And why not?" asked Fowler in an agitated tone.

"Well, like I said, he was wearing a hood and he was brandishing a powerful rifle with a scope. He took me by surprise, grazing me with one shot. To escape him, I had to do a daredevil jump from a high train trestle. By the time I came to, Ron was long gone." Conveniently for himself, the agent left out the part about leaving his gun behind in the seat of his car.

"Okay, agent. You know that I'll want all the specifics later in a fully detailed report. What are your plans at this point?"

"Uh, Director, I think I have more than sufficient reasonable suspicion for us to take Ron in and interrogate him 'til the cows come home. Sheriff Niblock said he would ride with me this morning to Pelion and apprehend Ron. Hopefully, in the process, I'll find out what happened to Ortmann."

"Sounds fine, Jet. What do you need from me?"

"Can you have your army buddy give me full clearance to take Ron in custody and bring him back into North Carolina?"

"No problem there, agent. My friend will be willing to wink a blind eye in our direction, I'm sure. But Jet, for God's sake, don't kill an innocent civilian in the process. Watch your grandstanding, mister—no high speed chases, no gunfights in a public place. I owe my old acquaintance that much, agent. None of his agents have ever killed innocent bystanders in North Carolina. I don't want to start a new trend with a body count I'm going to have to explain to reporters."

"Understood, sir!"

Suddenly, a wet Cat, glistening with beads of water, came from the steamy bathroom, wiping herself off with a towel. "Nolan, who's—"

"Shh!" whispered the agent in a slightly admonishing manner. Holding the phone to his chest, he mouthed: *It's Fowler.*

Sorry... mouthed Cat back at Nolan.

Jericho winced a little as he put the receiver back to his ear, for Fowler knew a woman's voice when he heard it. "Agent, who's that woman I hear with ya? Is Cat—"

"Sorry, sir," interrupted the quick-thinking agent. "My door's open and a maid stopped by to check on my linen."

"Oh, okay. Anyway, check in with me tomorrow evening. Hopefully, this mess will be over with soon, and you and Cat can get your carcasses on back here to Raleigh."

"Sure thing, sir. Good day."

Upon hanging up, Jericho looked at Cat and let out a sigh while giving her the old that-was-a-close-one look. "Cat, you know better than that. You've got to be more careful! Thank goodness Fowler couldn't quite identify your voice. After all, he wouldn't expect us to be in each other's company this early in the morning, particularly in my room."

"Sorry, Tiger. Now, get on over here and help me dry off!"

"No problem at all," commented Jericho with a smile.

"For some reason, I'm cravin' pancakes this morning for breakfast," Cat said as she made a motion rubbing her belly. "Or do you think maybe I just have a warped desire to see a tree trunk of a man do a chicken dance?"

"Surely not, Cat. I always perceived you as a bit of a masochist rather than a sadist," responded Nolan in a dry, matter-of-fact tone.

"Well, all I know is I need a good breakfast before we set out toward Columbia."

"Uh, '*we*', Cat? Darlin', I'm afraid that you're under the wrong impression, and you're not gonna like what I'm about to tell you."

◆ ◆ ◆ ◆ ◆

"Yeah, Jet," said Walt, as his curly black hair danced frenetically in the wind. "I'll bet our Miss Cat wasn't thrilled at all staying behind at the motel on this go-round."

"No, quite frankly, she kicked up quite a bit of sand," acknowledged Jericho as he steered his red convertible on down the highway. "However, I stood my ground on this one. I mean, I don't know what's happened to our surveillance man, Ortmann. I just thought it was too dangerous for Cat to accompany us in consideration of Ron's blatant attempt at having me pushing up daisies while, I might add, having the audacity to parade his identity right in my face. That nut definitely appears to have gone totally cuckoo for Cocoa Puffs. Yeah, Walt, Ron has completely become a wild joker in the deck, so it was way too dangerous for Cat to have come along."

"I'll bet that *she* didn't see it that way," mused the sheriff.

"Walt, there are a good many things she doesn't see my way," affirmed the agent.

"Jet, I hate that you're using your personal car to drive all this way. I would have been more than happy to have used one of our department's vehicles."

"Call me a hopeless romantic, Walt," said Nolan, "or just call me claustrophobic. But after the kind of evening I spent yesterday, I just needed to feel the sunshine against my face and the breeze slappin' me around a little. You can call it my self-prescribed therapy—my own home remedy, if you will. But driving just makes my sore body feel a little better than merely sitting in a passenger seat. Besides, Ortmann already has one of our state cars down there somewhere around Pelion and when we find out what in the world he's been up to, I'll have him haul Ron back in it with us following him."

"Sounds like a plan, Jet. Yeah, I have to admit that it is kinda fun zipping along the road in your Sting Ray. Oh, by the way, there's something big I hadn't told ya about. . ." said Walt, leaving his friend hanging.

"What, you enrolled Deputy Hodges in a class about the handling of wild animals?" Jericho responded while giving his partner a sly look.

"Nah, ol' Hodges learned far more from the bear than sitting in a class would ever teach him," answered the sheriff.

"Then what?"

"I let Dreama go early this morning—you know, gave 'er her walkin' papers. I stopped by her place before going on to my office and asked her to turn in her badge, her uniform, and her gun. The funny thing was she had bubble gum crammed in the barrel of her gun!"

"*Hmm!* Bubble gum, huh? You don't say!" remarked Jericho, knowing full well how the gum ended up in the gun. Although Cat hadn't told him specifically about her inspired little undertaking, a bubble gum-filled pistol did reek of something that Cat might do if her ire was raised enough. "Well, Walt, it was certainly a long time in coming. How did Dreama take it?"

"Surprisingly well, Jet. It's like she kind-a predicted that her days were numbered. I dunno—I mean, I'm not the best at reading people sometimes, but it's like Dreama has the soul of a gypsy. I think she's just one of those people who is happiest being restless—you know, constantly searching for a happiness that I'm not sure she'll ever find."

"A very astute observation, Walt, and just remember that your obligation has totally ended in assisting Dreama in her ongoing quest for her happiness. You're running a law enforcement agency, not an adult rehabilitation clinic. Consider Dreama gone, a done deal. Forget about 'er."

"I'll try, Jet. Although I realize that she was the biggest staffing mistake I've made since becoming sheriff, I'll have to admit that there was a kind of kinetic energy about Dreama—a spunkiness, if you will—that I'm going to miss having around the office. When she wasn't causing my wife to go out on a wild shooting spree, she did kind-a brighten up the place a little, being all pretty as a pea. It's quite amazing how much she reminded me of Miss Cat, even though the resemblance is totally coincidental, of course."

If you only knew, my old friend . . . if you only knew. "Well, Walt, until we arrive in Pelion, just sit back and enjoy the breeze," suggested the agent, having a blast in his beloved Anna as the miles rolled along.

The trip did not seem to take long at all. After arriving in Pelion, Walt looked at Jet and said half-seriously, "You know, I've passed that big peanut enough this week to do me for a while."

"Hey, what about me, friend? This is only your second trip down here. I came Tuesday to interview Ron, then we came here Thursday to search his place, and now we're here again to haul him in. I'd safely say that my three trips to Pelion have definitely knocked this location off my list of vacation destinations for next summer," said the agent with a grin.

◆ ◆ ◆ ◆ ◆

The Christmas homestead seemed more dormant than ever, totally lifeless. The light blue Galaxie was sitting in its usual spot and this was good, for it meant that Ron should be home. But something about the place on this late Saturday morning right before noon seemed like a purgatory . . . a netherworld . . . a grim depository of good memories long gone and bad karma now embracing it.

As the two lawmen stepped out of the red convertible, they were immediately struck by just how dead the property seemed. "Man, Walt, ya hear that?" asked Jericho.

"Hear what, Jet? I don't hear anything—anything at all," replied the confused sheriff.

"That's just it—there's nothing. This place offers about the loudest silence you'll ever hear. I mean, it's just like the first day I came here to interview Ron, with the place seemingly deserted. Everything was so lifeless—that is, until Ron appeared out of nowhere with a pitchfork."

"Let's keep real alert, partner. No telling where he's hiding now or what he might be thinking," suggested the sheriff.

"Right, especially considering the fact that Ortmann still hasn't been seen or heard from. I was really banking on seeing the department's car parked somewhere back up the road a ways or maybe even right around here. I sure hope that John's okay."

"Yeah, Jet, isn't it funny how a particular person you work with can make your skin crawl, but you still hope for his well-being in the long run? I'm sure he'll turn up. Perhaps his car just broke down somewhere."

"Perhaps, but surely he could have flagged somebody down and gotten to a phone. Surely Fowler would have known something by this morning when I called him. I dunno, Walt, I fear that he might have fallen asleep at the wheel and, God forbid, perhaps run off the road into a swamp or something. Who knows?!"

"Jet, before we go a-knockin' on Ron's door, let's walk over and check out his car—you know, see if the keys are in it. You never know, maybe there's some evidence in the car, such as the sock monkey with the handwritten message on it that he used as bait to lure you onto the trestle."

"Good idea, Walt, why not?!," agreed Nolan.

As they neared the Galaxie, Walt said, "Jet, do you smell that?—a *baaad* odor of some kind?"

"Yeah, I do smell it," concurred Jericho, opening the car door. "Something putrid smelling. Well, Walt, the keys *are* in the ignition. At a glance, however, I don't see any visible evidence up front."

Having already opened the back door, Walt stood up straight and wiped the sweat off his brow. "Nothing in the back either except, of course, that rank smell in the air."

"Okay then, I'll take the keys and open the trunk. I'd love to find some handy evidence in there, say the sock monkey or the rifle with the scope on it. That would be way too convenient, however."

As the two men positioned themselves at the trunk lid and Jericho placed the key into the lock, he paused for a second. "Oh-oh, Walt, bad news! The smell is way stronger here."

"Yeah, Jet, almost sickening."

"Walt, hold your breath, I'm opening 'er up. I know that smell all too well. There's a body in here."

As the trunk lid was lifted, both men took a step back and cupped their hands over their noses. The sudden release of the foul odor from the decomposing corpse was downright nauseating, as the hot July heat had played havoc with the fluids and tissues of the body. And it didn't matter how prepared each man was to see the macabre scene they were now witnessing, the initial glance still sent a message of shock to their brains and a jarring jolt to their guts.

"John . . ." said Nolan quietly, nearly choking up. "Dear Lord, Walt, it's John Ortmann, and he appears to have shot wounds."

"What's weird, Jet," interjected Walt somberly, "is that your boss only sent him out here two days ago—you know, when you called him on the payphone Thursday after searching this place. I mean, Ortmann couldn't have gotten here from Raleigh until the wee hours of the morning on Friday."

"Yeah, Walt, what I figure is that Ron easily spotted Ortmann's car as he was departing yesterday, I've no doubt, on his way to attempt getting rid of me at the train trestle." Jericho suddenly gulped deeply and sighed, temporarily placing the palm of his hand over his forehead. "DAMN! If only Fowler had listened to me. I knew that John wasn't right for this kind of assignment. The poor soul probably died in his sleep!"

Immediately feeling remorseful for the dig at Ortmann in his last comment, Jericho gently closed the trunk lid and look heavenward. "I'm, uh, sorry about that remark, John—and my apologies to you too, Walt. I know I must seem insensitive with my implications of John falling asleep on the job. However, his excessive narcolepsy did make solitary surveillance very risky for him. Maybe I shouldn't blame Fowler. After all, manpower is becoming very sparse these days, thanks to the budget. I guess Fowler didn't feel he could afford two men for this gig."

"I'm really sorry about your friend, Jet," said Walt, placing his hand on Nolan's shoulder.

"Thanks, Walt. Now, enough with the helplessness! It's time to do what we came to do and haul in this murderous imbecile. Walt, I'll check the house—and don't worry: today, I have my gun. Would you check the outbuildings and the barn just as you did the other day? If this creep is on this property at this moment, he's going in as of now!"

"Sure thing, Jet, but be careful."

"You too, partner. Remember, he tends to like farm tools," said Jericho, alluding to the pitchfork incident.

As Walt walked toward the chicken coop, Jericho stepped lightly onto the porch and proceeded to the screen door as quietly as a ninja. He opened the screen door and peered through one of the panes of glass on the wooden door. There was no sign of life inside—no movement, no lights on, and no noise to be detected. Recalling Ron's surprise attack with the rifle at the train trestle, Jericho decided it was now his turn to do the surprising and chose not to announce his arrival. He slowly turned the door knob, gave a gentle push, and, allowing the door to swing open slightly from its own momentum, eased inside without making a noise.

The house was as silent as a tomb. Having chosen to leave his gun in his holster and remain free-handed, Nolan still reached inside his jacket to ensure that his firearm was there and ready for action. With a nod to logic, the agent decided to search the kitchen first as it had the only other outside door on the first floor. He paused in the doorway and, per his inclination, looked at the top of the refrigerator, as if the cigarette carton might magically materialize for his benefit. Glancing away from the fridge, Nolan's attention was immediately drawn to a single piece of paper lying on the dining table. He could tell by the jagged edges of the paper that it was a page that had been ripped out of a book. It was apparently somewhat aged, displaying some moderate discoloration, similar to that of old newspapers.

The curious agent gently lifted up the yellowed piece of paper, which was full of handwriting in black ink. At the top of the page was something of a descriptive heading followed by a date. Jericho's eyes widened immensely as he realized just what he was holding. *Oh, man! A diary entry—-this is a torn-out page of a diary!*

Linda's Thoughts   Feb. 4, '43

Tonight, Ron asked me to marry him this summer. Wow! I told him I would, and he actually had tears in his eyes. It was the most emotional I have ever seen him. I love Ron so. So much has happened this year!

I really have enjoyed my friendship with both Ron and Paul over the last three years. Both boys are so different. I really love Paul, too. For some strange reason, I dread telling him that I've marrying Ron, but I doubt it will bother Paul in the least. Paul just never sits still and he always has so many people around him.

I feel I've made the right decision in saying "Yes" to Ron. I never really cared for crowds of people and being in the spotlight like Paul does. I hope Paul finds a woman who doesn't mind sharing him with the world. Although I care greatly for Paul, his energy simply wears me out. Ron and I have so much more in common that I believe I could have a much happier life with him.

I will probably tell Paul about our plans tomorrow. I'm sure he will be happy for us as he simply does not seem the least bit interested in settling down with anyone at this point. In a way, the difference between the boys made my choice for me, and I'm glad of that. Thank goodness for you, diary. You're always the best listener!

Well, well, well! It looks like Mary Christmas was spot-on about Ron and Linda's relationship. Chalk one up for a mother who keeps up with what is happening in her kids' lives. Although Linda seemed a little confused or torn when writing this entry, her thoughts definitely document the choices that Ron and Paul were making for themselves during their senior year. Evidently, Ron is still so obsessed over his late wife that he continually replays the memory of Linda accepting his proposal by reading her diary entry over and over. Ron uses Linda's written declaration of love to constantly re-energize his obsession and justify his unhappiness.

Folding the enlightening artifact in quarters, Jericho tucked the paper in the pocket of his jacket for safe keeping. The agent quickly searched the remainder of the first floor rooms and closets for Ron, but, as he expected, no fugitive was found in hiding. *I gathered from my last visit that Ron spends much of his time upstairs, as most of his furnishings seemed to be up there. I'll bet Ron saw Walt and me coming in and ran to higher ground. Although not guaranteed, I'll bet he's hiding either under the bed or in the bedroom closet.*

The agent slowly crept up the stairs, his stealth permitting no creaks or groans from the time-worn steps. Continually monitoring the balance of his body with each step, Nolan ensured that the varnish-deficient floorboards in the hallway were equally cooperative in avoiding disclosure of his presence.

Jericho could feel his heartbeat accelerating as he placed his left hand on the doorknob to Ron's bedroom while extending his gun hand toward his holster. Having been nearly pitchforked, stoned, and shot by the maniac who was hopefully on the other side of the door, there was no way the agent could play his next moves too cautiously.

Gently pushing the door open, Jericho was ready for the madman possibly hiding behind it. What he couldn't have anticipated was the thin, nearly-invisible fishing line attached to the other side of the door by means of a paneling nail which, in turn, trailed across the room to a 55-gallon oil drum sitting against the wall. With the door open about eight inches, Jericho noticed the fishing line, but it was too late! His eyes immediately followed the line to its terminus and, spotting the oil drum against the wall with some equipment sitting on top, he nervously took two steps toward it.

From a distance of about six steps from the drum, Nolan now ascertained that the jerk on the fishing line from opening the door had tilted the glass tube to which it was attached. He quickly deduced that mercury placed inside the tube had slid downward, closing the electrical circuit wired to the bomb. At a glance, the observant agent could also see a timing mechanism within the apparatus, and the moving indicator on the timer passed from the number 'six' to the number 'five' in the duration of a second!

Five seconds . . . Realizing he had only seconds to live if he remained in the house, Jericho's survival instincts kicked in.

Four seconds . . . his internal clock told him. He lunged forward eight feet at lightning speed and dove outward with all his might.

Three seconds . . . his mind counted down for him.

KUH-RASH!

Crashing through the bedroom window face-first in a perfectly horizontal position, the desperate agent's body immediately descended three feet in mid-air.

Two seconds . . . came the mental notice.

KA-WHAMM!

Landing on his belly, Jericho smacked hard against the sloped tin roof over the front porch of the house.

Standing at the barn about to lift the crossbar fastening the doors, Walt's head jerked immediately toward the house upon hearing the crash of the window and the harsh slam of the agent's body upon the tin sheets of the porch roof.

One second . . . his internal timer informed him.

Upon impact with the tin roof, Jericho's body continued streaming downward fast as he slid face-first across the smooth, slick tin toward the edge of the overhang, much as a baseball player sliding in belly-down to home base. Careening over the edge of the precipice, the agent suddenly found himself sailing toward the ground from about twelve feet in the air.

ZERO . . . he reckoned.

Like a falling cat, Jericho was able to twist his body in mid-air, thus achieving enough in-flight contortion to somewhat invert his body position.

BUH-RROOOOMM!!!

The noise was almost deafening, causing Walt to recoil backwards and fall against the right-hand barn door.

The tremendous explosion occurred at the moment the agent's body was about three feet from the ground. Although his toes touched the ground first and somewhat broke his fall, Jericho couldn't quite manage to land on his feet. His knees took the brunt of the fall, and, with the debris from the explosion in full descent, the agent immediately flattened himself face-down on the ground, using his arms to cover his head.

Hugging the ground as tightly as possible, Nolan felt rushes of air and heat. Then stuff began pelting him at random points all over his body. Sometimes it felt as if someone were simply touching him, sometimes as if someone's finger were poking him firmly, and sometimes as if he had received the line drive of a tennis ball. Luckily, the sensation he feared might be forthcoming failed to materialize—that of being hit by a portion of a toilet or a chunk of a bed's headboard or some other significant piece of flying rubble.

Suddenly, Nolan's left foot began to sting and he lifted his arm left arm off his head just enough to look back and survey the problem. The bottom of his left pant leg was on fire! Evidently, a cinder of some kind had managed to ignite the cloth on contact. The agent instinctively began pounding his leg against the ground, moving it up and down rapidly until the flame was extinguished.

After the heavy debris ceased falling, the agent sat up and began to dust himself off, although ashes and dust particles continued to envelope him. He noticed a small, paper-like object gently wafting through the air and stayed attuned to its presence as it floated down into his lap. It was a half-burnt photograph. He closely examined the charred image: it was a picture of Linda Christmas!

Walt was in the process of standing up, having also hit the dirt by anchoring himself on the ground against the barn and covering his head with his arms—for he, as much as Jericho, had been in jeopardy of being hit by any explosion-launched projectiles.

"Jet!" hollered out the sheriff, "Are you okay?"

"Yeah, Walt, I'll live," yelled back Jericho, as he also rose to his feet. "No sign of Ron, though."

"I'll bet not," said Walt loudly as he began to walk over partway to Jericho. "If Ron was anywhere inside that house, he was propelled clear to Timbuktu by that blast. If you're up to it, let's go check inside the barn. That's the only building I hadn't gotten around to."

"Okay," shot back Jet. Taking his first steps since standing, the agent began hiking toward Walt.

No one could have predicted what was to happen next. No one could have heard the car being turned on by a sleazy hand manipulating the ignition key at the exact moment of the blast. No one could have heard the momentary idling of the car due to the ambient noise of the house burning and collapsing after the blast. As Walt stood about fifteen feet from the barn with his back toward the doors, a thumping crash ensued.

BUH-ROMMMP!!

Nolan watched helplessly as the startled sheriff whipped around to the spectacle of the two large barn doors ripping from their hinges and hurtling toward the ground. Out of the darkness roared an ugly olive-green Ford LTD, as if it were some ill-tempered beast exiting a cave after a long hibernation. With time seemingly frozen-framed, Walt struggled desperately to lurch sideways out of the awakened monster's path, but was only half-successful. The front corner on the driver's side of the car cut short the evasive attempt of the sheriff, clipping his left thigh and spiraling him into a clumsy somersault to the left side of the roaring vehicle.

Seeing Walt tossed helplessly like a rag doll. Nolan immediately drew his gun and took aim as the Ford zoomed past him. He fired three times. All three shots were delivered through the rear windshield toward the driver's seat, but the green monster failed to decrease its speed. Evidently, the driver had estimated some valiant attempts at marksmanship by the crack shot and, in the way that Jericho had avoided decapitation by a concrete block, had used that same ducking-down maneuver in the front seat.

Once the agent realized that his shots had failed to bring home the bacon, he lowered his gun toward the right rear tire of the car and fired twice more. Again, no dice! The car had simply out-distanced the range of Nolan's shots, with no lead of a bullet reaching the rubber of a tire.

"Damn!" shouted Jericho in frustration, mostly cursing himself for delaying too long before shooting at the tires after his fruitless bids at the driver.

Nolan rolled his eyes at the teasing sight of the rude Ford as it bounced across the ruts of the rugged drive toward freedom on the paved highway.

Immediately, he shot a glance toward his friend, yelling, "Walt, are you hurt bad?"

Sitting up on the ground with both hands clutching his left thigh, Walt answered, "I'm okay, I'm okay—only my leg's broken, I think! I'll just sit here." Instantly pawing at the air furiously with his left hand in a gesture signaling his partner to get moving, the injured sheriff shouted, "Go, go, go! Catch the jackass! I'm fine, just go!"

Jericho completely cleared the passenger door of his convertible as he broad jumped into the driver's seat. After a rapid turn of the ignition key, the agent floored the accelerator, flinging a smoke screen of powdery dirt from the spinning rear wheels as the red Sting Ray propelled itself forward like a rocket sled down the rut-infested drive.

"NO! Not again, Ron!—not this easily!" shouted Nolan angrily as he slid sideways out of the dirt drive into a quick right turn onto the hard surface of the secondary road. Having seen the direction Ron had headed from his already lengthy distance behind the fleeing Ford, the agent could still sight the olive-green blob far up ahead. *I thank my lucky stars for these lengthy, straight, flat stretches of South Carolina highways. They sure make car chases a damn sight more convenient than in most of North Carolina.*

The wind tunnel, as Cat liked to call it, was incredibly exhilarating as the red convertible sailed down the highway with its engine revved to the max. An almost wicked smile crossed Nolan's face as the green blob appeared to be growing larger and larger, for he was fully confident that his quarry would soon be in the bag.

Suddenly, an "a-ha moment" hit the agent. *Now I know how this lunatic easily passed through the dragnets that I had Walt set up yesterday evening in North Carolina. He had Ortmann's car! And since law officers were screening the highways for a Ford Galaxie, they readily ignored the Ford LTD with its permanent state license plate. And all the while yesterday, Ortmann was lying dead in the trunk of Ron's car. I swear by all that's holy, I'm gonna walk Ron Christmas personally to the gas chamber!*

Jericho held the red Sting Ray at 140 miles per hour, even though the speedometer of his '67 crown jewel allowed measurements of speed up to 160 miles per hour. The agent felt it best to maintain a slightly subdued speed because of the hidden danger in such long stretches of highway. Although mostly flat, the road tended to contain some dips and rises that were visually undetectable from a certain distance away, and Jericho was wise enough to know that it really wasn't prudent to become outright airborne. In other words, today was not the day to end up on the highway upside-down as had the anteater-snatching airplane pilot in front of the Dagenhart's house back in Icy Springs.

Yep! Gotcha now, old boy! thought Jericho confidently as his car narrowed Ron's lead to around a half-mile. *This will validate the on-the-job use of my Sting Rays to Fowler, for here I am, about to overtake one of his own precious department cracker boxes!*

Without fair warning, fate lent its fortuitous hand, casting good fortune to the driver of the LTD. Just as the ugly green vehicle passed by a herd of cattle lined up beside the road, a farmer opened his gate for the waiting cows to cross the highway. A twice-a-day routine for the herd, they marched back and forth between a fenced-in milk barn on one side of the highway and a fenced-in pasture offering shade and a deep, cool creek on the other side of the highway. Whether the partially blind farmer didn't see the approaching red convertible rapidly flashing forward remains unknown; whether the farmer didn't bother looking, relying totally on the *Cattle Crossing* signs posted in each direction on the highway, remains unknown. From a pragmatic standpoint, neither reason was relevant to Jericho. All he knew was an immediate need for hitting his brakes.

As rubber burned against the already hot highway, Jericho begrudgingly brought his Sting Ray to a dead stop less than a half-tenth mile from the clueless herd. "Son of a—"

Beeep . . . beeeep . . . beeeeeeeep!!! The frustrated agent leaned on his horn even though he realized that it wouldn't exactly serve as polite encouragement for the brainless bovines to expedite matters. Instead, his tantrum on the car horn was perhaps a lashing-out against fate for having chosen to root for the bad guy. It was his way of saying "I've got a killer to catch here! *A little help, please?*"

The farmer's eyes never made contact with the "damned ol' rude Yankee driver always in a hurry." Perhaps his partial deafness played a factor in not being attentive to such a purpose-driven man behind a wheel. Or perhaps, the old guy ignored Jericho because he just flat out didn't give a rat's ass. Again, it was all irrelevant, for this Red Sea of cattle wasn't going to part for such an impatient Moses, even one in a red Sting Ray, and only in the world of James Bond could one jump a sports car over an entire herd of cattle.

As the last cow trotted across the road, Jericho mashed the accelerator and, steering Anna off the highway, arced around the moseying moo-cow. Flirting dangerously with the edge of the ditch, Jericho immediately re-took the highway while keeping the accelerator floored. The flustered agent quickly re-established his speed at 120 miles per hour while feverishly looking for the green blob to re-appear in the horizon. Nothing was revealing itself on the highway facing him, and he started feeling a sick sensation in the pit of his stomach, sensing that Ron had possibly ended up with the upper hand, yet again!

In desperation, Nolan started scoping the terrain ahead panoramically and noticed a highway jutting out within the horizon to his right, skewed at roughly a forty-five-degree angle from the road he was on. Twisting his head backwards even further to the right and looking across the fields lying between the two highways, he spotted the green blob on the other highway moving in practically the opposite direction. *Thank goodness, a second chance! There's got to be an intersection up ahead for that fool to have accessed the other road.*

Sure enough! In several seconds, the agent spotted a *Stop Ahead* sign in the distance. He could now see the upcoming intersection comprising the vertex of a enormous, sharp wedge formed by the two highways. From an airplane, the angle formed by the two highways would actually resemble a giant, single slice of pizza. And lying within the area comprising the sharp wedge between the two highways was a huge cornfield.

A slightly bizarre flash of inspiration hit Jericho, and he slowed his speed to around eighty miles an hour. Surveying the thin, dry, yellow stalks left behind as victims of a recent drought and eyeing the rock-hard soil baking in the July sun, he decided to cut corners and bypass the intersection. *Sorry, Anna, but hold on, girl. This is going to be one helluva ride for both of us!*

At a portion of the highway where the ditch was nearly non-existent, Nolan entered the cornfield at nearly seventy miles per hour. As Anna rocked and rolled among the corn stalks, dust and pieces of the plants flew about in a frenzied mixture. The agent vigorously swiped at his face and hair to prevent the gritty, hot cloud of dirty, brittle plant matter from clinging to him. *I swear! What a time to be driving around without my top up.*

Exiting the cornfield, Jericho once again slid his car sideways into a sharp right turn and swerved onto the highway. Having made up for some lost time by circumventing the intersection, the agent inhaled deeply out of much relief that he had not lost Ron completely, or so he hoped. If lucky, the elusive killer was only two, maybe three miles ahead and hadn't yet left the highway, as alternative routes in this area weren't exactly a dime a dozen. Flooring his accelerator yet again, Nolan decided to throw caution to the wind. *Forget the freakin' tiny hills and valleys in the road. I can only catch him if I give it all this baby's worth. Come on, Anna!*

The red convertible's engine again roared loudly as Nolan accelerated to 150 miles per hour. About five miles on up the highway, the unpredictable road offered one of those invisible little rises, and without warning, for about four seconds, the agent could feel his stomach leave him as his convertible went airborne. As he was now literally *flying* at 150 miles per hour, Nolan knew he needed to keep a firm grip on the road. If he lost control of Anna upon landing, there would be no need to send out an ambulance. All they would need to do to clean up the mess would be to bring out some brooms and dustpans to sweep up the pieces. The agent breathed a sigh of relief the moment he felt the wheels of the car bounce back onto the highway in perfect evenness.

Still piloting the Sting Ray at meteoric speed, Nolan strained to catch sight of the LTD, praying that he hadn't somehow missed it again. So it was with great relief that he soon spied the green blob up ahead once again. *Anna, you definitely outdo those molasses-mobiles! Unless he's been flying beneath the radar so as not to attract attention to himself from some random state trooper? Oh, who cares, ol' girl—there he is! Let's git 'im!*

Closing in on Ron within about three-quarters of a mile, Nolan suddenly caught some movement out of the corner of his eye on the horizon to his left. The endless, caterpillar-like image of a distant train gliding across the fields came into focus. As the train's line of movement appeared to be not quite parallel with the highway, Jericho quickly deduced that there was a very strong likelihood of a railroad crossing not too far up ahead.

Jericho kept it floored, but unfortunately the driver of the LTD apparently noticed the red flash of a Sting Ray re-approaching him from out of nowhere. Once again, the driver of the Ford gunned it as fast as an LTD can gun it. *Damn, he's speeding up again!* acknowledged Jericho, as his peripheral vision could also see that the train was now angling toward the highway at a sharper trajectory. *Oh-oh, Jericho! you definitely have a train about to cross the road.*

Up ahead, red lights started flashing, with bells sounding and wooden arms lowering to a horizontal position across the highway. With the train roughly a half-mile from crossing the road, the green Ford crashed through the crossing arms and zipped across the railroad track with plenty of time to spare. Jericho knew that he had no such wealth of seconds to play with, for he was around two-thirds of a mile from the crossing, and it was going to be incredibly close. He floored Anna for all it was worth. *I'm gonna make it! I'm gonna make it!— NO!!!*

Jericho had waited as long as possible, but with the intersection of the railroad track and the highway quickly approaching, he could now sense that he was headed toward a dead-on collision with the front end of the lead diesel engine. The agent rode the brakes so hard that he felt he was about to push his foot through the floorboard. The smooth surface of the highway did not embrace the rapidly decelerating Sting Ray readily as smoking wheels fought for traction. Nolan gritted his teeth and braced himself as the front of the convertible started sliding to the left. Turning his steering wheel into the slide, the nervous agent now saw the train engines crossing the highway as he stared at them from *across his passenger door!* Long black skid marks continued flowing outward from the tires amidst the pungent smell of melting rubber. Finally, Anna came to a halt sideways on the highway alongside the railroad track. Nolan inhaled very slowly and very deeply as he looked across the passenger door at the train whizzing by, roughly eight inches from Anna's red exterior.

Looking down the track, Jericho could see that the train went on . . . and on . . . and on . . . possibly having as many as two hundred cars. Realizing that waiting out the train would definitely require more time than needed to wince through a small herd of cattle, Nolan crossed his arms, laid his head back against the seat, and closed his eyes. *I swear! Cows and trains! Ron Christmas must have a freakin' Leprechaun in his pocket! There's no way to catch him now, no way at all! He's done it again!*

Looking around at the wide expanse of open fields threaded by a train track and a deserted highway, the agent looked at himself in his rear view mirror. *Okay, genius—now, where on God's green Earth are you?*

CHAPTER 28

Collateral Damage and Sock Monkeys

It seemingly took forever in the rural "wilds" of South Carolina, but Nolan managed to come upon a crossroads community, comprising a small store and three farms. He politely but urgently commandeered the phone inside the store for official use and immediately contacted the Sheriff's Office of Lexington County. Luckily, Sheriff Gordon West was in and, being fully acquainted with the Ron Christmas situation, instantly agreed to grapevine an APB across all South Carolina highways for an olive-green Ford LTD with a permanent North Carolina license plate. Sheriff West also offered to contact law enforcement officials of Mecklenburg County to get the ball of vigilance rolling around the Charlotte area in case Ron attempted flight into North Carolina. Lastly, the sheriff also said the fire department would be dispatched to the Christmas farm if they hadn't already been, and that Jericho could also count on emergency personnel arriving to attend to Sheriff Niblock. Now came the part the agent dreaded, that of informing Fowler of Ortmann's death.

As if he had been waiting by the phone for bad news, Fowler answered after only one ring. "Hello, Fowler speakin'."

"Jericho here, sir."

"Okay, Jericho, spit it out. What's goin' on?"

"Well, sir, Ron Christmas managed to get away from me after I chased him for some miles. He sped away from his property after blowing his house to smithereens with some explosives. Luckily, Sheriff Niblock and I escaped the blast. Sheriff West of Lexington County is putting out a state-wide APB on the suspect and also extending it into the metropolitan area of Charlotte. The APB is on an olive-green Ford LTD with a permanent North Carolina license plate."

"On an olive-green—hey, wait a minute, Jet! It's sounds like you are telling me that Ron is getting away in one of our cars. Just why is it that you are telling me that, agent? And this'd better be good!"

"Well, you see, sir, Sheriff Niblock and I found Ortmann's body at the Christmas homestead. John is, uh, dead, sir." There was approximately six seconds of silence before Jericho interceded. "Uh, sir . . . did you hear me?"

"Yeah, Jet, I heard ya. I just, uh, don't know what to say. I definitely don't know how I'm going to explain this to Ortmann's family. I should've never sent him down there alone."

"Sir, don't blame yourself. You could have never predicted Ron's bizarre behavior."

"I know, agent. It's just difficult being the one responsible for where your agents are sent and what they're sent there to do and why some of them, God help us, don't come back."

"Well, sir, there's a saying within the works of Shakespeare, I believe: 'Heavy lies the head that wears the crown.' You deal with life-and-death decisions constantly, and there is no way you can control all the variables out there in the field. There's no way in this business for any of us to have a perfect record in what goes on out here, you know that."

"I know, agent, but that doesn't mean I can live with it or that I can or should ever grow comfortable with it. It's still always gonna sting like hell."

"Yes, sir, I understand."

"Jet, how did he die?"

"Shot several times, sir, with his body deposited in the back of Ron's Ford Galaxie. That's how Ron got around undetected the remainder of the day yesterday. He was using our car, the car that John had requisitioned."

"The rotten bastard! Jet, ya gotta get this guy, ya hear me?"

"Yes, sir, loud and clear. I promise you and, uh, John's family."

"*Good*! Good, agent, you do just that! I will get some guys down there to Lexington County to bring home John's body."

"Sir, I'll keep you notified as to my progress."

"Thanks, agent. My prayers are with you." And Fowler hung up.

Never had Jericho heard Fowler this emotionally off-balanced. *Man, there's a lot more under that gruff exterior than I have given him credit for. I never realized he took the loss of one of his own so personally. The crown of which Shakespeare spoke definitely must bear an unwieldy weight. My prayers are with you also, Director.*

Jericho looked over at the old store owner and his wife, both seeming entirely mesmerized by the content of such official conversation. "Sir, ma'am, would you mind if I make one more call?—and then I'll be on my not-so-merry way."

"Sure thing, young man, you take your time gettin' all your arrangin' done. There's no reason to hurry!" replied the husband of the gracious hosts.

Nolan picked up the phone and dialed yet another number scribbled down on yet another piece of paper. However, he dialed this number with a little more trepidation than with his previous two calls. "Room #4, please," said Jericho in a slightly impatient tone. *Okay, c'mon now, Kitten. You'd better be in your room as I requested!*

The recipient of this call exhibited far more anxiety than had Fowler, answering before the completion of the first ring. "Hello, Nolan? Nolan, this had better be you!"

"It's me, Cat. Calm down, love. I'm okay, I don't have a scratch on me." *Well, not too many scratches*, thought the agent when considering he had just served as a pin cushion for a crap-load of projectiles in an explosion.

"I've been so worried. I've been imagining the very worst, of course."

"Oh, Catherine—have no fear, your precious Nolan is alive and here."

"Okay, Underdog, cut the rhymes. I really have been worried."

"Yeah, but the way you answered the phone—tsk, tsk, darling! How did you know for sure that it wasn't Fowler calling?"

"To hell with all that! I guess I'm comin' around to your way of thinking, Tiger, you—make that, *we*—are too important to keep dancing around the constraining expectations of others. So, you promise you're okay?"

"Yeah, I'm fit as a fiddle, although slightly out of tune as always."

"Okay, so I take it that you have Ron in custody?"

"No, not quite."

"What do you mean, not quite!?"

"He eluded me yet again at a train crossing. Anyway, we've got an APB going out on him and he should be in the ol' hoosegow soon."

"Now *that* makes me very nervous. I mean, he's such a maniac—"

"—which is *precisely* why I'm calling you at this very moment, Cat! Now, listen closely and, for your own good, please adhere to the following instructions. I'm sure you'll be okay there in your room at the hotel. Don't leave your room under any conditions, and keep your door locked! Don't stay in my room! Call the guy at the front desk and instruct him to not disclose to anyone that either of us are currently checked in at the motel in case a certain someone would happen to call or stop by the desk and ask. Although I've never explicitly informed Ron that I've been staying at the Chat & Nibble, you just never know. I mean, there are only so many places in the Icy Springs-Sharpton area to stay, and Ron could easily figure it out. So, consider my room a danger zone for the time being. Remain in your room and keep the television and radio off. Only keep one lamp on and play cards or something. Keep the curtains closed. Remember, keep that door locked and chained!"

"Your wish is my command, O Jericho!"

"Good girl! Cat, I don't mean to alarm you with any overkill on the precaution, for I'm sure we'll nab this jerk. However, I don't like him being on the lam, and I particularly don't like being away from your side."

"Well, what if I call over to the café and get Father Nature to come over and protect me?" asked Cat in quite a teasing tone.

"*Caaaat,*" exclaimed the agent, drawing her name out in disgust. "Cut the comedy! Now, this is serious. I mean it!"

"Yes, sir," responded Cat in an unusually sincere tone of submission. She knew just how much she could push her lover's buttons, and she knew when he had about had his fill. "I promise you, Tiger, I'll be a good girl. Hurry on back here as soon as you can. You know that I get cabin fever worse than any human being on this planet, and I fail to find the charm in the these rustic little motel hell-holes that you evidently do."

"Yes, ma'am," replied Jericho, matching Cat's submissive demeanor. "I'll be back to my Sweet Polly Purebred before you know it."

"Okay, Shoe Shine Boy," whispered Cat lovingly. "You just make sure you do."

Hanging up the phone, Jericho felt a little guilty that he hadn't disclosed everything to Cat. Yes, she would want to know that Walt had been injured, although it wasn't life-threatening. And yes, she would definitely want to know that John had been murdered. However, what she didn't know for the time being would not hurt her. After all, she felt paranoid enough with Ron being on the loose, so there was no need to fuel her paranoia or anxiety even further. *Oh, my gosh, Walt!*

Turning to the good Samaritan couple, Jericho bowed his head slightly and said, "Thank you both for the use of your phone. Before I leave, I have just one more favor to request of you—that is, if you don't mind."

◆ ◆ ◆ ◆ ◆

The little store in the middle of God-knows-where turned out to be only seven or eight minutes from where the high-speed chase had begun. Beginning at the intersection where Jericho had toured the cornfield, the Ford LTD had actually led Jericho back in the general direction of Pelion. The Good Samaritan store owners eagerly apprised the grateful agent of a nearby road offering the quickest access to the secondary road running right by the Christmas homestead. Nolan was most anxious to get back to Walt's side and check on his condition.

Not far from the entrance to the homestead, law enforcement officials had already cordoned off stretches of highway a half-mile in each direction to guarantee public safety and ensure that efforts of emergency personnel remained unobstructed. Flashing his identification for access, the agent slowly proceeded up the rough dirt drive toward the seeming war zone lying ahead. With a huge, billowing pillar of black smoke as a centerpiece, the area was busy with flashing lights, hoses and water, and lots of people running around barking out commands and following orders. The smoke pouring out skyward from the hollowed-out, flaming husk of the farm house had actually been visible as soon as Nolan left the little store at the crossroads. Therefore, it had not been necessary for the Samaritan couple to assist the agent with directions, for Jericho could easily have followed the smoke straight to the farm. At any rate, the red Sting Ray was now in the middle of the all-hell-broken-loose scenario.

Nolan parked Anna at a spot where he perceived she would be out of the way of the emergency vehicles. Stepping out of the convertible with his brows furrowed out of concern, the agent began visually scouring the landscape for his partner. A rescue vehicle had backed up to the side of the barn with its front now facing Jericho, but there was no sign of life in that area. The worried agent was about to head in another direction when a medical technician walked out from behind the vehicle and opened the driver's door. Grabbing something, the technician disappeared once again behind the truck. With curious hope, Nolan walked briskly over to the site and rounded the corner of the truck.

"Well, well, well . . ." exclaimed Jericho, quite relieved at the sight of his friend sitting upright on a makeshift chair in the form of a rusty oil drum. Walt was positioned with his left leg straightened out, the left pant leg cut off at mid-thigh, and a bandage wrapped around it. "Walt, when you requested that I come from Raleigh last week, I never realized the party would get this wild."

"Hey, partner, neither did I!" responded Walt. Even though Walt had on his usual happy face, Nolan could tell that he was fighting pain by the wincing in his expressions and the flinching of his muscles. "Hang on a minute, Jet, this nice fella here wants me to sign a form, and then he and his cohort are heading off."

Jericho perceived that a quick departure of the rescue vehicle was good news for Walt, or at least he thought it was. After Walt had thanked the two men and watched them drive off, the agent instantly began his interrogation. "Okay, Sheriff, spill the beans! What's the prognosis?"

"First, Jet," shot back Walt, turning the tables on his friend, "you tell me. Did you catch the sorry jackass?"

"What do you think?" replied Jericho with a look of disgust.

"I would say by your face that the slippery ol' eel slipped and slunk away successfully."

"You would be correct in your assessment, Walt. Call it bad luck or whatever you wish, but it came down to a *loooong* train crossing the road, with Ron on one side and me on the other. Anyway, I found a phone and called Sheriff West. What a man-of-action he is! He's put out an APB all across South Carolina for the Ford LTD and contacted Mecklenburg County just in case Ron pushes northerly toward Charlotte. He even summoned the guys that just attended to you and mobilized the rest of these jokers running out here."

"What about Cat, Jet? Have you contacted her?"

"Yeah, buddy. Even with all the precautions, I told her to hole-up at the Chat & Nibble, just to stay put in her room with the door locked."

"Well, partner, that's about all we can do for the moment," offered Walt with a voice of consolation. "Jet, don't blame yourself for Ron getting away. You can't help that."

"I know, friend, *I* know," responded Jericho in a voice indicating that he didn't quite subscribe to the notion that Ron's continuing flight was not his fault. "I also called Fowler quickly and told him what was going on. You realize, don't you, Walt, that the car Ron used to do the hit-and-run number on you was our SBI car from Raleigh?—the one John had driven?"

"Yeah, Jet, I did manage to catch a glimpse of the permanent plate in the middle of my gymnastics exhibition. Boy, he sure did flip me like a pancake, didn't he?"

"He sure did, Walt, but now it's my turn to do the flippin'. Anyway, I thought I heard you say that your leg was broken, and here you sit cocked up on this oil drum like nothing's happened. However, you can't fool me with your bad acting, fella. I can tell you're experiencing quite a bit of pain."

"Jet, after the top edge of that car slammed against my thigh bone, it hurt like holy heck. The pain was so bad that I really thought it was broken. The good news is that, according to the ambulance guys, my femur wasn't broken. In fact, it really wasn't fractured in the least. It was what they called a bad bone contusion. In other words, my femur was badly bruised. The guys told me that bone contusions are often as painful as breaks, and will leave a guy limping for awhile. The short guy said that, as far as femur injuries go, he wasn't that impressed and that I should be able to get around, although my whole left thigh will probably turn a pretty shade of purple."

"Hey, Walt, that's good news for the most part! So, uh, what are you supposed do for it?"

"Ice it, massage it, and go easy on it as far as vigorous movement. The medical guys said I would be okay riding back to Icy Springs with you, but they recommended you drop me by the hospital in Sharpton. They said it would be a good idea to acquire some crutches for those times I might not feel like putting my weight on my left leg. The biggest reason they said I need to stop by the hospital is to pick up some pain killer. According to them, the next week or two is going to be pretty rough, with a lot of throbbin'."

"No problem at all, Walt. We'll definitely go by there. Let's see, now . . . it's about four o'clock. With you in the condition you're in and with Cat by herself in Icy Springs with that maniac on the loose, I say we head on back now. I really wanted to cart that scum back in handcuffs personally. However, there's no telling where he is at this point. I guess it really doesn't matter anymore which law enforcement officials manage to nab him. I mean, as long as Ron is taken into custody by somebody, we can have him sent to us by UPS for all I care."

"Yeah, Jet. Surely to goodness he ought to be easy to sight and apprehend, driving around that big ol' dark green clunker with its permanent North Carolina plate."

"Yeah, surely!" echoed Jericho, although deep down he remained only half-convinced that Ron wasn't slick enough to elude his pursuers. "You sit tight, Walt. I'll pull the car right over for you."

Upon backing right up beside Walt, Nolan started to hop out so he could assist his partner in getting situated on the passenger side. "You stay put, friend," requested Walt. "I'm not *that* invalid, I'll make do. Hey, what's with all the corn stalks in your back seat?" As the two lawmen began rolling forward, they stared somberly at the crater-like remains of the Christmas house still rendering massive plumes of ominous black smoke.

"Well, Walt," said Jericho, "I guess this explosion served two purposes for Ron: one, it was a good opportunity to get rid of me, and two, it was a way of psychologically slamming the door shut on his past."

"Yeah, Jet, I'd say that he definitely shut that door with quite a bang. It's a miracle that you made it out of the house alive, but it certainly didn't hurt matters that the miracle man you are has such quick reactions. By the way, partner, what kind of bomb was it, in your educated opinion?"

"ANFO, Walt—ammonium nitrate mixed with fuel oil. Of course, I only had a second to glance at it, but in my experience being around the bomb squad in Raleigh, it definitely looked to be that kind of explosive."

"Ammonium nitrate?" asked Walt with a look of surprise. "You mean, as in common fertilizer?"

"Yep, that's precisely what I mean. However, due to the potency of the explosion, it's likely that the mixture might have been a little more sophisticated. I speculate that the ammonium nitrate might have also been combined with some nitro-methane."

"Zowie, Jet! Living in a small town, the biggest bombs I see are M-80 firecrackers used by our high school boys for various pranks. Recently, a boy named Robert put an M-80 under a metal bucket and stood on the bucket after lighting the fuse. It turned out that he had wanted to launch himself to the roof of his house using a strategy like James West in the TV show *The Wild Wild West,* but he damn near blew his legs off his body. Man! Nitro-methane, huh?"

"More than likely, Walt. Like I said, I didn't hang around too long to analyze it."

"Why didn't he rig it so that when you entered the room it would go off immediately? I mean, why did he give you that window of opportunity, those few precious seconds, to get out of the room?"

"Well, Walt, he used a tilt fuse, much like that used in car bombs and such, in which the shift of mercury in a container closes the electrical circuit to the bomb. However, most people dabbling with this stuff are smart enough to incorporate a timer which will delay the electric current from detonating the explosive. When you're working with something so volatile, you would want a little time to run likes blazes in the event you happen to accidentally trigger the reaction prematurely."

"I get where you're coming from," commented Walt. "It's a little preventive measure to keep one from involuntarily becoming a suicide bomber."

"Right! I'm estimating that Ron had built in a safe harbor of around ten seconds to enable himself to flee down the stairs and out the door in case of a mishap. I'm sure I used up at least five seconds just trying to get my bearings on what was up with the trip wire leading to the oil drum against the wall. Once I had mentally processed things by seeing the tilted tube of mercury and the timer, I had five seconds to get out of the room. Ron knew I could not have reacted quickly enough in that handful of seconds to run down the stairs and get out of the house. What he didn't figure upon was the possibility of me generating a much quicker escape route through the window."

"Man, Jet, I'll never forget the sight of you sliding down the tin roof and diving for the ground. Tell me, which was worse: falling about a dozen feet to dry land from a porch roof or plummeting around forty or fifty feet toward two or three feet of water, *à la* train trestle?"

"Walt, uh, neither one was a walk in the park. I could probably go the rest of my life without the need to duplicate either experience."

"I'm sure you could, ol' buddy," said Walt in a half-laughing voice, followed by a bit of wincing from the pain he still felt from his femur. "I'm gonna put my head back and try to relax in the sun and breeze a little while you drive. Wake me up when we get there!"

◆ ◆ ◆ ◆ ◆

Cat shot a worried glance at the clock on the nightstand. *C'mon, Tiger! It's 7:30, and it won't be long until dark. Why haven't I heard from you? I realize that I'm perhaps twice as worried as I should be due to you not coming back yesterday evening from the trestle. But I simply can't shake the feeling that I'm close to losing you for good. I just feel so helpless. And, I feel so hungry! Why is it that I have to be one of those women who eats like a horse when being stressed out?*

Walking into the kitchenette area of her room, the beautiful lass encountered the worst of sights: a bare counter, with nary a morsel of snack food to be seen. There was no use in opening the cabinet doors, for she never found shelves worth the bother when staying on the road. Everything always went on the counter—that is, if the place where she was staying even had a kitchen. Turning the Cheetos bag upside-down, she managed to catch one lone Cheeto in mid-air and chucked it into her mouth as if it were a vial of precious antidote to a deadly poison within her body. *God, there's nothing around here! The Cheetos have simply vanished! The Chips Ahoy and defenseless Cracker Jack never stood a chance! How in the world am I going to get out of this predicament?*

Frustrated by foodlessness, Cat flung the door of the fridge open. *Oh, crap! I thought I had brought more of the Canada Dry over to my room. I didn't notice earlier that there was only one left. The others are sitting next door in Nolan's refrigerator since I've been spending so much time over there. I swear! No drink, no food . . . hey, wait a minute!* A serene look suddenly crossed the face of the hunger-stricken damsel, for she suddenly visualized a smorgasbord sitting on the counter in Nolan's kitchenette. Now dancing in her thoughts were a bag of Tom's barbecue potato chips plopped between some packages of Lance peanut butter crackers and a box of Cap'n Crunch.

I know I promised Nolan I would stay put. But c'mon, let's get realistic! I mean, it would take me fifteen seconds—twenty, at the most—to raid my baby's kitchenette and be locked up back in my room once again all safe and pretty. With aspirations of plundering the neighboring village of Room #5 now formulated, Cat walked to her door and put her ear against it. *Hmm, it sounds quiet enough. There's no talking, no cars pulling up . . . It definitely seems safe enough. Boy, how I hate sneaking around all-scared and silly, like a four-year-old during a thunderstorm; but I promised the worry-wart I would be really careful. Actually, I promised him I would stay put. No, wait! The more I think about it, I'm sure I promised him I would be extra-careful if I had to go over to his room for anything.*

Grabbing the key to Room #5 off the dresser, Cat undid the chain on the door and turned the lock. The pretty plunderer dashed like a lightning bolt and quickly unlocked the door to Room #5. As if it on a midnight raid in an enemy camp, Cat swooped into the kitchenette. She flung open the door to the fridge and snatched up two cans of Canada Dry, tucking them under her right arm. After slamming the fridge door shut with a swing of her hips, she grabbed two packs of Lance peanut butter crackers with her left hand and swooped up the Tom's barbecue potato chips and Cap'n Crunch with her left arm, cradling them against her abdomen.

Cat hustled back to Room #4, moving rather quickly, considering all the loot she had pilfered. *I'll just have to scurry back and shut Nolan's door after I dump all this stuff on my counter. I doubt that the team of Mission: Impossible could have pulled this off any more efficiently than I did!*

Cat deposited the motley collection of snacks on the counter while reveling in her own ingenuity. In her mind, this was a moment of triumph for the hungry soul of Room #4, and she was relishing it. Amidst the noise of clanking cans and crunching bags being set on the counter, the distracted beauty had neglected to notice the shadow appearing on the carpet behind her or the smell of cheap cologne beginning to permeate the air. What she did notice was the sudden grasp of an arm around her neck and the slap of a handkerchief against her face, completely covering her nose. It was too late for her feeble attempts at struggling, for her muscles seemed to be turning to jelly as any desire to resist began fading away. Oh, yes, she did also notice the sweet smell of the chloroform as her body turned traitor, refusing to muster the strength she needed to fight the good fight. However, does anybody ever truly notice the darkness at the very moment of losing consciousness?

◆ ◆ ◆ ◆ ◆

The red convertible pulled into the emergency room entrance of Sharpton's Ireland Memorial Hospital at around 7:30 p.m. Nolan was particularly road-weary because the traffic had been unusually taxing in both Columbia and Charlotte. The heat of the day had eased up somewhat in the late evening, and Walt was still snoring like a baby when Jericho turned off the ignition. "Wake up, Rip van Winkle! You have some medical affairs awaiting you," snapped the agent in an chiding tone, pretending to nag the dormant sheriff.

"Wha—what? Are we here already?" asked Walt with a big yawn and rubbing his eyes.

"Sure are! Walt, for the life of me, I don't understand how you can sleep so well with a bone that's aggravating you so badly. I noticed you wincing in pain while you were sleeping."

"Jet, it's like this—between solving this murder, firing Dreama, and the business with Hodges and the bear, I haven't slept hardly at all lately. I guess I'm flat-out worn out."

"You must be! Do you need me to escort you in?"

"No, Jet. You go on and check on Miss Cat and get some rest yourself. There's no telling how long it'll take here. But you can do me a favor, however."

"What's that?" asked the willing agent.

"If you don't mind, wheel by my office on your way back to the Chat & Nibble and tell Sanford not to go anywhere. He's minding the store today. Just tell him I'll call him in an hour or so to come and pick me up. Hey, maybe by now he's heard some information over the radio about the progress toward locating our fugitive from justice. Hopefully, they've reeled him in by now."

"Hopefully," agreed Nolan as the sheriff stepped out of the convertible. "Take care of that leg, Walt. Tell 'em to load you up on as much of that pain medicine as you can carry."

"Will do, good buddy. There's no sense in not asking for it and wasting my investment on insurance premiums," remarked Walt with a devilish grin.

◆ ◆ ◆ ◆ ◆

Jericho hardly noticed the usually agitating bell as he entered into the Sheriff's Office. Desiring to make this little visit a quickie, he was anxious to get on to the Chat & Nibble so he could make sure Cat was okay and, of course, assure her that he was. "Good evening, Deputy Sanford. Uh, I've got a message for you from Sheriff Niblock, and then I'm outta here."

Deputy Sanford had been quite engrossed in the local newspaper before the agent burst in like a whirling dervish. Quite startled, the lawman jumped slightly and dropped the section of the paper he was reading. "Oh, uh, hello, Mr. Jericho. What is it that the sheriff is needing?"

"He's at the hospital in Sharpton. His leg got a little banged up in an altercation with Ron Christmas, but he's gonna be just fine. He just needed to pick up some pain killer. He said for you not to go anywhere. He will call you in the next hour or so to come and get him. Sorry I'm in such a hurry, Deputy. Our suspect successfully eluded capture, as you probably know. I've got some things I need to get about checking on."

"Understood, Mr. Jericho. By the way, I've been monitoring periodic reports of the pursuit on our scanner. The Ford LTD with the permanent plate was found about forty-five minutes ago."

Jericho immediately brought his hasty exit to a complete halt. "Really?! Where did they find it? Did they apprehend our suspect?"

"They found the car right outside of Columbia. He had forcefully switched cars with another driver."

"I don't doubt it, Sanford," replied Jericho as his mind generated flashes of his former colleague's body in the trunk of Ron's Galaxie. "The suspect has a strong penchant for taking illegal possession of vehicles. Is the other driver okay?"

"Yeah, bless her heart. The driver was a sixty-two-year-old woman. He forced her into the trunk of the LTD and left it in the parking lot behind a restaurant, then drove off in her '63 white Rambler station wagon. She nearly suffocated, being crammed in the trunk for several hours in the heat, but they think she'll fully recover."

"A Rambler station wagon, huh? I just can't figure him out," remarked the agent, bearing a puzzled expression. "He picks a not-so-inconspicuous car with two states on the lookout for him. And, it seems like it would have been just as easy, not to mention potentially useful, to take the lady hostage. I mean, with the insanity he's currently demonstrating, what would he have to lose in having a bargaining tool? At any rate, I'm glad for the woman."

"Yeah, I am also. Anyway, just to be on the safe side, Maness is patrolling the area south of here at this very moment—you know, keeping an eye out for the station wagon. The way he and I see it, Ron fled from y'all—uh, from Columbia—hours ago. The APB put out on him was only amended forty-five minutes ago, so law enforcement in the Charlotte area had been looking for an LTD up until then. Maness said there's a good possibility that Ron might have made it through Charlotte in the Rambler—"

"—before the amended APB informed them to search for a white station wagon!" interrupted Jericho. "In other words, Ron could very well be in this area. Thanks, Sanford, I'm on my way to check on, uh, things."

"Yeah, and there's one more thing that I almost forgot to tell you, Mr. Jericho. Some guy called about you a little earlier. Hold on a minute—I wrote down his name. Yeah, here it is. He said his name was Agent DeMarco and that he was an SBI courier. He wanted to know where you were staying because he had some important information he had to hand-deliver to you, and he said it was imperative. I told him you had a room at the Chat & Nibble, but would probably not be back yet from Columbia."

"Are you sure his name was DeMarco?" asked the agent with an extremely worried look.

"As sure as I know my mama's name, Mr. Jericho. Why?—uh, what's wrong?"

"Well, Sanford, for one thing, our agency does not have a courier *per se*, other than the occasional errands run by Miss Marshall. I've never heard of a DeMarco in the Bureau. And, why would an SBI representative have to ask where I could be found? My director is well aware of my lodging arrangements!" Upon that revelation, a look of panic came across Sanford's face as Jericho wheeled around, reaching for the door.

"Uh, I'm sorry, Mr. Jericho. I hope I haven't jeopardized anyone's safety."

"You'd better not have, Deputy," shot back Jericho in an unforgiving tone before slamming the door behind him.

The fuming agent could feel his heart racing as his red convertible sped along the several miles to the Chat & Nibble. *Oh, God! Cat had better be okay. I suppose I could have called her room from the Sheriff's Office, but it really doesn't take much more time to get to the motel, and each second earlier that I can arrive in person might be crucial. I swear! Too much information, Sanford! And dammit, Walt! Who trains those mouse-keteers you have for deputies? Walt Disney!? Maness seems to be the only one worth his weight in salt. Lord, I pray that Cat is all right.*

The red convertible shot into the parking shot and slid across the gravel to a halt in front of Room #5. Nolan's heart started beating even more furiously when he saw that the doors to both rooms, #4 and #5, were standing wide open. *There's no reason the doors should be open like that. There's no maid service at this time of day and, even so, Cat should've refused all comers anyway, per my instructions. If that nutcase has been here and harmed Cat in any way . . .*

The agent first glanced in Room #5 and hollered out, in case Cat was back in his kitchenette area or in his bathroom. "CAT! Are you in here??" No response! He then zipped over to her room, preparing to yell for her once again. However, Nolan's voice was instantly cut short as he beheld the empty room and the most shocking of sights. The agent stood with his mouth open and his heart pounding like a kettledrum, wishing that what he was now seeing was simply a hallucination, but it wasn't. In the middle of the bed was Cat's stuffed white Shetland pony and sitting atop the pony was the sock monkey that Ron had positioned on the trestle as bait and then later retrieved. The message written on the sock monkey, *DIE, SBI*, still burned to the core of the agent's soul. Affixed to the monkey was a handwritten note, which Jericho frantically snatched off.

Big Blue's,

Come alone

or I'll kill her!!

Yes, on the bed before Jericho sat the stuff of which nightmares were made. What had been the worst of nightmares activated by a hallucinogenic barbecue sauce on a Monday evening was now a stinking reality. For Nolan, it was quite apparent Ron had pushed the fast-forward button toward the hour of reckoning. It was now time for someone to die.

CHAPTER 29

And the Walls of Jericho Came Tumblin' Down

Jericho was well aware that the ten-mile section of Highway 64 from the Chat & Nibble to Big Blue's Feed Mill lacked the generously long, straight stretches of highway like those he had encountered around Pelion. Furiously zooming through Icy Springs, the agent could risk only ninety miles per hour with the slightest guarantee that the challenging curves would not fling his Sting Ray from the highway.

Nolan realized that it would not be too long until darkness staked its claim on the village, remembering that a late-July sunset in this area of North Carolina occurred sometime just after eight-thirty. As he sped down the slope of highway leading to the Atkins River Bridge, the agent could see his ominous-looking destination sitting about two hundred feet off the left side of the highway on the opposite side of the river. During business hours, Big Blue's Feed Mill and Fertilizer Warehouse was a virtual beehive of activity, but after five o'clock on Saturday afternoon, the noisy behemoth of commerce went into hibernation. Situated in the shady hollow, there was something just downright spooky about the old mill as twilight loomed closer.

Crossing the bridge and looking sideways to his left, Nolan had a straight-on view of the establishment's front side. The main part of Big Blue's, the feed mill itself, was a complex of three conjoined buildings. On one side of the facility were two enormous metal silos and, on the other side, a loading area featuring a gigantic, bucket-like hopper under which large trucks could park to receive their grain.

Roughly fifty feet across the gravel drive from the loading area was Big Blue's fertilizer warehouse, a large, three-story cinder-block building. This was the oldest building on the property, having served many functions throughout the decades. Interestingly, a creek ran underneath the building, entering a large

289

corrugated steel pipe on the back side of the building and running out of the pipe on the front side of the building toward the river. Large strands of ivy clung to a wide portion of the outside wall, which over time had become saturated with cracks of all lengths and widths running in all directions. The cinder blocks of the warehouse had been painted quite a few times and, more than likely, one could readily document the building's maintenance history by walking up to the wall and pulling off layers of different-colored paint chips. For the past two decades, the building had suffered an aesthetically offensive paint job, a dreary dark beige. However, one could not criticize the hideous paint or underestimate its importance for, more than likely, the paint was the only thing holding the precarious structure together.

As Jericho passed by Big Blue's, he studied the front intensely, but detected no sign of life. *According to the note left by that psychotic idiot, I'm supposed to come to the back of the mill. Okay, that's fine and dandy, but I'm not going to simply amble back there with the likelihood of being picked off by his rifle. I won't save Cat that way. I think a quiet entrance by sneaking up is in order, perhaps allowing me to survey the battlefield a little. Who knows? Even though he's expecting me, providence and swift thinking still might allow me to take the bastard by surprise.*

Having driven on past Big Blue's, Jericho waited until his view of the establishment was obstructed by a small, wooded area to the left of the highway—to be more precise, the agent was actually ensuring that *he* could not be seen from the feed mill or the fertilizer warehouse. Nolan slowed down, crossing the other lane and pulling Anna off on the left side of the highway in front of the woods. He kept his fingers crossed that he had not been seen parking the Sting Ray from the private residence he remembered being on up the highway beyond the trees, a beautiful house in the style of a log cabin, which Jericho had always figured was Big Blue's home; he really didn't wish to jeopardize Cat's life by getting Big Blue involved.

He took one deep breath and stepped out of the car while glancing at his watch. *8:15, not many more minutes of daylight left, agent. Let's get Cat out of here alive and wrap this thing up once and for all.* Jogging down into the woods and looking through the trees on his right, Jericho could faintly make out the carport side of Big Blue's house. Apparently, Big Blue was home, judging by several lights in the house being lit. His biggest fear was that Big Blue might have a platoon of hunting dogs or some kind of hounds in a kennel ready to earn their Alpo for the day by sounding an alarm. The agent's heart raced madly knowing that, at any second, a symphony of canine howls might ring out, spoiling his opportunity to stage an intimate showdown with Ron and rescue his damsel in distress. Deeper into the woods, Jericho could make out a small corral behind Big Blue's house and noticed that it had roughly a half-dozen Shetland ponies! The miniature horses were of several colors, including the shocking white which had sent chills up his spine ever since that wicked, gut-wrenching dream of Cat on the beach.

To Jericho's left, he could see several mammoth forms taking shape through the trees. He breathed deeply several times and clenched his fists as the buildings of Big Blue's mill and warehouse became clearer with each step. Coming to the edge of the woods beside the creek winding toward the fertilizer warehouse, the agent paused completely for just a moment, then stepped out of the woods at a length of two paces.

Nolan could not have anticipated the visual shock awaiting him. As a rush of terror seared straight through his gut, the agent's heartbeat escalated rapidly and his psyche furiously battled to sustain rational thought. He was paralyzed instantly in his tracks, for dangling against the wall of the fertilizer warehouse at approximately three stories high was his beloved Cat. Hanging from outside a window with the panes missing, her hands were bound by what appeared to be fragments of burlap twisted into a strap, more than likely from feed sacks. Nolan grimaced as he viewed the thick strap of burlap extending from one arm to the other. Worse yet, the burlap alone was supporting her weight, for her captor had arranged for the abrasive strap to encircle the rusty metal frame of the glassless window. The raw peril enveloping his lover exceeded any degree of horror that the agent could have possibly imagined. Indeed, it was the most harrowing of sights, but at least she was alive!

Resisting the urge to immediately holler out to his lover, the agent glanced quickly along the unstable-looking wall of the old warehouse. He could see that the rusty frames of the other three windows also lacked panes of glass, but he detected no movement, no barrel of a rifle jutting out through the openings. *Where is that psycho? Has he gone momentarily to retrieve something? Or, has he gotten cold feet and simply decided to get out of Dodge, perhaps deciding not to have a Mexican standoff but instead fleeing while I'm busying rescuing Cat? WHERE IS HE?*

As Nolan walked forward another five or six paces, Cat happened to look downward and spied her hero closing in. "Nolan!" hollered Cat, struggling to speak in between her grunts of discomfort from being suspended. "Nolan, you've gotta get me down from here."

"Cat, other than hanging there, have you been hurt in any way?"

"No, he snuck up behind me at the motel and chloroformed me. Then, the next thing I knew, I was hanging up here." Cat paused for another second to release another grunt or two. "My wrists and arms are killing me. That scratchy cloth-stuff is tearing up my skin, and my muscles hurt so much from the hanging."

"Don't worry, Cat, I will have you down in a minute. I'm going inside and I'll be right up. Hold on!"

"Whoa there, Agent Jericho. Perhaps it's *you* that needs to hold on."

Jericho jerked to a halt and swiveled his head back and forth rapidly in an effort to determine the location of the strident voice. With a harshness echoing through the woods behind, the mysterious voice-out-of-nowhere was evidently amplified. At any rate, the echoing quality of the modified voice made it difficult to discern its point of origin, and the agent still detected no movement behind any of the windows.

"Okay, Mr. Christmas, what's it all about? Why here? What do you hope to accomplish by all of this?" shouted the agent while continuing to scan the area panoramically.

"Let's just say you weary me, agent, and weary men resort to quick solutions."

"Why the lady, Mr. Christmas? She hasn't dealt any cards in our game. Why not let her go?"

"Oh, agent, that's where you're wrong. You see, she's my trump card in this game—for I *know*, agent! I know how much she means to you."

"You do, do you?" replied Jericho, now shaking with fury that Cat was being tortured so. She was now grunting more often and kicking her legs around somewhat to relieve the ever-intensifying pain.

"Yes, agent, I know this lady means a *lot* to you. You see, the day that the two of you paid me a little visit, I was watching you two lovebirds through my window, and I saw the two of you locked in a sickeningly passionate kiss as you were about to leave."

Jericho's heart immediately sank and, if he could have punched himself senseless at the moment, he certainly would have done so. What a mistake he had made, letting down his guard and providing the man he was chasing inside knowledge about the relationship between Cat and him! What a mistake to have even taken Cat along to search the Christmas homestead, solely for the reason of satisfying his desire for her company! If the two of them managed to get out of this sticky situation and Fowler fired him on the spot for his stupidity, well, he certainly deserved it!

Nolan knew he needed to regain his composure for Cat's sake. Taking a deep breath and pulling himself together, he shouted "Okay, so you're nosy! But you still haven't answered what this is all about. What are you trying to do?

"Trying, agent? Did you say 'trying'? I'm doing it, agent. Before I head off into parts unknown, I'm going to get rid of you once and for all. You see, if I didn't kill you, I'd go crazy imagining you hiding behind every tree and lamppost trying to catch me. AND, the beautiful part of it all is, I'm going to kill your wonderful little beddy-bye partner in the same fell swoop. In other words, agent, the two of you are going to die with that nauseating, loving little fondness for each other thrown back in your faces. Or, should I say 'blown' back in your faces?"

"Okay, I give. What do you mean by that?"

"Well, Agent Jericho, I take it by now that you are well aware of my attraction for things that go 'boom'. The sad thing is that I probably wouldn't have bothered at all with your lady friend here if you had simply cooperated and allowed yourself to be blown up in my house. Your refusal to die really pisses me off!"

"Sorry to disappoint you, Mr. Christmas."

"You have a continual habit of disappointing me, agent. You just never seem to perish on schedule. But no matter, I eventually learned my lesson after you played Houdini on me the first couple of times and escaped the inescapable. So last time, I had a backup plan in case you miraculously got out of my house. You see, agent, at this moment there are some explosives inside the building against the wall to which your lady fair is attached. Oh, it's not going to be the incredible array of fireworks I managed to mix together in Pelion. It's merely a couple bundles of dynamite I brought along just for the occasion. But in the shape these walls are in, it'll be sufficient to get the job done, I assure you of that. If you'll pardon the pun, agent, you might say that the walls of Jericho shall surely come a-tumblin' down."

"Very clever, Mr. Christmas, very clever. Pardon me if I find it difficult to appreciate your sense of humor. I must say, though, your humor is quite *à propos*, being it is of a religious nature—PAUL CHRISTMAS!!"

Even Cat, who was suffering by this time from severe rope burns and arm cramps, completely stopped moving upon hearing the revelation contained in Jericho's startling outburst. There was complete silence, with the loud, echoing voice offering no immediate comment.

The voice rang out once again, but this time with a tone indicating its bearer as having been somewhat startled. "Uh, very clever on your part also, agent. I, uh, guess I've underestimated you in more ways than one. And just what brought you to this grand epiphany that you and your lady friend are about to die at the hands of that noble do-gooder, Paul Christmas?"

"Well, I must admit, Paul, you've put on a marvelous performance as your lonely, bitter brother, such as in the barn that day acting like we had never met. You really had me fooled for a while, just like you've evidently fooled the entire village of Icy Springs for quite some time with your veneer of Godliness complete with the entire phony 'love-of-your-fellow-man' shtick to which you evidently didn't ascribe. You even had your own mother completely in the dark. Like everyone else, I was so mesmerized by your sparkling reputation and your lifetime of Christian service that considering you anything less was unthinkable. So, honestly, it really was only today, while driving that long trip back from Columbia, that some small bits and pieces came together in my mind suggesting that Paul Christmas was still among the living, having murdered his own brother, Ron!"

"So, agent, you tell me—what gave me away?"

"Oh, several little clues in the past several days had sparked my curiosity, Paul, and admittedly, these things had me confounded at times. For example, the widow's mite I stumbled across at the railroad trestle outside of Spartanburg. I didn't even know what the coin was at first, but yesterday a reputable source informed Miss Marshall that it was a widow's mite, and widow's mites can be plentifully acquired as souvenirs. I asked myself, 'Why a widow's mite?' And then I remembered that someone had mentioned to me briefly that Reverend Paul once took a trip to the Holy Land. But, so what?! By itself, this wasn't enough to draw any big conclusions. After all, alas, the great Paul Christmas was supposedly dead!"

"Go on . . ." urged the mysterious voice, sounding most intrigued.

"Then there was the simple matter of you attacking me on Paul's—on *your*—home turf. Yes, I know I goaded you quite a bit into your desire to exterminate me. But, for supposedly being Ron, or more precisely, for supposedly being someone who had never bothered to set foot in Icy Springs through the years to visit his brother, you really had an amazing inside knowledge of this area. I mean, in such a quick turnaround time after we searched your house in Pelion, you managed to select such a viable, out-of-the-way place at Beaver Junction to eliminate your main adversary, the kind of isolated place which was perfect for a private execution and the kind of place that only a long-time local would be aware of. Paul, let's just say that being lured to the train trestle at Third Fork Creek suggested to me that the guy in the purple hood was mighty comfortable operating in and around Icy Springs."

"Anything else before you die—after all, we all need to learn from our mistakes. I might be able to use what you're sharing with me in the future."

"Paul, I guess my biggest 'a-ha' moment came from what I saw earlier today lying on the table in Ron's kitchen, the entry which had been torn out of Linda's diary. It's funny when you think about it. When I read it at first, I inferred that a heartbroken Ron had been bathing constantly in Linda's declaration of love for him by obsessively reading her words over and over and over. However, on the way back from Columbia, it hit me: What if it was Paul who was obsessively reading Linda's words about how she loved both boys; about how she just couldn't accept Paul's nature of being so people-centered; and about how she was afraid of hurting Paul in the process of accepting Ron's proposal? Up until I read that diary excerpt, everyone—and I mean *everyone*, including your mother—had convinced me of how lonely Ron was after the loss of his wife and his fortune and how happy and fulfilled Paul had been throughout his life. So, seeing the diary was when my big 'a-ha' moment occurred. What if it was Paul who was obsessively reading Linda's words over and over, constantly dwelling on how close he might have been to winning Linda's hand, instead of his brother? What if it was Paul dwelling on how he had been punished through the years by being the type of person Linda didn't desire to choose for a mate? What if Paul was the lonelier and more miserable of the two brothers? I mean, this truth would certainly correlate well with the widow's mites and the assassin's thorough knowledge of the Icy Springs region. That is right, isn't it, Paul?! You loved Linda all of these years, didn't you?! And Ron most certainly had to die for taking her away, didn't he?!"

By this time, Cat's chin was against her chest and her eyes were closed. Nolan bit his lip and inwardly said a small prayer that she was not dead, that she had merely passed out, having become light-headed from the loss of blood circulation to her wrists.

"I now understand why you're on your state's payroll, agent. You're evidently the Sherlock Holmes of your dull bunch. Yes, I loved Linda. She was the only one I ever desired to play the part of the preacher's wife. It's been very hard living all these years with the fact she chose a more shallow lifestyle to share in as the wife of my Godless brother. He didn't deserve her, but yet she chose him!"

"How could you fault *Ron* for Linda's choice, Paul? Did Ron deserve to die simply because she wanted him instead?"

"No, Supercop, he didn't deserve to die for that alone! Why do you think I allowed them to be married for as long as they were? I was able to reconcile life's hideous injustices to a certain degree, but a man has his limits. I let him have her hand in marriage and attempted to live with that for as long as I could. So, at least give me that much credit. But what did my foolish, ungrateful brother go and do? He killed her. He simply tossed aside a treasure granted to him so undeservingly, as if she were nothing more than trash. She died because of him!"

"That's not the story I've heard, Paul. I heard she died in an accident boating on Lake Murray."

"Call it whatever you wish, agent. She died because of Ron's negligence in that sordid, morally distasteful world he had created for the both of them. They were drinking and partying, agent, in celebration of Godlessness, of immoral hedonism brought about by Ron's servitude to the false idols of wealth and power. Take it from me, agent, Ron killed her, all right! Maybe he didn't pull the trigger that night on Lake Murray, but he provided her with the loaded gun. He's the one who pushed her over the edge of the boat. For God's sake, agent, you would think that after I had the decency to accept his marriage to her, he would have at least reciprocated with the decency to keep her alive. I ask you, was that too much to expect?"

Jericho knew the dialogue between him and Paul was nearing closure, for he realized that nothing more could be said at this point to scratch the surface of the crazed reverend's insanity. Many people spend a lifetime of loneliness without taking the lives of others, so Paul's actions in no way could ever be justified or excusable. But the agent could at least fathom the loneliness which had plagued this so-called man of God, and he well understood how the chisel of time can chip away at a person's rational mind, eventually rendering that person as a tragic, soulless shell of humanity. A paraphrased Biblical quote immediately came to Jericho's mind, a phrase that Reverend Paul had probably uttered more than once from his pulpit: "*O how the mighty have fallen.*"

"Paul, uh, tell me, what was Agent Ortmann's reason for dying? Why did he deserve to be shot to death and left in the trunk of your car?

"Agent, c'mon now! I could have easily killed that little old woman whose station wagon I borrowed today. But at least *she's* still alive, or I guess she's alive if she hasn't suffocated to death in that trunk. I feel you should at least give me a little credit for my thoughtfulness toward her well-being. So, perhaps not having killed her might, uh, cancel out my impulsive little boo-boo with your agent friend?"

Throughout the entire conversation, Jericho had eased forward step-by-step. Having gradually brought himself closer to the wall from which Cat was hanging, he was still standing right beside the creek which ran underneath the warehouse. The agent helplessly glanced down toward the trickling water and immediately back toward Cat. He then clenched his fists tightly and spoke even louder. "Paul, you truly are a sick, demented creature. Why don't you just walk on out here and end the running for yourself? Come on out and let me take you to some people who can help you cope with all the demons eating you up inside."

"Oh, agent, there you go being inconsiderate yet again. It's really gettin' close to my bedtime and you're still alive, standing there doing nothing more than stalling for time and begging for me not to kill you, like the sniveling coward you are! Now, I need you to walk forward about another dozen steps."

"What's in it for me?"

"DO IT!" shouted Paul impatiently, "Or the lady dies NOW!"

The agent realized he had no choice. Bantering with Paul had only seemed to postpone the inevitable, and Jericho could think of nothing in his disadvantaged situation to get Cat down safely. Being the sharpshooter he was, Nolan had considered shooting at the burlap strap around the metal window frame which was supporting her weight. But, he knew one shot wouldn't completely sever the thick bond, so, how many shots would it take? . . . three? . . . four? No, it would simply be too risky firing that many shots so close to his lover's body. Anyway, Jericho concluded that, after he had fired the first shot alone, Paul would surely have activated the explosive destiny for them that he had in mind.

Jericho obediently walked closer to the wall, step by step beside the babbling water. As his heart beat rapidly, his mind raced supersonically in an effort to design and execute a miraculous escape for Cat and him. There was no time at all to analyze whatever plan would come to him, no time to calculate odds. Now painfully obvious to the powerless agent, Paul's death trap for his two victims-to-be was seemingly escape-proof. Halting on his twelfth step forward as directed, Nolan was now eight feet from the three-story-high wall. Looking to his right, Nolan's eyes beheld the creek flowing into the opening of the corrugated pipe which was jutting out about four feet from underneath the warehouse. Glancing upwards diagonally to his left, Cat's feet dangled motionlessly around twenty-five feet above his head.

Breaking through the morbid silence, Cat's voice seemingly filled the air in spite of its anemic projection. "Nolan, I will . . ."

"Will what, Kitten?" asked the confused agent, with his heart and mind still racing franticly.

"Marry you," replied Cat, with her voice becoming progressively weaker. "Now, Tiger--get me out of here." After her declaration, Cat again appeared to slip into unconsciousness. Nolan, while joyfully acknowledging the declaration within his heart, knew that the next minute or less in their lives would determine whether Cat's intention to be his wife would stand a chance of becoming a reality. But what could he do!?

"How sentimental, Agent Jericho. Now, back to the matter at hand, your deaths! Please allow me to quote the following on your behalf: 'to everything there is a season, and a time for every purpose.'"

"Yeah, yeah, Paul, I know! 'A time to be born and a time to die'—from the third chapter of Ecclesiastes. I'll tell you one thing about yourself you might wish to improve, Paul. You're definitely unoriginal. I can't tell you how many villains I've seen in movies and on television who quoted that passage to the flies caught in their webs. I think that the last time I heard it was about three weeks ago on a re-run of *The Wild Wild West*.

"Well then, agent, how's this for some originality and streamlining the scene in my script involving your death—after all, I certainly wish not to bore you senseless. Here we go, then. Uh, goodbye! You have three seconds to live, starting NOW!"

The frustrated agent knew that there was nothing he could do to help his beloved Cat. At that moment, he wished that he truly was a Superman as Cat had always referred to him. Then perhaps, he could have zoomed through the air, forcefully yanked her away from the wall, and flown away from the blast with time to spare, but alas, not in the real world.

Three seconds passes by quickly, yet it's amazing how time can appear to be in slow motion during those three seconds. In a hyper-accelerated state of consciousness, a person's reaction time to events thrust upon him can seem like an eternity, such as when a concrete block is tossed off a bridge toward that person's windshield. Like a cat clawing frantically to escape an adversary, a man in jeopardy often claws away at all options set before him during those precious last seconds, and Nolan's mind was desperately clawing at the possibilities, trying to snag onto the slimmest chance of survival. *What to do? Where to go?*

Jericho's survival instincts kicked in, as the only solution he could generate left him one second to spare—that is, one second according to Paul. The sharp-witted agent leaped toward the creek and landed with a solid splash, his face breeching the opening of the conduit into which the water freely flowed. Upon impact, he immediately initiated a forearm- and elbow-driven belly crawl similar to that of soldiers in a field under enemy fire.

BAA-RRROOOOMMM!!

As the avalanche of cinder blocks roared downwards, Jericho remained undeterred from entering the pipe, which was approximately three feet in circumference. The thunderous pelting of the block against the corrugated steel rang out tremendously, to a point the agent found practically deafening. In what was the slimmest margin of error the agent could afford, Nolan felt one of the blocks graze the sole of his right shoe just as he was pulling his foot inside the pipe.

Jericho now felt a wave of fury throughout his body, for fate had possibly dealt him the worst of hands, the death of his beloved Cat! This painful moment of reality was infinitely worse than the harmless little nightmare he had experienced in which Cat had perished in the path of the collapsing sand castle, for this was not a dream which could be laughed off and forgotten. It was a true-to-life event which would leave him hurting and empty forever. *God, I don't ask much of you, but I'm going to ask this one miracle of you. Please! I ask you, please, let me find Cat alive when I get back to that pile of blocks!* Of course, Nolan realized that this was indeed the tallest order of a miracle that he was requesting. How he wished it was sand rather than the brutal cinder blocks under which Cat was probably now buried!

With the thunder around him now having quieted down, Jericho glanced behind him toward the sudden darkness beyond his feet. There was no way he could exit the opening from which he had entered the pipe, for it was now sealed up by the landslide of cinder blocks. Looking ahead, the agent could see the opening of the pipe on the other side of the warehouse, appearing as an illuminated pinhole lying roughly sixty to seventy feet ahead. Nolan again began belly-crawling, which was propelled greatly by his newfound fury. *I fear*

Cat is dead, for I don't see how anybody could have survived that. Since Cat's dead, then so is he!

Jericho was now drenched and feeling some lacerations on his arms and abdomen from rubbing across the sharp pebbles washed along by the creek. Luckily, tarantulas and scorpions weren't indigenous to the Piedmont area of North Carolina. Jericho hoped that his crawl through the pipe wouldn't involve crawling through some black widow spiders or, worse yet, brown recluse spiders. He was also keeping his fingers crossed that some copperheads weren't using the artificial banks of corrugated steel alongside the creek as a base of operations, for the dark, moist tunnel would certainly appeal to a band of venomous vipers. As he looked ahead, the light provided by the opening at the other end of the pipe seem to shift a little, as if something was suddenly there, then suddenly wasn't, and then suddenly there again. Nolan stopped crawling momentarily, attempting to focus his eyes in an effort to determine the source of the motion. *That movement up ahead in the light, what is it? It's definitely too broad to be a snake of some kind. I don't think it's a small dog—a groundhog, perhaps? Well, I certainly can't go backwards!*

Suddenly, the dark blotch of movement appeared to be lunging toward the agent in a kamikaze run. The form averted a head-on collision with Jericho, instead brushing against his face and coming to an abrupt halt at his right pant leg. *A rat! A damn rat! My God, it's the size of a cat—and a fat cat, at that!* Nolan shook his leg vigorously in a effort to scare the large rodent. Undaunted, the rat began nibbling at the agent's pant leg, and he began to feel the teeth of the creature piercing through the cloth and rubbing against the skin. Jericho knew it would be only seconds before the rat had completely cleared the fabric upon which it was chewing and began to make a smorgasbord out of the agent's flesh. Reacting quickly, he reached out with both palms and scooped up a double-handful of sediment and stones lying beneath the creek atop the bottom of the pipe. Twisting around as much as he could and taking aim, he catapulted the significant clump of sludge toward the hairy varmint.

SPUH-LAT!

Bull's eye! That'll teach you, you filthy critter! Evidently, the faceful of dirt and pebbles slamming against its head was more than the rat could handle, for it scurried away into the darkness on behind the agent. *You'd better be glad that worked, rat. The next option I was going to exercise was to get out my gun and blow you into rodent-heaven! Now, to get on out of here!*

Jericho resumed crawling on his abdomen through the creek. About halfway through the pipe, he encountered an iron grate in the top of the pipe that evidently served as an opening right onto the main floor of the warehouse, perhaps for ventilation? Or perhaps for dumping waste into the creek to wash on into the river? Whatever the reason, the agent thought it prudent to now exit the pipe if he could. He pushed against the rusty grate with his right hand—and it didn't budge. Nolan shifted his weight slightly in an attempt to achieve more leverage, then struck the grate three times with his forearm. Again, it didn't budge. *Well, I guess I'll just head on out the exit that seems the most inviting at the moment.*

Nolan looked at the thirty to thirty-five feet of pipe lying ahead. The once-brighter pinpoint of light was now diminishing in its illumination as the after-effects of sunset were beginning to take hold. As he prepared to crawl on toward the end, some erratic movement now appeared at the opening of the pipe. At first, the agent could not discern what in the world this sudden flurry of activity outside the conduit might be. *What the—?! What now?*

To his horror, Nolan's curiosity was immediately answered in the worst way. A bundle attached to the edge of a lengthy wooden pole was being ushered in through the pipe's opening. And, sparks were flying on one side of the bundle. *O my God, he's at it again. Dynamite! He's going to blow me up in here!*

Once the hands at the opening of the pipe had fed the pole inwardly as far as it would go, the hands laid the pole on the ground beside the creek so that only the bottom edge of the bundle inserted within the conduit sat in the water; the primary portion of the dynamite and its fuse hugged the corrugated steel bank of the creek, leaning against the dry wall of the pipe.

Without blinking, Jericho knew he now had only one exit for survival and only the briefest margin of time in which to utilize it. He scrunched up into a cannonball-like contortion as much as he could, given the limited space, with his toes in the creek and his back against the iron grate. Pushing with all his might, he prayed that the rusty structure would give way to his brute force. He could hear the grate groaning from the pressure he was applying, but it just didn't seem to want to budge in the least. Thinking about Cat buried beneath the cinder blocks, he gritted his teeth and exerted as much force as he could muster. They say that providence opens gateways, and Jericho sensed that providence was on his side, increasing the leverage from his severely straining back and legs.

SNAP-PANG!

The iron grate immediately ceased its stubborn resistance against the agent's efforts and flipped open, slamming against the floor of the warehouse above. Without missing a beat, Jericho shot upward out of the pipe, sprawling along the dusty warehouse floor on his back. *FUHH-WOOOOMMP!*

The floor shook extensively as the explosion rattled the pipe underneath. Jericho held his breath for a second, hoping that the vibrations from the blast would not bring down any of the remaining warehouse walls or ceiling on top of him. Although the steel pipe absorbed the blast as one would expect, the shaky remainder of the fragile warehouse wouldn't tolerate much more in the way of seismic activity.

Snapping to his feet, Jericho caught his first glimpse of the pile of rubble that had been created by the fallen portion of the wall. Staring intensely at the small mountain that had swallowed his lover, he felt so powerless. Oh, how he wanted to run over and start flinging cinder blocks left and right, but he knew he had to stop Paul first. If there was the slightest chance Cat could be alive under the blocks, it would do her no good if the agent was killed in the process of digging her out. Paul was relentless and simply wasn't going to give it a rest. No question about it: he had to stop Paul here and now! Only then could he see if Cat was still alive.

The agent darted toward an old wooden door at the front of the warehouse. Not bothering to see if it was locked or not, he kicked it open with a single thrust from his left leg. As he exited into the twilight, Nolan looked across the lightning bug-illuminated gravel drive toward the feed mill. It was getting much harder to see in a landscape which was becoming darker minute by minute in the arms of dusk. His eyes managed to catch the quick motion of a door closing on the side of the mill. Without hesitating, Jericho sailed across the drive like a phantom and purposefully slammed his back against the wall of the mill next to the door which had just closed. Retrieving his gun out of its holster, he quietly turned the door knob and gently pulled the door open. Upon entering, he heard the hum of the overhead lights as the inside of the mill was now half-lit. With Paul evidently having flipped a master switch, the florescent lights would gradually come to life much like the staggered luminescence of a school gymnasium.

Nolan crept along without making a sound, hoping to catch the maniacal killer off guard. However, this would prove to be quite a challenge, as the feed mill was a home turf of sorts for Paul. Having worked part-time at the mill for the past so-many years definitely gave the home court advantage to Mr. Christmas, for he surely knew every nook and cranny of the place. Nolan definitely felt like a sitting duck, for he was surrounded on all sides by somewhat tall, bin-like metal structures with ladders attached to their sides. Knowing that Paul could be hiding around a corner of one of the structures or, worse yet, on top of one, the agent kept his gun extended fully outward in firing position.

God, not a sound! Where is that crazy son of a bitch hiding!? Easy, agent. Since he knows every foot of this establishment, he could lash out from any direction. Keep alert! Finish this creep off so you can get back to Cat.

Walking by the last metal structure, Jericho now stood on the edge of an immense open area. Ahead of him was a ladder extending to a high catwalk running halfway across the length of the large indoor arena. In the middle of the floor right underneath the end of the catwalk were multiple stacks of burlap sacks containing feed. Underneath the catwalk and all along the walls of the open area, there was a vast array of machinery. Nolan could only begin to imagine what kind of grinding and crushing went on within the impressive arsenal of machines, but he could well imagine being tossed into one of the sinister-looking devices if Paul managed to get the upper hand on this round.

In Jericho's defense, he could not have kept his eyes on all angles at all times, and he couldn't have seen what was about to hit him. Hearing a creak above the last metal bin he had just passed, he looked upward toward the sound and—*FOOMMP!*—was greeted in the face and chest by a fifty-pound bag of chicken feed. Having been chucked downward from about twenty feet high, the bag immediately kayoed Jericho.

The next thing Nolan could sense happening was a form kneeling beside him. As the agent barely squinted his eyes to an imperceptibly open position, he could see Paul holding *his* gun, which had just been wrenched from him by the vicious blow from the bag of feed. Jericho was aware that the lights had kicked in and the place was now fully it. He also sensed that Paul was talking to him, but he was still too stunned to process any of the killer's ramblings.

"Too boring! Yeah, I may have shot your friend in Pelion, but I've got something extra-special in mind for you, agent." Paul tossed aside the gun and declared, "Yes, my friend, after claiming I'm so unoriginal in your recent critique of my work, I'm going to make sure you appreciate the innovation I'm incorporating into your death."

Although Paul's gabbing sounded more like garbled nonsense to the dazed agent, it had managed to stimulate Nolan enough to keep him half-conscious. Nolan slipped backed into unconsciousness the moment Paul finished his deranged dialogue. Almost immediately, the agent snapped back partially into consciousness upon detecting that he was being dragged backwards. He could feel Paul's hands lifting his body by his underarms as the overhead lights of the mill seemed to sting his eyes a little.

The agent's eyelids closed involuntarily for a third time since his rude union with the bag of chicken feed. He was soon awakened by the sound of a tractor starting and, still in a groggy state, attempted to determine where Paul had positioned him. Glancing around, he found he was sitting upright with his back against a stack of burlap sacks bloated with feed, one stack among the hordes of stacks located just under the end of the catwalk.

Shaking his head and banishing the last of his grogginess, Jericho saw a huge Massey Ferguson tractor careening his way. The large machine had been fitted by Big Blue with three forks extending from its front end, enabling the tractor to serve as a forklift, among many other purposes. Now fully alert, Jericho realized that the Massey Ferguson was about five seconds from making a shish kebab out of him with the gigantic, pointed tines coming right at him.

Without flinching, Jericho instantly identified his escape route. Leaping upward while extending both hands, he caught hold of a hook on the end of a chain hanging from the catwalk with his right hand. The agent knew there were about three seconds left until contact with the tractor. He shimmied up the chain at a phenomenally quick rate, ending up about twelve feet in the air. "Damn you, Jericho!" shouted Paul as the tractor plowed into the sacks of feed, causing bags skewered by the forks to eject cascading grain. "Why don't you just die, SBI?"

"Because, you have too much to answer for!" shot back Jericho. "Consider me your personal Grim Reaper, Paul Christmas."

"Never!" hollered Paul. Backing up the tractor away from the stacks of feed, the crazed man proceeded to elevate the forks and tilt them at roughly a seventy-degree angle so he could attempt some mid-air skewering of the pesky lawman. The wily agent immediately sensed what the determined reverend was up to. Oh, he could have easily climbed on up to the catwalk. But, since he had no gun at the moment, he would be at a stalemate with Paul, and he was determined that this time the murderous pastor would not attain freedom.

Jericho extended his left arm sideways, grabbing the end of a shorter, lighter chain hanging from the catwalk. Choosing to execute his next maneuver on the smaller chain in lieu of the heavy-duty chain, Nolan began undulating his body back and forth in a swinging motion. In the meantime, Paul had finalized his adjustment on the front-end loader of the tractor and was moving forward again toward Nolan.

Twisting his body somewhat, the agent managed to swing between two of the approaching forks. Upon witnessing Jericho's evasive maneuver, Paul proceeded to throw the tractor in reverse, but Nolan had let go of the chain at about fourteen feet in the air and was now plummeting downward toward Paul. A powerful collision of their two bodies ensued, with Paul knocked off the tractor as if he were nothing more than a billiard ball. Having somehow remained halfway in the seat of the tractor, Jericho immediately brought the tractor to a complete halt from its slow-moving reverse motion.

Leaping off the tractor, Jericho landed on both feet at about three paces from Paul. But, unbeknownst to the agent, the crafty clergyman had managed to secure a handful of the spilled grain. Seemingly from out of nowhere, flying morsels of grain showered Nolan's face, with some of the smaller particles entering his eyes.

Running desperately in the opposite direction, Paul ended up at the other end of the catwalk and chose to seek higher ground. He had no plan at this point; he just wanted to keep out of Jericho's reach.

Quickly swiping the grain from his face and rubbing it out of his eyes, the agent saw Paul at the bottom of the ladder and ran in that direction.

Nolan glanced upward at Paul, now halfway up the ladder. "Give it up, Paul. You know you can't escape me. You know you're a dead man."

Now at the top of the catwalk, Paul looked down at Jericho. "This was not my doing, agent. I've been cheated like no man has ever been cheated. I promised God years ago I would serve him faithfully. I gave him my life, and what did I get in return? Loneliness! A wonderful lady leaving me who wanted more than what a preacher has to offer! A congregation that would only offer me a pauper's pittance of a salary, leaving me to have to slave away many long, hot hours doing part-time work in this hellhole! You can blame God for it all, agent! I did my part! He's the one who didn't deliver."

By now, Paul was backing up about midway down the catwalk as Jericho was stepping onto the metal walkway from the ladder. "You can't blame God for this one, Pastor. Many, many other people have spent lifetimes doing service in the name of religion and have experienced far more hardship and pain than you, and it didn't turn them into heartless killers." Jericho knew that Paul had gone as far over the deep end by this time as anyone could reach. The glazed, soulless look in the minister's eyes indicated that he was within the realms of total insanity.

"But God and I had a bargain, and he reneged on it."

"That's where you made your mistake, Reverend!" replied Jericho, looking him straight in the eyes. "You don't bargain with God; you only deal with the Devil!"

"Well, then, maybe Satan will be appreciative once I deliver you to him personally!" shouted Paul with the maniacal look of a wild man. The tall man suddenly reached over the rail to his right and grabbed a long pole with a hook on the end. Attached to a clip on the rail, the implement was frequently used in the mill as an extension enabling one to reach chains, the levers of machines, and other objects. "It'll be my extreme pleasure to run you straight through, agent."

An amusing look of disbelief suddenly crossed Jericho's face. "Uh, Paul, have you forgotten the lack of success you experienced in challenging me with a pitchfork back at the barn in Pelion?"

Paul stared at Jericho for a few seconds with a confused look. He then glanced down at the stick he was holding for a second and looked back at the agent. "Oh, yeah, the knees. I almost forgot." With that reminder, Paul chose not to walk toward Jericho with the intention of impaling him. Instead, the desperate man drew back and hurled the stick with all his might at the agent.

By this time, all the cobwebs from the bag of feed were clear and Jericho was at the top of his game; he was now in control. With his disciplined mind in complete focus, he watched the stick as it almost seemed to glide through the air in slow motion. It was no problem at all for Nolan to lean a little to the right, allowing his straightened left arm to lash outward and deflect the six-foot-long projectile.

Seeing the determined, steely look in the agent's eyes, the reverend gulped deeply. "Okay, agent, you very well might have me. But at least, I'll either go to jail or go to my grave knowing I've deprived you of the one you love so much. I relish the thought of her corpse lying there, buried by those heavy blocks. So, come on, do your darnedest! It's too late for her, no matter what you do!"

At those remarks, the agent felt as if all the atoms inside of his body had suddenly exploded. Nolan could literally feel time come to a complete halt as the totality of rage, pain, and horror experienced by all of his ancestors began to swirl within him. His blood began seething with the fury and torment of four different races encoded within his genetic memory. Images of faces past flashed in his mind—images of great-grandparents, of grandparents, and, most notably, of his late father, presumed missing during the Korean War.

Christmas, it is your time to die—

Seeing the intensity in Jericho's face, Paul knew he had really screwed up with his last tirade. "Now, now, agent. I, uh, take back all that stuff I said about—"

"*Ni mara yako ya kufa!*" chanted the agent with fire in his eyes. The machine of a man known as Jericho began stepping forward toward the now panicking Paul Christmas. Nolan could feel the pride and perseverance of his African ancestors flowing within him. His Kenyan grandfather was looking down upon him at this moment, blessing his actions.

"Okay, you! Now . . . seriously, I was just . . . uh . . . kidding with all that stuff about being glad your lady's dead. What say we just shake and make up, huh? No harm, no foul, agent?"

"*Es su hora de morir!*" chanted Jericho, this time translating the Swahili phrase he had just uttered into Spanish. Continuing his forward motion towards Paul, Nolan could feel the fiery, passionate nature of his Latino ancestors flowing within him. His Puerto Rican grandmother was looking down upon him at this moment, blessing his actions.

Still backing up and holding out his hands in a gesture of truce, Paul tried a different strategy. "Okay, agent, I'll turn myself in to authorities . . . you lead the way!—No wait, I forgot: you don't like me being behind you. . . Well, you just let me ease right by you there, fella, and we'll climb down that ladder together. . . I promise, no tricks this time. Huh, whad'ya say?"

"*Sore wa shinu anata no jikandesu!*" chanted the robotic Jericho yet again, this time in Japanese. Still advancing toward the cowardly killer, Nolan could feel the tenacity and resiliency of his Japanese ancestors flowing within him. His Japanese grandfather was looking down upon him at this moment, blessing his actions.

Pulling out all the stops, Paul ushered in yet another approach. "All right, Mr. Jericho. Surely you must have a pragmatic side, being an underpaid agent and all. With my brother gone, the family farm will be left in my name—uh, minus the house, of course, seein' as I blew it up and all. . . But there's lots of acreage there. I'll be more than glad to have it all put in your name. You could sell it and get you a place at the beach."

"*Zhé shi ni de si!*" chanted the unflinching agent for a final time in Chinese. Only six feet from his backwards-walking adversary, Jericho could feel the nobility and determination of his Chinese ancestors flowing within him. His Chinese grandmother was looking down upon him at this moment, blessing his actions.

Realizing he was nearing the end of the catwalk, the desperate pastor fell cowering to his knees. "Jericho, I beg of you . . . I implore you! Have mercy upon me! Forgive me for the actions I committed against your lady friend and your agent friend, the one in the ugly green car. I beg of you, please don't kill me!"

As Nolan was stretching his arms out to choke the life out of his enemy, he suddenly felt a powerful surge of reasoning from within. It was as if the sundry bits and pieces of his heritage had suddenly unified within his soul and the positive aspects of each lineage were now in control. There was just something about seeing the sniveling man cowering before him and begging for his life that sparked a repulsion within the agent. Under no circumstances would he sink to the level of Paul Christmas and become the type of scum kneeling before him.

Now fully in control of his emotions, Jericho had finally reached a new level of understanding. For the first time, he truly grasped the practices of sound reasoning his bi-racial parents had adopted as a way of coping with life. His mother and his father each had the best and worst traits of two completely different ancestries flowing within their blood, so some internal reconciliation and psychological sense of order had certainly been necessary for them to survive. Nolan could sense his mother and father within him, now guiding him in his decision making. NO! This was logically not the time and place for Paul Christmas to die. For one thing, why make things that easy for the killer? After all, he had much to answer for here on Earth before departing.

Nolan backed off, his eyes now vacant of the fierce stare that had illuminated them only moments before. With his arms now lowered by his side, the agent softly said to Paul, "Get up, I'm not going to kill you. I'm taking you in."

Sensing that the agent had calmed down immensely, Paul misinterpreted Jericho's switch to a restrained, tranquil mood as the act of letting his guard down, perhaps a sign of weakness. A wicked smile came across the face of the kneeling minister, for now was the time to lunge forward and shove the unsuspecting agent over the rail for a high tumble from the catwalk.

Paul sprang from his crouching position with stiff arms extended outward, but the cautious Jericho was ready for such. The agent's left arm extended forward in a lightning-fast motion, his left palm connecting firmly with the pastor's chin.

POP!

Paul suddenly found himself reeling backwards toward the waist-high rail at the end of the catwalk. As he collided with the rail, the dazed minister's momentum carried him on over. Nolan lunged out with his right hand in a desperate attempt to snag at least one of Paul's flailing feet as they pitched over the rail, but he just missed doing so. As Paul plummeted from the catwalk, Nolan's heart raced somewhat. *No, it's not his time to die! Before St. Peter gets a hold of him, he needs to answer to his fellow man for what he's done. Besides, the stacks of feed are below. What if he has a soft landing and bolts for freedom? Not again!*

Nolan walked forward to the short rail and looked down. He nearly did a double-take of disbelief at the morbid sight below. There was Paul's body, suspended in mid-air, impaled on one of the forks jutting out from the raised arms of the tractor. Paul's fall had tossed him over the rail into a backwards somersault, and his body was facing the ground. Jericho could see no movement out of his adversary. There was a lot of blood spilling onto the mill's floor, but no movement.

Scurrying down the ladder of the catwalk as fast as he could, Nolan dashed to the far side of the building toward a small, glassed-in room appearing to be an office. He kicked the door in and immediately grabbed for the phone sitting on the desk and dialed "0" in one motion. "Hello, operator, send emergency personnel down to Big Blue's in Icy Springs at once! No fire trucks, just medical personnel—ambulance, emergency medical team—and *hurry*! Send the sheriff, too!"

Nolan then flew out of the mill back toward the fertilizer warehouse. As the darkness had now firmly taken root, the powerful security lights on the poles outside of each building at Big Blue's had come to life. The illumination of the compound was further enhanced by the brightness of the moon on such a clear summer night. Arriving at the collapsed wall of the warehouse, Nolan hollered out, "Cat, can you hear me? Make any kind of sound or movement if you can!" Nothing! No sound, no movement . . .

Glancing around, Jericho suddenly saw what looked like some strands of brown hair flowing out between some blocks at the top of the pile. "CAT!" he yelled as he furiously began ascending the mountain of cinder blocks. *God, please let her be alive! Please let her be alive!* The agent kept chanting the little prayer in his mind as he grasped his way to the top of the fickle, unsettled pile of rubble. Reaching the apex of the rubble, Nolan screamed "CAT!" as he saw her face with closed eyelids pointed upward at the night sky. "Don't worry, Kitten," Nolan said aloud. "I'll get you out of this mess."

Putting his ear to her nose, the agent managed to detect the faintest trace of a breath being exhaled. *Thank you, God!* "Cat, hang in there! Fight, baby, fight! You still have a chance, but you've got to keep breathing." Of course, Jericho realized that she was unconscious and that the cheerleading was probably more for his benefit than hers. Tossing aside block after block, Jericho finally uncovered her frail, seemingly lifeless body. He wisely did not attempt to move her, saving that action for the emergency medical crew to handle.

Cat was a painful sight for the agent to behold. There was blood mixed in with her beautiful brown hair, obvious scrapes on most of her exposed skin, and deep purple bruises rearing their ugly heads. Of course, who could ascertain by just looking at her which bones were broken? Most assuredly, some were; there had to be. But again, she was at least breathing, even though very shallowly. That was a huge victory at this point, certainly beating the alternative.

As Nolan stared at her, he struggled to maintain his balance on the precarious debris. The agent concluded that it was best to climb back down since the rubble tended to shift under his weight. He didn't wish to potentially damage her any further in case particular bones had been compromised, such as in the critical areas of her neck or spine. Easing back down to the ground, Nolan began staring helplessly at his lady lying atop the dusty mound. He thought long and hard about the 'what-if's' of recent events, not being able to shake the feeling that the pile of debris resembled a funeral pyre right before being lit. *Dammit, rescue squad, c'mon! Some rescuing needs to be done right here and right now, so HURRY UP!*

Nolan was so wrapped up in Cat's condition that he didn't notice the footsteps approaching him. As a hand gently rested on his shoulder, the familiar voice of a good friend accompanied it. "Is she alive, Jet?" asked the caring voice.

"Barely, Walt. I think she's barely clinging with every breath she takes. It's amazing that she survived it at all. The rescue personnel should be here any minute."

"I'm, uh, sorry about Miss Cat, Jet. When I called Sanford from the hospital, he radioed Maness and had him pick me up. The deputy and I stopped by the motel to check on you and, uh, Miss Cat. We saw the calling card Ron left on the bed asking you to meet him here at the mill. I was already on the way when I heard them calling for me on the radio. I also heard that the emergency squad is on its way. When we got here, we saw your car parked beside the highway on past the mill. That's why we decided to come in here rather quietly."

"How's the leg, Walt?" asked Jericho, struggling for something else to occupy his mind other than *Where's the ambulance?*

"Oh, the same diagnosis as from the ambulance guys at Pelion. I'll be fine! It's just going to be a little sore for a while. They gave me a butt-load of pain killers. So for right now, it's all about Miss Cat. She's the one to worry about."

"You're so right, Walt, you're *sooo* right!" agreed the agent.

"Jet, if you don't mind me supposing, I suppose ol' Ron got away again, didn't he?"

"No, Walt. You and Deputy Maness will find a body right smack in the middle of the mill."

"Had to kill him, huh?"

"Actually, Walt, he died of his own accord. He took a dive off of the catwalk. Unfortunately for him, he didn't choose the right place to land. You won't have any trouble finding him; he's the one with a tractor jutting into his stomach. Just make sure you don't have any degree of nausea before you enter the mill—it's, uh, quite a mess. I'm turning all that over to you as of now. I'm going to follow the ambulance to Ireland Memorial and stay with Cat this evening."

Finally, the emergency personnel arrived. Nolan was nearly sick to his stomach while the technicians looked Cat over. Although she continued breathing, they could not get her to open her eyes. The crew examined her extensively before placing her body on a stretcher. Just as Nolan had prudently done, they wished to avoid causing any permanent paralysis or other damage by shifting body parts situated in a potentially perilous position. Once they were satisfied she could be moved, it seemed like forever as the technicians carefully navigated their footsteps in lowering Cat to ground level. While Cat was being loaded into the emergency vehicle, the lead technician turned to Jericho. "Sir, she's evidently one tough lady. By all rights, she should be dead. She didn't respond at all to anything we tried. We couldn't rouse her. As I'm sure you're already aware, the poor gal has multiple concussions to her head. I can't tell you the extent of damage done to her head or to the rest of her body. They'll determine all of that in the hospital. All I can tell you at this time is that she appears to be in a coma."

"Thank you," replied Jericho softly as his eyes began to well up slightly. "I'll, uh, follow you guys to the hospital."

"Jet," interjected Walt, "I'll drop by the hospital in just a little bit after I get the mess cleaned up here and talk to Big Blue."

"Walt, I'm surprised he hasn't come over here with all the activity going on tonight. I saw the lights on earlier in his house."

"Oh, Big Blue goes country dancin' on Saturday evenings at Sloan's Wagon Wheel outside of Monksville. He always leaves some lights on to discourage burglars."

"Ah, well. Anyway, Walt, I have two requests. I realize you have quite a bit of clean-up to do here, getting in touch with Big Blue and taking care of, uh,

Ron's body. My first request is please don't come to the hospital tonight. Just let me administer to Cat. I'll stop by and fill you in tomorrow morning, I promise you that."

"Okay, partner, but only if you're sure of it. What's the other request?"

"Hold off the media—no comments to the press until tomorrow afternoon at the earliest. Try to keep a lid on this thing."

"Uh, okay, I'll do my best on that one. I'm sure having to trust you a lot here." With tears slightly misting his eyes, the sheriff then addressed his friend in a more somber, philosophical tone. "You know, Jet, isn't it simply astonishing that all of this even happened to begin with? And so needlessly, I might add. I find it unbelievable that the man lying dead in that mill could have completely lost his grip on reality and been the cause of all this heartache."

"I feel the same way, Walt," responded Jericho as he began walking to get his car. "'*Quis custodiet ipsos custodes?*' as the saying goes."

"Huh?" asked the sheriff in confusion, watching the agent disappear into the darkness.

CHAPTER 30

Playing God

RING . . . RING . . . RING . . . "Hello, Fowler speakin'."

Jericho really dreaded this, and not because it was an early Sunday morning phone call. "Director, uh, Jericho here. I guess I'm through down here in Icy Springs."

"Great news, Jet! So ya got the killer, and I assume it was the guy who was on the lam yesterday—the victim's brother, right?"

"Uh, yeah, it was the brother, the same guy that also killed Ortmann." Jericho wasn't bothering at this time to inform Fowler that it was Paul who had committed the murders, that it was Paul who had left Ron's body on the church steeple. After all, the agent hadn't even shared that knowledge with his good friend, Walt. For all the sheriff knew, the man impaled on the forklift of the tractor last night in the mill was Ron, not Paul.

"Great news, Agent! Great news! You can't imagine how rough it was last night makin' the call to Ortmann's loved ones, definitely one of the toughest things I've had to do lately. His family will be relieved to know ya got him!"

"I'm sure it was most difficult, sir. And, uh, sir, I didn't take Christmas in alive. He was killed trying to elude me."

"What? Did ya have to shoot 'im?"

"Uh, no sir. He had baited me to the local feed mill in Icy Springs. I was in the process of chasing him on the catwalk in the mill. He lunged at me and I knocked him good in the chin, causing him to stumble backwards and fall over the rail. I tried to grab him so I could haul him in alive, but I just missed reaching him. When I looked down, he had speared himself through his torso on the prong of an improvised forklift of sorts. He died instantly."

"Well, Jet, we do what we can do, and that's all we *can* do. So don't be hard on yourself. Yeah, it's better for many reasons to bag 'em alive, but sometimes they just won't let us do that. I certainly have no problems with your actions."

"Uh, thank you, sir." Now for the part Nolan really dreaded, the part of yesterday's events that Fowler would take great issue with, and certainly for just cause. "Uh, sir, there is something that happened last night I need to tell you about—something terrible that happened."

"Okay, Jet, ya got a captive audience." Fowler's voice didn't sound all that concerned. After all, Ortmann was already dead and he had been the only agent assigned to a dangerous case at this time other than the man to whom he was now talking.

"Uh, it's Cat, sir. I really don't know how to go about telling you . . ."

"WHAT? What happened to Cat, Jet?" Boy, now Jericho really had a captive audience.

"Well, sir, that maniac managed to stop by Cat's room at the motel and chloroform her. He, uh, took her to the mill and tied her to a wall near some dynamite. Then, he set off the explosives and brought the wall down on her. She's in a coma at the hospital in Sharpton."

"You'd better be performing a late April Fool's on me, Mister!" shouted the angry director.

"Uh, no, sir. I'm afraid it's not a joke. Cat's lying in a rather tenuous condition at the moment."

"How could ya let that happen, agent? You know the only reason I send that young lady out in the field is for purposes of relaying information and doing legwork for you agents, errands that should be far out of harm's way. She has had no specialized training for being involved in engagement activities of the first level. She's not supposed to have *any* contact with your suspects. They're not even supposed to know of her existence. So, how did he know about 'er, huh? And how would he have known where she was staying?"

"I, uh, can't tell you at the moment, sir. I just don't have it in me. I will give you a full report when I get back to Raleigh."

"You bet your ass you will, son! I don't know what you've been doing down there this week, but you evidently put her life in jeopardy as no other agent of mine has done."

"Understood, sir." There was nothing Jericho could say in his defense, for Fowler was totally correct.

"In the meantime, agent, what are the doctors saying?"

"Well, from what they could figure through x-rays and scans, there is hopefully no paralysis—no damage to her neck or spine. Her body sustained a massive amount of cuts and bruises. The bones they have detected being broken are her collarbone and three ribs. I suppose if you're going to have broken bones in your body, those are among the most preferable, self-healing bones to break. I guess the major battle facing her is the coma she's in."

"How bad did the doctors say the injury to her head was?"

"Uh, they're still unsure, sir. The chief physician, Dr. Allen Mebane, said that she suffered quite a bit of head trauma. He said she had some hemorrhaging, but luckily it appeared to be all exterior of the brain rather than interior, although he wasn't one-hundred percent sure. Dr. Mebane spent most of the night trying to minimize the potential swelling of and pressure on her brain. I'm no doctor and a lot of what he said was way over my head, but that's the gist of it, sir."

"What did he say her chances were in waking up from the coma?"

"Well, sir, it seems that comas still baffle even the medical profession. Dr. Mebane said that comas are truly wild cards and are extremely individualized, with results varying greatly from patient to patient. He said that Cat could wake up tomorrow . . . next week . . . in a decade . . . or never. He did say that, as comatose patients go, all of her vitals appear to be reasonable and everything seems to be functioning okay."

"I, uh, don't even know how to respond to any of this, agent." For once, Fowler indeed sounded at a loss for words.

"Sir, there is one bright spot in all of this, something positive which totally surprised me."

"And just what would that be, agent?" asked the director, interested in anything resembling a better outcome than what he was now imagining.

"Uh, Dr. Mebane said that if she remained stable throughout the day today on into noon tomorrow, he would see no reason why she couldn't be transferred—carefully, of course—to Mary Elizabeth Hospital in Raleigh. I was amazed that they would try to move her so soon, but Dr. Mebane told me he would feel more comfortable with Cat being near home. He said that stronger sparks of awareness tend to occur within comatose patients when they have more access to friends and family and vice versa. He thinks that Cat's sister, along with other familiar faces and voices, might accelerate Cat's journey toward consciousness."

"So, she'll be in Raleigh by tomorrow evening if things remain stable, right?"

"Yes, sir. Uh, sir, I know you're not very happy with me at the moment, but I have one favor to ask."

"And what might that be, agent?" asked the director with a hesitant tone.

"Sir, I really would like to have tomorrow and the next day off, although I've not requested those days as vacation days. Uh, I really desire the time to visit and tend to Cat and also coordinate efforts with her sister, seeing as how I am responsible for Cat being in the state she's in. Unfortunately, I don't even know how to get hold of her sister at this point. You know that Cat has all those cats at her place, so there are some matters to attend to."

"Agent, don't worry about the sister, I'll have people on my end track 'er down and inform her as to what's going on. We'll tell her sister that Cat should be at Mary Elizabeth tomorrow evening if all goes as scheduled. However, I will grant you the two days off because I realize you need a couple, but in the books it will be as two days suspended with pay. Until I find out what-all in the hell happened for Cat to end up in a coma, I want your days off to be reflected as a disciplinary action. I can always reverse the decision later if I find out that your actions were not responsible for her being placed in jeopardy."

"Good enough, sir. I, uh, understand."

"Jet—" said the director in a radically different tone, as if he were now speaking to a favorite son he was having to bend over his knee. "You've really placed me between a rock and a hard place. I'm at a loss as to what to do with you."

"Uh, what do you mean, sir? You could simply fire me and be done with it, I suppose," responded Jericho in a matter-of-fact tone.

"It's, uh, not that easy, son. Ya see, you're by far my best agent. I couldn't have sent any of the rest of these goons to Icy Springs and had them end this business any quicker than you did. And, don't get me wrong, I am thrilled that you've solved the murder and ended that crazy joker's killing days, even if he basically killed himself in the process. What I'm not happy with is some of your judgment lately, such as putting Cat in danger—which I know ya did, since ya said there are some things ya've yet to tell me. So, what do I do? I mean, my best agent is acting rather erratically and being extremely high maintenance, and at a moment when I really might be needin' his services."

"What do you mean, sir? What's happening now?" asked the agent, with his interest piqued.

"You've probably not been watching the news, seeing that you've had your hands full and all. It's the biggest news story these days, that is, when they're not running that story about some idiot lawman who stood underneath a falling bear."

"What story, sir? inquired the agent once more, impatiently.

"A serial killer or, at least officially for the time being, a serial kidnapper. No bodies have turned up yet, but we've have had three adult women that we know of disappear from the Raleigh area in the past week-and-a-half. The first one actually disappeared the night before you left for Icy Springs. At the moment, we have no leads—zilch!"

"Is there anything that the three missing women have in common, sir?"

"Yeah, Jet, they were supposedly homosexual women—uh, lesbians, I guess you would say."

"Hmm, fascinating, sir. No missing homosexual men, huh?"

"No, just homosexual women, and we're completely stumped. That's the dilemma you've placed me in, Jet. I really would like to get you on that case, but I really need some major debriefing from you to make sure I'm not assigning it to someone who's in need of a long vacation. You're great at what you do, Jet, but even great people can hover too near the edge at certain times. There's a helluva lot of anxiety mounting in Raleigh over these missing women and therefore a shit-load of pressure on me to find out what's going on. But I've got to ensure that I only put people on this case who are operating on all cylinders at the moment."

"Yes, sir, I understand."

"You've got Monday and Tuesday off, Jet. I'll give you a call on Tuesday afternoon."

"Thank you, sir."

CLICK.

Jericho took several deep breaths and threw his body backwards upon the bed. He really couldn't tell at the moment what-all was in the director's mind. He really didn't know if the call had gone well or not. These days, it was really hard to define what "well" meant—or even "normal."

After lying still for several minutes, the agent stood up and walked over to the dresser. Opening the drawer, he pulled out the ring which had yet to adorn his fiancée's hand. He stared at it as tears came to his eyes. It had indeed been an extremely long night at Ireland Memorial for Cat *and* him. There's nothing settling at all about a hospital waiting room, such an area being somewhat akin to the likes of a dental chair, the principal's office, or the other side of a desk during a tax audit. Time had passed *so* slowly while the agent faithfully awaited news provided by periodic pop-ins from a slew of medical personnel. Throughout the night and into the wee hours of the morning, Jericho's perceptions of what it was like to be alive and what it was like to be dead had wavered as updates on Cat's comatose condition played havoc with his mind. At first, he had absolutely despised the word "coma." But as each agonizing minute ticked away and phrases such as "isolate the hemorrhaging," "reduce the swelling," and "minimize the pressure" were tossed at him, Jericho had practically begun to cherish the fact that Cat was even left alive to be in a coma. Therefore, Nolan eventually compromised with his baser instincts and made peace with the fact that, for the time being at least, being comatose was God's way of providing a limbo of sorts for Cat, a safe haven, a place to be on hold, while her body and the medical profession fought for her recovery.

Well, I guess I'd better get on to the Sheriff's Office. It's time to bring my good friend up to speed on everything. He gently placed the ring back in its box and tucked it back into the drawer for safe-keeping. *God willing, Cat, you will be walking around with that ring on your finger someday. I know you will.*

Ten minutes later, the bell tinkled above the door as the man in all-black casual dress entered. Immediately, the tall body behind the center partition popped up and walked out, having evidently been eagerly awaiting the agent's arrival. "Okay, Jet, how is she, buddy? I've been dyin' to know, but I've stayed put as you requested."

"I know, Walt. Thanks for all of your cooperation. I appreciated the note you left on my door this morning, letting me know you'd be here in the office. I realize that you usually like to be in church on Sunday morning."

"Yeah, but this isn't just any Sunday morning. So, out with it—is she going to be okay?"

"Cat's got a long way to go to be out of the woods. Walt. She's now stabilized within a comatose state, and her vital signs and everything else appear to be okay. They've got any swelling and pressure involving the brain under control. She's had some internal bleeding due to her head trauma, but at the moment, they don't think she's bleeding within her brain."

"That's good news, I guess. I don't think I've ever known anybody personally who has been in a coma. When do they think she'll wake up? She will wake up, uh, won't she?"

"That is what they can't tell me, Walt. They said that every coma patient reacts differently, so there's no way to tell. However, they are going to go ahead and transfer her to Mary Elizabeth Hospital in Raleigh tomorrow so she can be near her sister, if her condition doesn't worsen."

"Wow, that's soon!" said the sheriff with a surprised look.

"Yeah, that's what I thought, but they're gonna send her on. I talked to Fowler a little earlier and he's giving me the next two days off to attend to her and get some rest, I suppose. I'm going back to Ireland Memorial this evening and tomorrow morning to sit by Cat's side, and I'll probably return to Raleigh myself not long after they transfer Cat out tomorrow afternoon."

"What did Fowler say about you catching Ron? I imagine he will give you some kind of commendation for it."

"I'm sure he's glad the killer was caught. But like me, he's worried quite a bit about Cat. He's not happy at the moment about her being in a coma."

"Jet, while I'm thinking about it, the guy from the garage outside of Spartanburg called here yesterday and left a message, saying you had left him with this number. He said your Sting Ray looked brand-spankin' new and was good to go. All the glass has been replaced and everything."

"Good, Walt. Thanks for the message."

"How are you going to get it back to Raleigh?"

"Oh, I'll call Agents Flagg and Donnelly. Flagg owes me a favor and he's remarked for quite some time now how he'd love to take a spin in my 'pretty blue Ray,' as he calls it. I'm sure he never imagined that the spin I would offer him would involve the distance from Spartanburg to Raleigh, but I certainly don't think he'll mind. Both of them can ride down together, and Donnelly can follow him back. Donnelly won't mind, either. He likes to get away from his wife and nine kids."

"*Nine*! Lord, I can't imagine having nine kids."

"Walt, I don't think he ever did, either. However, if you ever saw him and his wife together, you'd understand. They're like two rabbits humpin' in a field of clover."

"Man! If I get overly frisky, Sarah gets out the rolling pin. She can only stand so much of me slobbering over her," said Walt while smiling.

"Walt, what's been going on publicity-wise about what happened at the mill last night? Were you able to keep the hounds at bay?"

"Yeah, Jet, nothing's out yet. I asked Big Blue to keep mum about it today. I'm sure that it's gonna have to come out in tomorrow's newspaper at the very latest. I can only stay on this type of thing for so long. You remember the saying you once shared with me, don't you? 'In the absence of good information, people create their own information.'"

"Yeah, partner, I remember."

"So, Jet, I've just been waitin' here this morning so you and I could put our heads together on all of this. This is all such a big deal that I only want it publicized the way you recommend. I contacted Ron's mom at the rest home early this morning and told her what happened. She was understandably torn up. She did say, however, that she would like us to go ahead and have Ron buried beside of his brother. The people of this area are not going to embrace the idea of a great man like Reverend Paul being buried next to his killer. But I think our citizens will also place much stock in the wishes of a mother regarding the loss of her children. Ultimately, they'll probably bless her request. At any rate, Jack the coroner has Ron's body at the moment, so you tell me what's next. You know that when it comes to your recommendations, I always hear and obey."

"Walt, I didn't exactly come clean last night with you. There's something startling you need to know . . ." said the agent softly.

"What, Jet? We got the killer——case closed, right?"

"Yeah, we got the killer all right. But it wasn't who you thought it was."

Sheriff Niblock's mouth flew open, for he knew that it wasn't Jericho's tendency to joke about matters such as this. "Okay, partner, consider me stumped! If that wasn't Ron Christmas we plucked off of those big ol' prongs last night, then who, pray tell, is lying on Coroner Jack's table at this very moment?"

"Paul Christmas, Walt! It's Paul, not Ron."

"Okay, Jet, I give!" said the sheriff in disbelief. "Where's the hidden camera? I know Allen Funt's going to pop out at any moment and go 'Surprise! You're on *Candid Camera*!'"

"I wish that were the case, Walt," replied Nolan in a regretful tone, "but Allen Funt's nowhere around. It's Paul that's lying on Jack's table, I swear to you, not Ron."

For a minute, Walt was speechless. In dealing with this sudden revelation from Jericho, he sat down on a wooden chair at a nearby desk. Nolan followed suit, pulling over another chair and sitting face-to-face with his old friend.

"Yeah, Walt, Paul came clean with me last night and confessed to it all after I pinned him down on several things."

"Like what things, Jet?"

"Well, I told him what Cat had found out about the coin, about it being the replica of a widow's mite that one could find at gift shops. I told him that I had become a little suspicious about this when considering that you, Walt, had told me about Paul having once gone to the Holy Land. Then, I told him about how weird it was that Ron, a guy who had supposedly never been around this area, had no trouble at all in finding his way around and nearly killing me at such an isolated place as the Third Fork Creek train trestle."

"You know, Jet, that was also eating at me. I was amazed at how slick Ron seemed to be in maneuvering all around us. Just when did you figure this stuff out?"

"As you put it, Sheriff, several of these things had been eating away at me also. But, the kicker for me was the diary entry of Linda's I read before being nearly blown up in Ron's house. This helped bring it all home for me. I pretty much had it all pieced together while you slept on the way back from Columbia."

"What was it about the entry that gave Paul away, Jet?"

"Well, I had been looking at everything from Ron's perspective. I assumed he was still mewling over Linda's death and his misfortune by burying himself in her diary. It just hit me on the way back from Columbia that maybe Paul had been in love with Linda and that he was the resentful one, even more so than Ron. I concluded that just maybe it was Paul who was lonely and bitter, angry at Ron and life and God and, well, everything and everybody."

"Why didn't you clue me in, Jet?"

"Walt, I still wasn't sure. My thoughts were still in the incubation stage. And, the first order of business was dropping you off at the hospital so you could see after your leg. The second order of business was checking on Cat, for Paul definitely had time to get here from Columbia ahead of us. Seeing as she had accompanied us when we searched his house, I wanted to ensure that she was okay. To be honest with you, Walt, I never was one-hundred percent sure that Paul was the killer until he opened up. The bits I had managed to piece together simply made more sense if Paul was the killer, but I still had my doubts. You see, Walt, I had been fooled by Paul's charisma and persona as much as you, the villagers, Paul's mother, and everybody else. I had held Pastor Paul up to such a high standard that him being the killer was unimaginable."

Trying to take it all in, Walt sat back in his chair with his arms up and fingers of both hands locked behind his head. He looked toward the ceiling for around twenty seconds and then back at Jericho.

"Jet, I still can't comprehend this. Paul seemed so happy and so productive, so driven to serve God. You hardly ever saw Paul without a smile on. Why did he resent his brother so much? I mean, why turn into a killer, even if he did once fall in love with Linda?"

"Walt, there are no easy answers. I mean, a person wears many masks—a mask hiding his private self from the general public, a mask hiding his inner self from the people to whom he's closest, and even a mask burying certain qualities of himself of which he himself is totally unaware. It's why you have evangelists who can rake in a fortune in the name of God while it's the money they're worshipping. It's why you have a teacher who can put in a thirty-year career with a sterling reputation of all smiles and many apples on the desk, but yet that same teacher inwardly can't stand kids. I could go on and on, but it all comes down to the fact that certain people can become experts at putting up a front. They can convince others and/or themselves that they are who they appear to be, when in reality they aren't."

"What do you think made Paul so unhappy?"

"I'm no psychologist, Walt, but I have a feeling that he had a strong need as a male for a lifelong bond with a female. I theorize he had settled on Linda in his mind for that lifelong bond. So when Linda decided on Ron for a mate, Paul tucked away that cinder of rejection which burned for so long. They say that time has a way of healing, but I also think it also has a way of tearing away, especially regarding loneliness. We both know how lonely serving the public can be, and being a minister can also be lonely, I'm sure. Just because a person is surrounded by people all the time doesn't mean he is getting the inner nurturing he needs. That's what I meant last night when I said to you '*Quis custodiet ipsos custodes?*'."

"Yeah, I wondered what that meant. I never understood Spanish."

"Uh, it's a Latin phrase, actually, meaning 'Who guards the guardians' or 'Who watches the watchmen?' The saying was originally intended to imply the possibility that those looking after our well-being or property might perhaps take advantage of us for their own benefit, so maybe the guards themselves merit guarding. However, I like to twist the phrase a little and think of it more from the guard's perspective—you know, if they are guarding others, then who is taking care of them? Think about it, Walt. Who protects those protecting us? Who cheers for the cheerleaders? If anyone was seen as the guardian or cheerleader of this village—other than its noble sheriff, of course—it was certainly Paul."

"Wow, I guess you have me convinced that Paul must have flipped his lid. As they say, 'It can be lonely at the top.'"

"Yeah, Walt, that it can!"

"But still I ask: why kill Ron?"

"That I really can't answer, Walt. Yeah, I know that Paul resented Ron for being the one to win Linda's hand and for letting her die in that boating accident, but it goes much deeper than that. Subconsciously, Paul was mad at God for a lifetime of lonely service characterized by celibacy, whether intended or not. I think he also loathed the village of Icy Springs for being what he perceived as his prison, for exhausting him of all his time and energy in having to visit them, preach to them, comfort them, and save them spiritually."

"God in heaven, who would've thought?"

"Nobody, Walt. Do you remember me telling you at the crime scene that the body hung on the steeple might have been the killer's way of sending a message to the villagers?"

"Yeah, Jet, I do remember you saying just that."

"Well, that was part of the total package Paul was hoping to accomplish on that most unholy of mornings. In one fell swoop, he murdered his despised brother and then hung his brother's body on the church steeple as a way of raising his middle finger at God, the church congregation, and the entire village of Icy Springs. Only after that could he slither back to his childhood home of Pelion to spend a lifetime in isolation dwelling on what could have been with Linda."

"There's one thing I'm very ashamed of, Jet. You must think we are a complete bunch of yokels. Jack should have picked up on the fact that it wasn't Paul's body to begin with when he did the autopsy. After all, I'm sure dental records and fingerprints would have confirmed that it wasn't Paul."

"I know, Walt, but go easy on Jack. I recommend that you don't go requesting that he be fired or reprimanded. Think about it and remember how much we *all* were fooled by Paul. I mean, if I had been Jack, I probably would have thought presumptuously in the same manner. Everyone was so definite that the guy in the minister's robe hanging at the top of the steeple who looked like Paul was Paul. And why not? Who would have ever dreamed that Paul would go to Pelion, kill his brother, drag him back to Icy Springs, hang him on a steeple, and then set about pretending to be his brother? I certainly wouldn't have and didn't until the very end."

"Yeah, Jet—as usual, you're right. I don't blame Jack for not checking more thoroughly."

"Sure. I mean, you had a whole village crying out 'Here's our dead hero, our great martyr!' Jack had no reason at all to doubt it was Paul and go to any lengths in confirming his identity. Walt, I've usually found it to be the case that, in small towns and rural areas, citizens are trusting of each other. When a significant enough number of people declare an acquaintance of theirs is dead, the coroner usually has no reason to contradict them, especially if the dead

320

person doesn't seem to be re-appearing anywhere else. Yeah, Walt, it's indeed different in small towns than it is in large cities. Small town coroners don't worry much about the identity of the dead. They are usually more wrapped up in the time of death and how the person died."

"Okay, Jet, you've now convinced me as to the *who* and the *why* in this murder. It's now the *how* that's what I'm left wondering about. What about the *how*? How in the world do you suppose Paul got to Columbia without his car? I mean, after all, his car was still in the garage at the parsonage."

"I've already figured that one out, Walt. You remember that Paul was last seen on his visitation rounds at the hospital on the Tuesday evening prior to his, uh, 'death,' right?"

"Sure," replied Walt, hanging onto Jericho's every word.

"Well, he casually drove home that evening and parked his car in the garage. Then, several hours later, after dark, he called for a taxi in Sharpton to come out and pick him up on the short stretch between Doc's Store and Switzer's Hardware. It was easy to imagine him resorting to a taxi, for I used a similar strategy to get back to Icy Springs from Charlotte the night my blue Sting Ray was smashed up. Before I called Fowler this morning, I called Body Hauler's Taxi Service and, sure enough, their logs indicate that one of their taxis picked up a man in Icy Springs at about 11:15 p.m. on Tuesday night. The man had them take him to the bus station in Charlotte. I'm venturing that he had on a disguise of some sort for the taxi ride. I'm also venturing that from Charlotte, Paul caught a bus to Columbia just as I had caught a late-night bus from Spartanburg to Charlotte. I'm also sure we'll find in the records of some taxi service in Columbia that a male passenger was dropped off early Wednesday morning on the secondary road near the Christmas homestead. Once Paul had arrived, it would have been easy for him to take his brother by surprise and drive the body back to Icy Springs in the trunk of Ron's Ford Galaxie after it turned dark Wednesday night. Funny thing, I even considered calling the bus company in Charlotte this morning to check on their passengers to Columbia at around one o'clock early Wednesday morning. But then I remembered, most bus companies around these parts don't keep a manifest listing names of passengers, as do ships and jetliners."

"Thanks, partner, that certainly addresses the *how*."

"Yeah, Walt. I wish the taxi service in Sharpton had thought it suspicious about picking up a late-night passenger in Icy Springs and had at least informed us of that after Paul's death. I mean, how often does a person take a taxi ride from Icy Springs to Charlotte?"

"Not often at all, Jet—hardly anybody in Icy Springs has any need of a taxi."

"Well, evidently the taxi service thought little of it, since it happened two nights before 'Paul's' body was discovered and the passenger they picked up was leaving the area instead of arriving. "

"Jet, there's just one more question bothering me about all this mess."

"What's that, Walt?"

"The cigarettes, Jet. What about the cigarettes? Did they end up being important to you at all in the long run? Why were they so important to Ron—uh, Paul, I mean?"

"Great question, Walt! The cigarettes didn't have to be important at all, but Paul subconsciously assured himself that they were. In the long run, I suppose they were the most important element in this whole affair."

"What do you mean, Jet?"

"Well, they served as a catalyst of sorts for the events that followed throughout the week. You see, Walt, it was like this: All I knew initially was that the victim's body was believed to be Paul's and that Jack had confirmed the victim was a heavy smoker up until his death. And we had found a package of Kool cigarettes at the crime scene with a South Carolina tax stamp on it. It could have all ended right there if Paul hadn't let it work on his paranoia. You see, I had no more to go on than what I just told you when I went to interview him in Pelion. But Paul could never really be sure of what I knew and what I didn't know."

"So, I take it you're saying that the cigarettes might have sparked his paranoia a bit, fanning it to a point where his behavior burst into flames—with him, uh, taking some desperate measures?"

"Bingo, Walt! You see, nobody knew for sure what either brother's smoking habits were at the time of Paul's—make that Ron's—death. Supposedly, Paul had been trying to quit, but nobody really knew if he had successfully accomplished that, as he had begun keeping the habit as private as he could on account of his congregation. Likewise, no one really knew about Ron's chain-smoking, as he was virtually a hermit. So, just the fact that the dead body was currently a heavy smoker in no way pointed the finger in either direction. But, for all Paul knew, I could have dug up some information on Ron somewhere that confirmed Ron was a heavy smoker, or I guess it's even possible that someone might have been able to verify that Paul was now a non-smoker. Paul could never be one-hundred percent sure of those things and that made him nervous when I visited him in Pelion."

Walt thought for a second while looking at the floor. Scratching the side of his head, he looked back at Jericho. "What difference would Ron being a heavy smoker have made? Ron being a heavy smoker didn't mean that Paul couldn't also be a heavy smoker. I mean, it wouldn't exactly eliminate the notion that it was Paul's nicotine-saturated body which had been laid to rest, would it?"

"No, Walt, it wouldn't have, necessarily. But again, Paul had no way of being absolutely sure of whether I was aware that he had become a non-smoker. When I went to Pelion, the first thing I noticed about the house was that there was no hint of a cigarette odor. When I confronted Paul about it, he claimed—as Ron, mind you—that he had kicked the habit in order to explain the lack of tobacco smell. And, kick it he had, Walt. Indeed, Paul had finally managed to kick the smoking habit that the women in his congregation had chided him about for so long."

"So? Again, the body in the grave could still be—"

"—I know, Walt, Paul's body. Just hang on, we're getting there. So, Paul moved into the house at Pelion, pretending to be Ron. The first thing he did was to deodorize the place as much as possible—you see, once someone kicks smoking, it simply kills them to be around cigarette smoke or cigarette smokers. So, he got rid of the smell. What Paul didn't get rid of in those five days between Ron's death and me visiting him at Pelion was Ron's cigarettes on top of the refrigerator. Oh, I'm sure he would have gotten around to it eventually, but having a lot to think about and worry about, he'd simply neglected to toss out the cigarettes."

"So, when you mentioned seeing the cigarettes that day in his house, it—"

"—yeah! It threw him for a loop, for he had painted himself in a corner. You see, Paul—pretending to be Ron—said that he had kicked the habit a year ago. He explained the cigarettes on the fridge by saying he had not gotten around to throwing them away yet, *blah blah blah*. However, I made sure he knew that I had access to the pack of cigarettes found at the crime scene, and he was smart enough to know that the date and state of the tax stamps on the cigarettes atop the fridge would match the date and state of the package at the crime scene. He knew that if I ever gained access to the cigarettes on the refrigerator, the jig would be up. He would be caught with his pants down. I mean, if he had quit smoking over a year ago, why would the tax stamps on the cigarettes atop the fridge say July 12, 1972? Immediately, I would know that the supposed non-smoker currently in that house was a liar."

"Okay, I'm following you."

"And, here's the good part: if a non-smoker in that house claiming to be Ron truly did have no use for the cigarettes, it would mean that the cigarettes at the crime scene were the victim's, not the killer's. In other words, Walt, the cigarettes truly were those of the chain-smoking South Carolinian named Ron Christmas. They had fallen out of his pocket while Paul was attaching his body to the steeple. At any rate, no matter which twin was living in the house or which twin was lying in the grave, the twin in the house definitely would have been fingered for his brother's death if I had gained access to the tax stamps on that carton."

Walt started laughing slightly and shook his head in disbelief. "Man, now that would have been poetic justice!"

"Yeah, and if you think you were lost in this maze of mind-blowing 'if's about the cigarettes, think about how ol' Paul was sweatin' it. Like I said, Paul had really painted himself in a corner of sorts. How ironic it would have been if Paul, pretending to be Ron, had been indicted for murder anyway as 'Ron' for killing 'Paul,' the charge being based on Ron's corpse, which was misunderstood to be that of Paul's. Boggles the mind, doesn't it?"

"Sure does, Jet, it sure does!"

"So, Walt, the cigarettes themselves didn't tell me anything since I never saw the tax stamps on the packs on top of the fridge. It was the other clues later on that implied to me that the killer was Paul. But, without Paul becoming paranoid enough over the cigarettes to attempt ending my life at the train bridge outside of Spartanburg and to persist in his efforts to kill me, the other clues such as the widow's mite would never have materialized. At any rate, the cigarettes served a great purpose for us."

"It's still crazy though, Jet. If he would have just played things all calm and cool-like, you really wouldn't have had much to go on after he got rid of the cigarettes on the fridge."

"Yeah, Sheriff, but you remember Edgar Allen Poe's 'The Tell-Tale Heart,' don't you? Those cigarettes on the fridge sure acted like the heart in the story hidden beneath the floorboards. Boy, the ghost of Ron sure talked to Paul through those cigs, didn't it? It goes back to what I've told you before, friend. It's not the content of an inquisition that drives fear into the guilty; it's merely the fact that the inquisition is happening and the guilty knows not what lies in the mind of the inquisitors."

"What about Ron using fertilizer in his explosives, Jet? Were you able to connect that in your mind to the fact that Paul had access to a lot of fertilizer, working part-time at Big Blue's as he did?"

"No, that wasn't nearly as obvious to me as the other clues that I put together. In the rural Carolinas, you find people in about every square mile who have bags and bags of fertilizer sitting in a shed. Unfortunately, just about any schmuck can access the materials for making a homemade bomb with fertilizer as easily as he can the ingredients for baking a cake. Walt, I fear that our country is going to experience much trouble in the future with juveniles and other crackpots making such weapons of destruction."

"I sure hope not, partner. I sure hope not. Jet, I, uh, can't thank you enough for putting a stop to all of this. I feel now just as I did when you ended the cotton gin murders, except I hurt for our little missy. Again, I'm sorry about Cat."

"She'll be fine, Walt. I know she will," replied Nolan, his voice choking up slightly.

"And I also meant to tell you, Jet, that Sanford came clean this morning about disclosing the location of your lodging to a mysterious caller yesterday claiming to be an SBI courier. I told him to go home for now and I would get with him this evening. I'm going to fire the little pipsqueak."

"No, Walt! Don't, please. Let's say that all of the ill-feelings, hatred, and 'what-if's' died last night on the front of that tractor. We really can't blame Sanford's misjudgment for Cat being in a coma anymore than I can blame myself for having taken her with us to Pelion or Fowler for sending her down here in the first place. I want so desperately to blame myself, but that won't do Cat any good. No, the one who did this to her ended up dead last night. If you would, keep Sanford on your force. He's a good man. Tell him that I, uh, forgive him totally and in no way hold any ill will."

"Sure, Jet. I most certainly will."

"Now, Sheriff. About the publicity, you realize by now that you are facing a great dilemma, don't you?"

"Yeah, I guess you're referring to how I go about informing a community that their precious spiritual leader of a quarter of a century was not the victim or a martyr as we all thought, but a killer."

"Yeah, Walt. That's why I said nothing to you last night and hoped you could keep a leash on the media. As guardian of your community, you have a lot to consider. It's not just a dilemma, it's a *moral* dilemma."

"Okay, partner, help me think here. You know I certainly don't consider myself fit for playing God with people's lives. I know the obvious reason I would let people think that it was Ron who died last night. I mean, it's gonna take the people around here eons just to get over the fact that a man they held in such high esteem was murdered so viciously. Can you imagine how long it will take for them to cope with the fact that it was actually their hero who was the vicious murderer!"

"I know, Walt, they'll never get over it. I fear it will shake the very foundations of religion in this village for generations. I fear that the faith of so many who ascribed to Paul's teachings will be severely damaged and that the souls of the many whose lives he touched in God's name will suffer confusion and erosion."

"So, supposing I did leave it with Ron as the killer, Jet? How would it affect those in Ron's world?"

"Well, Ron really had no others, Walt. The only other person in his life of any matter was his mother—and even she, I think, would be more prepared to accept Ron having committed the unthinkable than Paul. In fact, I believe a small part of her has already prepared herself for Ron to have done it, due to my visit with her. She knows that Ron was always an outcast and was at a point in his life where he was bitterly self-absorbed in his own down-and-out state of being. However, Mary thought that Paul walked on water. To desecrate his memory now and indicate otherwise—I don't think that she could handle it."

"Okay, Jet, so now we get to the philosophical argument of the matter, the *'can a lone man on an island be a sinner?'* kind of stuff, right? What about Ron? I know he's dead, and I know he was a miserable whelp when he was alive. But what do I owe Ron, knowing he was innocent? It's true, maybe he would have taken a shot at killing Paul during certain times of his life. In our minds, we all get angry enough to kill someone else at times. Even though Ron never amounted to much in the end, would it be fair to him—to his memory, that is—to have him footnoted in the pages of criminal history as having murdered the person who actually killed him? Would it be just for an innocent man to be blamed for the death of a psycho who is probably, in the next year or two, going to have a statue erected somewhere around here in his honor? Is it *fair*, Agent Jericho, to publicly make a saint out of Paul and a hell-hound out of Ron, when in truth it is the other way around?"

"I, uh, can't answer that, Walt. I was sent down here to stop the killings—to catch the killer—and that I did. I realize that you have to consider the needs of your many citizens as opposed to justice for one man in this case. That's why I didn't correct the falsehood of Paul's death until I saw you this morning. It has to be your decision, for it's your community. Nobody knows about this dilemma but you and I. Even Fowler still thinks that Ron Christmas was killed last night."

"Boy, what a moral mess I'm in," said Walt woefully, as if he had just lost his best friend.

"I wish I could answer for you on this one, Walt, but, as I said, it's your people. It's your call. As your friend, I will respect you equally, either way you decide. If it makes it any easier, government officials play God with people's lives all the time. For example, there's a lot of hubbub going around about the Kennedy assassination being an in-house undertaking by certain political interests. Who knows what information will surface in the future concerning the assassination. Will it be the part that's shared with the public or the actual truth? Take the Roswell and Kecksburg UFOs: We may never know whether or not there are really little green men up there. From government officials in Salem trying to protect their constituents from witches to witch hunters during the McCarthy era trying to save Americans from the communists, you've always got someone acting as Big Brother in this country. Someone's always trying to protect us from ourselves by censoring the quantity and quality of information we receive. They're always operating by the principle of *'What they don't know won't hurt 'em,'* constantly filtering what and how much we know. Of course, some of the information imparted is not always for the good of the common citizen, but rather for the good of the imparters—you know what I mean, Sheriff? Just because you're paranoid doesn't necessarily mean that someone's *not* out to get you. All that aside, Walt, if you do make a decision that involves imparting the wrong information for what you perceive is the good of your people, you certainly won't be the first to have done it—or the last."

"I, uh, understand all of that Jet—well, most of it, at least. I'm not wanting to manipulate my fellow citizens or keep them controlled like a bunch of cattle. I just want them to be happy and feel loved."

"Then, Sheriff, make your decision accordingly. It truly is your decision to make, and I can't think of a more worthy man to make it."

"Thank you, Jet. I, uh, have a helluva lot of thinking to do before I make some calls."

"I know, my friend. And I shall leave you to do so. However, I feel a little guilty. As I prepare to depart, I realize that I am privy to the secretive moral dilemma that is now weighing so heavily on your heart. You are exhibiting such trust in me, my friend, that I feel it only fair to reciprocate with the same trust. Do you mind if I share something with you that no one else knows?—something that is weighing heavily upon my heart? I feel that we would be even-Stephen, as the old saying goes. And it might help me a little in the upcoming days to know that someone else is helping to carry my load."

"Sure, Jet, anything you need to tell me! Fire away!"

"Uh, Cat and I are more than co-workers, more than merely agent and assistant. She and I are, uh, seeing each other, and we have been together for some time now. The only problem is that fraternization with fellow employees is not allowed in the SBI."

"I knew it! I knew it!" shouted Walt joyfully, as if Jericho had just pulled a rabbit out of his hat. "I knew you two were an item, the way you argued lovingly and picked with each other. Like I said earlier, you'd think you two were married."

"Okay, Walt, but remember: this knowledge is only for Cat, you, and me at the moment. I'm sure Fowler is going to figure it out eventually, and we'll both be fired when he does."

"Well, partner, if you get fired, you just come right back down here. Imagine that! Deputy Jet Jericho working for Sheriff Walt Niblock! Boy, people would really walk the line in this county—no more askin' for too many beers at Keaton's Chicken Parlor, that's for sure. Hell, I'd even demote myself to deputy if you'd be willing to be sheriff here, Jet!"

"Walt, as enticing as Icy Springs would be to re-locate myself, I'm really hoping to hang in there with the SBI. At any rate, I'll definitely keep in touch and let you know what's happening with everything, especially Cat's condition."

Walt's temporary foray into a cheerful disposition slipped quickly back into a somber one. "Yeah, Jet, it appears that you and me both have a lot of praying to do for each other. I'll keep my prayers out for you and your lady. Just pray for me that I make the right decision when I make my call to the media in a little while."

"Well, old friend, take care of yourself and the people here. Tell Sarah goodbye for me!"

"Sure will, Jet. Be careful going back. Whisper in Miss Cat's ear that ol' Walt and all the people at Icy Springs are pulling for her."

"Sure thing, Walt. She'll come through. Goodbye."

"'Bye now."

As Jet took a final glance at the sheriff's office while stepping into his red convertible, he sighed enormously. Even in the throes of his own emotional tribulations and turmoil, the agent sympathized deeply with Walt. He could only imagine the agonizing soul-searching the trustworthy sheriff was now undergoing in coming to a decision about what was best for the citizens of Icy Springs. It had been a hell of a week for the two lawmen, and it certainly wasn't destined to get any better in the next few days.

CHAPTER 31

The Warm Shadow

There's just something about seeing a loved one lying unconscious that sends tremors to the very soul. Nolan always thoroughly enjoyed staring at Cat while she slept, for she had such an innocent, nearly childlike look about her. Her angelic face always seemed to be at its most tranquil when her exotic eyes were at rest. But looking at his lover in the hospital bed was almost more than the agent could bear, for in no way did her comatose state resemble a peaceful repose. She seemed so lifeless and vulnerable, giving Nolan the impression that every breath she took was the unlikely outcome of an internal, ongoing war being waged against Death itself, a confrontation in which Cat was assigned the role of an underdog.

Without a doubt, Jericho was tired. After all, he had spent the remainder of Sunday on through Monday at noon sitting by Cat's side at Ireland Memorial. Dr. Mebane told him at around ten o'clock a.m. that she seemed stable enough and was scheduled to leave the hospital at sometime around four that afternoon. As much as he wished to follow the ambulance, Jericho was justifiably exhausted and knew he had to have a least a little rest before driving back. He was confident that Cat was in good hands regarding the transfer to Mary Elizabeth. For that matter, she was in far better hands at the moment than she had been with him to have ended up in this situation in the first place. Anyway, it was time to head back to the Chat & Nibble for a little rest and an extremely late checkout, pending upon the owner's permission. Then, he would check in on Cat later that night once getting to Raleigh.

◆ ◆ ◆ ◆ ◆

Although needed, the nap was had not been that restful, so Jericho decided to walk over to the café and digest a meal that would not be that tasty. Nolan was a man who savored both his food and his sleep, but ever since the wall at Big Blue's had come down, nothing seemed to relieve his tormented, active mind or his bone-weary body. It was now that he truly realized just how thoroughly Cat had claimed dominion over every fiber of his being, for his heart, mind, soul, and body were solely her property. Would she ever rouse from her dormant world to enjoy the love he was willing to yield? Until now, the agent had never realized how painfully slowly a minute hand could make its way around a clock.

Sitting down in what was now "their" booth, Nolan was lost in the menu as a large form approached the table. "Why hello, little fella, I was about to think I wouldn't see you around here again."

Jumping slightly, Nolan looked up at the hulking waiter. "Oh, hello there. Sorry, Father Nature. I didn't mean to seem so startled—just real tired, I guess. What are you doing here? I thought you just worked here on weekends. Where's Lora?"

"Oh, she quit. She moved to Winston-Salem. I hear she's talking about opening up a massage parlor that serves men only."

"It figures. What about your Krispy Kreme job?"

"Oh, that? They fired me, little fella. They caught me eatin' too much of the product and said I was diggin' into their profit. Anyway, I'm here full-time during the day and still world wrestling champion at night. Hey, where's that cute little gal that you were dining with the other morning?"

"Oh, uh, she's not feeling too well. She just can't seem to stay awake these days, but I'll tell her you asked about her."

"You do that, little fella. And you tell her something for me. If it'll make her feel any better, I'll be glad to do my chicken dance for her when she comes back in. She really seemed to get a kick out of that."

"Yeah, we both thought it was most entertaining."

"Then if you would, sir, voice your opinion to the owner on the way out. He asked me to stop doing the dance, saying that I looked like a complete idiot and it didn't fit his vision for the café."

"Father Nature, a man would have to be quite a visionary to come up with a dance like that. Besides, I'm sure nobody has pulled the wool over your eyes and gotten an undeserved third round of pancakes, have they now?"

"No, sir. People hardly take issue with me at all on matters concerning my table service."

"Well, Father Nature, as stalwart and muscular a fellow as you are, I'd about be willing to offer free pancakes to any man crazy enough to contradict you on any matter at all."

"Thanks a lot, mister. By the way, it was great that they got the reverend's killer, wasn't it?"

Jericho suddenly snapped to full alertness. "Why, uh, I've not caught wind of it yet. What have you heard?" Having been consumed with Cat's well-being, Nolan hadn't even thought about checking out a newspaper.

"Oh, it's big, mister. Here, it's right here in the paper they dropped off at noon." Easing two booths over, the giant man snatched up a copy of the paper lying on one of the seats. Easing back over, he handed the newspaper to Jericho. "See, front page! Pastor Paul can rest in peace now that his killer's dead. I tell ya, it's hard to believe that a man would murder his own twin brother, especially with Paul being a man of God and all. Boy, ol' Ron sure had a gruesome ending on the forks of that tractor, didn't he?"

"Yeah, Father, ol' 'Ron' sure did," echoed Jericho grimly as he surveyed the article.

"And I'd really like to meet that Jericho dude who put an end to Ron's killin'. He must be one hell of a man. I wish they'd had his picture in the paper, 'cause I've never seen him. I've heard people talk about how he solved those murders out at the cotton gin and of how unbeatable that guy is. There's hardly anybody I'm afraid to go up against, but that guy sounds like a tiger that I sure wouldn't want to get by the tail. Maybe someday I'll get a good look at him."

"I'm betting good money on that, Mr. Nature. I'd venture to say you might have already met him and didn't know it."

"Nah, little fella, I've got an eye for tough people. I've never seen anybody around here that looks as tough as that guy sounds."

"Well, you never know. Anyway, thanks for letting me in on the big newsflash."

"You're welcome, mister. Now, what can I get you?"

"If you would, Mr. Nature, just bring me a Coca-Cola and a basket of hushpuppies, please."

"Sure thing, sir."

"And, uh, I don't see any ketchup on the table. If you would, grab some ketchup for me."

"Ketchup, sir?" said Father Nature.

"Yeah. I like to, uh, dip my hushpuppies in a pool of ketchup."

"Sure thing, sir. Have a great week."

"I'm sure hoping it'll go uphill from here on. Thanks, Father."

One would think that Father Nature would be a pain in the ass to have as a waiter when one was in a downer of a mood. On the contrary, Nolan found the good-natured, well-intentioned oaf to be a quite colorful diversion, if only momentarily. The meal served its purpose also, managing to put at least *some* sorely needed nourishment—if you could call it that—into the agent's bruised, starving body. Not really getting into his meal as he often did, Nolan kept on eating the ketchup-dipped hushpuppies until he was out of Coca-Cola. Normally, he would have ordered more drink until the food was gone, but in this case the agent interpreted the absence of soda as a sign that it was time for him to leave Icy Springs.

Nolan took one last glance at the newspaper article before exiting the café. The only mention about Cat was that "an associate of the agent was injured in an explosion set off by Ron Christmas, and she is currently recovering at Ireland Memorial Hospital." The article's minimization of her involvement was probably for the best at the moment, for Walt had done his best to handle everything with prudence. Nolan really felt for his friend. Although he knew Walt had labeled the killer as Ron for the good of his village, he speculated that Walt was now agonizing with the decision he had made and feeling as if he had betrayed the memory of an innocent man.

Heading down 64 through Icy Springs, the agent sensed that the once-timeless village had now transformed into a place far unlike that which he customarily visited for a friendly hunting trip with Walt. Yes, prior to this assignment, Jericho did have the haunting aura of the '67 cotton gin murders glaring at him every time he passed by the defunct ginning company. But now, the old gin would be joined by a pair of sister sites in Icy Springs sitting by the cursed highway, two newly appointed places hosting an unshakable stigma of infamy which would last for generations. The workers at Big Blue's would certainly be talking for years about that crazy guy who fell from the catwalk and speared himself on the prongs of the tractor. The citizens passing by Icy Springs Lutheran would always be prompted by its steeple to recall a black robe flapping around like a flag in the breeze. Yes, now there were three places forever tarnished by the after-shocks of sinister events, three places whose lingering reputations would serve as the fodder of local spook legends bandied about from campfire to campfire.

Passing through the holler at Bud Holly's, Jericho grew apprehensive as he ascended the slope just before Viola Krenshaw's on the left and the Lutheran church on the right. The agent especially feared for the church's future, for he thought about how the citizens now feared the shadows of the steeple, of how the church now emanated such anguish over its recent entanglement with evil, of how the people of Icy Springs must now feel such despair with their spiritual leader vanquished from the Earth.

As the agent crested the hill and approached the curve at the church, a slight smile came across his face, and into his heart spread a warmth of a sort he hadn't felt since Cat said "I will" at Big Blue's in answer to his proposal. An elongated shadow was stretching outward from the majestic steeple of the church in the late evening sun. And what a sight it was, for the cross was firmly planted flat in the middle of the highway.

What made the sight even more awe-inspiring was that several of the villagers had meandered over and were standing on the center line of the road. Jericho looked in amazement at the handful of villagers, of whom he recognized only Miss Eden and Miss Krenshaw. All were looking toward the steeple while basking in the sun, with their feet firmly planted on the silhouette of the cross. Miss Eden and Miss Krenshaw had their eyes closed as it they were offering a prayer of some kind.

Jericho brought his red convertible to a quick, non-screeching halt and exited the car without saying a word. He walked over and stood in the midst of the villagers, joining them in feeling the comforting heat in the shadow of the cross. No longer did the shadow present itself as an icy menace. The doorway from ground to heaven had once again been propped open in the villagers' hearts.

Miss Eden and Miss Krenshaw opened their eyes and saw the agent standing nearby. They eased over to him without saying a word and both gave him the tightest hug a person could imagine. Each woman kissed his cheek and whispered, "*Thank you.*" After that, each lady took one of his hands and the three of them stood there in the shadow of the cross, savoring the warmth of the moment.

CHAPTER 32

Have You Ever Ridden a Bike in the Rain?

After bidding the villagers adieu, Jericho headed on down the long road to Raleigh. He now understood that the church would have a future; that the death of one man was not going to quash the existence of Icy Springs Lutheran. Too many people powered by the blessings of a provident God had put too much effort into keeping the church alive and thriving through the years. A church is never the work of one man nor is a village. In Nolan's eyes at least, Walt's decision had truly been vindicated by the joy he had witnessed in the faces of the villagers. What difference did it make if they believed that Ron was the killer and Paul was the saint? God knew the difference. Neither man was dealing at all with the people of Earth anymore, so neither man could care less. The spirits of both were now dealing with unearthly powers, above or below.

Thoughts of Cat were starting to gnaw at him as he began to imagine the worst. He even imagined the attendants not latching the ambulance door properly, resulting in the wheeled stretcher rolling out of the back as if Cat was trapped in a silly *Little Rascals* production. And, although he tried to talk himself out of his fears, he was only successful for brief moments.

Eventually, Jericho knew a distraction was essential to help keep his mind on his driving. He flipped on the radio right in the middle of a newscast.

"—and Mr. Christmas had used a mixture of fuel oil and nitro-methane combined with ammonium nitrate—common fertilizer—to destroy his house near Columbia, South Carolina. It appears that he used several bundles of dynamite to do extensive damage to Big Blue's Feed Mill and Warehouse in Icy Springs, injuring an SBI employee, her named as yet undisclosed. It is said that SBI Agent Nolan Jericho pursued Mr. Christmas across a catwalk in the feed mill, from which Mr. Christmas fell to his death, impaling himself on the prongs of a forklift. We'll have more details as they unfold. On a lighter note, the deputy of the Sheriff's Department in Icy Springs who recently found himself

underneath the posterior of a falling bear seems to be recovering and will soon—"

This station just wasn't doing the trick, so Jericho began fiddling with the radio again.

"—and officials in Raleigh are still baffled about the disappearance of the three young women. Director Jackson Fowler of the SBI said that all forces are currently mobilized in an effort to locate the women. When asked if he thought they could still be alive, he offered no comment—"

Okay, I'm already up on that news. Let's try this station.

"Hey, gang, it looks like the cool front that's moving in tomorrow is going to bring a lot of much-needed rain with it, about two inches of it. The farmers certainly will be glad. After all, we've had this drought going on for quite some time now. So listeners, enjoy the cool and enjoy the wet—"

Oh, well . . . let's see what's on my favorite music station. . .

"Oh, won't you stay just a little bit longer . . ." It was Cat's favorite song, "Stay," by Maurice and the Zodiacs. He hadn't heard it since that night in her bedroom which had ended up in a man-versus-feline war. As much as he needed something to keep him from worrying about Cat, there was a part of Jericho that felt he would be betraying her in some manner if he changed channels to avoid the song.

Although he feared that listening to Cat's song might be somewhat macabre, considering the circumstances, the words immediately struck his soul as being *so* appropriate. *Yes, Cat, won't you stay on this Earth just a little bit longer?!* The more the melody and the words played along, the more comfort the agent seemed to be finding. Images of his lady-love ran rampant through his mind—*Ahh, there she is, standing in front of Fowler's office the day we met; man, there she is in that silver string bikini, jumping into the water from that high ledge in Jameson's Quarry outside of Greensboro; oh, there she is in that gorgeous green velvet dress, serving me a slice of lasagna; yeah, there she is in that black négligée, ooh-la-la! Wow, now she's pulling up in my red convertible wearing that cowgirl outfit; oh, there she is fighting with Dreama in the hotel room—Yikes! Get that out of your mind right now Jericho, Cat doesn't like you picturing that scene!—Man alive, there's Cat in that long, flowing wedding gown!*

Suddenly a radio announcer cruelly dared to interrupt the tail-end of the song. As if a black hole had sucked him right out of his fantasy world, he suddenly pictured Cat underneath the huge mound of sand from the collapsed sand castle. Then his mind involuntarily switched to an image of her lying atop the pile of cinder block at Big Blue's and, ultimately, lying comatose in a hospital bed. *She's gonna pull through this thing, Jericho! She's just gotta!*

◆ ◆ ◆ ◆ ◆

It was very late, and visitors were discouraged at this time of the evening in the intensive care unit of Mary Elizabeth Hospital. It's quite amazing, actually, the number of doors that are opened up for an agent without question upon flashing his SBI identification! Nolan pushed the door to Cat's room open ever so gently, as if he would startle her, as if startling her would be a bad thing. The agent nervously tiptoed to her bedside and looked down at her lovingly. He began talking to her in a quiet whisper.

"Kitten, you're home now; at least, you're near your home, your friends, and your loved ones. I know you're still struggling to forgive me for letting Paul do this to you. But he's dead now and can't hurt you anymore."

Nolan looked around the room in a secretive fashion to ensure the couple had complete privacy for what was to follow. *"Kitten, I'm going back to my apartment for the time being to get some rest and let you get some rest. You'll be fine here. I'm the happiest and luckiest man alive to have you as my fiancée. I can't tell you what that means to me. I promise you will never regret accepting my proposal. I promise I will make the best husband a woman could ever find. Our love is blessed by so many stars above, at least 213 of them. I love you, and I promise you that you'll always be proud to be Mrs. Catherine Jericho."*

At that, Nolan bent over and kissed Cat lightly on the cheek. He stood up and looked at her, as if he was hoping they were simply trapped in a fairy tale and all it would take to wake her up would be his kiss. But, alas, it was not to be. After standing there for a half-minute, Nolan reached into his pocket and took out the ring box. Opening the box with care, he extracted the ring and held it to his chest. Then, he gently took hold of her right hand, leaned over, and kissed it. Following this gesture, the agent slid the ring onto her fourth ringer. *"See you tomorrow . . ."*

◆ ◆ ◆ ◆

Jericho actually slept well that night; he needed to. Maybe it was because he had finally slept in his own bed, but, more than likely, it was because Cat was back in Raleigh—not safe and sound just yet, but at least close to home. The agent wasted no time dressing in his "Jet-casual" and heading back over to the hospital.

Once again, Nolan pushed the door to Cat's room open gently, but this time he was surprised to see a figure standing by her bed. It was a woman who looked to be perhaps in her early- to mid-thirties, with straight hair that was flaming red. She had on jeans adorned with flowery patches and peace signs, a breezy little top of some kind, and sandals. A beautiful woman actually. Nolan noticed upon making eye contact with her that she had those slightly asymmetrical-looking eyes similar to Cat and Dreama. "Oh, uh, I'm sorry, I didn't mean to barge in on you like that, Miss, uh—"

"It's quite all right. Actually, I was just about to leave. And it's Miss Marshall. I'm Krystle, Cat's older sister. You can just call me 'Krys', although some people call me 'Starbaby.'"

"Yeah, I was actually beginning to catch on that you might be Cat's sister. 'Starbaby'?" inquired Nolan with a puzzled look.

"It's a long story," replied Krys, "and something I tell people on a need-to-know basis. I'll probably enlighten you sometime down the road," she teased, with a slightly mischievous smile.

"*Hmm,* Starbaby!" mused Nolan. "At any rate, Cat's talked a lot about you. You're one of her heroes, next to your late father, that is."

"She and I are rather close, always have been. We were there for each other during some crucial times. Now, I'm not psychic, I promise; however, I know for a fact that you must be *the* Nolan Jericho."

"Uh, yes, ma'am," responded the agent in a surprised tone.

"Nolan, if I may call you that, you're all that Cat talks about. Let me tell you, you are *it* in her book," said Krys with a big smile.

"Wow, usually the only thing I'm *it* on is the list people keep when they're out to get someone!"

Krys laughed aloud while playfully twirling her hair with her finger. "I see immediately what she enjoys about you. She's said that you are so serious, but yet you have a marvelous, dry sense of humor that comes through without any effort."

"Well, I try my best not to exert any effort."

Chuckling again, Krys said, "See, that's what she means. You are definitely one to get to know! Uh, Nolan . . ."

Krys' demeanor took a more serious turn. Even though Nolan felt comfortable in her company, he still found it unsettling for her to call him Nolan, for that privilege generally went to only Cat and his mother. "Krys? Are you okay?"

"She is going to pull through this, isn't she, Nolan? My sister will come out of this alive, won't she?"

"The doctors seem to think there's a chance, but as to when she will wake up and what condition she'll be in, they have no idea. Uh, Krys . . ."

"Yes, Nolan?"

"It's all my fault. Cat was helping me on an assignment and I stupidly, albeit unintentionally, placed her in harm's way. I invited her to be at a place where she really didn't need to be. I take full responsibility for your sister and I am so sorry. If I had to do it all over again—"

"Aw rats, Nolan, come here!"

Nolan was confused by the nature of Krys' reaction as well as the command following it, for he was only used to Cat being bossy with him at a sentimental time. Obeying, he walked three steps and stopped right in front of her, as if to indicate *Okay, I'm here like you asked!*

Krys unexpectedly reached out and gave him a tremendous hug. She kissed him on the cheek and then pulled away quickly. "Okay, you listen here, Nolan Jericho. I'm not going to let any man my sister is so fond of beat himself up with guilt. You know Cat would pitch a fit about that. Cat doesn't like to live in the past; she's a here-and-now gal."

Nolan's thoughts then flashed to the moment when Cat had shared many of her tormenting memories with him. If Krys only knew how much the past actually haunted her sister. "I, uh, thank you for that perspective, Krys. It's hard not to blame myself, as there will certainly be others who will hold me accountable for her condition and my actions. So, thank you for obviously being an ally I can trust."

"Well, I just know my sister—she always likes to be right in the thick of things. She probably could have exercised the option to say 'no' to being in harm's way if she had wished, but you probably couldn't have kept her out of harm's way if you had tried. Cat is just, well . . . uh . . . she's just *Cat.*"

"That she is, Krys, *that* she is," said Nolan with a smile.

"Well, I had best be on my way," said Krys, grabbing a small sack that perhaps functioned as a handbag. "I'm going with some friends to a protest rally."

Nolan had been suspicious about the flower child get-up. From the moment he had walked in the door, Krys had struck him as a late-blooming hippie, a sort of ghost-of-Woodstock past. "What exactly are you protesting?" asked the agent with a curious look.

"Why, inequality and oppression of course, what else?!"

"Inequality for whom? Whose oppression?" inquired Nolan, with an even more curious look.

"Anybody's! Everybody's! Anybody that is discriminated against because of race, gender, religion, nationality, sexual orientation, whatever!"

"Interesting," mumbled Nolan while nodding his head. "Krys, before you go, are you going to feed Cat's kitties for awhile?"

"Sure am, Nolan! I'll take care of them for the rest of the week. What say you and I alternate weeks?—you take next week?"

"I guess that would work for me. So you feel okay with me helping to look after her cats?" asked Jericho in a humble, somewhat puzzled tone.

"Why not?" exclaimed Krys, walking towards the door. "After all, you're the one whose ring is on her finger!" Smiling, Krys opened the door and turned back around to the blushing, stunned agent. "Don't worry. Until you're ready to announce it to the world, it's our little secret. Toodle-oo!"

Whoa! Now I see where Cat gets her spunk, her spontaneity, and her headstrongness. Something tells me to count my lucky stars that Krys is on my side. I think she'd be one hellcat to deal with if her ire was raised.

◆ ◆ ◆ ◆ ◆

Nolan decided to go home for the afternoon with the plan of checking back on Cat sometime later in the evening. On his way home from the hospital, the rain heralded by the regional forecasts began to fall. Nolan knew the rain was a blessing from up above, yet he just wasn't in the mood for the dreariness it would bring being compiled with the dreariness of his current situation. *Lord, I know we're lucky to have the rain you're sending. But could I have just a little sunshine opening up in my life pretty soon? I'm feeling a little low at the moment.*

Grabbing a couple of Almond Joys and a Nehi grape soda, the agent sat down on his couch and flipped through the *TV Guide*. *Nothing! No* Star Trek . . . *no* Mission: Impossible . . . *no* Wild Wild West . . . *no nothing! . . . not even* a Secret Agent*!* Flinging the *TV Guide* behind the couch, he hunkered down with his candy and his grape drink, munching and sipping while looking at the dreary rain falling outside his window. Some claps of thunder rang out, appropriately accentuating the current mood of the day. If anything, listening to the thunder was at least more interesting than watching re-runs of *That Girl*. After a while, Jericho settled into the rhythmic pattern established between the sipping, the munching, and the thunderclaps.

RING . . .

Oh, great! Okay, Fowler, like I'm ready to be chewed out!

RING . . .

All right, all right, I'm comin' . . .

RING . . .

"Jericho here!"

"Hey, Jet. It's me, Walt."

"Hi, Walt," Jericho responded almost cheerfully, so grateful was he not to have to be talking to Fowler. "How's it going for you out there?"

"Well, Jet, actually not bad at all. I guess you've seen or heard the news about the decision I made."

"Yeah, Walt. As a matter of fact, I did. I even happened to run into some villagers on my way out of Icy Springs. Judging by the mood they were in, it was as if that veil of gloominess had been lifted off of them; as if they believed in justice and goodness again. Sheriff, I think you made the right decision. Can you imagine how harshly they would have dealt with the reality of Paul being a murderer?"

"No, Jet, but I still try to imagine it every now and then to justify having identified an innocent man as the killer."

"I know, buddy, I know," responded Jet sympathetically.

"Well, that's not why I called Jet. I—"

"Oh, Cat? She hasn't come out of her coma yet, Walt. But at least she's still stable. She seemed to do well, as well as could be, on the trip from Icy Springs to Raleigh. She has her loved ones around her up here. I met her sister Krys this morning."

"Wow, everything sounds good, Jet—under the circumstances, that is. Keep talkin' to Cat and, while you're at it, keep reminding her I'm cheering for her. However, believe it or not, that's still not the main reason I called."

"What then, Walt?" asked Jericho with a worried tone, seeing as how Icy Springs was still in a somewhat fragile state.

"Uh, it's Dreama!"

"Oh, Lord! What about 'er?"

"Well, you know how I fired her, right?"

"Right."

"Her landlord called and asked me to stop by her apartment. Mrs. Phifer said Dreama had moved out and had left behind something she thought belonged to the Sheriff's Department."

"What's that?"

"Uh, Dreama had accidentally left a pair of handcuffs lying behind the headboard of the bed with the initials 'S. D.' etched on them—S. D. for 'Sheriff's Department'."

"Handcuffs behind the bed, huh? Sounds like Dreama. I wouldn't have expected anything less of her."

"Well, that's not the news you'll be interested in, partner. Mrs. Phifer said that Dreama indicated she was moving to Raleigh. According to Mrs. Phifer, Dreama said she had a half-sister who was seriously injured the other night by some madman at Big Blue's. She said her half-sister was in a coma, that she had been transferred to Raleigh, and she needed to be by her side. Jet! There's no doubt that you know Dreama and Cat are half-sisters. Why didn't you let me in on that little fact?"

"Sorry, Walt. As much trust as I have in you, I promised Cat I would say nothing of it. As you've witnessed, there's certainly no love lost between her and Dreama. Cat still hurts greatly over the anguish Dreama has caused her in the past."

"Well, I guess I can understand that, seeing that Dreama's been such a burr under my butt in the short time I've known her. Anyway, Jet, Dreama said that there were some others close to her half-sister that she could probably be of, uh, 'great comfort' to at a time like this. I thought you'd find that piece of information most intriguing. Basically, I wanted to give you a heads-up."

"Thanks, Walt—as always, I appreciate you watching my back."

"Hey, the feeling's mutual. Anyway, keep in touch, Jet. Keep me up on what's happening out there."

"Sure will, Walt. Goodbye."

"'Bye now . . ." And Walt hung up.

Oh, just GREAT! Dreama!—wanting to be of 'comfort' to Cat's loved ones. I definitely know of one loved one she has her sights set on comforting. I really don't need her antics around here during these tough times ahead.

RING . . .

Lord, who's calling now?

RING . . .

"Jericho here!"

"Jet, Fowler here—"

Great, Fowler! With Walt's revelation about Dreama, Jericho had temporarily put Fowler's intention to call out of his mind.

"Yes, Director?" replied the agent in a slightly perturbed tone.

"Jet, I still want ya to come in tomorrow. Although it's not on the news yet, we believe another woman was kidnapped on Sunday night. We've had to give it some time, of course, to officially declare her as missing."

"Was she homosexual?"

"Purportedly—" The director hesitated for a moment. "Jet, you're my best, and I really need ya on this case, but—"

"I'll do my best, sir!" responded Jericho in earnest.

"—*but*," continued Fowler, "as I told ya earlier, you've really put me in a bad position, you and Cat."

"Please continue, sir."

"Well, Jet, I didn't get to be SBI director because I'm a clueless dummy. I mean, I may not know my flowers, but I did find out recently that a proboscis is definitely not a flower—it's a nose, of all things. Jet, it doesn't take a rocket scientist to figure out that you don't have as much as a daisy growing in your apartment. I felt there was something fishy going on, and it all became verified from Cat's injury that you've been keeping her a little too close to you—and, a little too often."

"I, uh, can't deny that, sir," offered the agent, beaten down by the implications.

"Well, what ya didn't know was that I've actually been a little suspicious for some time now about you and Cat. I'll take some of the blame on how far this has gone, because I should have called the both of ya into my office at the first sign. I should have known better than to have sent her to you in Icy Springs."

"First sign? What sign, sir?"

"Engelbretsen saw you and Cat dining together one night at The Butcher Block. He ratted on ya the next morning. He said the two of you were simply eating, not cuddling or kissing or anything. So like an idiot, I gave my two best employees the benefit of the doubt, fooling myself into thinking that maybe, just maybe, it was a one-time gesture of appreciation or friendship from one of you to the other or some other cockamamie reason."

Engelbretsen, what an asshole! What was he doing at the Butcher Block? He claims he's a vegetarian!

"Uh, sir, I realize you're not to blame for my actions. However, having this knowledge, why exactly *did* you send Cat to me at Icy Springs? Why have you not yet seen me behind closed doors about the matter?"

"Like I said, Jet, the two of you are my shining stars, and I was willing to risk not pursuing the issue out of blind faith in you. Besides, if I had not done business as usual and not sent Cat to assist you in Icy Springs, that alone could have raised some eyebrows here among the boy scouts. It would have looked funny if it appeared I was going out of my way to keep you two apart. I guess, deep-down, I was trying to avoid forcing the issue at a time in my life when I wasn't willing to deal with it. I just didn't need this crap, Agent!"

"Well, sir, I really have no other comment on the matter at the moment. Where, uh, do we go from here?"

"Like I said, Jet, I have a lot of pressure on me right now to end this string of kidnappings. The governor is really on my back to end this mess, and I know you'd come closer to doing it than anybody. So, consider yourself on the payroll temporarily."

"Thank you, sir—"

"But Jet, after this case, I'm probably going to fire you. I'll have to fire Cat, too—if she pulls through, that is."

"Isn't that a bit drastic, sir?"

"Jet, ya know the rules and ya know why rules have to be followed in an organization. As leader, the others are going to be watching me to see how I handle this, to see if I set any precedents. Ya know very well that the exception always becomes the rule when an exception is made. If I let you two get by with this, a can of worms would be opened all around the state government. If I let you two get away with this, it would eventually be handled at a level somewhere above me. In the long run, the three of us would be fired."

"I understand, sir."

"I'm really sorry, Jet. You two are good people."

"Sir, you say Engelbretsen's the only one who saw us, right? What if he has an accident of some kind?"

"Okay, Jet. Quit tryin' to be funny."

"Who says I'm tryin' to be funny!?"

"Jet, Engelbretsen may be the most unlikable jerk in the department, but he is a decent agent—when I'm not having to clean up a lot of brushfires due to his rudeness. I'm sure he's not the only one that knows. You know what a blabbermouth he is. He gossips like a preacher's wife."

"Yes, sir. I suppose you're right that it's out in the open."

"Anyway, Jet, get some rest the remainder of the day. Show up tomorrow morning, and I'll brief you on the case."

"Okay. Thank you, sir."

CLICK.

Well, I could blame Engelbretsen all night long. But, the fact is, it was me who was so careless about treating her out publicly amidst Cat's warnings. And it was me who was careless with her well-being at Icy Springs. Way to go, Jericho!

The dejected agent reached for another sip of Nehi and started to open another Almond Joy.

RING . . .

Good grief, it's like Grand Central Station around here.

RING . . .

"Jericho here, and this had better be mighty important!"

"Oh, the average person would consider this call very important, Nolan Jericho," said the deep voice with rich clarity.

Ay! It's Dr. Rob, wanting an answer to his earlier proposition. This is definitely not the time for this! "Well, Dr. Rob, suppose I'm not the average person?" asked the agent wryly.

"I would greatly agree with that supposition, for average you're not, Nolan Jericho, or you wouldn't even know of my existence. I wouldn't have even bothered to call you if you were average. Have you come up with a definite answer regarding the little arrangement I have waiting for you?"

"It's like this, Dr. Rob. I simply have too many irons in the fire at the moment. I have too many loose ends left untied, so I'm afraid I must decline your offer."

"If I were you, Nolan Jericho, I would *think* your decision through rather than *feeling* it through. I realize you desire to remain by the young lady's side in her current state. But, Nolan Jericho, she could be in that coma for decades."

Damn! How <u>does</u> he find out this stuff so quickly? He surely must have me followed or tap my phone or something!

"As I've indicated to you earlier, sir, the young lady is my business!"

"Yes, Nolan Jericho, she's your business, and the two of you are the business of Director Fowler. You do realize, don't you, that you and the young lady are going to lose your jobs anyway after you finish Fowler's dirty business for him regarding the disappearance of the four lesbians."

"Well, uh . . ."

"You tell me, Nolan Jericho: how does it feel to be used by another man to do his work for him and make him look good?—and then only to be tossed aside like yesterday's news once you've served his purpose? You realize that's the road you're heading down, don't you?"

"I, uh . . ."

"Nolan Jericho, if you go back in at this point and knock a home run for Fowler, he's only going to throw you off the team after the game is over. If you do that, Nolan Jericho, you realize that you will not have furthered the cause of your African ancestors, don't you? After all, if you do another man's work for him and he can treat you anyway he wishes, what's the difference between that and picking cotton for a day under the supervision of a man on a horse with a whip?"

"Not that much, I suppose . . ."

"So, Nolan Jericho, think about what I've said. Time is running out on my offer. It may already be a moot point, for the opportunity may have already been terminated in my absence during the length of this phone call. If not, I'll get back with you sometime in the near future."

CLICK.

At this point, the agent felt sick to his stomach. He walked stiff-legged, like a zombie, over to the window and leaned against it, pressing his nose against the glass. He watched the cars slowly passing by in the dreary rain.

Nolan knew that Dr. Rob had some good points about getting out of Dodge and going to Washington while the gettin' was good. After all, how many days . . . months . . . years . . . or decades would it be until Cat came out of her coma? Would she ever come out of it? Whether she did or didn't, the agent's days with the SBI were certainly numbered. As Dr. Rob noted, Fowler was just keeping him around so that a photo showing the director shaking hands with Governor Scott would eventually appear in Raleigh's *News & Observer* when the case was solved.

Yes, when ending a lengthy drought, rain can seem a blessing to some. But for others, "when it rains, it pours" is just dreariness stacked upon dreariness stacked upon dreariness. Keeping his nose pressed against the windowpane, Nolan closed his eyes in an effort to make the rain stop, but in his mind it continued to pour, drenching his soul. The sad part was that here stood a man who could rush into the worlds of other people, such as those of Icy Springs, and save the day, restoring everything to as close to status quo as possible. But these days, he felt so powerless, so emasculated, to keep his own world from falling apart.

God help me. My fiancée's in a coma; her hot-to-trot, busybody sister's coming to town; Fowler intends on firing me; and the voice on the phone is urging me to take another job which would involve me leaving Cat behind. I just don't have the strength to handle any of this.

Opening his eyes, the agent spotted a boy on a bicycle shooting down the avenue with his mouth open, catching whatever drops happened to be at just the right spot in front of his face. Out of the corner of his eye, Jericho caught a glance of his red convertible sitting in the driveway. *Hmm, I wonder if that old myth is true that if you drive fast enough with the top down, the rain won't hit you; that you won't get wet. I've never really tried it.*

Nolan's thoughts once again began rotating from Cat to Dreama to Fowler to Dr. Rob. As the images pounded in his head, he looked back at the red Sting Ray. *Lord, I ask you, is there any way I can outrun the rain?*

COMING SOON!

The Sequel
THE BLUE PEOPLE

Join Jet Jericho in the nail-biting sequel to Icy Shadows. With his fiancée Cat lying in a coma, Agent Jericho and his partner Bennett James attempt to put a stop to a series of disappearances targeting female homosexuals in the Raleigh-Durham area. Complicating matters are the arrival in Raleigh of Cat's half-sister Dreama and the mysterious Dr. Rob's persistence that Jericho leave his SBI assignment for a CIA position. You'll learn more about Cat's older sister, a political activist targeted as one of the kidnapping victims. AND, the identity of Dr. Rob will be revealed in this startling conclusion of the trilogy.

The Prequel
GIN!

See how it all started! Join Jet Jericho as he visits Icy Springs for the first time to solve the infamous Cotton Gin murders. The readers will be treated to the roots of Jericho's acquaintance with many characters first appearing in Icy Shadows: *Cat, Fowler, Agent James and other members of the SBI ... Sheriff Niblock, Doc Lassiter, Paul Christmas, and other citizens of Icy Springs ... and, of course, the shadowy Dr. Rob. The origin of Jet's departure from the NYPD will be revealed, resulting in his placement with the SBI of North Carolina. But foremost, be sure to enjoy Jet's electrifying first encounters with Cat.*

BONUS FOR READERS
An outtake scene from *Icy Shadows*

Dear readers, just as in the final edits of movies and television shows, books often have "scenes" that don't make the final cut. Often these scenes may be cute, amusing, or interesting, but they are deleted because they slow down the established pace or do not advance the story sufficiently. Out of my appreciation for your readership, Warren Publishing and I have included a short scene from Chapter 20 at Ireland Memorial Hospital when the Sheriff, Jericho, and Cat dropped by to visit Deputy Hodges, still recovering from the bear incident. I hope you enjoy this short outtake!

Knocking on the door of Room #313, the trio heard a woman's voice beckoning, "Come on in. He's awake!" Sheriff Niblock and his two comrades tiptoed into the room and beheld the fallen deputy on his back with a pillow under his head, two pillows under the calves of his legs, and his right arm in a cast, positioned on a pillow. Standing on the far side of the bed near the window was the quintessential church lady, a plump, gray-haired older woman in a flower-patterned dress and hose, wearing a little black hat with a strange ornament of some kind on top. At the foot of the bed was a rather chubby man in overalls who favored Hodges quite a bit in appearance, yet seemed a little too young to be Hodges' father or the plump lady's husband.

"Hi, Mrs. Hodges. Hello, Wendell. How are you feeling today, Deputy?" asked the sheriff.

"Real sore, sir, but don't worry! I'll be back in action soon. I guess I got that bear, didn't I?"

Leaning slightly toward Nolan, Cat whispered, "*I think the bear got him instead.*"

"Yeah, Deputy," assured Walt. "Ol' Smokey's up in the Brushy Mountains as we speak. When did the doctor say you could leave?"

Mrs. Hodges spoke up. "Well, Sheriff, they said if nothing was messed up in his back, he could probably go home tomorrow. After all, he's in a cast and there's not too much these quacks can do for broken ribs and collarbones, is there?"

"No, ma'am," replied Walt. "I don't suppose so. Oh, I almost forgot: Ma'am, Wendell, these are two friends of mine from Raleigh, Agent Jet Jericho of the SBI and his assistant, Catherine Marshall. Jet, Cat, I know that the two of

347

you know Deputy Hodges. This is his mother, Clara Hodges, and his older brother, Wendell."

"Oh, it's nice to see you in person, Mr. Jericho," exclaimed Mrs. Hodges in a humming voice. "My Benny here has told me all about your exploits in helping the Sheriff and the other deputies with the cotton gin murders back in '67. I remember seeing your picture in the paper, too."

"Yes, sir, I'm thrilled to meet you, too," said Wendell, extending his hand toward Jericho. Turning towards Cat, Wendell followed with, "Ma'am, it's a pleasure to meet you, too. Gee, you're a honey!"

"WENDELL!" shouted Mrs. Hodges, embarrassed.

"Sorry, ma'am," offered Wendell, backing off with a slightly red face.

"It's a pleasure to meet the two of you also," added Jericho. "You seem to be quite proud of, uh, Benny here."

"Yes, there's no deputy like Bernard B. Hodges," beamed his mother. "You know, Mr. Jericho, it takes a heck of a man to catch a bear. Benny said he didn't want the poor critter to break his neck, so he ran up to catch him and broke the poor animal's fall. I'm proud of my son, for he's a genuine hero!"

"And proud you should be, Mrs. Hodges," commented Jericho, glancing over at Cat and slightly winking his right eye. "It's not every town that has a true-to-life bear catcher living in it."

"Darn tootin'," agreed Wendell. "Why, those news guys seem to love Benny. They show the film of Benny catching the bear every five minutes, and those news guys just smile real, real big when they're talkin' about Benny. He's getting to be real popular. Hey, look! It's comin' on right now! I'll turn up the sound. . ."

Nolan and Cat followed Wendell's lead and looked up at the television mounted on the wall.

"_. . . Okay, thank you, Marla. Now, for all you who haven't seen this spectacle yet, boy, are you in for a treat!_ [chuckle] _This is a grizzly_ [chuckle] _example of local law enforcement at work. In Sharpton, Deputy Bernard Hodges was in the process getting a bear out of a tree at Mitchner Community College. It seems the poor creature had wandered down from the Brushy Mountains and—well, as you can see—couldn't find his way back. This footage was shot just after Deputy Hodges put the bear to sleep with a tranquilizer gun. Now watch this, viewers! You have to see this to believe it. Watch carefully as the deputy walks up and stands underneath the limb holding the dozing bear . . . watch . . . watch . . . SPLAT!_ [chuckle, chuckle] _Now, that's one deputy who really knows his bear-ass-entials!_ [chuckle, chuckle] _I'll tell you now, viewers, it's a good thing for the deputy that a hippopotamus or an elephant hadn't got stuck in the tree._ [chuckle, chuckle] _Keep tuned to Channel 9. We'll have an update on the condition of our bear-taming_ [chuckle] _deputy on this evening's news. . ._"

"That's my Benny!" crooned Mrs. Hodges. "Best lawman in the county! It's so wonderful that he made the news!"

Nolan glanced over at Walt, who had both hands over his face and was exhaling a long breath. Removing his hands from his face, the sheriff began shaking his head. Leaning over once again to the agent, Cat whispered, "*I would say the sheriff definitely needs to get out of town today!*"

"*Lord have mercy, I agree*," whispered Jericho, slightly rubbing his Oriental eyes as if he couldn't believe what he had just seen. "Uh, Walt, I guess we'd better be heading on to Columbia. Deputy Hodges, I'm glad you're on the road to recuperation." The agent then turned and politely bowed toward Mrs. Hodges and her older son. "It was really nice to meet you, ma'am, Wendell."

"And you also, Agent Jericho and Miss Marshall," replied Mrs. Hodges.

"We'll check on you later, Deputy," added Cat. "And it was nice to meet the two of you."

"And *you* for sure, ma'am," responded Wendell. "You sure are quite a honey!"

"WENDELL!"

About the Author

Rob Robertson

Living in the Statesville/Salisbury area north of Charlotte, N.C., Dr. W. Dwayne "Rob" Robertson is an author, musician, and award-winning educator. Dr. "Rob" has performed services for school systems, colleges, and universities throughout the Carolinas and has performed piano concerts around the United States. Having served as consultant for N.C. state departments, he was appointed chair of a national focus session on education with his research having been published internationally. Rob considers himself a "Renaissance man." *Icy Shadows* is his maiden voyage into the world of fiction, the first novel in the Jericho Trilogy. Rob welcomes all to the exciting world of Agent Nolan Jericho.